Also by Cathryn Grant

NOVELS

The Demise of the Soccer Moms ◆ *Buried by Debt*

The Suburban Abyss ◆ *The Hallelujah Horror Show*

Getting Ahead ◆ *Faceless* ◆ *An Affair With God*

THE ALEXANDRA MALLORY PSYCHOLOGICAL SUSPENSE SERIES

The Woman In the Mirror ◆ *The Woman In the Water*

The Woman In the Painting ◆ *The Woman In the Window*

The Woman In the Bar ◆ *The Woman In the Bedroom*

The Woman In the Dark ◆ *The Woman In the Cellar*

The Woman In the Photograph

THE HAUNTED SHIP TRILOGY

Alone On the Beach ◆ *Slipping Away From the Beach*

Haunting the Beach

NOVELLAS

Madison Keith Ghost Story Series

Chances Are

SHORT FICTION

Reduction in Force ◆ *Maternal Instinct*

Flash Fiction For the Cocktail Hour ◆ *The 12 Days of Xmas*

Cathryn Grant

HAUNTING THE BEACH

Haunted Ship Trilogy Book Three

D2C Perspectives

This book is a work of fiction. References to real people, events, establishments, organizations, or locales are intended only to provide a sense of authenticity, and are used fictitiously. All other characters, and incidents and dialogue, are drawn from the author's imagination and are not to be construed as real.

Email Cathryn at Cathryn@SuburbanNoir.com or visit her online at SuburbanNoir.com

ISBN: 978-1-943142-22-4

Mary

Before the concrete ship cracked and her mother died and everything changed, Mary wondered if she would ever know the truth. There were so many secrets, so many things they didn't want her to know because she was just a child.

After she saw the ghost, she kept it to herself. For a very long time, she never told a soul that a ghost haunted the concrete ship. No one would listen to her because most people didn't believe in ghosts.

Haunted

I*'ve been here for a long time — alone on the California coast, near the center of Monterey Bay, on the shore of Seacliff Beach. I'm the ghostly breath of fog that blows across the water, first hugging the horizon, quickly shrouding the blue sky, blanketing the sand. I'm closer than the pebbles and sand and broken logs of drowned trees. Only a handful of the millions of beachcombers and surfers, swimmers and sunbathers have felt my presence. Only those with eyes. Not the eyes in their heads, but internal eyes.*

I'm here, watching. I'm here, listening. I'm here, speaking, if anyone wants to pay attention.

It's commonly believed that ghosts haunt a particular place because they're looking for closure, they want to find rest, they need release from something unresolved so they can pass on to the afterlife. But the truth is slightly different.

Winter 1930

One

Normally, Lorene would have been eager to walk to the beach with Mary, despite the thick layer of fog keeping the temperature in the mid forties. She relished breathing fresh air into her lungs, stretching her legs, feeling her daughter's small, firm hand in hers. But the unfinished argument with Henry twisted in her stomach like spoiled meat. No matter how many times she tried to wait silently for his attention, restraining herself in the same way one kept her distance from a cat until the animal made the first move, she ended up losing her temper. It was unseemly for a woman, and worse when there was a chance their daughter might overhear.

It seemed to Lorene that Henry was more upset by the chance of Mary overhearing harsh voices than he was by the argument itself. His concern made Lorene feel as if he cared more for Mary's feelings than hers. Not that Lorene wouldn't be horrified if Mary heard raised voices or slammed doors or, during that awful moment two nights ago, a thrown teacup shattering on the parlor mantelpiece.

Right now, Henry could be anywhere in their twelve-room house. Keeping his distance from Lorene and her rage.

She loved their Victorian-era home, perched on a cliff above Monterey Bay, but sometimes she thought a smaller home would be more…homey. The house had too many rooms, too many doors and windows and verandas. If she called his name, Henry wouldn't hear.

She pulled on her cloche hat and checked her reflection in the mirror on the armoire.

"Where are you going?"

She turned. Henry stood in the doorway. Dark stubble covered his face, making it look as if he was standing in a shadow. He wore trousers the color of caramel with a white shirt, the top two buttons open. She imagined him striding across the room, wrapping her in his arms, telling her in a voice broken with emotion how much he loved her.

"To watch the ship coming in."

"It might rain."

"I don't think so," she said. "But I'll bring an umbrella."

"Why are you going out in such nasty weather?"

"Mary wants to see it."

"You're feeding her imagination. She'll never set foot on it."

"She's excited."

"You need to squelch that."

She slid the center button on her cape through the hole. "Can't you imagine how it is for her? It's all anyone talks about, so it's difficult to think of anything else."

He stared at her. She waited to see if he would mention their argument. He folded his arms across his ribs and angled his body in the doorframe as if he thought she might change her mind when she saw the doorway was blocked.

"Will you come with us?" she said.

"No. And I don't approve of you taking Mary out there."

"Please," she said. "Please understand."

"I understand that she'll want to stand there all day in chilly weather. She'll talk about it constantly, and she'll invent all kinds of stories, and she'll pester us even more for a chance to go aboard."

"Is it called going aboard if the ship isn't floating?" she said.

"Don't change the subject."

"I told you we were planning to watch them tow it in. Claire's going too."

He unfolded his arms, moved away from the doorframe, and slid his hands in his pockets. "Make it clear to Mary that the dancing and dining will be for adults. No children allowed."

"She knows that."

"I don't think she does. Have a nice stroll."

"Please won't you come?"

He laughed. "It's not as if a concrete tanker races up to the pier like a motorboat. It's going to take them all day to maneuver it into position. Possibly several days. There will be a lot of standing around. It's a waste of time. We can all see it when it's settled into place." He turned and disappeared from sight. As he descended the stairs, she heard his footsteps, solid and evenly paced, like everything about him.

The conversation felt like a continuation of their argument, or another thread to be woven into it. Every conversation was a new thread. A cocoon was forming around each of them, layers and layers of string and knots, delicate fibers growing into something coarse and impenetrable. Soon, she would shout. and he wouldn't hear her voice at all. If he spoke, she wouldn't know.

When he'd been standing in the doorway, she'd wanted to run to him and press the side of her face against his chest. She wanted him to put his hands on her head, pulling her closer. She'd wanted to say different things, although she wasn't sure what those things would have been.

The cocoons had grown tighter and more solid since Claire came to live with them. It was hard enough that their mother died only five weeks after they discovered she was ill. Now Lorene was left to finish her mother's job — overseeing Claire for the foreseeable future. She had no idea how to raise a sixteen-year-old girl. Guiding a ten-year-old was all-consuming, and Lorene navigated carefully, taking cues from Mary with whom she had a bone-deep connection. Claire might as well be an adult already. She kept her thoughts to herself, even her grief over the loss of her mother. She was a virtual stranger. She'd been a child when Lorene married and moved away from San Francisco.

With Claire in the house, there was always someone walking into a room, always someone drinking tea with her and Henry, a near-adult listening to the things they said over dinner. When Mary was their only companion, Lorene and Henry could sometimes talk around her, carrying on a separate conversation. Mary chattered to herself or stared out the window at a bird. It wasn't like that with Claire.

The only place Lorene and Henry were alone was in their bedroom, but he kept late hours, closed up inside his study finishing the day's correspondence or making notes in his ledger, or simply reading the newspaper. He often ate in restaurants with his business partners and didn't come home until after midnight. She tried to stay awake, but most nights, she failed. It was cool in their bedroom and she burrowed beneath the covers with a book. The warmth of the quilts and the comfort of the pillows made her sleepy. The book ended up on the floor. In the morning, she'd find it closed on her nightstand, a bookmark in place, often the wrong place.

She finished buttoning her cape and went downstairs.

Henry wasn't in the parlor or his study. The living room was also empty. She wasn't sure why she was looking for him. He'd been firm that he wasn't walking out to the cliff with them. She went into the living room and looked out at the front garden, the path, and the curved driveway. The car was parked in its usual spot. He was somewhere close by.

Annie was in the kitchen peeling potatoes. "I'm making stew for dinner, if that's alright."

Lorene nodded.

"It's so cold. And gloomy."

"Stew is a perfect choice," Lorene said. "Do we have sourdough rolls?"

"That's what I was thinking." Annie smiled.

Unlike the household help that lived with some of Henry's business partners, Annie came six mornings a week to cook breakfast and clean, staying through dinnertime. Once a week, Annie's sisters joined her for heavy cleaning. Annie was only a few years older than Claire, but she managed an entire household. Claire couldn't seem to manage much more than a walk to the shops for a new dress. It wasn't the cost of her clothing that was concerning, there was plenty of money, but it seemed as if Claire cared only about her appearance. Lorene worried about the effect on Mary.

"Have you seen Henry?" Lorene said.

Annie shook her head. "The car's in the drive."

"Yes, I saw."

"He's probably working."

"I suppose so. We'll look forward to the stew."

"I'm glad." Annie put a pale, smooth potato in the bowl and picked up another. She ran the knife along the side, removing the entire length of skin. She made peeling potatoes look satisfying, calming. Lorene hadn't peeled a potato since she was a child.

"If you see Henry, tell him we went for our walk. To see the ship." It was a meaningless piece of information. He already knew where she was going, but it felt wrong to leave the house without saying goodbye.

She went into the foyer to wait for Claire and Mary to come downstairs from their bedroom on the third floor. Sharing a bedroom wasn't for lack of space — it was Mary's fascination with her young aunt. The moment Claire had set her suitcase on the foyer floor, Mary started pestering for her aunt to sleep in the same room. "I'm lonely up there by myself."

Claire had smiled, a distant look in her eyes, maybe her own loneliness and grief, maybe something else.

"We have the second-floor bedroom ready for Claire," Lorene said.

"She'll have to come all the way upstairs to see me," Mary said. "How can we get to know each other if she's in another room?"

"There's plenty of time for getting acquainted." Lorene

started to pull off her glove. It caught on her diamond. She plucked at the fabric, pulling it away from the stone and the sharp prongs securing it. She felt Claire staring at her hand. She removed the glove quickly and folded her hand around it.

"Please," Mary said. "Please, please, please."

"Don't beg," Lorene said. "It's not nice."

Mary gave her a coy smile. "I'm not begging. I'm asking nicely."

"Claire needs her own space," Lorene said. "She's not a little girl." She glanced at her sister. "Isn't that right?"

"It doesn't matter," Claire said. She smiled at Mary.

Against her better judgment, Lorene had relented. There was no good reason why they couldn't share a bedroom for now. Lorene looked small and petty saying *no* when it had nothing to do with her. But she didn't like it that Mary had learned a subtle lesson — begging paid off. And she felt slightly manipulated, although she wasn't sure why. It seemed as if Claire had forced her hand, yet Lorene didn't really believe Claire wanted to share a room with a little girl. She didn't believe Claire wanted to share a room with anyone. Lorene certainly wouldn't have chosen that when she was sixteen. Still, Claire was suffering. She was a child herself and she'd lost her mother. Now she was living with a sister she hardly knew, torn away from her home, her friends, everything familiar. Forced out of an exciting city into a sleepy, slow-moving beach town. Claire said it didn't matter where she slept because there were so many other things that mattered more to her, things she couldn't change.

Later, Lorene had pulled Claire aside and thanked her for indulging Mary. Claire gave her the same vacant smile. "It's not a bother," she said.

It doesn't matter — It's not a bother. Lorene was left feeling as if she'd been accused of considering her daughter a bother. Claire adopted an image of being pure and good-hearted when compared with her older sister. It hadn't been a good start to their shared lives.

Lorene sat down on the parson's bench and unbuttoned her cape. She should go upstairs and hurry them along, but what was the rush? As Henry had pointed out, it would take the entire day for the crew to move the concrete ship into position. There was plenty of time.

Two

Jacob Archer walked along the gravel path at the edge of Seacliff Drive where the King family lived. Seacliff Drive was occupied by the wealthy — enormous homes that looked more like hotels, many of them hoarding panoramic ocean views, automobiles in every drive. Better to stay away from that area, his brother told him. But he couldn't. He'd seen Mr. King's sister-in-law emerge from his sage green and black Packard, its ostentatious white rimmed spare wheels displayed on either side. The flashy car distracted him for only a fraction of a second — he'd known he had to meet her. Not only meet her, but court her, if that wasn't too old-fashioned a word. He would find a way to show a privileged girl that she couldn't do any better than Jacob Archer. He might not have a lot now, but he would. Once he figured out a plan, once he found a job that paid more than working at the apple-packing barn, he would be able to afford wool suits and leather shoes. He'd own a car, people would pay attention to him.

There was an eerie beauty about her — pale, silky hair that hung several inches past the hem of her fitted jacket with its brown fur collar. The story around town was that Mr. King's sister-in-law was an orphan. He'd heard she was only sixteen, but she looked as wise and knowing as the twenty-year-old girl who worked in the diner on Trout Gulch Road. If Jacob didn't make a move soon, some other man would win her attention. He thought she'd looked in his direction once when he saw her outside of the market, one of several businesses her brother-in-law owned. But Jacob had been standing a block away, near the newspaper stand, and it wasn't likely she was able to make out much of his face from that distance, if he stood out at all.

Yesterday, when he'd mentioned it to his brother again, David shook his head slowly, playing the wiser and more cautious older brother. "Keep walking up and down that street, and someone will notice. They'll report you as a peeping Tom."

"That's ridiculous. A peeping Tom looks in windows. I'm just taking a walk."

"Henry King won't like some lollygagger eyeing his sister-in-law."

"She's not a piece of property."

"To a man like Mr. King, you can bet that's exactly what she is. Be careful," David said. He slid a Chesterfield out of the pack and held out the box. Jacob took one. David struck a match and lit both.

They smoked and walked toward the cliffs.

"The concrete ship's coming in tomorrow," Jacob said.

David nodded. "I know."

"Should be something to do. Watching them get it situated."

"Like watching paint dry," David said.

"Better than that."

"Sounds boring."

Jacob put the cigarette between his lips and shoved his hands in his pockets. The air was damp and cold. His fingertips were numb. He mumbled around the cigarette. "Everyone wants to see it."

"When it's lit up and filled with music, sure. But watching them drag it to the pier? I'll pass."

Jacob curled his hands into fists. The cotton lining of his pockets was doing nothing to warm his fingers. He should have worn gloves. "A lot of people are going to watch."

"Not me."

They walked in silence until they reached the edge of the cliff. "Oh, I get it. You think your little tomato will be out here watching a ship get towed to the beach."

"Maybe."

"Absence makes the heart grow fonder," David said.

"What does that mean?"

"If she sees you everywhere she goes, you'll blend into the scenery."

Maybe David had a point. David was the worst kind of cynic, but every so often, he said something worth considering. This might be one of those moments. But had the girl even noticed him? Jacob wasn't sure.

She was so beautiful he could hardly bear to look at her for more than a few minutes at a time without his body aching to be near her. It was as if she'd drifted down from heaven on a cloud, with that shimmering hair, and her slim figure, and those eyes. They looked right inside of you and through you. He'd only passed her close enough to see her eyes on two occasions. They'd been full of so many things he thought he could sit beside her and hold her hand and listen to her talk for a hundred lifetimes and not grow bored with those eyes. He'd never heard her speak, but he imagined her voice sounded like birds greeting the dawn in the springtime. He was stupid with wanting her. He couldn't say any of that. David would laugh until he was sick.

Jacob took a drag on the cigarette and tapped the ash to the ground. He wanted to see the boat towed to shore. It sounded interesting, whether she was there or not. Was he risking looking like a goof, following her around? Walking past her house? He thought he'd been cautious. He'd go out to watch the ship, and after that, he wouldn't walk past the house for a week. Five days, maybe. There had to be a way of getting introduced to her. He'd been working on that problem for three weeks. So far, his mind remained blank.

On January twenty-second, he was out on the cliff before dawn. A thick layer of fog made the sunrise an uneventful fading of charcoal gray to white. The ship was a speck of black on the horizon as it moved farther into the bay, dragged along as if it were something dead, all the power coming from the tugboat. It was disheartening watching a brand new, well-engineered vessel pulled along like a useless hunk of concrete. And that's what it was — absolutely mind-boggling that a 434-foot slab of concrete was able to float. He lit a cigarette.

By mid-morning, the ship's progress toward the pier had been minimal. He'd already smoked four cigarettes and was about to give up. From the corner of his eye, he saw Mrs. King, her angelic sister, and Mrs. King's daughter. They stood at a point where the cliff jutted out slightly, but they kept well back from the edge. Mrs. King was closer to where Jacob was standing, effectively blocking his view of her sister. Every few minutes, he saw a wave of blond hair as the wind lifted it off her back.

Another hour passed, during which the movement and activity of the woman and the two girls were as minimal as the ship. They stared out at the bay, occasionally speaking to one another, words he couldn't begin to hear, standing fifty or sixty feet away, partially obscured by a Cypress tree. What were they saying? Did they discuss the design of the ship? The marvel of floating concrete? Their plans for dancing and dining? The clothes they would wear to parties on the ship? The little girl — Mary — looked like she wanted to run to the beach and tow the ship to the pier herself. He imagined she must be disappointed that the dance parties wouldn't admit children.

The grand opening would be an expensive evening, but he planned to buy a ticket. Next week, he was starting a second job at the newspaper stand to supplement his work at the apple-packing barn. If he restricted himself to a single meal a day, if he stopped smoking…he took a drag on his cigarette. This would be the last for today. How many would David allow Jacob to borrow before his failure to reciprocate was noticed? He shoved the pack into an inside pocket of his jacket, hoping it helped him stop thinking about them. The trouble was, standing around, watching a boat inch across the water, turning this way and that, *was* as boring as watching paint dry. The idea of it had been interesting, and he was glad he hadn't missed such a remarkable event, but the actuality was dull.

Watching the girl was anything but dull. Having her at least partially within sight, not suddenly disappearing into a store or being driven off in the car, or leaving the front garden to go inside the house, made him want her more. It was worse, seeing her so close but lacking any appropriate method for introducing himself. Instead of walking past her house, filling his thoughts with longing, he should direct his mental energy back to thinking of ways to secure an introduction. Maybe her brother-in-law would come to the newsstand and buy a paper.

Three

The dresser top was hardly visible, covered as it was with Claire's things. She had three hairbrushes! Mary couldn't understand why she needed three, even though her blonde, almost white hair, reached past her waist. The brushes were kept on a silver tray. The tray was surrounded by bottles of perfume, jars of creamy things that smelled delicious, combs and barrettes and cloisonné containers of costume jewelry.

Before Claire moved into Mary's bedroom, it had smelled of ocean air. Mary liked the window open, even when it was cold and her father asked her to close it because all the warmth was escaping. She often tiptoed to the window and slid it up so it was barely noticeable, sitting some of her dolls in front of the gap. Claire preferred the window closed, and now the room smelled of Lavender water and talcum powder.

Still, it was worth it. She loved sharing her room with

her aunt who wasn't like any of her friends' aunts. Claire was like a whole separate person with no identified place in the family — a stranger. She wasn't old and full of rules like most aunts, and she wasn't someone to fight with like a cousin. Claire made Mary feel more grown up, even though Mary preferred not to smear perfume behind her earlobes and dab it on the insides of her wrists. Mary believed brushing your hair three times a day with three different hairbrushes was a lot of unnecessary effort. All of that aside, Claire was fun. She told stories that were unlike anything Mary had heard from her parents or her friends.

Mary's dresser was almost bare. The polished wood gleamed. There was an oval mirror that was attached to wood arms and tilted to give different views of yourself, just like Claire's. On top of Mary's dresser was a wooden bowl filled with small purple and white seashells and gray pebbles she'd collected on the beach. Beside the bowl was a blown glass horse with a red mane.

"Hurry," Mary said.

"I need to brush my hair."

"It'll get mussed up in the fog."

"Not as mussed as it will if I don't brush it first."

"It's already smooth. It looks beautiful."

Claire smiled at the mirror. Mary couldn't tell whether the smile was meant for her, or if Claire was smiling at her own self. Smiling at one's reflection was vain. Her mother told Mary never to gaze at herself in the mirror. She should only glance at the mirror. It was more important to think about what was inside, the beauty of her heart, not her skin and hair and eyes. Still, Mary often looked at her reflection when she was alone in her room. Secretly, she had a thought that she worked hard to push aside, but she kept trying — the mirror suggested she was prettier than Claire. It was a secret she'd have to keep to herself forever. Claire's hair was longer, silkier, maybe, from all that brushing, but Mary's eyes were nicer. Mary's eyes were large and deep blue, her eyelids only visible when she lowered them. Claire's eyes bulged out, her lids more prominent than the pale blue, reminding Mary of a frog. It was an unkind thought, and her mother would be disappointed she was having it, but it was the truth. And her mother also liked her to be truthful.

Claire bent forward and flipped her hair over her head. She ran the brush from the nape of her neck, over her scalp, and down the length to the ends.

"We're going to miss the ship," Mary said.

"No, we won't."

"I don't think your hair needs any more brushing." Mary unbuttoned her coat. Even with the window open, it was too warm for a wool coat.

"It's important to look your best."

"The ship doesn't care what you look like. And if you think boys will be watching you, they'll be way out on the tugboat, they won't even see you."

"I'm not trying to impress any boys."

"Yes, you are."

Claire straightened and began brushing her hair from the top again.

"Come *on*!"

"Don't accuse me of flirting. I like to look my best. A woman's crowning glory is her hair."

"My mother might change her mind, and then we won't get to see it."

"She's not going to change her mind. She wants to see it brought to the pier as much as we do."

Mary went to the window. She looked across the backyard, a thin line of the ocean was visible in the distance. She loved having the only bedroom on the third floor of the house. She loved the alcove at the front of her room, a single window facing the driveway. She loved the size of her room and the large closet that gave plenty of space for all of Claire's beautiful dresses alongside Mary's. The other room across the hall on this floor was used for storage. There was even a bathroom connected to her bedroom. The only thing she didn't like was the shelf lined with dolls. Claire's possessions might be too grown up with all her creams and perfumes and combs, but the shelf near Mary's bed made her side of the room look like it belonged to a little girl. She wasn't so little anymore, only six years younger than Claire — too old for dolls.

Every year on her birthday she was given a new doll.

Her mother thought she loved them. And she had, when she was seven, even eight. She didn't want to hurt her mother's feelings by complaining about the dolls. It wasn't only that they belonged in a little girl's room — they scared her. She felt they were watching her all the time. They seemed to know what she was thinking. They stared at her with unblinking, disapproving eyes when she had unkind or selfish thoughts. She heard them whispering at night. No one knew the dolls could see her thoughts and no one knew they spoke to her. Such a story would be dismissed as a childish fantasy, but it was the truth.

Finally, Claire was finished. She wove a green ribbon down the left side of her hair and clipped it with a gold barrette. She smeared cream over her hands and put on her gloves. "Are you ready?"

"Of course I'm ready," Mary said. "I've been waiting forever."

Claire smiled. "You're such a precious…"

Mary was glad Claire managed to bite her tongue. She'd remembered Mary didn't like being called a child.

They took their coats and went downstairs.

They stood on the cliff above the newly constructed pier. The S.S. Palo Alto was far out in the bay, but even from all that distance, Mary could see it was huge.

Her father had taken a brick, since he didn't have any slabs of concrete, and put it in a tub of water. It sank immediately. Everyone expected a concrete ship should do the same. He'd explained that if the density of a ship is lighter than the density of the amount of water it displaces, the vessel will float. Concrete had qualities that made it better than steel ships in some ways. It made the ship immune to fire and corrosion, offered better insulation, and provided greater stability. At the beginning of the Great War, it was discovered that concrete ships were less costly to build. Her mother had read an article out loud to Mary, describing the ship's brass fittings, tiled galley, and decks made of white Norwegian ash.

Looking at it now, it was hard to tell if the ship was moving, it turned so slowly as the tugboat pulled it this way and that, backing it up to where it would join the pier, the bow facing out to sea. Once it was filled with water and settled onto the ocean floor, it would never go anywhere again. She felt a little sad for it, knowing its life as a ship was over.

After a while, her feet grew cold even though she wore thick socks and tightly fitted leather boots tied up to her ankles. She didn't want to complain. After she'd begged every day for so many weeks to see the ship towed to shore, her mother and Claire would think she was ungrateful if she told them she wanted to go home and drink cocoa. But it was cold, and for the past twenty minutes, the tugboat and the concrete ship hadn't moved at all.

She walked closer to the edge of the cliff. She kicked a stone and watched it bounce on a larger rock and fly off into nothing. She stopped walking, trying to hear the stone hit the ground a hundred feet below. There was no sound. She walked back to where her mother and Claire were standing.

Claire had been right that Lorene was just as excited about the ship. She hardly moved, staring out at the horizon. It seemed as if there were tears in her eyes. Mary slipped her hand into her mother's. "Are you crying?"

"It's so beautiful, but it's so sad. It was never allowed to make a voyage."

Mary felt the same, but she didn't like knowing her mother was upset. She wanted her to smile and feel excited about the ship. "But there will be parties," she said.

"Yes. You know children won't be allowed."

"I know. You already told me. But maybe it will change."

"It makes me sad that she never crossed the ocean, was never used as she was designed. She's so majestic, and now she'll be humiliated, trying to see the Pacific Ocean from where she's sitting. She must feel useless."

Claire laughed. "It's a hunk of concrete."

"But beautifully made," Lorene said.

"It's a boat. It doesn't have feelings."

"Everything has feelings," Lorene said.

Claire turned slightly. Her lips were twisted in a smirk.

If she could see herself in the mirror now, she wouldn't be admiring her beauty. Turning her lips like that made Claire's eyes bulge more, and the lids were tinged red from the cold.

"Everything has feelings," Lorene whispered.

Mary wasn't sure who she was talking to, maybe no one. Mary shivered, even though the wind had died back and the fog was simply a thick quilt of white and gray.

A few days later, Mary and her mother went without Claire to watch as the boat was filled with water. She sank slowly and settled onto the sea floor. The captain, assigned to her when she was commissioned, was there to watch her come to a final stop. He stood at attention, his face covered with tears. He patted her side one final time and left her to her fate.

Four

After Jacob finished his first day at the newsstand, David met him on the opposite corner of Aptos Street and Trout Gulch Road.

"Let's get a bottle of pop and walk out to see the concrete boat," David said.

Jacob shook his head.

"Why not?"

"Saving my money."

"What for?"

"I'm going to the grand opening."

David laughed. "You won't get to dance with that doll."

"I just want to go. I want to see the ship. It's a big deal — the opening night."

"You can't fool me." David shook two cigarettes out of his pack. He handed one to Jacob. "I suppose that means you can't afford these anymore?"

"I guess not."

"I can get us some pop," David said. They walked toward the market. "Have you seen Mr. King's car go by this afternoon?"

Jacob shook his head.

They stopped in front of the market, finished their cigarettes, and dropped the butts in the gutter. "Let's go," David said.

"I said I'm not getting any."

David pulled his hat on tighter. "My treat."

They went into the store. Jacob followed his brother to the refrigerated case.

"What kind?" David said.

"Lemonade. Thanks."

David opened the door and pulled out a lemonade and orange pop for himself. He took a few steps toward the aisle to his left. "I have to check out something else. Wait for me by the front."

"It's fine, I'll stay here."

"Look at the magazines or something."

Jacob laughed. "I spent all day with magazines, there's nothing I need to look at."

David turned. He pinched the bridge of his nose. "Can you just go wait up front? I have to look at some, uh, medicine and stuff."

Jacob moved back toward the refrigerated case.

"Hurry up, will you?" David turned down the next aisle.

Jacob strolled to the front of the store. David had seemed nervous. He must be buying something for itching, or laxative syrup, maybe. The clerk nodded at Jacob and turned back to a woman buying milk and a bag of potatoes. He took the woman's coins, made the change, and put the food in a sack.

Jacob glanced at the magazines. It was a small rack, and all they had was *Life*, a few detective and science fiction magazines, *Time*, and *Good Housekeeping*. The newsstand carried three times that many. It was getting too warm. He unbuttoned his coat, but it didn't help. He rubbed the back of his neck, pulling the collar away from his skin. What was taking so long? He stood on his toes and tried to see over the shelves, but David was nowhere in sight.

The clerk folded the top edge of the sack and handed it to the woman. "Thank you. Have a good day."

"Thank you, George. I'm sure I'll see you again tomorrow." She walked toward the door. Jacob reached for the handle and opened the door. "Thank you." She smiled.

A moment later, David was walking down the aisle, headed toward Jacob. His arms were stiff, as if he was cold, trying to keep his jacket tightly wrapped around him. He must be feeling…

"Go," David said. He walked past Jacob and opened the door with too much force. The blinds clattered against the glass. David stepped outside.

"Hey!" George rapped the heel of his hand on the

counter. "Hey, did your friend have something there? Inside his coat?"

Jacob stared. From the corner of his eye, he saw David break into a slow run. "I don't think so." Jacob opened the door and walked out.

"Hey!" George shouted. "Come back here."

What was David thinking? It wasn't as if this was a big city and they could sneak around unrecognized. Had he changed his mind about wanting something to drink, or had he stolen the pop? And the laxative syrup? Jacob ran after him. They would be recognized. Henry King owned the market. The clerk would report them, he'd be watching for them, their faces tattooed on his brain. Jacob's more than David's after all that time loitering by the magazines. He ran faster.

David slowed to a fast walk, but Jacob didn't catch up until they reached the edge of the cliff. "Why did you do that?" Jacob said.

"You wanted pop."

"I didn't! You did."

David grinned. "Don't get in a lather."

"That guy knows who we are," Jacob said.

"No, he doesn't."

"Maybe not you, but he sure knows my face. I was standing there like a goof for five minutes."

"He'll forget." David pulled the bottles out of his inside pockets. He handed the lemonade to Jacob. "Cheers."

"I'll be worrying every time I go in there."

"It'll give you something to think about besides that doll."

"Very funny." He held the bottle, staring at it. For a moment, he considered hurling it over the side of the cliff. That would make his point. But there was a chance of conking someone on the head. He didn't need that kind of trouble.

David offered his pocket knife to pry off the cap.

Jacob shook his head. If he told David what he needed to do, David would try to talk him out of it, laugh at him, but Jacob knew he had to return to the store. If luck ran against him, and George and Henry King were ever in the store together when Jacob walked in, if George pointed Jacob out to Henry, he'd never get a chance with the mesmerizing girl. He stuck the bottle in his pocket.

"Aw, come on. Drink up," David said.

"I'm not thirsty."

A gust of wind swept in a circular motion along the edge of the cliff, stinging Jacob's face with cold air. He pulled his coat tighter.

David shrugged. The wind didn't seem to bother him. His jacket hung open, and he gulped down the orange icy liquid as if it were a cloudless summer day.

The street was nearly empty on a rainy Monday morning. Jacob thanked Providence, if there was such a thing, for bringing rain to clear out curious onlookers.

When he stepped into the shop, George was handing a large bag to the same woman Jacob had seen before. She must come in every day. George glanced at Jacob. His smile slid to a straight line and his jaw tightened. The woman took the bag and left.

"You owe me five cents," George said.

"I know. That's why I'm here." Jacob pulled the bottle of pop out of his pocket and set it on the counter. "I'm sorry for what my…friend did."

"I want him in here paying what he owes."

"He's not coming. You got me." Jacob reached into his other pocket and took out two nickels. He placed them beside the bottle of lemonade.

The clerk glared at the coins and the bottle, covered with fuzz from Jacob's pocket.

"I can't sell that."

"I'm paying for it, and the other one, so do what you can with it. I just wanted you to know I didn't drink it. I'm sorry for what he did."

George cupped his hand over the coins. He hesitated, then dragged them across the counter. They fell into the open palm of his other hand. "I'm not going to thank you. All you did is what you should have."

"I hope you don't mind if I shop here again."

"Your friend is not welcome."

Jacob nodded. "Good-bye, then." He walked to the door

and turned the knob. He pushed it open slowly. As he stepped outside, Henry King was getting out of his Packard. Jacob turned and hurried down the street, yanking on his hat as he walked, bending his head to keep the rain off his face. He hunched his shoulders. The rain was biting cold on the backs of his hands and still managed to drip on his face. Behind him, someone was shouting. He prayed George hadn't ratted him out to Henry. He lengthened his stride. The corner was only a few more steps.

"Hey, kid! Wait a minute."

He slowed. Running was a bad idea. George knew what he looked like. He might as well stop and face whatever was going to happen.

He turned.

Henry King was striding toward him, holding a huge black umbrella with a glossy wood handle over his head. He came up close to Jacob and stopped. He tipped the umbrella so it covered both of them. "Your honesty is impressive."

"Thank you," Jacob said.

"I won't beat around the bush. I'm looking for an employee I can trust."

"Is that right?" Jacob wiped rainwater off his face and looked into the man's eyes.

"I have a lot of businesses. I need an assistant who can help keep me up to date on what's going on, do some clerical work, run errands. Someone I can trust."

"I can see that," Jacob said.

"Trustworthy workers aren't too hard to find, but someone who might eventually become an insider to all of my operations…that's another story."

Jacob nodded.

"If you're interested, I'd like to start you out running errands. Where are you working now?"

Jacob told him about the newsstand and the apple processing outfit.

"Can you get away from them by next Monday?" Henry said.

"I think so. Yes."

Henry nodded. "I'll pay you six dollars a day."

Jacob swallowed. Six dollars! It was crazy. It was like the man was offering him tickets to an evening on the concrete ship. If he could be introduced, if she was interested, he could buy a ticket for the girl as well! He tried not to flop his head about and pant like a puppy. Business. Henry had approached Jacob, there was no need to kowtow.

"Is that agreeable?" Henry said.

Jacob nodded. "Yes. That's fine. Thank you."

Henry moved the umbrella to his other hand. He shook Jacob's hand. "I didn't just pick you up from one incident. I've seen you around town. You and your brother."

So David wasn't safe after all.

"I won't do anything about your brother, but make sure

he stays out of my store."

"Yes, sir."

"I'll see you Monday. At the market. Seven a.m."

Jacob felt he should salute. Instead, he shoved his hands in his pockets. "I'll see you then, sir."

Henry turned and hurried up the street. When he reached the Packard, he snapped the umbrella closed and climbed inside. Jacob stood in the rain until the car disappeared from sight. He didn't think David needed to know about this right now. He'd wait a bit, see how things unfolded. He wasn't just one step closer to the beautiful girl, more like fifty steps closer.

It almost seemed too good to be true. He hoped it wasn't.

Five

The argument had started mildly enough, as most of their disagreements did. Lorene and Henry were sitting in the parlor after Sunday dinner. She'd made a pot of tea, but only she was drinking it. The tea in Henry's cup was lukewarm, maybe colder, since he'd been pouring scotch whiskey out of the flask he kept behind the volume of encyclopedias on the second shelf in the corner.

She didn't like him drinking scotch, and he knew it. It might be legal to have it in your home, but there was no way to purchase it without breaking the law. She didn't want to think what kind of people he'd met up with to keep up his steady supply. Even if it had been legal, which might happen again since it was rumored Congress was considering an amendment to Prohibition, she didn't like him drinking it. The odor on his breath was pungent, and when he kissed her after he'd had a drink or two, his mouth secreted excess saliva. His lips were loose and sloppy on hers, and she had to resist the urge to pull away, trying to turn her mind away from the nausea wiggling through her intestines. He must have sensed her disgust because it had been quite a long time since he'd tried to kiss her.

Before Prohibition, she'd often had a glass of wine with dinner, or sipped champagne at parties, but that was different. Hard liquor was nasty. It made men do stupid things. They became crude and boorish.

All she'd done was ask why he wasn't drinking the tea she'd made. She supposed he'd recognized her question for what it was — unsubtle criticism.

As if to taunt her, he put the flask to his lips and tipped his head back, swallowing twice. He lowered his hand. "I've told you a thousand times, I like a drink in the evening. Tea keeps me awake. Scotch helps me unwind."

"It's illegal."

"So you've mentioned. The law is idiotic. I'm not allowed to buy it, but I can have it in my home?"

She kept her voice low, her tone conversational. "I don't think we should ignore laws just because we don't agree with them."

"In this case, we should."

She'd dropped it after that, but her timing had been all wrong, bringing up the subject of Claire the moment he folded the business section of the newspaper and tossed it on the coffee table. Things were already brittle. "I wonder if we should have Claire move into a bedroom by herself."

"I'm not sure why you allowed her to stay in Mary's room to begin with," he said.

"Mary was so excited to have her living with us. And I thought it might be nice for Claire, when her grief was so fresh. But now…" She took a sip of tea.

"Now, what?"

"Claire is sulky. I know she's grieving, and it's much more intense for her than it is for me. She's essentially alone in the world, but at the same time, I feel as if she's taken over our home. I don't think it's good for Mary to spend so much time with her. Claire is so much older…"

"You're the one who wanted her to live here." Henry stood up and went to the fireplace. He took the poker out of the rack and stabbed the flaming log, breaking it apart with ferocious jabs.

"There was no other choice," she said.

"There's always another choice." His tone sounded as if he'd figured out that other choice.

He was wrong. Lorene was Claire's only living sister. Both of their mother's sisters lived in Chicago. The two aunts were in their sixties, and it was too much to ask them to raise a sixteen-year-old girl. "I'm worried."

"Then tell her to move to the other bedroom."

"It might be better coming from you."

"That's your domain," he said.

"She listens to you more. She needs that male authority. Especially with my father being gone for so many years.

She hasn't had enough supervision."

He shook his head. "Child-rearing is your responsibility."

"You give firm guidance to Mary when she needs it."

"Sleeping quarters aren't guidance. If you don't like the current arrangement, tell Claire she needs to move."

"Mary will be upset."

He walked to the coffee table and picked up his flask. He took a sip. "You know, now that I think about it, you're right. You should take care of it immediately. She's had plenty of time to get settled. Mary needs to be around children her own age. And I don't want her head filled with all those Quaker fancies. I don't know why I didn't think of it sooner."

"Please don't," she said.

"We agreed she'd be raised in The Church."

"She is."

"I don't want Claire whispering any of that blasphemous nonsense about following the whispers inside your head, growing up with the notion that God speaks directly to people. It makes for an unstructured, lawless society."

"It worked out fine for me. I'm sensible."

"A fluke." He poured the dark gold liquid into his glass. It looked beautiful and dangerous, glowing as it captured the light from the roaring fire.

"How can you drink illegal liquor and accuse Quakers

of being lawless? It makes no sense."

"Don't talk to me like that."

"You're my husband, can't I tell you my honest thoughts?"

"I'm not going to debate religion. This household belongs to The Church of Rome. I don't want Mary confused."

"I'm not debating religion."

"Is that why you let Claire stay in Mary's bedroom to begin with? Were you led by some voice inside your head? Or your need to keep everyone happy?"

"I don't want to fight," she said.

"We're not fighting."

"I think we are."

He took a swallow of whiskey. He licked his lips.

She felt tears sliding across her eyes. Her vision blurred. She moved the crochet hook and the doily she was working on off her lap. She picked up her teacup with both hands and took a sip.

"Don't start crying," he said.

"I'm not." She blew gently on the surface of her tea. It didn't need cooling at all, but the movement of her breath past her lips helped dry the tears away from her eyes. She drank the rest of the tea and put the cup on the saucer. "I don't even know why we're arguing. We agree that Claire needs to be in her own bedroom."

"Mary should be the one to move," he said.

"She loves that room."

"She should be near us, your sister is the guest."

"That's been her room for years. She loves being on the top floor. She loves the alcove and the..."

"It will be better that way. You can keep a closer eye on her."

"I don't spend the day in our bedroom, so I wouldn't be keeping a closer eye." She couldn't imagine telling Mary she'd have to give up her room. And it wasn't fair. As he said, Claire was the guest, why should Mary be put out of a place she loved, as if she were being punished? The conversation was going in the wrong direction. How had this happened? She stood up and walked to where he was standing. She kissed his chin. "I'll tell Claire to move to the second floor. Tomorrow."

"I said I want Mary to move."

"I thought this was my domain?"

"It is, but I don't know why I didn't recognize it before. With a stranger living in the house..."

"She's not a stranger. She's my sister."

"You hardly know her. She was a child when you last lived with her. We have no idea what things she's saying to Mary." He looked truly horrified, as if it had never occurred to him until this moment that Mary and Claire might be whispering to each other at night, sharing confidences.

"She could be filling Mary's head with all kinds of sordid things, dishing out all that *waiting for the spirit to lead* nonsense."

"It's not nonsense. It's no different from seeking God's will in prayer."

"It's very different," he said. "God speaks through the Pope. And He's laid out everything quite clearly. We don't need to go pestering him for personalized information. It's one step from that to following the Devil."

"That's not the way it is. Not at all. Everything isn't black and white. Sometimes the Inner Light speaks to your heart and shows you a more truthful path. I know in my heart I should follow the laws of the land, even if I don't like them."

"It all gets taken care of at confession." He sipped his drink. He held it up, turning the glass.

She couldn't help thinking he looked at the drink and the light changing color in the cuts of the crystal as if he were looking at something divine. "You think we can do whatever we want and get rid of it at confession? That's a terrible attitude." She picked up her teacup and put it to her lips, trying to hide their trembling. She didn't understand what had happened to their love. He never used to speak so harshly. He used to think her beliefs were charming, even if he didn't agree with them. He used to touch her arm or her cheek when they had a difference of opinion, and that softened everything.

"That's how it works," he said.

"I don't think that's the intention."

"Are you questioning God?"

"I'm trying to talk to you. Don't act as if you're the only one who has thoughts and opinions."

"I know you have thoughts and opinions, Lorene. Believe me, I know. You shovel them in my ear every time I walk in the door."

She took the cup away from her lips and flung it at the mantelpiece. It shattered. She started to cry.

"Well. Isn't that nice." Henry picked up his flask and the glass and walked out of the room. She heard the thud of his study door closing.

She fell onto the sofa and put her face in her hands. Her tears ran out across her fingers.

Lorene hadn't been much older than Claire when she met Henry at an Independence Day celebration. She'd seen him for the first time at the parade along Market Street. She stood on the wide sidewalk beside her older sister. Horses clopped their iron shoes on the pavement as they marched by, seemingly filled with pride at their inclusion in the parade. Large gleaming cars filled with dignitaries followed. The number of wealthy people using the parade as a chance to show off their automobiles increased every year.

The sun was out, which wasn't always the case in San Francisco in the summer, and Lorene's face was damp with perspiration as the sun moved toward the center of the sky.

Her older sister's face was damp and red. Every few minutes, Sylvia flapped a cardboard fan printed to look like the American flag in front of her face. Sylvia was twenty-three and anxious about her unmarried condition. Their parents constantly reminded her to look inside her heart and allow the Inner Light to guide her to the right man, to wait for the man who was designed for her. They told her fretting wasn't seemly and accomplished nothing. But Sylvia couldn't manage to quiet her heart for more than three minutes at a time. She'd never been able to do that.

Before the parade was half over, Sylvia grabbed Lorene's elbow. She dragged her away from the curb, headed toward the corner of Market and Fourth Street. She stopped beside a man who appeared to be watching the parade without a companion.

"I want you to meet Henry King," Sylvia said. Her voice was shrill, as if introducing him to Lorene was a matter of life and death. Maybe it was.

Henry King was tall, dressed in a charcoal gray suit with a white shirt, not the silly white holiday pants and bright shirts some of the men wore. The bright sunshine and warm air seemed to have no effect on him. His skin was smooth and looked cool to the touch. Lorene had to curl her fingers to resist a strange desire to stroke his cheek.

Henry bent forward in a slight bow. Sylvia giggled. "A pleasure," he said.

"It's nice to know you," Lorene said.

"Do you know me?" He lifted his left eyebrow.

She stared at him, admiring his trick of moving one eyebrow independently from the other. She'd never seen anything like it. "It's an expression," she said.

He smiled, leaving the eyebrow arched.

Sylvia's fingers fluttered over the cuff of his jacket. "I met Henry at the library." She smiled up at him. "He was reading a book about the Civil War. I've never met anyone who reads history books when they're not in school." She glanced at Lorene, then looked up at Henry again. "You're so intelligent."

His eyebrow was no longer raised. He gave Sylvia a half smile.

Watching Sylvia shoot small, phony smiles at Henry, stand a few inches too close, touch his sleeve with her fingertips, was embarrassing. She laughed too loudly and smiled too often. Did he notice?

Sylvia was frantic to keep the conversation going, to remain at the center of his attention for a moment longer. She seemed terrified he was losing interest and would turn away. "Will you join our family picnic?" Sylvia said. "We have two kinds of potato salad. I made one of them."

"Very impressive," he said.

Lorene felt he was mocking her sister. She didn't like it, but at the same time, it made her smile. Was he cruel, or just trying to be polite to a woman who was eager and not very interesting? She didn't want to know a man who was deliberately unkind, but her sister was behaving like a silly child.

Sylvia turned to Lorene. In a stage whisper, she said, "He's had so much tragedy in his life. We should make sure he enjoys the day, so he can forget."

"I'd love to join your family. How many of you are there?" he said.

"You make us sound like a herd of cattle," Sylvia said. "Just Lorene and me and baby Claire. And our parents, of course. They'd love to meet you."

"How do you know?" Henry allowed Sylvia to rest her hand on his forearm and they began walking toward the small park where the picnic was being held. Lorene followed, studying the exaggerated sway of her sister's hips. Sylvia was wasting the effort — Henry couldn't see her movements as she walked beside him.

Their mother and father gushed over Henry in the same way Sylvia had. Lorene could barely eat for watching all of them treat him as if he were a European dignitary. When her plate was finally empty, Lorene took Claire's hand and led her to a temporary play area set up to keep smaller children entertained. For nearly an hour they cycled between the slide, the swings, and the circular platform that turned when you held the bar and ran beside it. Claire climbed onto the platform and Lorene ran as fast as she could to keep it spinning. After a few minutes, she stopped, and several more children joined Claire. Lorene resumed pushing the merry-go-round. Sweat broke out along the sides of her nose. She laughed — Sylvia would be horrified by her lack of concern for her appearance. For a moment, she wished she were still a child and could ride the merry-go-round with the others. There was plenty of time for boys, and men. Henry was a man, much too old. She was in no hurry to find a boyfriend, and she was confident that even when she was Sylvia's age, there would be no rush. She liked waiting for the Quiet Voice to speak inside her, moving as gently as a spring breeze, sweet and clear. The presence of the Inner Light was more pleasurable than the attention of boys. She laughed harder, and the children, thinking she was laughing at the fun of pushing them around, echoed her laughter.

After a while, her arms ached. She felt as if steam were rising up from the layers of cotton clothing and her damp scalp. She stopped. "That's all for now." She stepped away from the merry-go-round, turning her head away from the six whirling children who stared at her with hopeful smiles. Claire clapped her hands. "More."

She heard the merry-go-round pick up speed. She turned back.

Henry was bent over, gripping one of the iron bars. He walked with long strides. Already it was turning faster than she'd been able to make it go when she was scurrying in a circle, wearing a flat ring in the grass.

She moved away from the ride. The children shrieked

and clung to the bars, their fingers white from the pressure. Henry pushed them for several minutes until terror crept into their shrieks. He slowed, and the shrieks faded again into sounds of pleasure.

When he stopped, there wasn't a drop of sweat on his brow. Lorene wiped her finger along the side of her nose. He reached into his coat pocket, pulled out a handkerchief, and handed it to her. She patted her face and handed it back to him.

"Keep it," he said.

"My perspiration offends you?"

He smiled. "To the contrary. But you might need it again."

She wasn't sure what that meant, but she tucked it into the tiny purse strung over her wrist.

At twenty-nine, he was nothing like the boys her age, who acted like goofy children to get a girl's attention. He looked at her, holding her gaze rather than nervously turning away, his eyes as dark as his nearly black hair.

After that day, when she went for walks in the park, Henry often happened to be there, and they walked together. Soon, they were arranging to meet. When she spoke, he considered her words and responded to her thoughts rather than changing the subject to his own interests. He listened to her enthusiasm over the books she read — histories and stories of London and Paris and Rome. Moscow and Tokyo. She wanted to go everywhere, see all of the cities that rivaled San Francisco in their beauty and importance. He said he'd never thought much about traveling. He was occupied with business, with the shops — a clothing store and a market — he owned in the small seaside town of Aptos, and the secretarial service he managed in San Francisco.

Then, Henry invited her to a dance. Her mother reminded Lorene to seek the Inner Light. Lorene wasn't sure she wanted to be courted, but maybe it was too late for that. Sylvia had hardly spoken to her after observing Lorene and Henry at the merry-go-round. Once Sylvia heard about the dance she would be furious. And hurt. Lorene looked inside and felt the Inner Light splitting in two. She was drawn to Henry. He consumed her thoughts, and she felt slightly bored when he wasn't around, but she didn't like to see any living creature suffer. Seeing the pinched, worn expression on Sylvia's face was painful.

But Henry made her laugh, and he loved to hear her talk. He was fascinated by the unfamiliar beliefs of the Quaker faith. He asked her repeatedly to explain how she recognized when the voice of God was speaking to her. "How can you really know?" She assured him it took practice, and maturity. He seemed to bristle at that. The muscle in his forearm tightened and a rigid look formed around his lips.

"I suppose there's always some uncertainty," she said.

He smiled, and his face relaxed.

She'd planned to tell Sylvia privately, gently, about the dance, but flowers and a note had been delivered the week before. Sylvia took the delivery and read the note.

As Lorene descended the stairs to the foyer, Sylvia turned slowly. She threw the lilies on the marble floor. They made a soft but horrible sound, like flesh slamming to the pavement after falling from a second-floor window. Lorene paused. She hugged herself and opened her mouth to speak. She walked slowly down the last few steps.

"You trollop!" Sylvia's face was the shocking white of the wounded lilies. She stamped her foot on the flowers.

Lorene cried out as if Sylvia had stomped on her rapidly beating heart.

"How dare you steal him from me! He's mine. He was courting me and…"

"I don't think he was," Lorene said.

"What do you know? You're a child." Saliva flew out of Sylvia's lips. "You flattered him and acted helpless and lured him away from me. I was behaving with decorum, letting him know I'm a lady and that he had to woo me."

"Decorum?" Lorene laughed. She knew it was unkind. She heard the Quiet Voice admonishing her gently, but she couldn't listen to that right now. Decorum was the last thing her sister had shown. "You threw yourself at him. Maybe he didn't like that."

"What do you know about men? He's a man, not a silly boy. You're much too young for him."

"That's not your decision," Lorene said. She knelt to pick up the flowers. She took the card in her fingers and opened it. *Looking forward ~ Henry King.*

She touched two of the lilies that had avoided Sylvia's boot.

Sylvia lunged forward and slammed her foot on the back of Lorene's hand. Lorene cried out and tried to tug her hand from beneath her sister's boot.

"Apologize," Sylvia said.

"For what?"

"For stealing him. For insulting me."

Lorene laughed.

Sylvia released Lorene's hand from beneath her boot. "Send him a note and tell him you can't see him." She kicked the flowers, scattering petals and broken stems across the floor.

Lorene shoved the note in her pocket and stood up. "I'm not doing that."

Sylvia never forgave Lorene. A few days after destroying the lilies, she began speaking to Lorene again, but only words that were required during meals, or when they had an unfortunate chance meeting in the hallway.

For several weeks, Lorene looked inside her heart, seeking the Inner Light, asking herself what she could have done differently, questioning her feelings for Henry. She couldn't find any evidence that she'd done something wrong, or unkind. There was no guilt, only the pain reflecting from her sister's eyes. Sylvia had loved the wrong man because she didn't look into the alcoves of her own heart. Lorene hadn't stolen Henry. It wasn't possible to steal a human being. Those accusations came from Sylvia's unenlightened mind, filled with fear and want, without regard for the truth.

Two months after Henry escorted Lorene to the dance, Sylvia was dead. The flu pandemic swept around the globe, taking Sylvia, along with more than half a million other Americans. It wasn't until Sylvia was locked inside her coffin and lowered into the ground that Lorene remembered Sylvia's mention of Henry's tragic life. When Lorene asked him about it, he said it was nothing. When she asked a second time, he said it was too difficult to talk about.

A month later, their father slipped away just as quickly, without a sound.

Lorene knew she was too young to be married, but when Henry lowered himself down on one knee and said he worshiped her, she thought she might faint. The words and the look of adoration in his eyes filled her with a glow that spread its warmth through her entire body. She thought about her plans for visiting other parts of the world, but who would accompany her? Seeing the cities she'd read about would have to come later. Henry adored her. He insisted his life would be empty without her. He needed her. And didn't her mother and her baby sister need a man in the family to step into her father's place?

The day before they were married, without prompting, Henry finally told her about the tragedy of his past. "I was married once before. My wife died." He looked away from her and swallowed. He continued in a low voice. "The cliffs were unstable after weeks of heavy rain. The soil and rock collapsed, and she fell." He wouldn't say anything more about her. Lorene didn't want to spoil the happiest days of her life digging for details about a woman who was dead anyway, but every night of their honeymoon, she saw a shadow in her dreams — the faceless, unformed image of Henry's other wife.

Spring 1930

Six

Jacob had been employed by Henry King for nearly three months, with gradually increasing levels of responsibility. He ran errands between Henry's shops and his home office, and to his partners. He delivered packages to the post office and picked up packages for Henry. He oversaw deliveries to the market and the dress shop. Occasionally he took the train to San Francisco to make a delivery, but other than that, Henry kept the secretarial service under his exclusive domain and Jacob had little information about what it entailed. He was plenty busy with the operations in Aptos. He distributed paychecks to employees, helped with inventory tracking for the market, and hired the window cleaners for both establishments. It was enjoyable because every day, every hour was different, and there was no more back-breaking labor. The money was nice too. He bought new clothes and got his hair cut more frequently.

When Henry asked him to start taking cash deposits to

the bank, Jacob knew he was a trusted insider. It was time to make his move toward the girl he longed to know. Possibly he'd waited too long, but he hadn't wanted Henry to think accepting the job had only been an excuse to get near his sister-in-law.

Over the past few weeks, Jacob had been given more opportunities to steal glimpses of her. And he'd learned her name — Claire Farmington. The name was perfect for her. The delicate, melodic sound of it in his mouth echoed her beautiful hair and eyes, her slim heart-shattering figure.

He visited the King house every business day and most Saturdays. He walked up the hill carrying letters and invoices in his satchel. He went around to the back veranda, always glancing to his right to see if Claire was sitting in the screened porch. Now that the weather was growing warmer, she often was. He tried not to stare, turning quickly and knocking on Henry's office door at the opposite side of the veranda.

It was a cool, windy day. The sky was streaked with white clouds, swatches of pale blue between. He climbed the steps and glanced at the screened porch. It was empty, but it was early, only eight-thirty in the morning. Maybe she'd be there when he left. A week ago, he'd tipped his hat in her direction as he went down the steps. She hadn't acknowledged him, but it wasn't as if he'd been able to stand around, peering through the screen to see whether she was aware of his gesture.

He knocked on the office door.

"Come in."

He went inside and put his bag on the corner of Henry's desk.

Henry was writing in his ledger. Without looking up, he said, "Do you have the shipping invoices?"

"I was too early, George didn't have time to get them sorted," Jacob said.

Henry nodded and continued writing. "You'll have to come back later. I need them today."

Jacob placed the other paperwork in the appropriate trays on the desk. When he was finished, he strapped the bag closed and hung it over his shoulder. Henry was still writing. Was it too risky to interrupt him? But he was always writing, or talking on the phone. There would never be a time Jacob wouldn't be interrupting or abruptly changing the topic of conversation. "Sir? Mr. King?"

"Yes?" Henry continued writing. He didn't seem perturbed, but it was uncomfortable, talking while someone was busy with another task.

"I have a question to ask. A favor."

Henry put down his pen and looked at Jacob. He pushed his chair back slightly.

"I'd like your permission to invite your sister-in-law to go for a walk with me. Along Seacliff Drive, maybe out to the cliff to look at the ship."

Henry picked up his pen. "Why are you asking me? Ask her."

"I thought…"

Henry waved his hand. "She has a mind of her own. It's not as if she's my daughter."

"I thought you were her guardian?"

Henry shook his head. "Invite her wherever you want. But you should know, she has strange beliefs — Quaker."

Jacob knew nothing about Quakers. He'd heard of the sect — they weren't baptized or absolved through confession and communion, but what did any of that matter? He didn't pay much attention to the Church, he hadn't been to confession since he was a kid. "Thank you, sir."

"Don't mention it. Just watch out for that Quaker thing. They think God speaks to them."

Jacob opened the door. "I'll be back with the invoices this afternoon."

"Thanks."

Jacob let the office door fall closed behind him. He looked across the veranda to the porch. The sun was hitting the screen, turning it to a solid gray wall. He couldn't see whether anyone was sitting there. He squinted, but it did no good. He crossed the veranda, his boots thudding on the planks. He went down the steps to the yard and around the side of the house. He wasn't going to stand there trying to peer through a screen, his eyes watering from the glare.

When he approached her, it should be with assurance. Now wasn't the right time. He needed to think it through.

It was three o'clock by the time he headed back to the King house with the invoices.

He'd been so preoccupied with presenting his request to Henry, he hadn't given any thought to how Claire would respond. She might already have her eyes set on someone else. She might consider Jacob beneath her — an employee of her brother-in-law, and a low level one. Jacob had no doubt he was valuable to Henry. He had a lot of responsibility and was paid well, very well, compared to most, but in Claire's eyes, he might be nothing but an errand boy. He was a decent looking guy, so he didn't need to worry about that. She'd never heard his voice — everything but his face would be new to her. What made a girl interested in a guy? Looks were part of it, but beyond that, he had no idea.

His boots crunched on the gravel path as he rounded the side of the house. The sound was like glass breaking. It seemed terribly loud and made him walk slowly, aware of the give of the gravel under his weight. He reached the back steps and looked toward the screened porch.

She was there, reading a book. She wore a dark green dress, and her hair was in a single braid, hanging over her shoulder. She fiddled with it as she read, wrapping it around her wrist, then sliding it off her arm.

He went up the steps and knocked on the doorframe.

She looked up.

"Hi, Claire. I don't know if you recognize me…I work for your brother-in-law. My name's Jacob Archer. May I come in?"

She put the book on her lap and flipped the braid behind her shoulder. "I know who you are. Come in."

He opened the screen door and stepped inside.

He should be more firm. He wouldn't ask for permission to sit. There was a wicker chair across from her. He pulled it away from the low table and sat down. He'd forgotten to remove the bag from his shoulder, and it prevented him from sitting back in the chair. He probably appeared over-eager, perched on the edge, leaning forward as he was.

If he looked awkward, she didn't let on that she was amused.

"I've seen you around. I saw you the day they brought the ship to the pier," he said.

She smiled.

"Would you like to go for a walk with me? Maybe out for a cup of coffee?"

"Sure. When?"

He blinked. He felt foolish as his eyes fluttered up and down. Twice in one day, he'd received a response he hadn't anticipated. He should stop being so hesitant. Starting now, he wasn't going to think and debate with himself and imagine endless scenarios and craft his words ahead of time. Neither Claire nor Henry hesitated for a single moment before they spoke. It was as if they always knew what they wanted and the words came out on their own.

"Saturday afternoon? I have to work in the morning."

"Saturday afternoon will be nice." She smiled. "What will we talk about?"

"Probably quite a lot, since we don't know anything about each other."

She laughed.

Yes, not thinking was definitely his new plan. It was working already. It made things much more interesting and exciting. No more mental debates, no more discussions with David. He hadn't seen David as much since he was working so many hours for Henry King Inc. David was envious, although he tried to pretend he wasn't. He wondered what David would think of this. Maybe he would invite Claire to the grand opening of the ship after all. And David had laughed at him for dreaming of such a thing.

He stood up. "I'll come around on Saturday at two o'clock."

"I'll look forward to it," she said. "Come to the front door."

He nodded. "See you then."

He left the porch and went to Henry's office door, resisting the overwhelming pressure on the back of his head, urging him to turn and see whether she was watching him.

On Saturday the sun came up in a cloudless sky. It was sixty-five degrees by noon. The weather was a good omen, the sun shining on him and Claire. No one was there to see, and no one was privy to his fanciful thought, but his face grew warm, blushing at the way he imagined the natural world caring about his hopes. The heat on his back and shoulders was intense as he walked along the road, uphill to the King home. The green and black Packard was still covered by shade, making it look sleek and dangerous for some reason he couldn't explain. Someday, he would own a car, and he wouldn't have to worry about walking uphill, sweating under his cotton shirt and wool jacket, worrying his face looked like a boiled red onion. He took out his handkerchief and swiped it across his forehead. Rather than refolding it, he stuffed it in his pocket and patted it flat.

It was two o'clock exactly when he rang the doorbell. A young woman with short dark hair, wearing a blue dress covered by a darker blue apron opened the door.

"Jacob Archer," he said. "I'm here for Claire."

She opened the door wider. "Come in and have a seat." He stepped inside, and she gestured toward a parson's bench on the left side of the foyer. Across from the bench was a staircase leading to the second floor. The sound of a piano, notes shivering at the high end of the keyboard, came from a room somewhere behind him.

A moment later, Claire appeared in front of him. He

hadn't heard any doors, couldn't determine from which direction she'd come. It didn't matter. She was here. He stood up.

She wore a cream-colored dress that flowed around her like liquid. Her legs were bare, and she wore black shoes that looked like the little slippers he'd seen on dancers. Her hair was braided, a cream-colored ribbon woven through the braid.

They walked along Seacliff Drive and out to the edge of the cliff. The ocean was glassy dark turquoise, dotted with gulls and pelicans sitting on the barely moving water.

He told her about the work he did for Henry and about his brief stint at the newsstand. He left out his job picking apples. He shouldn't try to hide it, there was nothing shameful about being a laborer, but he'd save it for another time. He said nothing about his childhood or his family. It wasn't important, and he'd rather listen to her voice. She did like to talk. She described the exterior and every room of the house where she'd grown up in San Francisco. She talked about her mother's sudden illness, her death, and the lonely taxi ride that brought her to Aptos. When he asked about her father, she shrugged. *I don't remember him.*

He couldn't imagine what it would be like to have no memory of his father. "Do you think of Henry as a father?"

She laughed. "No."

She told him about her friends in San Francisco and how eager she was to finish school, hopefully moving back to the city once she was eighteen. "I feel like an adult already," she said. "After all the things I've experienced. I'm too old for school."

They agreed on that. He'd been out of school for five years now, and sometimes, it was hard to remember what he'd learned there. He never thought about it.

They walked along the edge of the cliff, talking about the boat and the ocean. She told him stories about her old friends and the number of letters she received from them and how desperately she missed them. The three hours flew past, and he felt it had only been a few minutes since he was escorted into the foyer to wait for her.

"Next time, I'll take you for coffee," he said.

"That will be nice."

He swallowed, and his heart thudded against his ribs, thinking about sitting across from her at the diner, everyone seeing them together.

"And pie or cake," she said. She slipped her hand around his arm and rested it on the crook of his elbow.

After Claire went into the house, Jacob turned and walked down the steps. In the few moments he'd been standing on the porch, the sun had dropped suddenly, sending a chill through the air and covering the garden with shadows. Henry sat on a bench near a lemon tree. His form was barely visible in the dim light.

"I didn't see you," Jacob said.

Henry stood and walked toward him. "I'm not checking up on you."

"I didn't think you were."

Henry handed him a small, square box. "Will you take this to William Sharp? He needs it tonight."

"It's dinner time."

"He's expecting you. He'll interrupt his dinner."

"Okay." Jacob took the package. It was light enough. It wouldn't require much effort.

Henry reached into his pocket. He handed a bill to Jacob. "For your trouble. Working on a Saturday evening."

"It's no trouble." Jacob peered at the bill. Five dollars. "That's a lot of money just to deliver one package."

"It's an important package. Consider it symbolic of how much I trust you." Henry turned and walked toward the porch. He seemed to glide up the front steps. A moment later, the door opened and closed.

Jacob shoved the bill in his pocket. It was unsettling to be paid so well for a simple delivery. There was something he was supposed to understand. About trust. He expected he wasn't supposed to mention the delivery to anyone. But who would he tell? And why?

His life was getting better and better. So much money. And he was sure that Claire liked him as fervently as he did her. The next time he saw her, he'd invite her to the grand opening of the S.S. Palo Alto. His veins seemed to swell until he thought he could feel the blood moving through them, filling him with enthusiasm. He'd never had so many good things happen to him in such a short time. He hoped it wasn't all too good to last.

Jacob had been fourteen and David was fifteen when their mother died, and their father retreated to the Church and a life of silence. Sam Archer began attending mass daily. He spent his evenings sitting in the living room clutching his rosary. An enormous painting of his wife hung over the fireplace, and when Jacob and David came home after school, Sam was often on his knees, staring up at the painting as if the image portrayed God Himself.

A table in the corner was cluttered with her ceramic angels. Sam dusted them every day, taking each one in his hand and gently wiping it with a linen cloth. Her jewelry was laid out on the top shelf of the bookcase, surrounding a framed photograph of her on their wedding day. The second shelf featured a photograph of her as a child. It stood beside her lavender rosary beads with their bloody crucifix.

Unless he was saying the rosary, Sam no longer spoke. The house was achingly silent. Neither Jacob nor David felt they could speak about routine matters. When they did, it was in whispers. A neighbor woman came every afternoon and silently prepared a stew or a soup or a pot of chili and left it on the stove for the two motherless boys and their father.

David resented being called motherless. He wasn't a

little brat with a runny nose who needed mommy to wipe all the things coming out of his body. He quit going to school and got a job at a nearby farm. He was a man, and he was going to prove it to that woman next door, and to their father.

"I don't think she cares whether you're a man," Jacob said. "What difference does it make?"

David glared at him and pulled out a pack of cigarettes.

"Where did you get those?"

"I have my ways," David said.

"It's not allowed. He'll be angry."

"He won't know. It's not as if he comes close enough to smell the smoke. And we'll do it away from the house. On the cliff."

"We?" Jacob said.

"People respect a man who smokes. Not a pansy who spends his life on his knees, begging God for something he can't have."

Jacob couldn't argue with that.

David never doubted his own opinions or decisions. He was brimming with authority. It seemed as if he'd sucked it right out of his father, left the husk of the man kneeling on the floor, beads sliding through his dried fingers, and was now set on telling Jacob how to live his life.

The year after Jacob graduated from high school, their father died quietly on the living room couch. Through mysterious laws and reports of debts that neither boy understood, they were told the house no longer belonged to them. They found single rooms to rent, and although they lived at separate addresses two blocks away from each other, David's influence continued. He appointed himself the overseer of Jacob's life.

Now, things were changing. Jacob made more money than David. A lot more. Jacob had a girlfriend. Jacob had responsibilities and no time for hanging around smoking cigarettes and drinking soda pop, trying to find sources for illegal beer.

David had become sulky. Every few weeks, he asked to borrow money.

"It's not to buy beer from a bootlegger, is it?" Jacob said.

David insisted it wasn't. "Just a bit to tide me over. For smokes and whatnot."

Jacob opened his wallet and slowly pulled out a dollar. He handed it to his brother, ashamed for both of them. He wasn't sure whether or not David was lying. He didn't really want to know. He needed to keep himself free from illegal activity. Henry trusted him, that's why he had this job with increasing responsibilities and levels of trust. And that's why he had Claire. He wouldn't allow his brother to bring anything into his life that would jeopardize his standing with Claire.

Seven

It hurt to think of ripping Mary out of her beautiful bedroom. Lorene still hadn't told her she would have to move. Mary had blossomed up there — it was her private palace. Even when the room was empty, Lorene felt her daughter's presence when she walked through the door. But now that Claire was going on dates, Lorene was more concerned than ever about what she might be saying to Mary. What if Claire had allowed boys to touch her in places they shouldn't, and so much worse — what if she'd told Mary about it? Did the two girls lie awake telling secrets? That's what she and her older sister had done, until Sylvia was seventeen or eighteen. None of her sister's stories were scandalous. Now, girls knew so much more about the world. Over the past few years, restrictions on women had loosened. Girls socialized freely with boys and wandered farther from home with other children and no parental supervision.

Lorene really had no idea what Claire's life had been like for the past twelve years. She didn't know whether Claire had already gone around with boys. She didn't know a thing about the girls Claire exchanged letters with. Some of the return addresses listed only the street and city. Possibly, some of the letters came from boys.

A small voice, not the quiet whisper of the Inner Light, whispered that she might look through Claire's correspondence and read some of those letters. She thought about it often, too often.

She stood in the doorway.

The window was open. Outside, songbirds twittered and in the distance, gulls cried out to each other, their squawks carrying across the cliffs. A breeze as soft as a baby's sleeping breath eased its way into the room, lifting the curtain away from the windowsill.

She could straighten Claire's dresser. It was covered with a tangle of loose hairs billowing over hairbrushes, clusters of combs and perfume bottles and jars of cream. A white smear of cream ran along the top edge, and the whole surface needed dusting. Particles were collecting in the drying cream.

She stepped into the room. Looking through her sister's belongings wasn't right. She turned. Claire stood in the doorway.

"Are you looking for something?" Claire said.

Lorene shook her head.

"What are you doing in here?"

"It's my daughter's room, I have a right to be here."

Claire smiled. "Well, what do you want?"

"Please let's not argue."

"Are we arguing?" Claire walked in an exaggerated arc around the spot where Lorene stood. "I need to get ready, so will you leave, please."

"Ready for what?"

"I'm going for coffee and dessert with Jacob."

"Are you planning to see him more?"

"I just told you, we're going out."

"I meant long term."

"None of your business."

"It is my business."

"How?" Claire smiled. She went to the dresser and looked at her reflection. She pulled the comb out of her hair. It spilled and tumbled like a waterfall down her back.

"He's old for you, Claire. I think he's twenty-two."

Claire was silent, looking into the mirror as if she saw something that Lorene did not.

Lorene touched her throat, feeling for her necklace. It had fallen inside the neckline of her dress. She fished around for it. She couldn't discern any guidance for how she should handle this. She had no idea what her next words should be.

Claire spun around. "He's not too *old*. I'm almost an adult."

"Almost."

"And how old is your husband?"

Lorene shivered. Did Claire lean heavily on the *your*, as if she were considering Jacob for a husband?

"How *old*? Eleven years older than you? Twelve? Jacob is only eight years older than I am."

"It's different when…"

"It's not different."

"He's…I'm not sure he's right for you."

"You don't know him. And you know nothing about me. It's not your decision."

Lorene couldn't argue. She continued searching for the chain around her neck. She wasn't concentrating, and her fingers refused to locate it on their own. "I don't know about his character."

"You're a snob. It has nothing to do with his character — you don't like that he's Henry's employee. Not in our class, is that what you think?"

"I didn't say that."

"But you think it."

"You can't know what I think," Lorene said.

"Stop clawing at your throat."

Lorene pulled her hand out of her dress. "I'm not. I was looking for my necklace."

Claire smirked. "You looked like you were going to throw up."

"I've seen him smoking cigarettes."

"So what?" Claire picked up one of her hairbrushes and began pulling it through her hair. There was no need, the brush slid through the strands like a piece of ivory sliding over silk. "You're not my mother."

"I'm not trying to pretend I'm your mother."

"Of course you are. You stuck me in this room with your child, treating me like I'm ten."

"You said you wanted to share a room with Mary. Although now might be a good time…"

"I never said that."

"You didn't object."

"Because I could see that's what Mary wanted. And I know you want what Mary wants."

"I asked for your preference."

"No, you asked if I *minded*."

"Well, maybe we should think about…" She paused. She didn't want to talk about the bedrooms, not yet. She wanted to talk about Jacob.

"Your precious daughter wanted it."

"Why do you make that sound so awful? She is precious to me."

"You worship her."

"I don't."

Although Claire was watching and would accuse her again of clawing at her throat, she stuck her fingers behind the neckline of her dress. She ran them over her collarbone and found the fine gold chain. She pulled it gently and settled the tiny pearl on the outside of her dress.

"Feel better?" Claire said.

"About what?"

"That you found your necklace."

Lorene took her hand away from the pearl. The conversation was running all over the place. "I saw Jacob accost Henry in the garden. After you went out walking. It was unnerving."

"What are you talking about?"

"It was dark. Henry was sitting in the garden and Jacob walked over to him. Very aggressively."

Claire laughed.

"Why is that funny?"

"You make it sound so ominous. He *accosted* Henry."

"I don't know what they were talking about. After dark like that."

"Why don't you ask your husband?"

She felt trapped. She couldn't let Claire see the hairline fractures in their marriage, couldn't let her know that Lorene was afraid to ask Henry, afraid to upset the relative calm that had settled over them again. Afraid to pry into his business, putting her nose where it didn't belong. He'd said that once when she asked a question about his work. Then he'd laughed and told her not to be concerned with his business. She was well taken care of, and he had everything under control.

"I think you're right," Lorene said. "I'm sorry I took

your ambivalent answer as a yes that you wanted to share a room with Mary. You deserve your own space."

"I think what you mean is you don't want Mary sleeping with a girl who's out cavorting with boys."

"Don't put words in my mouth."

Claire smiled. She removed a silver ID bracelet engraved in tiny, delicate script with something Lorene had never been able to read. Lorene didn't want to ask what it said or who it was from.

"I hope Mary won't mind moving downstairs. She seems to like being up here close to the birds." Claire placed the bracelet on the dresser, hiding the engraving. She began unbuttoning her blouse.

"She does." Lorene felt as if the walls were moving closer, the curtains wrapping themselves around her arms and legs, binding her limbs to her body, preventing her from doing anything of her own free will. Mary would not want to move to the second floor, and Henry would be annoyed if she didn't. It was better when she'd allowed the situation to remain unresolved, hoping blindly it would work itself out. No matter what happened now, someone was going to be angry with her. "I thought Mary would stay here, that you would prefer the second floor."

Claire took off her blouse. Her skin was smooth and creamy. She unzipped her skirt and let it fall to the floor. She stepped out of it and left it lying in a puddle of dark blue. "Why would you think that?"

"It's not as stuffy. The heat rises, and this room gets quite warm."

Claire laughed. She pulled her slip over her head.

"You don't need to be getting undressed right now."

"I told you I need to get ready. Don't you like seeing your baby sister's body?"

Lorene's skin was suddenly warm. When had she become the prudish older woman? How had that happened? Every word out of her mouth sounded like her mother or one of her aunts. "You shouldn't leave your skirt on the floor." It seemed she couldn't stop. She was going to be the middle-aged mother to Claire even though neither one of them wanted it.

Claire kicked the skirt.

"Don't be childish," Lorene said.

"I prefer this room. It's more private."

"Why do you need privacy?"

"Everyone needs privacy."

"The room on the second floor is private."

"It's right across from yours."

"The door isn't across from ours." Lorene's skin grew warmer. She touched her neck.

"Am I embarrassing you? Sorry. Anyway, I want this room."

"It's been Mary's since she was four."

"Change is good, don't you think? It will make her more adaptable. More flexible. That's important. You never know what's going to happen to your life. Your mother might die, and you're an orphan, and then you get tossed about by relatives as if you were an unnecessary piece of furniture."

"We didn't intend to make you feel that way. That's not how we think of you."

Claire reached behind her back, unhooked her bra, and dropped it on the pile of clothing at her feet. Her breasts were round and soft, larger than Lorene had realized. She turned slightly.

"They're pretty, aren't they?" Claire said.

"I suppose it would be better for Mary to be near us. That's what Henry prefers."

"Well then," Claire said. "It all worked out. Hopefully, Mary won't throw a fit."

"Mary doesn't throw fits."

"Are you sure?"

"Enjoy your coffee date," Lorene said. She walked to the door and turned back.

Claire stood in the same spot, her hands on her hips. She arched her back, moving her shoulders so her breasts wobbled slightly.

"Just be cautious. Don't give up your heart too easily," Lorene said.

"Thank you for the advice. I think I know my heart better than you do."

Lorene stepped into the hallway and closed the door.

She'd been bested at every turn. She dreaded her conversation with Mary. At least Henry would be happy.

Mary didn't throw a fit in the classic sense, there was no screaming or flinging herself to the floor. Of course, she was a bit old for those kinds of theatrics. What she did was far worse. She inched away from Lorene to the end of the sofa and picked up a small round pillow. "Do you love Claire more than me?" she said.

"Of course not." Lorene moved over and wrapped her arms around Mary, pulling her halfway onto her lap. "Moving you out of that room has nothing to do with love."

"But I love my room. I love the trees. And the birds. I like my alcove. It's like two rooms in one. I like seeing the sky."

"You can see the sky from the other room. And there are trees outside the window, with birds."

"I can't see as much sky. And I can't see the birds fly, just sitting on the branches hopping about."

"Claire needs her own room."

"Why?"

"Because she's a big girl. Almost an adult."

"Doesn't she like sharing my room with me?"

"See. That doesn't make her feel welcome — thinking of it as your room."

"I won't say that again."

"It's better this way."

Tears swam across Mary's eyes. They didn't spill over but they turned her lashes damp and dark. Her voice trembled. "Why is it better? I like my room. You must love Claire more. She got to pick. She got to have my room that I've loved all this time. Ever since I was born."

"Not since you were born. You were in our room, and then in the room across from ours."

"Ever since I can remember."

Lorene held Mary tightly, breathing in the light, sweet aroma of sweat on her scalp. The baby smell of her head was so long gone, she couldn't even recall it. All she remembered was the knowledge that it was heavenly. But even now, she loved the feel and look and smell of her daughter. It wasn't worship at all. She loved her daughter and wanted to give her all the happiness she could. Part of being a mother was teaching hard lessons. Happiness eluded those who never learned you couldn't have everything you wanted. Lorene wasn't as good at the hard lessons.

Removing Mary from her bedroom seemed wrong, but a small part of her thought Henry's instinct might be right. It was better to keep their family sleeping together on a single floor of the house. Let their visitor have her own de facto apartment instead of inviting her to infiltrate their tiny family. Besides, Mary couldn't always have what she wanted, and she did need to learn that lesson. It was unfair but unavoidable.

"I love you more than anything," Lorene said. "Your father and I both do. And Aunt Claire loves you. But she's all alone in the world, and we want to make her feel loved, too. I let her choose that room. And it's the best place for her, so she'll have her own home within our home."

"She picked my room?" Mary twisted sideways, leaning away as if she wanted to break free of her mother's arms. "Why would she take my room away from me? I thought she liked me?"

"That's not what happened."

"But you said you let her choose."

"She suggested it first."

"It's the same thing."

Where was the Inner Light, why did everything in her heart seem dark when she'd spoken to Claire, when she tried to explain to Mary? She was stumbling blindly, leaving a trail of misunderstanding and hurt feelings. "Showing generosity to people we care about is important. Can you think of it as giving something special of yours to someone you love?"

"I suppose," Mary said.

Mary's body still felt stiff in her arms. Mary didn't understand at all. But why should she? Lorene understood it in her mind, but not in her heart.

Something inside of Lorene silently ticked off the location of each person in her household.

Claire had left the house without saying goodbye to any of them. She must have looked out the window of the alcove and seen Jacob walk through the front gate. She'd been on the porch, winding her silk scarf around her neck before he rang the bell. Henry had gone to San Francisco for the day to meet with his associates, and Mary was playing at her friend's home nearby. Annie was in the kitchen, rolling dough for a pie crust.

Lorene's feet moved deliberately up the stairs. At the second floor, she turned and glanced into the bedroom that would become Mary's. It was a pretty room, full of light. Mary would adjust.

Henry was planning to ask Jacob and a handyman to move Mary's furniture to the second floor. It seemed inappropriate for Jacob to be in Claire's bedroom, but when Lorene mentioned that fact to Henry, he stared at her as if she'd gone mad. As she started up the second flight of stairs, she thought maybe she had gone mad.

The bedroom door was closed. She opened it and went inside, leaving it open, already planning that she'd look less furtive if she were discovered with the door open.

A small writing table near the window had a pen and a box of stationery but no half-finished letters. She picked up the address book and flipped through it. Her assumption had been correct. There were four boys' names and addresses in the book. Boys? Or men, like Jacob? She had no way of knowing. She put the book back on the desk and went to Claire's dresser. She pulled open the top drawer. It was filled with slips and silk stockings and underwear. She ran her hand along the bottom of the drawer. The silky fabrics drifted across her wrists and the backs of her hands. All she felt was the lining paper. She removed her hand and closed the drawer. The second drawer contained sweaters and socks and three pairs of gloves. The next drawer yielded folded nightgowns. A few purses, a wool scarf, and a box with pieces of jewelry that had belonged to their mother were in the bottom drawer.

She stepped away from the dresser. Claire received mail every few days. Did she destroy every letter the moment she read it? Lorene went into the closet and looked through hat boxes and shoe boxes and Claire's luggage. There were no letters.

She returned to the bedroom and sat on the window seat. She hated the swimming sensation in her stomach. The Inner Light splashed across her thoughts with an ache of disappointment.

She stood and went to the bed. She knelt down and slid her hand between the mattress and boxspring. There was no paper, nothing but the edges of sheets and blankets. Near the head of the bed, her fingertips bumped a small box. She pulled it out. She sat back and removed the cardboard lid. Fitted inside was a blue velvet jewelry box. She turned over the cardboard container and let the box slide out into her hand. She snapped open the lid. Inside was a diamond the shape of a teardrop on a silver chain. She held it up to the light. It was a very nice diamond. Brilliantly cut. The stone was larger than her engagement ring. She put it back in the box and returned it to its spot under the mattress, hoping she'd put it close to the original location.

As she walked down the stairs, she tried to think of a reason why Claire would hide something like that. She hadn't worn it since she'd lived with them. Was it new? Surely Jacob couldn't afford such exquisite jewelry, and even if he could, they'd only seen each other once that Lorene knew of. She was pretty sure she would have noticed Claire slipping out of the house after dark to meet a man. Wouldn't she?

It hadn't belonged to their mother.

Claire was so young! Who had given her such an expensive piece of jewelry? There were so many things Lorene didn't know about Claire's life. Was she promised to someone? Had she stolen it? There was no answer that satisfied her more than another. Every possibility was equally unfounded and equally upsetting.

There was nothing to do but keep a closer eye on her. It might be difficult, once she was alone in the third-floor bedroom. Claire could climb the stairs at night without going past Lorene's bedroom door. She had assumed Claire went to bed and stayed there, but did she really know? And now that Claire didn't have to be concerned with disturbing Mary, there was no telling what she might be up to.

Eight

Mary sat in her window seat. Usually, when she curled up on the cushions, she looked out at the sky. Today, she kept her back to the window and surveyed her room. It was the most wonderful bedroom in the world. It was filled with light because it had two windows. The blue carpet and pale blue walls made it feel like she lived in the sky. She loved the alcove with its own window looking over the driveway where no one could see you because it was under the peak of the roof. On the opposite side of the stairs, across the hall, was a storage room. It was filled with furniture they no longer used and furniture from her grandparents' home. There were trunks and boxes full of clothes from the late 1800s, including racks of dresses that had belonged to Mary's grandmother. She loved to close the door and pretend she lived in a different world. She reclined on the fainting couch and batted her eyelids. She pretended she couldn't make up her mind which of the beautiful dresses she should wear. She'd tried on all of them. Her favorite was red velvet with rhinestones sewn along the neckline. A pale blue gown had a huge skirt with layers of gauzy fabric underneath. When she wore it, she walked about the room carrying the matching parasol. She liked it that no one in the entire world knew where she was, as if she'd slipped out of her house and been transported back in time.

The only thing she didn't care for in her bedroom was the shelf of staring, listening dolls. They would be moving with her to the second floor so she wouldn't be rid of them.

Now, she wouldn't get to hear any of Claire's stories. During dinner, Claire sat with a pleasant smile on her face, chewing ever so slowly. She answered questions posed by Mary's mother, or her father when he was home. She nodded and murmured *hmmm* when they were speaking, but that was all. The stories she whispered in the darkness would stay in the third story room, flying out the window to the passing birds. If Claire even kept the window open at night once Mary was gone.

The first story Claire had told her was the night after she'd come to stay with them.

"I noticed your father drinks whiskey," Claire said.

"What's whiskey?" Mary said.

"Alcohol."

"What's alcohol?"

Claire's twittering laugh sounded like wind chimes.

"It makes you feel good. It makes you laugh and have a

good time."

"How come I've never had it?"

"Only adults can drink it. And really, no one is supposed to drink it because it's against the law."

"My father wouldn't do something against the law."

"It's okay. A lot of people break that law. They think it's silly."

"Oh," Mary said. "How do you know he drinks it?"

"I saw him. After dinner."

Often he drank from one of the expensive glasses, but Mary hadn't known what the liquid was. Her mother drank tea every evening.

"Sometimes alcohol makes you drunk. People do stupid things when they're drunk. Sometimes they do mean things or nasty things. Men get in fights. If you drink too much of it, that's what happens," Claire said.

Mary turned onto her back and pulled the covers up to her neck. "That sounds scary."

"It is. Sometimes it's funny."

"My father never got in a fight."

"He's probably careful."

"I think so," Mary said.

"I had alcohol once. Not whiskey. It tastes nasty. I had champagne."

"What's that?"

"It's like wine. Wine is alcohol too. Champagne is like white wine, but with bubbles."

"That sounds good," Mary said.

"It's delicious. I snuck out of the house and went to a speakeasy. It's a place where they have alcohol, but they're careful who they let in so no one tells."

"Who would they tell?"

"The police."

"How did you sneak out?"

"I put my dead sister's hairpiece on the pillow. I stuffed pillows under the covers so when my mother came to the door to check on me, she thought I was sleeping. I climbed out the window, and I met my friend Robert at the corner of our street."

"We went to the movies. We had to sneak in there, too. There was a big group of people going in, and we just bunched up with them and walked in. The ticket taker was too busy flirting with one of the girls who was really pretty."

"What's flirting?" Mary said.

"When a boy tries to make a girl laugh, and they tease each other."

"I hate it when people tease me."

"It's a fun kind of teasing, where you know the person likes you more than he likes other girls."

"Oh."

"So we went into the movie that we weren't allowed to see. I'm tall for my age, and so is Robert, so no one took any notice of us. After the movie, the people we snuck in with went to the speakeasy. Robert and I heard them talking about it, and we asked if we could go."

"I got a little drunk, but it was fun. I was dancing. When you have alcohol, you don't care what anyone thinks of you."

"I suppose that's good," Mary said. "My mother says you shouldn't be concerned with what other people think of you, only what you think of yourself."

"That's true," Claire said. "But you know how you feel stupid when you say something dumb and your friends laugh? Or when you ask a stupid question? When you have alcohol, there aren't any wrong things to say. And you can dance and not think about whether you're clumsy. It was fun. But then I threw up."

"Yuck."

"It was awful. But it was worth it. I'll do it again, I just won't drink as much of it."

Later, Claire told her more about Robert, and other boys she knew. She whispered in a lower voice, although Mary's parents would never hear her way up on the third floor.

As they lay in bed on the night they'd gone out to see the concrete ship towed to the pier, Claire had told her there was a boy following her.

"How do you know?" Mary said.

"I saw him watching me. He likes me."

"Do you like him?"

"Maybe."

"Why does he follow you?"

"Because he likes looking at me."

Claire sounded awfully sure of herself. Of course, she had beautiful hair, and she looked nice in her dresses — with slim legs and a curvy body. But all girls Claire's age had curves. Why did this boy prefer Claire?

"I see him everywhere. He's always looking at me, thinking I don't notice," Claire said.

"Why does he think that?"

Claire laughed. "He tries to turn away when I look at him. He pretends he wasn't looking. I've seen him walking past the house."

"How do you know if you like him?"

"He's sort of handsome," Claire said. "He's tall."

"Oh. But is he nice? Does he tell funny stories?"

"I've never talked to him."

"Then how do you know if you like him?"

"Never mind," Claire said. "You'll understand when you're older."

There'd been other stories, things Mary tried to put out of her mind, things she didn't want to hear about. She wouldn't miss those stories, really only one story. But she would miss hearing Claire's breath while she slept. She would miss waking and seeing Claire's exotically messy dresser and the promise of all the older girl things that were ahead for Mary.

Most of all, she would miss the birds and sky and her

room. She would miss feeling special because she was sleeping at the very top of the house in the nicest room of all. She tried not to cry.

Nine

It was thrilling to be Claire's dinner guest with the King family, but eating a meal with Henry and his wife and daughter was filled with potential difficulties. Jacob wasn't sure if Henry viewed this evening as a gesture to an employee or a social event with his sister-in-law's boyfriend. The air in the foyer was cool, but his neck was covered with sweat. His hands had the texture of dead fish, and he wasn't looking forward to shaking Henry's hand.

Claire answered the door. She wore a pale pink dress that swept across her legs above her knees. As Jacob entered the house and she turned to lead the way, he saw she had a hair ornament with pink ribbons hanging from it as if they were growing out of her head. She ushered him into an enormous living room that reminded him of a hotel lobby. There were three separate sitting areas. The fireplace dominated the room, large enough for a child to walk into without bending her head. Two sofas faced it at an angle. In the front, where the house curved out in a semi-circular bulge that rose to the second floor and was adorned with a cupola on its domed roof, were two armchairs, bathed in light from the setting sun. At the back of the room was a second arrangement of a sofa and several chairs. Claire gestured at the sofa.

"We'll have some tea before dinner." She seated herself beside him and placed her hand on the sofa cushion, so her fingertips were less than an inch from touching his leg.

If he took her hand, as he knew she wanted, Henry might walk into the room and be disturbed. Although considering again Henry's indifferent reaction when Jacob had asked for permission to take Claire out, it probably wouldn't matter to him. The disapproval might come from Lorene. But if he didn't take her hand, Claire would be disappointed. He patted her fingers, then rested his hand on his leg. Claire reached over and took it, pulling his arm close to her body.

Lorene and Mary came into the room. Lorene took one of the chairs across from the sofa. Her eyes went immediately to their intertwined fingers. Claire introduced him without letting go of his hand. There was no way for him to approach Lorene and shake her hand. Was that a mistake?

Lorene asked how he was enjoying the day. She asked about his family and said she was very sorry to hear that when he told her his parents were deceased. She didn't look particularly sorry, she looked as if having dead parents at such a young age allowed her to put him into a category in her mind — someone who hadn't been raised properly, who lacked financial resources.

The woman who had answered the door the first time he took Claire on a walk came in carrying a tray with a teapot and four cups and saucers. Was Henry not joining them, or was he simply not drinking tea?

Mary took over the conversation, chattering about the concrete ship, the grand opening in June, wondering what kind of food they would serve in the dining room and commenting that even though the ship was sunk to the sea floor, it seemed as if it might sway like any boat when people were dancing.

When their tea was gone, they went into the dining room. A table large enough to seat twelve people was covered with a white cloth. It was set with fine china and silverware that glinted from the light of the chandelier that blazed overhead even though it wasn't dark yet. Henry was standing in the far corner. He came toward them and kissed Lorene's cheek. He shook Jacob's hand. "Glad you could join us."

Lorene gestured to the single chair at her left. Mary took the chair to Lorene's right with Claire seated beside her. Henry walked around the table and pulled out Lorene's chair. When she sat down, he leaned over and kissed her cheek again.

Henry stood behind his chair at the head of the table while he prayed over their upcoming meal. He said *Amen* and marked the sign of the cross on his forehead, breastbone, and shoulders. Lorene and Mary did the same. Jacob tapped his forehead, a moment or two behind the others, making it appear like an afterthought. Claire smiled and kept her hands on her lap.

Dinner was some kind of golden brown bird surrounded by small roasted potatoes. There was a green salad, steamed peas, carrots glistening with butter, and soft, fluffy-looking rolls.

Jacob took a bite of the bird's crusty skin and the dark, damp meat.

"How do you like the duck?" Henry said.

"Very tasty," Jacob said.

"I don't like eating ducks," Mary said.

"God created them to be eaten." Henry spread butter on his roll, moving the knife slowly, making sure the butter reached to the edge. He took a bite.

"God is mean."

"Careful of blasphemy," Henry murmured.

Mary pushed the small piece of duck to the side of her plate and cut a potato in half.

Henry talked about the weather and the economic news. He went on for quite some time about how fortunate they were to have a solid financial situation, not subject to the stock market disaster and the resulting loss of jobs. When his speech wound down, he attacked his meal. Mary took over, telling them about a book she'd read at the library. It concerned a woman reporter who pretended she was mad and had herself committed to a hospital for the insane. When her employer arranged for her release a few weeks later, she wrote an exposé of the lack of warm clothes in near-freezing buildings, the filthy, ice cold baths, inadequate amounts of substandard food, and general cruelty inflicted on the inmates.

Henry looked at Lorene. "You shouldn't let her read things like that."

Lorene smiled. "I can't help what she finds at the library."

Lorene hadn't taken a single bite of duck. She put her knife and fork across her plate and nudged the white and gold china plate ever so slightly away from her. "You'll be seventeen in a few weeks, Claire. What should we do to celebrate?"

Claire's pale eyebrows were pressed down, mirroring her frown. There was a tightness to her lips that made her appear older than she was, although none of that diminished her beauty. She glared at Lorene. He hadn't realized she was so young, but what did it matter? Henry was considerably older than Lorene. Age meant nothing when you fell in love. As the idea of falling in love passed across his mind, he felt his skin grow warm. The heat was so intense he felt as if a log was blazing in the fireplace behind his chair. He hoped his red cheeks didn't betray his thoughts.

No one spoke. Mary glanced from Claire to her mother.

"Seventeen. You're growing up so fast," Lorene said.

"I'm a little old for a birthday party," Claire said.

"Nonsense." Lorene smiled at Jacob. "Seventeen is something to celebrate. You're no longer a little girl."

"I haven't been a little girl for a very long time." Claire put down her knife and fork. She turned the piece of duck over and pinched the crispy skin between her thumb and forefinger. She peeled it off the meat. She tore the skin in half and put a piece in her mouth.

"You're very much a little girl when you eat like that," Lorene said. "Where are your manners?"

Claire stuffed the other piece of skin in her mouth. Speaking as she chewed, she said, "The skin is the best part."

"So, no party?" Lorene said. "Mary was hoping she could help plan it."

"I was?" Mary looked at her mother.

"I don't want a party," Claire said. "Let's talk about something else."

Annie appeared in the doorway. Lorene took a sip of water and turned. "I'm finished, Annie. And will you bring the tea? We'll have dessert after everyone else is finished. Oh, and will you also bring a washcloth for Claire to wipe her fingers? Thank you."

Annie took Lorene's plate and nodded. She left the room.

Claire stuck her finger and thumb in her mouth and sucked loudly.

Jacob wasn't sure whether he should laugh. She was staring directly at him, managing a wicked smile despite the way her lips were wrapped around her fingers.

"Jacob," Lorene said. "I hope you know how much Henry values you. He's always talking about how trustworthy you are."

"Thank you." He glanced at Henry who continued slicing his duck into thin strips.

"You're such an asset," Lorene said.

Henry looked up. He put a piece of duck in his mouth and chewed, studying his wife as if he was considering Jacob's value for the first time.

Maybe Henry didn't consider him such an asset after all. Jacob took a sip of water.

"In fact," Lorene said, "I had a thought. If you don't mind my commenting on your business matters."

Henry nodded. It wasn't clear if he minded or if he was signaling her to go ahead.

"I know you don't normally like me to interfere…"

Henry waved his fork in the air. "Say what you want." He ate another piece of duck followed quickly by a piece of potato.

"I know your San Francisco business is sensitive, and

involves a lot more money than your local operations. It seems to me, Jacob would be a good person to oversee that so you don't have to travel up there quite as often."

Claire stabbed several pieces of carrot and put them in her mouth. She gripped the fork, holding it out in front of her, staring at the tines as if she wasn't sure what to do next. Her knuckles were white, the skin pulled tightly over the bones as she squeezed the fork more tightly. When she lifted her head and glared at Lorene, she looked as if she wanted to stab Lorene with the fork. "You haven't been busy enough telling me what to do? Now you're going to run your husband's business?"

Lorene lifted the teapot Annie had set beside her. She filled her cup. "It was just a suggestion. I'm not trying to run anything."

"Like hell you're not," Claire said.

"Claire! We don't curse in this house," Lorene said.

"It's a good suggestion," Henry said. He pushed his plate to the side. "Will you bring me a cup of tea, Mary?" He lifted the napkin off his lap and patted his lips. "An excellent suggestion, in fact." He dropped the napkin on the table and looked at Claire. "This is how it is when you're married. You know one another's minds. I'd already been thinking about this."

Claire placed her fork on her plate. She leaned toward Henry. She put her hand on his arm. "I know how that is — when two people have the same thoughts." She smiled. She left her hand on his arm, turned and smiled at Lorene. "Jacob and I are finished eating. We don't care for any dessert." She let go of Henry's arm, pushed out her chair, and stood up. She left her chair standing away from the table. She dropped her pale green cloth napkin on her plate. Immediately the pooled butter began to bleed across it. She looked at Jacob. "Let's go for a walk."

He stood up and turned toward Lorene. "Thank you for the delicious dinner." He looked at Henry. "Thank you, sir."

"Let Annie know if you want a cup of tea on the veranda," Henry said. "Or if you change your mind about dessert. Maybe Jacob would like apple pie."

"I don't think so. We're going for a walk," Claire said.

She waited for Jacob to move around the table. She put her arm through his and leaned against him. She led him out of the dining room into the breakfast room. She opened the French door, and they went onto the back veranda. They sat beside each other in wooden chairs that were shaped so his body was partially reclining, his legs supported in a gentle curve.

"It would be terrible if you worked in San Francisco," Claire said.

"Why's that?" If the job was more important to Henry, if there was more responsibility, there might be another increase in pay. He'd already had one raise less than a month ago — seven-fifty a day. Working in San Francisco would be so much more exciting than sleepy little Aptos.

"We wouldn't see each other."

"I wouldn't live there," he said.

"He might expect you to."

"I don't know if I can afford that." He saw his hoped-for raise slipping away before his eyes, as if the money were melting like the butter oozing off the carrots, absorbed by exorbitant rent.

"Even if you didn't have to live there, you'd be gone all the time."

"Not all the time."

"It wouldn't work," she said. "I'd have to find someone else."

Was she breaking it off? Simply because he might work in another city? If she liked him, possibly even loved him — he'd hoped she loved him — why would she do that? If she loved him, a different city wouldn't matter. Hadn't she said she knew what it was like for two people to have similar thoughts? And they did, on so many subjects. "When you turn seventeen, you could move to San Francisco. Your birthday's only a few weeks away."

"My inheritance from my mother's estate is rather modest. I don't think I could manage that."

He would certainly be earning more. And they could be married, if she was seventeen. Couldn't they? There were no parents who might prevent them. She wouldn't have to afford an apartment. "Let's wait and see," he said.

"I'm just telling you, I don't think it will work."

He stood up. "Should we go for a walk?"

"It's dark."

"We could sit in the front garden. There are lights on the path."

"What's wrong with this?"

"I feel like they're watching. That they can hear us," he said.

"They're still in the dining room."

"Please?"

"Okay."

They walked down the steps and moved along the path. The crescent moon, blurred by thin clouds, provided some light until they reached the front of the house where small lanterns around the edge illuminated the lawn. They made their way into the garden, dense with flowering shrubs and small trees. They sat on the bench. He liked it that he could see the house. If anyone came out the front, he would see them before their eyes adjusted enough to notice him and Claire. He put his arm around her shoulders. She didn't lean into him like she usually did. He put his hand on her face and turned her head gently. He kissed her lips. "I love you, Claire. I'm not going anywhere without you."

She kissed his lips and the tip of his nose.

"Do you love me?" he said.

"I haven't thought about it."

Her answer was unsettling, but he wouldn't push her. She needed more time. She was young, not as sure of what she wanted yet. It was clear that she liked him a lot, and she was clearly upset that she wouldn't see him as often if he worked in San Francisco.

"She's trying to split us up," Claire said.

"Who?"

"My sister. She doesn't like that I'm seeing you."

"Why not?"

"She thinks I'm too young for you."

"You seem much older than you are," he said.

"I feel older." She lifted her face and parted her lips slightly.

He kissed her again, longer this time. His body ached for her. Seventeen wasn't too young for marriage. Or maybe they didn't have to wait for a ceremony. It wasn't as if either of them adhered to Catholic doctrine, and these were modern times. Still, he did want to marry her. He adored her. His life would be dull and colorless without her. He'd never known it was possible to be as happy as he'd been the past few weeks. "To celebrate your birthday, will you go to dinner with me on the concrete ship? For the grand opening?"

"Oh. That would be wonderful." She put her hand on his thigh and squeezed the space above his knee. "I won't let her separate us."

"We'll find a way to be together, even if it's hard at first. If I have to go back and forth to San Francisco a lot, I still have my responsibilities here. I'm sure Henry wouldn't want me to stay up there all day every day."

"I suppose not." She leaned into him.

They sat quietly for a while, their arms wrapped around each other. Their hearts beat with the same rhythm, their breathing was synchronized. He knew exactly what Henry meant when he said two people have the same thoughts. He would marry her. There was no doubt she was the woman for him.

The light outside the front door came on. It spilled across the lawn but didn't reach the secluded bench. The front door opened and Henry stepped onto the porch. He stood for a moment, peering into the darkness.

"I think he's looking for you," Jacob whispered.

"Maybe."

Henry crossed the porch and stood near the steps. Although he seemed to be looking directly at them, Jacob was sure they couldn't be seen, partially hidden behind a trellis gripped by wisteria. The lawn lanterns didn't reach as far as the garden. It only seemed as if Henry saw them because of his self-assured posture and the direction he faced. Henry reached into his pocket and pulled out a cigar. He struck a match and held it to the end, puffing rapidly to draw the flame into the tightly rolled tobacco.

"That's nasty," Claire whispered. "I hate cigars. They stink."

"You can hardly smell it."

"I can smell it perfectly. It's covering up the lovely flowers."

Jacob hadn't noticed the aroma of flowers. All he'd smelled before Henry came outside was damp night air and dirt and a whisper of something sweet on Claire's skin. The cigar didn't smell any different from the dirt. It was rather pleasant. Men and women smelled things differently. He kissed her cheek. He leaned forward slightly, hoping to kiss her lips again. She pushed him away and wriggled out from under his arm.

He put his mouth close to her ear. "What's wrong?"

"He's right there. You can't kiss me now."

"He can't see us."

"He can hear."

"I don't think so."

"It doesn't matter. I feel as if he can." She stood up and leaned over, putting her face close to his.

With her face so close, he was wild to kiss her again.

"You stay here," she said. "I'll go inside, and when he's finished with his cigar, you can leave."

"I'm supposed to sit here in the cold and dark for an hour?"

"It's not that cold, and it won't be an hour. He won't smoke the whole thing. He never does." She touched Jacob's mouth with her fingers, turned and tiptoed across the garden, as if Henry might hear her footsteps if she put her feet too firmly on the grass. The tiptoeing was pointless because, in a moment, Henry would see her.

Jacob heard her speak, but couldn't make out her words.

"You were sitting alone in the dark?" Henry said.

She spoke again. She pinched her nose, climbed the stairs, and walked quickly to the front door.

Henry turned and watched her enter the house. When the door closed, he remained with his back to Jacob for a moment. Then, he turned slowly and blew out a long stream of smoke. He walked down the steps and crossed the lawn. He stopped a few feet from where Jacob sat. "She's like a child in that way," Henry said. "Believing she can fool me."

Jacob couldn't think of what to say. He should have laughed, but now it was too late.

"Mind if I sit?" Henry said.

"Not at all." Jacob moved to his right so there was plenty of room for Henry. He missed the warmth of Claire's body. He shivered.

"Does the smoke bother you?"

"No."

"Good." Henry settled on the bench. "A man who's offended by cigar smoke isn't fit for civilized conversation."

Jacob nodded, hating his eagerness to agree.

Henry stuck the cigar between his teeth. He held it there and slid his hand beneath his lapel. He pulled out a flask.

Despite the darkness, the silver container shimmered. He unscrewed the cap, removed the cigar from his mouth, and put the flask to his lips. He swallowed and sighed with pleasure. He held the flask out to Jacob.

"I don't know," Jacob said.

"Have you tasted scotch whiskey?"

"I've never had liquor at all. Just beer."

"You don't know what you're missing."

"It's illegal."

Henry laughed. He took another sip. "So is beer."

Somehow, beer didn't seem as dangerous. It wasn't shrouded in the same cloud of stories regarding gangsters and violence.

"Have a taste," Henry said.

Jacob took the flask. He touched the opening to his lips. Any sense that he didn't want to taste Henry's saliva was overcome by the strength of the alcohol. It was pure and clean and allowed no other taste or smell to get in the way. Even the odor of the cigar faded in its presence. He tipped the flask and let the liquid slide across his tongue. He coughed. It burned, setting his throat on fire. At the same time, the alcohol flamed beneath the skin of his face, taking the edge off his thoughts, erasing the fear of what he was doing, removing his unease toward Henry. They were business partners, almost. Colleagues, maybe even friends. The trust between them was mutual, and there was no risk in what they were doing, they were equal parties to it.

He handed the flask to Henry.

"Pretty damn good, isn't it," Henry said.

Jacob nodded, not sure he could speak. He coughed again.

Henry laughed.

"It's very good," Jacob said.

"One of the best." Henry took another drink. "Prohibition will be over in a few years. Finally, the morons in Washington are waking up to the tax potential, instead of being held hostage by a bunch of old women and religious fanatics."

"You're not religious?" Jacob said.

"That's not what I'm saying." Henry took a sip of scotch and handed the flask to Jacob.

There was a loose feeling to Jacob's lips, a numbness in the tip of his nose. He took several sips while Henry went on—

"People insert their own prejudice and prudishness into religion. They take doctrines of the Church out of context and twist them to fit how they already see the world. I believe God is one of those *live and let live* type of fellows. All you have to do is look around at the world, read a bit about its history, and you can see He takes a hands-off approach."

Jacob nodded. He'd never given God much thought. All he knew of God was the boredom of Sunday mass and the tedium of flicking rosary beads past your fingertips. It was true, there was no evidence that an omnipotent being who gave any thought to the suffering of the human race was in control — not with the stock market crashing and wars since the dawn of time. People dying too young and getting horrid diseases. For a man who was completely focused on making money, Henry had a lot of wisdom about life. He was surprisingly philosophical. Jacob handed the flask back to Henry.

"Yes, Prohibition will end, and we can return to sanity. Getting rid of it will get the economy back on its feet. Taxes, vibrant commerce, people enjoying life and spending money. Sure, businessmen who can tolerate heavy risk are making a killing now, but the government could rake in a lot of that profit." He took a sip from the flask and returned it to his pocket.

Although the stuff was delicious and made him feel warm and content, Jacob was glad to see the flask disappear. He wasn't confident he could walk home without staggering. The last thing he needed was an arrest for drunkenness. Henry might be certain Prohibition was on its way out, but he only had to walk up the stairs inside his house and fall into bed. Jacob regretted agreeing to even a single sip. How would he make it home?

"Which is why businessmen should take advantage of the current climate," Henry said. "Do you agree?"

"Take advantage?"

"Yes, men who see opportunities for profit. Especially

higher than average profit. Distributing alcohol."

"Bootleggers?"

"Such a derogatory term. It originated with men who were essentially pirates. It doesn't apply to educated investors and businessmen."

Jacob nodded. He realized Henry was staring at the house and didn't notice the movement of his head. "Oh," he said.

"The scotch is very good, isn't it," Henry said.

"Yes."

"It's ridiculous that it's illegal. It takes fine craftsmanship to make a beverage like this. Years of study, careful attention to the process and quality control."

"I suppose it does." Jacob hadn't thought about it that way.

"The same goes for vintners."

"Yes."

"And the government has turned those good men into criminals with the stroke of a pen. Trying to drive them out of business. It's shockingly unjust."

The alcohol burned in Jacob's chest, warming him even as the wind picked up. He felt the injustice to people who had spent a lifetime mastering the art of fermenting wine or distilling whiskey. It was an outrage that a bunch of old women could put peoples' livelihoods at risk. And what did it accomplish? It didn't stop people from drinking liquor. His brother had been procuring beer since he was fifteen.

"A man has to be smart to be in that business," Henry said. He puffed on his cigar. "Always on his toes, discreet."

"Yes," Jacob said.

"You have all those qualities."

Jacob's breath caught, but Henry rushed ahead before he could speak.

"Lorene was right in pointing out how valuable you are. I've never had a more trustworthy employee. Or business partner. And that's what I've come to think of you as. You're a partner in the most integral parts of my operations. I hate the thought of shipping you off to San Francisco. You have intimate knowledge of this area, how people operate around here. You can't buy that knowledge. It's worth a lot. In San Francisco, you'd be a fish out of water, at a disadvantage to our competitors."

Jacob's chest felt as if it were filled with concrete. Everything was riding on the allure of San Francisco. Sure, he'd still be here with Claire, but the short-lived dream of another lucrative raise was sliding through his fingers like water.

"I value how well you know this area," Henry said.

"I've grown up here. My brother and I spent a lot of time walking around, hiking, exploring. Getting into trouble." He laughed.

Henry echoed his chuckle. "I have a business proposal for you."

"What's that?"

"How would you like to see a significant jump in your income? Twenty dollars a day."

"*Twenty dollars*?" Jacob turned.

Henry's profile presented a noncommittal expression. He blew out a cloud of smoke.

It had been a mistake to react with such obvious shock and pleasure. It wasn't a good negotiating tactic at all, but what did he have to negotiate? *Twenty dollars?* "What would I…"

"You'd have to possess a high tolerance for risk. And the utmost discretion, as I mentioned."

"I'm not afraid of risk, sir."

"I'm in the liquor transport business myself. That's why I can get ahold of, and afford, I might add, fine scotch like this."

"Oh." Jacob was cold. His fingers were numb, and his bones were sticks of ice.

"It's not dangerous. And the risk isn't intolerable, if you're young and believe in yourself. All you would do is pick up cases of liquor at the beach and take them to my customers. It would mean working at night, of course. And once there's access to the concrete ship, that will open up more opportunity for getting it ashore more easily."

"Why?"

"They look for boats coming up to the beach. A boat approaching the bow of the ship wouldn't be seen easily. *As* easily."

"I don't know, I…"

"You've already done it. Remember the package I gave you to take to Sharp that night? A pint of whiskey. It was easy. You weren't nervous, no one was watching you." Henry laughed. "It was a test."

"I didn't know."

"And that's the same attitude you should adopt going forward, if you're interested in the proposal. I think you're a smart kid, but I don't know yet whether or not you have vision. In another year or two, it might not be as lucrative, depending on when Prohibition gets repealed. You can think about it of course, if you're hesitant. If you've never thought about your tolerance for risk."

"I don't have to think about it," Jacob said. "The way you've described it, I can see it's a good opportunity. And it was easy delivering that package. It's a stupid law, I agree. And why not profit from it while we can? It makes me angry that people who grow grapes and make wine are treated as if their livelihoods didn't matter."

"Exactly."

"What do I need to do?"

"We'll discuss the details tomorrow in my office. For now, why don't you sleep at the house. We don't need you catching a policeman's eye walking home inebriated." He laughed. "Annie can make up a bed in the screened porch."

"Thank you. And thanks for the opportunity," Jacob said. "I won't disappoint you."

Henry tapped the ash off his cigar. “I know you won’t.” He curved his fingers and cradled the cigar there, letting the end grow dark. After a few minutes, he stood up.

Jacob followed him around the side of the house to the veranda. He wasn’t sure he’d be able to sleep, even with the scotch causing his blood to creep languorously through his veins. His heart was pounding at twice its normal speed — it might keep him awake all night, his thoughts racing to keep up.

Ten

This was Mary's last night sleeping in the bedroom that Claire had stolen from her. The light by Mary's bed was still on, and Claire sat on the window seat, gazing out into the darkness.

"I know you're angry with me," Claire said.

"I'm not."

"Don't lie, Mary. I can tell when someone's lying to me."

"I'm not lying. I'm sad, that's all."

"And angry," Claire said.

Mary sat up. "I'm not angry. I'm sad to leave my room, and sad you don't want to sleep in the same room as me."

Claire turned from the window. She smiled at Mary with a look that said Mary wasn't very bright. "Of course I want to sleep in the same room. But your mother and father don't want it. Mostly your father, I think."

"How do you know that?"

"They want you sleeping near them, so they can keep an eye on you. I didn't *take* your bedroom, I just figured out why they wanted us to stop sharing a room. It's obvious that having me stay in this room was their only option."

"That's not true."

"Think about it. They're worried because you're a child and I'm an adult woman. Now that I have a boyfriend, they're scared I'll corrupt you."

Mary snuggled down beneath the covers again. She closed her eyes. She wasn't sure what to say to Claire. Of course, her parents didn't want her corrupted, although she wasn't sure how Claire would do such a thing. Really, it was Jacob who was corrupting Claire. Maybe her mother and father didn't notice that, they were too busy worrying about who slept where. Claire didn't laugh much anymore, unless Jacob was around. She never wanted to go look at the concrete ship or collect shells on the beach. She never wanted to do anything except go out with Jacob. And she was mean. She'd been mean to Mary's mother about having a seventeenth birthday party. Even what she was saying now sounded mean. She treated Mary like she was stupid. Claire was the one who lied. She thought Mary was too young to understand that. Claire had a choice, and she'd chosen this room. It wasn't because Claire might corrupt her. They wanted to do whatever they could to make Claire happy, even if it meant taking things away from Mary. And Claire wanted this bedroom.

"Why are you sulking?" Claire said.

"I'm not."

"I should show you something. But you have to keep it a secret. I'm not sure how good you are at keeping secrets."

"I'm very good at it." Mary forced her eyes to stay closed. She didn't want to talk. She wanted to go to sleep, wake up in the morning, and try to find things to love about her new bedroom. This was stupid, pretending they were friends spending their last night together. They weren't friends at all.

"Even if it's a secret about something that's considered bad?"

Mary opened her eyes. "What do you mean?" She turned her head toward Claire, but Claire was looking out the window again.

"I did something I shouldn't have. But it was too much temptation, I couldn't help it."

Mary sat up. She didn't want to talk, and she was tired of Claire being a know-it-all, but now she was curious. So curious she could feel herself drawn once again into Claire's power. Claire knew she was curious and was tricking her into talking, but she didn't care. "What did you do?"

"It's not horrible. I'm not going to have a baby or anything like that."

Mary had no idea what having a baby had to do with it or why that would be considered bad. Babies were wonderful, but she was not going to ask a question and have Claire treat her like she was too dumb to know things. Claire liked doing that, a lot. Mary wasn't sure if that was Jacob's fault, or Claire had always been that way and Mary hadn't noticed it right away. "Are you going to tell me or not? Because I'm tired."

Claire stood up. She smoothed her nightgown over her hips. "Promise you won't tell? You have to promise. Cross your heart and hope to die. You can *not* tell your mother. She would be furious. She might throw me out of the house. Not only for corrupting you, but for stealing. You can't tell your father, either."

"Did you steal something from my mother?"

Claire laughed sharply. "Of course not."

"Who did you steal from?"

"I can't say."

"Why not?"

"It's bad enough I'm showing it to you. Do you promise? On your mother's grave?"

"I promise." She didn't like the part about her mother's grave. What did that mean? Her mother was alive.

Claire went to her bed. She knelt down and slid her hand beneath the mattress. She reached farther until half her arm was buried. When she pulled it out, she was holding a small box. She took a few steps to Mary's bed and sat on the edge near Mary's feet.

Mary moved over to make room.

Claire took the lid off the box. She pulled out a dark blue velvet box and snapped open the lid. She held it toward Mary. "Isn't it beautiful? A teardrop."

"It's pretty." Mary touched the stone. It was cold and hard.

"It's a diamond."

"I know." Mary's breath felt heavy inside her lungs. "Where did you get it?"

"I said I can't tell you. But it was so beautiful, I had to have it. I like to think the teardrop is for my mother. And the person I took it from will hardly notice. I mean, the person will notice it's gone, but they can afford to buy another one."

"What are you going to do with it?"

"Wear it for a special occasion."

"Your birthday?"

Claire laughed. "Jacob invited me to the grand opening on the ship. I might wear it then. So everyone can see how special I am."

"You get to eat dinner on the ship?" Mary felt like crying. It was so unfair. Why did Claire get to go and she didn't? Claire wasn't truly an adult, she just liked to pretend she was. Claire knew how badly Mary wanted to go on the ship, so she was bragging about it. It seemed as if she was bragging about stealing. As if it made her special and important. It seemed as if Claire thought stealing meant she was smarter than Mary, although Mary couldn't figure out why she thought that.

Claire closed the lid on the velvet box and put it back in the cardboard container. “You better never touch it.”

“Why would I do that?”

“I just thought I should mention it.”

Mary wriggled down under the covers. Her feet shoved against Claire’s hip, but she didn’t care. She wished she was sleeping in the second-floor bedroom right now.

Eleven

Lorene woke suddenly. Had she heard a noise? She switched on the bedside lamp. The other side of the bed was untouched. She looked at the clock on the dresser across from the foot of the bed. Two-thirty. It was two-thirty in the morning, and Henry wasn't home? She sat up. She picked up her glass of water from the nightstand and took a sip.

Where was he?

She plumped the pillows and arranged them behind her. She leaned against the headboard and took another sip of water. He'd never been out this late. Had something happened? Had he been robbed and beaten up? An accident? Fire? She whimpered and tugged the blankets up to her neck. She didn't want to have such thoughts. Why had her mind rushed to the worst, almost the worst?

He was dining with William Sharp and a few others at the Sharp home. She could call Margaret, but that was so thoughtless. Hearing the phone ring in the middle of the night — past the middle of the night — would terrify Margaret. It was an ungodly hour. No good news came from a phone that began ringing hours after midnight.

Could they still be there, smoking and drinking whiskey in William's parlor? That had happened often enough before, but never this late. Never after ten or eleven.

She wasn't sure whether she should be scared or upset, or simply put it out of her head, knowing men often forgot the time, caught up arguing about politics or discussing the splintering, sinking economy. Every conversation eventually touched on the problems since the crash of the stock market — so many people had lost their jobs, their farms, their shops. Discussions went on for hours. She was lucky to have a husband who had so many business interests, who saved money and invested it carefully, who spent hours every night making notes in his ledger.

But two-thirty in the morning?

She pushed the covers off and got out of bed. There had to be something she could do. She shouldn't assume the worst. Worrying accomplished nothing, but neither could she remain in bed, blindly hoping for a reasonable explanation. At the very least, after all this time, Henry might be drunk. If he was, she almost didn't want him to come home. She put on her bathrobe and opened the door.

From the doorway, she could see Mary's bedroom door. It was closed. Was this something new — Mary sleeping with her door closed? Was this the price of forcing her out of her room? Now, Mary must feel like a second-class member of the family so she closed herself off from them. Lorene's heart felt as if a spider were creeping across it, dragging its chilly, delicate feet across the surface. What they'd done, what she'd done, was wrong. She'd gone along too easily with Henry's demand. The day-to-day attention to raising Mary was her job, Henry always said so. And it wasn't only that he said so, Lorene knew it was true. She wanted that responsibility, and she'd succumbed to his opinion and her sister's manipulation. No matter how much Claire had suffered, Mary should be first in everything. Claire was a guest, Mary's was the life Lorene was responsible for. She walked to Mary's door and rested her head against the smooth wood. Could she hear her daughter's breath? Maybe Mary wasn't even in there. The house felt too large and too empty. Maybe Lorene was its only occupant.

When Mary was an infant, Lorene had worried constantly her baby would die in her sleep. It was a fear that grew out of tremendous, overwhelming love. She was consumed by the tiny creature entrusted to her. Several times a night, during the months when Mary slept in their bedroom, Lorene climbed out of bed and touched her baby's nose to be sure she was breathing. She'd laid her palm gently on Mary's chest, to feel the subtle rise and fall. Even after Mary moved into the nursery, Lorene crept into the room at night, if only to watch her child sleep, marveling at the perfect skin, the pale lashes on her cheeks moving like tiny spiders themselves in response to Mary's dreams. If the hint of a smile on her tiny lips was an indication, her daughter's dreams were peaceful.

She put her hand on Mary's doorknob. If Lorene opened the door and Mary was partially awake, she might be frightened. It was doubtful at two-thirty, quarter to three, now. As far as Lorene knew, children slept through the night. It was adult life that brought sleeplessness. She turned the knob soundlessly and opened the door a few inches. Mary lay with her back to the door, her hair fanned across the pillow and hanging over the side of the bed. Lorene stepped away and closed the door, hoping the disturbance hadn't introduced an element of darkness into her daughter's dreams.

She went to the stairs.

On the floor above, the box with the diamond teardrop rested beneath Claire's head, waiting. For what? It drove Lorene mad, trying to think where Claire might have gotten it. She worried about all the things she didn't know about Claire, about all the questionable people Claire might have invited into her life. Like Jacob. Although, Henry had been the first to invite him into their lives. Jacob was nice enough, a charming, polite boy. But much too old for Claire. Even if the age difference was less than hers and Henry's, things were different now. Men took more advantage of women now that there weren't as many rules. Or maybe things weren't any different. It didn't matter for the simple reason that Claire was immature, despite her assertion she was an adult.

The first floor was completely dark except for a greenish watery glow coming through the stained glass window alongside the front door. The porch light was on. That meant it was unlikely Henry was in his study. She'd check anyway. It gave her something to do and kept her from thinking of fires and accidents and drunken fights. It turned her thoughts away from Claire. She moved her hand along the wall in the foyer and found the light switch. She moved through the foyer, past the entrance to the dining room, around the corner to the small space outside his study door. No light came from beneath the door, but she wasn't sure whether it would if he was using only his desk light. Knowing he wasn't in there, she rapped loudly on the solid wood door. After a moment, she put her hand on the knob. It was locked.

The more she moved about, the more any hope of returning to sleep evaporated. It felt as if the sun would be rising any moment. She went into the kitchen and turned on the light. The fixtures and counter glistened with the solid rubbing Annie had given them. Every night she polished the room as if she were expecting a presidential visit the next day. They were so lucky to have Annie. She deserved more appreciation. Henry should increase her pay.

As if she expected someone to lead her in the right direction, she stood in the center of the room, turning slowly, studying the familiar counters and ovens, the canisters of staples, the door to the pantry, the small white table in the corner. The notice for the grand opening of the concrete ship lay in the center of the table — as if they needed reminding. There were notices posted all over town. It was a constant topic of conversation.

She was cold. She rubbed her upper arms and considered boiling water for tea. Drinking a cup or two of tea would seal her sleepless fate for the night.

No matter how she pretended otherwise, she was worried. And she was utterly helpless to take any action to alleviate her fear. She might as well be a child herself, a child younger than Mary for all her ability to take charge of the situation. If she telephoned, she'd arouse unnecessary fear in others. If Henry knew she was trying to check on him, he'd be annoyed. There was nothing to do but wait. She turned out the lights in the kitchen and foyer, climbed the stairs, and returned to her room. The sheets were cold now and did nothing to comfort her. She curled into a ball and closed her eyes. It was futile. She was condemned to lie here with spinning thoughts — regrets for the day past, fears for the future, complaints about her marriage, sadness over things she'd lost — following after one another until her head and her heart ached. She would have thought she would fall asleep from pure mental exhaustion.

The soft hum of Henry's car drifted in through the partially open bedroom window. The bedside light was still on. Lorene leaned up on her elbow and looked at the clock. Three-fifteen. She turned out the light. It might be too late. He might have already seen it as he entered the driveway.

A moment later, she heard the front door open and close, then silence.

If she turned on the light and Henry was drunk, it wouldn't be a pleasant conversation. It wasn't as if he was a drunkard who couldn't control his liquor, but when he was with his colleagues, they sometimes overindulged. The chance of him being arrested worried her more than the fact he was drinking. Enjoying a drink was understandable, but it was illegal outside of their home. Why couldn't he control himself and obey the law? She managed to live without wine. It was for the good of the country, they said. Maybe, maybe not, but it was the law, and it bothered her that he was so dismissive of it.

Waiting until tomorrow to talk to him would be better. She closed her eyes and turned on her side, trying to find a comfortable position so that when he came into the room, she didn't move suddenly and betray the fact that she was awake.

Two days went by before she had a chance to speak to

Henry about staying out nearly all night. She started to worry it seemed out of place now that so much time had passed.

Claire and Mary were in Mary's bedroom, sitting on the floor playing Russian Bank. They had a plate of cookies and a pot of tea on a tray, cards spread out in even rows between them. Lorene didn't expect to see them for the rest of the evening. It made her happy that Claire was doing something wholesome, that she was giving attention to Mary, who clearly worshipped her young aunt. More than that, she was pleased that Claire wasn't out with Jacob, walking about, possibly finding a secluded spot to kiss, or more.

She found Henry in his study with the door open. She stepped into the room she rarely entered. "Are you almost finished?"

"Completely." He smiled and pushed his chair away from his desk.

"I can make tea. And we have snickerdoodle cookies."

He grinned.

The oversized smile filled her with warmth. He looked like a boy, not a man with so many responsibilities, worries to make his nights as sleepless as hers, even though she didn't know what his worries consisted of. Money, probably. Keeping employees in line. If she knew more about his work, they might feel closer to each other. Some wives advised their husbands on business matters. Their husbands kept them informed on all the details and so their wives were able to contribute knowledgeably. She wasn't sure why hers and Henry's relationship hadn't evolved that way. It was as if their world split in two after Mary was born. As Mary grew older, Lorene knew less and less about his life, and although she told him about her days, he seemed detached. She felt as if she was making a report to someone outside of their family.

Part of the problem was that she'd married a man so much older. Maybe that was her concern for Claire. Lorene wasn't just protecting a child from the worldly ways of a man. If a man's life was already established when you married him, it undercut the equality of building a new life together.

Henry came to the doorway. He kissed her lips. "I'll have a drink instead."

"Oh." She frowned.

"This is our home. I can do what I want in the privacy of my home."

She didn't want to speak, didn't want to start an argument before they settled in comfortably. "I know. You've told me a hundred times. But getting it into our home is illegal."

"Semantics," he said.

"It's not."

"Think of all the distillers and vintners put out of business through no fault of their own. Law-abiding citizens who provided a product until the law ripped the rug out from under them and turned them into criminals. It's not right. And it's done nothing to stop drunkenness."

"I suppose that's true," she said.

"Why don't I open a bottle of champagne. You like that."

She felt her resolve turning into something soft and limp inside of her chest. This *was* their home. And champagne was perfectly acceptable before Prohibition, nothing about the drink itself had changed. It wasn't as if it had suddenly become wicked because a new law was signed.

"I don't know. I…it's…what about Mary? And Claire?"

"We can go in the parlor. I'll lock the door."

"That sounds sneaky. And slightly dishonest. And…"

He wrapped his arm around her waist and pulled her close. He put his mouth close to her ear. "It'll be fun."

He smelled like fresh air, and his body felt warm and strong. A moment ago she'd been regretting they lived in separate worlds. Maybe she needed to take a step into his. "Okay."

He put his hand on the back of her head and pulled it toward his shoulder. She felt as if he'd been waiting for her to move closer to him, to stop putting up walls. Maybe it wasn't all him. Not everything needed to be a battleground.

"Go sit down and I'll be there in a minute."

"I'll still get the cookies. Or maybe some apple, that

would be better."

He stepped back inside the office and started to close the door.

"You don't have to close the door," she said.

"You shouldn't know where I keep it. In case there's a raid." He laughed. "You should see your face. Don't worry, I was kidding."

"I hope so." She went into the kitchen, took two apples out of the bowl, and cut them into thin slices. She laid them in a ring on a small plate and took it into the parlor.

A moment later, Henry came into the room with an ice bucket and a bottle of champagne. It was already opened. He held up the bucket. "I'll get ice and glasses."

By the time he returned, Lorene had nibbled her way through three apple slices. He was making this a nice evening. They were alone for the first time in weeks, and he was trying to be celebratory. She needed to keep her thoughts on his good intentions rather than the law or thinking about how he'd gone about acquiring the champagne…and the scotch he drank regularly.

Now, she didn't want to spoil the evening by asking why he'd been out until nearly dawn, but she couldn't let it continue to eat away inside of her. She wanted the air clear, their relationship pure. If she didn't bring it up now, it would be too late, too much time gone by.

As he poured, the champagne was transformed into a large column of foam before settling down in the glasses.

He handed one to her and touched his to the edge of hers. "To the saintly mother of my daughter."

She smiled. "Thank you." She didn't like it so much when he called her the mother of his child. It seemed to separate them further, making her into someone whose sole purpose in his life was caring for his child. At the very least, it relegated his passion for her to second place. She put a lot of effort into keeping her figure slim — gardening and taking long walks. She was careful to wear hats to keep her skin from getting rough. She left her hair long the way he liked it. She wanted him to notice her — not just her mothering. But maybe the champagne was his way. She shouldn't pick apart his words in her mind, turning them into something unsatisfactory.

She took a small sip of champagne. It had been a long time since she'd had any alcohol and she didn't want it quickly clouding her thoughts.

When he settled beside her, she took his hand. "This is nice."

"It is." He swallowed nearly half his champagne and put the glass on the table.

"Do you want some apple?" she said.

"No thank you."

She took a slice and bit it. She chewed quickly. "I was worried when you were out so late the other night."

"You're always worried." He touched her nose with his fingertip.

"I don't think I am."

"A little. Always a little worried. Most women are."

That was unfair, and she wasn't always worried. "It was almost dawn when you came home. The night you went to William's."

"We had a lot to talk about."

"For eight hours?"

"You know how Jack Sorensen can go on."

She did, but still. "You talked for eight solid hours?"

"Yes, Lorene. We talked for eight hours. We also had dinner."

"I don't always worry, but I was scared. It was so late, and I thought you had an accident, or there was a fight, with all that drinking over such a long evening."

He patted her leg and picked up the glass. "I'm sorry you woke up. If you hadn't, you wouldn't have had to be afraid."

"I wish you wouldn't stay out so late."

"Sometimes business demands it."

"I don't see why."

"There was a lot to go over."

She took several sips of champagne. She felt dizzy. She put the glass on the table and picked up the plate. She held it out to him. He shook his head, and she returned the plate to the table. She wasn't going to eat two entire apples herself. She picked up another slice. It seemed as if her concern wasn't going to be resolved. She wasn't sure why she'd thought it would be. If he had meetings, he had meetings. It *would* have been better if she hadn't woken up. Ignorance was bliss. She ate the apple slice.

"What else is on your mind?"

"When does Jacob start work in your San Francisco operation?"

"I've changed my mind about that. It was a good suggestion, and you were right that he's valuable to me, but I decided to give him more responsibility right here in Aptos."

She felt as if he'd punched her stomach. Jacob would continue pursuing Claire, and Claire would be smug that Henry hadn't followed Lorene's suggestion — proving that he didn't value her input after all. She was utterly defeated. Their lives would always remain divided, they would grow further apart until she felt she was shouting at him across an expanding chasm. "I suppose he and Claire may end up marrying," she said.

He shrugged. He stood up and went to the window. He looked out into the darkness.

She wondered what he was seeing. "Why don't you close the drapes? I should have done it when we came in," she said.

"They're fine for now." He returned to his place beside her. He finished his champagne and refilled his glass. "You've hardly touched your champagne."

She picked up her glass and took a sip. "I think she's

still too young, too immature."

"No younger than you were." He kissed her earlobe.

She giggled although it was more an involuntary reaction than real pleasure. "I was mature, serious."

He gave her a solemn look. "You are that."

She closed her eyes for a moment. "I'm concerned she's stealing." She hadn't realized she planned to tell him until she said it, but this might be a good thing. Their mutual desire to protect their home would draw them closer. It seemed the Inner Light was guiding her. This would cause Henry to finally realize her concern, it would prompt him to be more involved with overseeing Claire, although she couldn't say how that might actually happen. It wasn't as if Claire would listen to his guidance. Or maybe she would — a sudden image of Claire's hand on his arm during dinner, eager to convince Henry she'd understood what he was saying, flashed past her eyes. Claire respected him. She'd grown up without a father, and Henry needed to step in to fill that gap before it was too late.

"From us? Stealing from us?"

"No. No, not from us. I don't know where…I found something that I don't think belongs to her. It's under her mattress and…"

"You searched her room?"

"I know I shouldn't have, but I'm concerned."

He sipped his champagne. "Doesn't sound very moral. Kind of like drinking alcohol." He laughed.

"I know I shouldn't have. She's…"

He put his finger on her lips and took a quick swallow of champagne. "You wanted her here. You take care of it. You keep acting as if this is my problem when I have nothing to do with it."

"She needs a father figure."

"I think it's too late for that. And I already have a daughter. One's enough. A daughter I'm raising from scratch, not trying to fix what someone else did wrong."

Lorene took a sip of champagne. She held out her glass. "I'll have a bit more." Her heart ached for Claire, and for herself. How did he think he was raising Mary? He spoke to Mary at dinner and sat beside her during mass on Sundays. For the most part, that was it.

There was nothing she could do to prevent Claire marrying anyone she chose, or getting pregnant before she was married, or smoking cigarettes, or drinking liquor, or stealing. The only thing she could do was keep her sister away from Mary as much as possible. Maybe Claire should be considered a lost cause. It was a terrible way to think of a girl, but Lorene was powerless.

Summer 1930

Twelve

Jacob was up early. He planned to walk to the cliff and look at the boat — that spectacular, fascinating, stationary ship where he would ask Claire to be his wife.

The money he was earning meeting liquor deliveries on the beach was astonishing. It had piled up so quickly in his savings account, he was certain he'd be able to rent a nice cottage and buy some furniture within the next few months. Standing on the cliff and looking out at the ship whenever he got a chance cemented his view that it was the perfect location for his proposal. The night would be magical, lights glittering on the water, music wafting over the sea. Everything about the way she looked at him and touched his hand or his cheek, told him she would say yes without any hesitation.

He stepped onto the front porch of his boarding house. David stood across the street, staring at the house. Jacob had wanted to go to the cliff alone, but he supposed they could walk together. He waved without enthusiasm.

David crossed the street. “You’re a hard guy to find lately.”

“I’m working a lot.”

“And earning a lot?”

“It’s a good job. Interesting.”

“I came by three nights in a row, and you weren’t here.”

Jacob was annoyed that none of the other tenants or the landlady had mentioned it. He didn’t like being surprised, especially with what he was doing for Henry now. He liked to know when people came looking for him. He had to be on his toes, as Henry reminded him, frequently.

“Where were you?”

Jacob considered whether he should say he’d been with Claire. But that wasn’t difficult for David to check on, and if Jacob were caught lying, it would put him at risk for discovery. “Working.”

“At midnight?”

“You rang the bell at midnight?”

“Close to.”

“That’s rude.”

“The guy who answered said it was no bother. He was awake anyway. So why are you working at midnight?”

Jacob stopped at the corner. He glanced at his watch. He only had forty minutes. “I was going to take a quick walk to the cliff, want to come?”

“Sure, but I’m very curious about what business

operations are going on at midnight."

They crossed the street and headed toward State Park Drive. "There's a lot of paperwork."

"So you work all day *and* most of the night?"

"I get time off in the middle of the day sometimes, I take a nap."

"Sounds like he's taking advantage of you."

"I don't mind it."

"Does he need more help?" David took several long strides forward, turned to face Jacob, and stopped, blocking his way.

Jacob stepped to the left. David moved in the same direction. "I don't have much time, so can you stop blocking me?" Jacob started walking. David kept pace.

"If you're working around the clock, it sounds like he does need to hire someone else. I'm available. Have you ever mentioned that to him? That I'm only working seven or eight hours a week at the packing plant. I could really use…"

"He wouldn't hire you." Jacob walked faster.

David grabbed his arm.

"Hey. Let go."

"Why wouldn't he hire me?"

"He needs people he can trust, okay? It's a lot of exposure for him, a lot of money, bank deposits, important papers. Legal documents."

"Yeah, yeah. You're an important man. Why wouldn't

he trust me?"

"You know why."

"No, I don't."

Jacob walked faster, dragging David with him. "Let go of my arm."

"Not 'til you answer my question."

"You know why. You stole that soda."

"How would he know about that, unless you ratted me out!"

"Calm down. I didn't rat you out. George told him."

"How did he know who I was?"

"He knew you were with me. He saw your face clear as day. We've been in there before."

"Since we were both in there when I took the pop, why does Mr. King think you're so damn trustworthy?"

Jacob stopped walking. He should have mentioned it sooner. Now, David was going to be upset. Very upset. "I took the bottle of pop back to the store. And paid for it. For both of them, actually."

David thrust his face close to Jacob's. "Why would you do something that stupid?"

"That's why I got hired. Mr. King came by right after, and George told him about it."

"You made me look like a thief."

"You are a thief!"

"That guy is loaded. He can afford to lose two bottles of pop. You're supposed to be loyal to me, not sneaking behind my back trying to make yourself look important and all honest."

"That's not why I did it. I felt bad. Besides, George saw me. You left me standing there like a stooge while you were rummaging around in the back. George had his eye on my face the whole time. I couldn't have gone in that store again if I didn't pay for it."

"There are other stores."

"It was the right thing to do. And now I got rewarded. That's how life works."

"For you maybe."

"For people who don't steal."

David punched his shoulder. There was a cracking sound.

Jacob lunged around his brother, clutching his shoulder as if he had to hold it in place. It hurt like hell. He rotated his arm slightly. It seemed nothing was broken or torn. He walked as fast as he could, up the slight incline, cutting across the field toward the edge of the cliff.

David ran after him. "I'm not a thief."

Jacob started running. He'd wanted to look at the ship and fill his thoughts with daydreams, remembering Claire's hands on his skin, the sensation of her soft mouth, the silky strands of her hair…

"Stop running. I'm trying to talk to you."

He stopped and turned. "What do you want me to do?"

"Get me a job."

"I can't. I really can't. He knows he can't trust you."

"That's not my fault. It's yours."

He didn't want to say it was completely David's fault and invite another punch. He didn't want to fight with his brother. He'd given him money, there was nothing else he could do. "Maybe you can…"

"It's hard to find a decent job."

"I don't know what to say."

His brother looked like he might cry. Jacob swallowed. There had to be something he could say, a way to help. "I could…maybe I can…"

"What? What can you do? You owe me. I practically raised you."

That wasn't true, but again, David was mostly incapable of accepting opposing beliefs. The world was all worked out in his mind. Any suggestion that moved those pieces into an alternate pattern would earn another punch. It was David's answer to everything. Jacob had seen it happen with others, but until now, David had never turned on him. Jacob's relationship with the King family — Henry and Claire both — and his job, was driving a wedge between them. He didn't want it, but neither did he want to continue on the path he'd been following before that incredible day when he'd returned the stolen lemonade.

"Maybe you can do what?" David said.

"Pardon?"

David twisted his face into a mocking grin and repeated

— *Pardon?* — in a high-pitched tone. He laughed. "Aren't you high class now."

Jacob winced. He and David had spent hours laughing at people who acted superior. People who thought they were better, when all they had was the random chance of birth into a family with money. And as David liked to point out, half of those families acquired that money by cheating and taking advantage of others.

"You said *maybe I can*...maybe you can...what?"

"I'm not sure what I was going to say." He hadn't meant to blurt out his half-formed thoughts. David would be relentless trying to find out what Jacob had been about to offer.

"Liar."

It was true, he was lying. He'd been about to say maybe he could pay for David to get his high school diploma. Or more. He could certainly afford it, but his income belonged to Claire. Setting up a household was expensive — they needed a home, not just a room or two. And furniture. A wedding. Maybe Henry would pay for that, but Jacob needed to give her a ring. A nice ring. And Claire had a lot of beautiful dresses. She'd want more. They might need help around the house. He wasn't sure whether she knew how to cook.

He felt as if he were lying on the beach as his brother piled shovels full of wet sand onto his chest, burying him deep as they had when they were kids. When their mother was alive, when their father did more than kneel and beg God to change reality. It wasn't fair they'd been left to fend for themselves. Jacob marveled that Henry King had appeared out of nowhere and plucked him from the garbage heap and set him at the entrance to a beautiful garden, starting his life over as if all the things before had never happened.

"You have to help me," David said.

"I don't."

David grabbed his lapel. He twisted the fabric.

"You're wrinkling my jacket. I need to look good for work."

"That's your biggest problem? Wrinkles?" David twisted harder. The sound of breaking threads accompanied his tightened grip.

"Let go of my jacket."

"Then tell me what you were going to say."

"I don't know…I can't…"

"You owe me."

"Why?"

"If I hadn't taken that pop, you wouldn't have had a chance to look like a hero."

Jacob laughed. "Are you kidding me?"

"It's true."

The uncomfortable thing was, his brother's backward logic made sense. He hadn't intended his act of repentance to transform his life, he'd started out with pure motives, but it had changed everything. Maybe he did owe his brother. They'd stuck together their whole lives. He couldn't just let David starve. It wasn't that he was starving, but he was thin, his cheeks slightly concave, the sunken appearance emphasized by the scrub of facial hair that looked like it had been sprouting for three or four days.

"Maybe you should apologize," Jacob said.

"Apologize?"

"To Mr. King." He doubted David possessed the humility to do such a thing. If David did offer an apology, it could cause problems for Jacob. He wasn't sure what problems, but the suggestion was a mistake. What was it about his older brother that compelled Jacob to start talking before completing his thoughts?

"No." David released his grip.

Jacob straightened his jacket.

"I'm not apologizing for not having enough money to buy pop."

Jacob nodded. "Let me think about it."

"What's there to think about?"

"I need to figure out how I can help."

"I don't need your charity," David shouted.

"You just said…"

"Yeah, but you make it sound like I'm a charity case. I'm not. I'm as good as you, and it's not fair that you have this fancy job raking in all this dough. Don't think I can't tell how much you have stashed away."

"Okay. I wasn't thinking you needed charity."

"You were." David took a few steps back.

"Let's go look at the ship. I'll think about it, and we can have dinner together. Maybe Thursday…"

"Maybe *Thursday*? You think you can fit me in on *Thursday*? You better check your calendar. You might not have room for me. On *Thursday*." David lowered his shoulders and rushed toward him. He grabbed Jacob around the waist and plowed forward, pushing him down into the soft earth and the yellow oxalis that covered the field up to the edge of the cliff.

"Get off me," Jacob shouted. "I'm getting all muddy."

David sat on his lower legs, pinning Jacob's arms to the ground. Jacob closed his eyes. He was five years old again, his brother sitting on him, getting ready to lean over and drool saliva on his face, or sneeze on him, smearing snot all over his mouth and eyes. He whimpered.

"Crybaby."

He made his mouth tight, his teeth clenched. "Get off me. Now."

"Says who?"

"I'm not going to help you if you treat me like this."

"Awww. You don't think you deserve to be treated like this? Fight like a man."

"I don't want to fight. I don't even know what we're fighting about." He wasn't fighting, he was defending. He was defending his job and his success and his growing bank account. He was defending Claire and the secret business that Henry had invited him to be part of. David couldn't find out about that, especially. He'd want to be included, and he had no concept of discretion. Otherwise, they wouldn't be wrestling in an open field, possibly observed by other men starting their workday.

David put his face close to Jacob's, his nose inches away. Sour breath laced with smoke and coffee steamed into Jacob's nostrils. He gagged.

"How are you going to help me? You say you will but I give you a suggestion and you tell me all kinds of reasons why it won't work. Mostly reasons that are attacks on me. I don't think Henry King is so damn perfect he can't give a guy a second chance. You peel the skin off bigwigs like him, and you'll find all kinds of stealing and cheating and lying. I know he drinks liquor. What's that about? He must get it somewhere, and we know that ain't legal."

"It's not the same thing." His legs ached with David's weight. Each time David spoke, the repulsive breath wafted across Jacob's face. He wanted to vomit. And he was late getting to the bank to pick up money to replenish the cash registers at the market and the dress shop. "Get off me. I need to get to work."

"Gonna get fired if you're late?"

"No. See, that's why I'm considered a valued employee. I don't want to be late because I know they depend on me and I have responsibilities. I want to take care of my responsibilities, not because someone is clocking me in and out."

"What are you going to ask him about me?" David said.

"Get off me, and I'll be able to think about it."

"I don't want any thinking. I want action."

"The first action is for you to get off me. I need to go home and change my clothes. And I'll think about it. That's how business works. You think and make plans. So I'll think about what I can do to work something out for you." The promise sounded ominous in his ears, offering something he might not be able to deliver. Even if Henry did consider hiring David for unimportant errands or stocking shelves, it would put him inside where there was a chance he could pick up on what Jacob was doing for Henry. This was not the kind of risk Henry would consider worthwhile, Jacob was sure of it. But he had to get David off him, and he'd figure out how to deal with the rest another time.

David let go of Jacob's arms and raised himself to a kneeling position. He planted his left foot in the weeds and pushed himself up to his feet. He reached out his hand.

Jacob took his brother's hand and allowed David to pull him up. He brushed at the backs of his pants, but the effort simply smeared mud across the fabric.

"Sorry about your fancy clothes," David said.

Jacob grunted. "I need to get home and change. Do you want to meet for dinner Thursday or not?"

"Sure," David said. "Your treat?"

"Yes, my treat. Of course."

David sneered at him.

Jacob started walking. He called back. "Are you coming?"

"I'll check out the ship and maybe head down to the beach. See you Thursday."

Jacob started a slow jog to State Park Drive. David had stolen the few minutes available to look at the ship and dream of his evening with Claire.

When he reached the road, he glanced over his shoulder. Lorene King was walking down the hill toward the beach. His skin turned cold and hard. If she'd been walking along the road for a while, she would have seen Jacob pinned to the ground. Had she seen David punch him? It would do nothing to help him find a place for his brother if they were caught fighting in public like a couple of thugs.

Thirteen

A breeze had been flowing through the yard when Lorene stepped into the back garden to cut off the dead roses that had gone to seed, but it died after only a few minutes. It was ten o'clock, and half of the rose garden was still in shade, but her forehead had begun perspiring beneath her sunhat. She lifted it slightly and patted her sleeve against her skin, careful to hold the clippers away from the hat, so they didn't snag the brim and yank it off her head. She wished she'd worn a short-sleeved blouse.

She cupped a dying white rose in her hand to keep the petals from falling all over the thorns below. She clipped the stem and dropped the handful of petals into the basket hanging from her right forearm.

Thirty white rose bushes grew in the area near the screened porch. She loved white roses, and she loved caring for them herself. The gardener did the heavy work — weeding, keeping them fertilized, and the bowls around the bases scooped out. She liked to do the watering, and she enjoyed snipping off the faded blooms. She liked the minor challenge of letting them go as long as they retained a hint of beauty, catching them at the right moment to end their lives before they scattered their petals. Hardly a day went by without her tending them, so each plant produced the maximum number of blossoms.

When she and Henry hosted dinner parties, she cut buds on the cusp of opening, leaving long stems. She plucked off some of the leaves, scraped off the thorns, and arranged them in tall vases for the table. There were always plenty. For years, she'd made a habit of cutting a single rose and putting it in a slender vase on Mary's bedside table every Sunday. Somehow, that habit had ended. It might have been right after Claire arrived to live with them. She'd no longer felt free to walk uninvited into her own daughter's bedroom. She'd still entered the room from time to time, but she didn't feel right about it. That was another reason why the new sleeping arrangements were better.

Although Mary's face had a sadness now, as if she'd left part of her soul behind in the third-floor bedroom, preserving her innocence was more important than any temporary sadness. She would forget about the old bedroom. This room was larger and had its own fireplace. The window seat in this room was spacious enough for Mary to share it with two or three friends, whispering secrets to girls her own age. The thrill of being alone on the top floor would fade and fall away like a dead rose petal. She snipped the stem and dropped the handful of petals into her basket. The top floor held a fascination for a small child, and Lorene saw evidence every week that Mary's childhood was slipping into the past.

"Mommy?"

She turned. The chosen form of address said Mary's childhood wasn't disappearing quite as fast as she'd imagined. Mary was still a little girl, confused about why she'd been snatched out of her room and away from the companionship of her young aunt.

"I'm over here," Lorene called.

Mary stood on the top step of the veranda, looking out toward the oak tree at the back of their property. She turned her head and trotted down the steps, her uncombed hair flying behind her. Mary insisted she wanted to brush her own hair, but on Saturdays, she left it unattended until lunch time. Lorene's fingers twitched with a desire to comb through the tangles.

Mary made her way along the narrow path that wound through the garden. "Can I help?"

Lorene removed the basket from her arm. Mary took a step back. "Not holding the dead ones. I want to use the clippers."

"It's dangerous."

"I know how to be careful. I'm not a baby."

"I know you're not, but…"

"Please."

"You should put on gloves, so you don't get scratched."

Mary ran to the gardening shed and emerged a moment later pulling on a pair of Lorene's gloves. The gloves swallowed her hands and the lower half of her forearms. The empty ends of the fingers flopped uselessly.

"Take them off," Lorene said. "Gloves aren't a good idea after all. You won't be able to manage the clippers properly."

Mary pulled off the gloves and handed them to her mother. She took the clippers and undid the clasp that held the curved blades together.

"Be very careful. Watch your arms when you go near the stems."

Mary nodded. She clipped a rose with brown-edged petals hanging to one side. A few petals fell to the ground. Lorene picked them up while Mary moved on to the next dying rose. They walked among the bushes, Mary clipping and trying to catch the disintegrating blossoms, Lorene picking up what fell to the ground. She was pleased with how cautiously Mary used the clippers, relieved that Mary recognized their potential danger.

When all the dead flowers were gathered in the basket, they emptied the dead blossoms onto the mulch pile behind the shed. They put away the basket and clippers. "Do you want iced tea?" Lorene said.

Mary nodded. She went up to the veranda and sat on the

wicker love seat.

Lorene went into the kitchen. She put two glasses on a wooden tray, filled them with ice, and placed the long-handled spoons next to them. She put out the sugar bowl and got the pitcher of tea out of the refrigerator. She carried everything to the veranda and set it on the table in front of Mary. She poured tea and added sugar, stirring vigorously. She took the seat facing Mary.

They talked about Mary's schoolteacher and the class picnic coming in a few weeks. When Mary's chatter quieted, Lorene considered asking about the new bedroom. After a few moments of silence, searching for the right words, she realized her desire to question Mary wasn't concern over Mary's happiness. She only wanted to reassure herself, to satisfy her guilty conscience. She said nothing.

"I wish I could go on the ship when you and Daddy go to dinner. And Claire and Jacob."

Lorene rubbed Mary's arm. "I know. Maybe someday they'll start serving lunch, and we could take you then."

"It's not fair."

"No, it's not."

"Then why can't I go?"

"Just because something isn't fair, doesn't mean I can change how it is," Lorene said.

Mary stirred her tea, clanking ice cubes against the spoon and the sides of the glass, moving her hand more quickly, trying to increase the racket. "Why are diamonds so expensive?"

"What makes you ask that?"

"I was wondering."

Lorene smiled. "Why are you wondering?"

"*Why* are they expensive?"

"Because they're difficult to get. They can't be manufactured, like a stone in a piece of costume jewelry. They have to be extracted from deep in the earth."

She felt Mary's eyes studying the diamond on her left ring finger. Mary's gaze bored into the stone as if she wanted to pull it off her mother's finger. Lorene moved her hand. The ring glittered in the sunlight that was making its way across the porch. Soon, it would be on their faces and sitting on the porch would be uncomfortable. "Why are you wondering about diamonds?"

"I just was."

"But why?"

Mary shrugged.

"Something must have made you think about it." She was pushing too hard, making Mary feel she'd done something wrong by asking a simple question, but she couldn't stop herself. Had Jacob given Claire a ring? Or was this about the teardrop necklace? Had Mary discovered it tucked between the mattresses? Sometimes, it was easy for Lorene to forget how curious she'd been when she was a child, how resourceful in discovering information, tuning into undercurrents in the household.

"Nothing. I just thought of it."

"They're pretty, aren't they?" Lorene held out her hand.

"I want one."

"Someday you'll have one."

"I don't want to wait until I get married. I want one now."

"It's not appropriate for a girl your age to have a diamond."

"Why not?"

Every answer generated a new question. More often than she liked, Lorene ran out of answers. She felt she was letting Mary down, never fully explaining the world to her. Did that mean Lorene didn't understand the world at all? No matter what subject, the depth of her knowledge was shallow. She was left wondering what had happened to her own curiosity. Diamonds were for adult women, but she couldn't say why that was or even how she knew it.

The question hadn't come out of nowhere. There had to be a way to find out without Mary feeling she was being pressured to reveal something she didn't want to.

"You have one," Mary said.

"Because your father and I are married." Lorene's earlier feeling returned — her daughter's childhood was evaporating before her eyes. How did she know so much? Want so much? Was this Claire's influence, or the normal course of development? "You have your pearl necklace, and when you're older, you'll have more nice jewelry."

"Pearls don't sparkle." Mary's eyes glittered.

It looked as if she might cry. What was she trying to understand that Lorene was failing to grasp? "You're awfully curious about diamonds." She smiled. "Do you want more tea?"

Mary shook her head. "They're pretty."

"They are."

"You're more special if you have one."

"I don't think that's true."

"It is."

"Did someone tell you that?"

Mary shrugged. She stirred her tea furiously.

"You're the most special girl in the world."

"That's not true," Mary said.

"To me you are. To your father."

"Not Claire?"

"Of course not. We love you so much it's hard to breathe sometimes."

Mary laughed. Her eyes continued to glisten.

Lorene stared at her daughter, desperate to understand what they were really talking about. How could a little girl be so complicated?

"Claire thinks she's more special."

"Why?"

Mary didn't speak for several minutes.

"Why does Claire thinks she's more special?" Lorene said.

Mary spoke softly, almost a whisper. "She must be, you gave her my room."

"We already talked about that. Don't listen to her when she says things like that. You should listen to me, I'm your mother."

Mary giggled.

"Why are you laughing?"

"I already know that."

Lorene refilled her glass and added a teaspoonful of sugar. There had to be a way to get Mary to tell her if she'd seen the diamond teardrop. She was certain now that Mary had seen it and been instructed not to mention it. "Do you miss talking to Claire, sharing your room?"

"Not really."

"But a little bit?"

Mary shrugged.

"You were excited to share your room with her."

"I don't like her as much now."

"Why not?"

"All she cares about is Jacob."

"That's normal. When girls get older, they like boys. Sometimes they forget about other girls, because boys are new and exciting."

"She sure forgot about me."

"When she grows up a bit more, she'll come back

around. She still cares about you."

"She cares about how she looks. And her things."

"I'm sorry she hurt your feelings."

"She's mean."

"Why is she mean?"

"She acts like I'm dumb. She was mean to you about her birthday party."

Her daughter had more insight than many adults. Lorene looked out across the garden. Her roses shimmered in the intense sunlight. If she let her eyes glaze over, the roses looked like a field of white diamonds. "Like I told you, it's hard for her, losing our mother. We should be kind to her, even if she isn't kind to us."

"She hides things." Tears spilled out of Mary's eyes.

Lorene stood up. She went to the love seat and sat beside Mary, putting her arm around her. "Why are you crying?"

"I shouldn't have said that."

"Said what?"

"That she hides things."

"Is there something I should know?"

Tears rolled across Mary's cheeks. She picked up her glass of iced tea and pressed it against her cheekbone. "I'm not supposed to say. I broke my promise."

"Promises are between people who are equal. Sometimes when an older person asks a younger person to keep a secret, it's not right."

"Why not?"

"Because when you're little, your parents are the best people to guide you."

"I'm not little."

Lorene took the glass out of Mary's hand. She put it on the table and pulled Mary close, pressing their bodies together. "You didn't do anything wrong. Adult secrets are confusing."

"I promised."

"Claire shouldn't ask you to keep secrets from me." She shivered, thinking of that day when she'd no longer be privy to so many of her daughter's thoughts. Of course, even now, she wasn't really. She just felt as if she was. There was an entire world unfolding inside Mary's mind — memories, thoughts about conversations she heard, people she observed, experiences with her classmates — things her mother would never know. For now, she should be grateful for the thoughts Mary shared. For all of Mary's life, she should be grateful for that.

"It's not important. I don't know why it's a secret."

"What is that?"

"Promise you won't tell her I told you?"

"Of course not."

"You won't break your promise, like I did?"

Lorene took her arm away from Mary's shoulders. She turned Mary's face up toward hers and held it in her hands. "Claire is almost a grown-up, and you're a little girl, a very grown-up little girl, but still young. She should not ask you to hide things from your parents."

"Like having champagne?"

"Claire drank champagne?"

"At a secret place. Then she threw up." Mary made a face.

Lorene sighed.

"She has a diamond necklace. That's why she's special."

"Did someone she loves give it to her?"

Mary shook her head.

Lorene put her arm back around Mary and shifted her position so Mary couldn't see her face. She felt the Inner Light fracture, no longer solid and warm. She'd rushed ahead to get the information she wanted, manipulating her daughter so she could get the upper hand with Claire. Not that she'd succeeded in getting it, really. She still didn't know where the diamond had come from.

Claire's bedroom door was closed. Lorene stood at the top of the stairs, trying to calm herself, to ease her thoughts, knowing her rapidly beating heart would follow her thoughts to a quieter place. She couldn't speak to Claire if her hands were shaking and her heart pounding so hard she couldn't breathe. She wasn't even sure what she wanted from the girl. She knocked on the door.

"Who is it?" Claire's voice sounded far away.

"It's Lorene."

"I'm busy. Do you need something?"

"I wanted to talk to you."

There was silence from inside the room. After a moment, she heard a drawer slam close. The bedroom door opened partially. Claire inserted herself into the opening so Lorene couldn't see anything in the room beyond. "What do you want to talk about?"

"May I come in?"

"I'm writing letters."

"Do you miss your friends from San Francisco?"

"Of course I do. Is this just a friendly chat about nothing?"

"I haven't seen you much except at breakfast and dinner, and I wondered how you're doing."

"I'm fine. I've been studying for end of year exams."

"Already?"

"Yes. It's important that I do well, don't you think?"

Lorene wasn't sure why it was so important, but she didn't want to imply that it wasn't.

"Is there something else?"

"I wanted to be sure you're doing okay. I wanted to let you know if you need to talk about boys, about Jacob, I'm available to listen and give you my thoughts based on my experience."

Claire laughed. "Boys?!" She let out a shriek of laughter.

"You're not my mother. I don't need advice on boys."

Lorene smiled gently. Claire might be confident and independent, she might have tasted alcohol and overindulged, but she was just now seventeen. She was naive. "There's a lot you don't know."

"I doubt that."

"You'd be surprised, Claire. I remember I thought I knew a lot at your age. And now, I wish I'd talked more to my mother. Our mother."

"Well I can't really do that, can I?"

"That's why I'm here."

"No. You're not going to pretend you're my mother. You're not going to interfere in my life. You're not going to stop me from seeing Jacob."

"We love you, sweetheart." Lorene put her hand on Claire's arm.

Claire stiffened and moved away from the opening. The door drifted open.

"Please don't shut me out," Lorene said. "You'll come to regret it."

"Is that a threat?"

"Of course not. It's the furthest thing from it. I want to help."

"I don't need your help."

"Did you have a boyfriend in San Francisco?"

"It's none of your business."

"I just want to make sure you're not in any kind of trouble."

"What kind of trouble would I be in?"

"I don't know. I…"

Claire narrowed her eyes into a scowl. "You have something in mind. What are you talking about?"

Lorene took a step back. "It's nothing. I just wanted you to know I'm available if you need a listening ear. Growing up is complicated."

"Not really. But thanks for your views on the subject."

"Claire, I…we…"

"It's nice of you to let me stay in your house, but I know there was money from the estate for that, so it's not like it's out of the kindness of your heart and your great love for me. I hardly even know you, if you think about it. And you certainly don't know me. We're strangers. I appreciate the room and the food and all of that, but you should put your effort into raising Mary. She seems a bit needy, if you ask me. And talk about naive! You'd better educate that girl, or her classmates will do it for you."

Lorene smacked Claire's cheek.

Claire didn't flinch. Her skin turned red, but her eyes stayed clear and hard. She laughed, one short sound, then closed her mouth into a tiny smile. "Feel better?"

"Don't ever speak about Mary like that again."

"I'm just telling the truth." Claire closed the bedroom door.

Lorene gasped, trying to catch her breath. Her stomach ached as if she'd been punched. She felt foolish, and very naive herself.

Fourteen

There was a soft knock, two quick taps. They were so quiet, Mary thought it was a bird outside the window. The taps came a second time. She stood up and shoved her diary under the pillow. She crossed the room, put her pen on the desk, and went to the door.

"Open up, it's Claire. I have a surprise, and I don't want anyone to see me."

Mary opened the door.

Claire pushed her way into the room. "Close the door."

Claire pulled her hands out from behind her back. She held a box of Chuckles candies and two BB Bat chocolate taffy pops. "Look what I got."

"Where?"

"Jacob gave them to me."

"They look yummy. But I'm not supposed to eat candy before dinner."

Claire laughed. "Just a few pieces. You can save the rest

until after dinner."

"Maybe."

"I never see you anymore except when your mother's hovering about, so I decided to drop by for a visit."

Mary shrugged.

"Let's sit in the window seat. Yours is enormous! It's like a separate room."

"Not really," Mary said.

Claire went to the window seat. She kicked off her shoes and curled up on the bench. She patted the cushion. "Come on. We can have a girl chat."

Mary joined her.

Claire placed the BB Bats between them. She opened the box of Chuckles and held it out to Mary. "Have one."

Mary pulled out two cherry pieces. She put them in her mouth and chewed slowly. They were so good. And she was hungry. A few more wouldn't spoil her appetite. She just needed to check her lips before they went down, to make sure they weren't stained red.

"How are you?" Claire said.

Mary laughed. "Fine. I just saw you at breakfast." She took another piece of candy.

"I mean in general. I know you're upset about the ship. That you can't go to the grand opening."

Mary turned her head and looked out the window.

"Sorry, I didn't mean to make you cry."

"I'm not crying. How's Jacob?"

"Oh, you sound so grown up." Claire scooted to the side, blocking part of the window, her leg touching Mary's.

"Do you have other boyfriends?" Mary said.

Claire laughed. "You're so charming."

"Don't treat me like I'm dumb." Mary took a lime candy and waited to see whether Claire would answer the question about boyfriends or try to change the subject. Claire was good at changing the subject when she didn't want to talk about something. Mary wasn't sure why she'd asked about Jacob. He seemed like a man, more like her father than a boy Claire's age. He smelled like a man — kind of smoky. A few days earlier she'd seen him come onto the veranda. There was a dark shadow on the lower half of his face, the start of a thick, heavy beard. The following day, the shadow had disappeared.

"Have you ever had a boyfriend?" Claire said.

"No."

"Do you know what a crush is?"

"Of course."

"Have you had one of those?"

Mary's neck felt steamy. Her scalp itched, and when she put her fingertips beneath her hair to scratch it, the skin was damp.

"You don't have to tell me." Claire held out the box of candy. "Have you ever played doctor?"

Mary shook her head. She should never have let Claire into her room. Claire tricked her, again. Mary had thought they would talk like sisters, eat candy that her mother didn't know about. She still had no idea why she'd asked about Jacob. It was something to say, something that made her appear interested in the things Claire cared about. Now, she felt trapped in the window seat, trapped in her own room.

"So you've never seen a boy's thing?" Claire stuffed a handful of the jelly candies into her mouth. It was too much, so she chewed with her mouth open, exposing red-stained teeth. It looked like blood, as if she'd been gnawing on an extremely rare piece of steak. Claire giggled. "Do you know what his thing is?"

Mary stood up. "I don't want to talk about this."

"Don't be silly. I've seen two of them. It's no big deal. It's just a thing where he pees. Right here." She pointed between her legs. "And he…"

"Stop! I said I don't want to talk about it."

"It's nothing to be afraid of."

"I just don't feel like talking about it with you."

Claire pouted. "Are you mad at me?"

"Why are you bothering me? Why did you come into my room? We aren't really friends. If we were friends, we'd still be sharing a room."

"I told you…"

"I don't believe you. And I don't want any more candy. It's almost dinner time."

"You can still have the BB Bats." Claire stood up. She

left both candy pops on the cushion. She folded the cardboard lid of the Chuckles box. "Don't be mad at me."

"You're not very nice since you started going around with Jacob."

"I'm the same person."

"You're not."

"Maybe you're just jealous of him. Or jealous of me, more likely."

"I'm not jealous."

Claire laughed. "You're always trying to make yourself look like you're such a good person. I know you're jealous of my room. Of my diamond. You hate that I have a boyfriend and you don't."

"I don't want a boyfriend."

Claire stabbed her finger against Mary's collarbone. "Everyone wants a boyfriend. I have one, and you don't and you're jealous. I get to go on the ship and wear a beautiful dress and go dancing. Everyone will notice my diamond and wonder who I am."

"Will you please leave."

"Why?"

"Because I asked you to."

Claire laughed. "You sound like your mother. If you want to know how to get a boyfriend, come to my room any time, and I'll tell you some things. But definitely, do not ask your mother. She pretends to know everything, and she knows nothing." Claire opened the bedroom door. She stepped into the hallway and ran up the stairs to the third floor, her footsteps echoing behind her.

Mary closed the door. She picked up the taffy pops and dropped them into the trashcan. She'd empty the trash herself before Annie saw it. She picked up her pen and pulled her diary out from under the pillow. She didn't want to write about the things Claire said. When Claire had told her that other upsetting story, about how much she liked it when a boy she knew touched her bare skin, Mary didn't write it down. Claire had even shown Mary the spot where the boy had touched her.

It was fun to write down some of her thoughts, and the things that happened to her at school, things her friends said. She opened to a new page. Maybe she would sneak out of the house and follow them to the party on the concrete ship. They'd all be so busy getting ready, they wouldn't notice she was gone. It was easy to slip past Annie. Most of the time when Mary was left in her care, Annie fell asleep by eight o'clock, trusting Mary to turn out her light when she finished reading her book.

She uncapped her pen. She wrote about the lights on the ship, glowing in the darkness. She imagined the dress she would wear and described how it moved as she danced. Then, she took a deep breath and wrote about the boy who sat in the front row in her class, walking up to her, taking her hand, and leading her onto the dance floor where they'd whirl in circles until after midnight.

Fifteen

The King family car sat in the center of the drive. It gleamed in the sharp rays that pierced the trees during the last few moments before the sun sank behind the house. Jacob went up the steps and rang the bell. He stepped back. A moment later, Claire opened the door. She wore a peach colored dress. The fabric was silky with lace over her breasts. The dress revealed the tops of her shoulders and her arms were bare, her skin creamy against the peach. Her shoes were the same color as the dress. Some of her hair was piled on top of her head and woven with peach ribbons, the rest hung over her shoulders and arms in curls that looked like pipes. She carried a shawl and a small purse. Circling her neck was a silver chain with a diamond hanging from it.

"You're so beautiful," Jacob said.

She smiled. "Especially tonight?"

"Always."

"But tonight, more than ever?"

He nodded.

She stepped onto the porch and closed the door. "Let's go."

Jacob took her arm. He led her down the steps and around the King's car to where his newly purchased car was sitting. He'd bought it from a colleague of Henry's. It was a 1926 Ford, obviously out of style compared to most vehicles on the road, but had been kept in excellent condition. He could hardly believe he owned a car. It was even more difficult to believe this beautiful woman would be riding beside him, eating dinner across from him, and dancing in his arms with so many people watching…after she promised to be his wife.

The diamond around her neck was unsettling. He could never afford jewelry like that. Except for the small ring he had in his pocket, he wouldn't be buying gems for a very long time. She already owned a diamond that was larger than the one he'd purchased. Was it a gift from her parents? Or a former boyfriend? When he held out the ring to her, would she feel he didn't love her that much after all, comparing it to what she already possessed? He'd never seen her wear this necklace and she'd never mentioned it. Now it shone in his eyes like the setting sun.

He opened the car door, and she slipped into the passenger seat.

When they reached the bottom of the cliff, there was

already a line of cars moving slowly, drivers looking for open parking spaces. After several minutes following the others, worrying about the gas he was consuming, he found a spot. It seemed as if everyone for miles up and down the coast wanted to spend an evening on the concrete ship.

As they walked along the pier toward the entrance at the back of the ship, Claire shivered. It was a clear evening, but now that the sun was down, a chilly breeze came over the water. He had to hold his shoulders tight to keep from shivering himself. She pulled her wrap more tightly. He put his arm around her. She leaned against him, and they stepped onto the ship. It didn't feel any different than walking on the pier. Even though it was solidly placed in the sand, unsusceptible to the surf splashing against the sides, he'd expected to feel he was on a ship.

They walked along the edge, gazing down into the water. When they reached the entrance to the dining room, Jacob gave his name to the maître d'. They were seated at a table for two near the center of the room. Claire seemed pleased with their table, and immediately shrugged the wrap off her shoulders.

The maître d' held out his hand. "May I take that for you?"

Claire smiled. "I think I'll keep it, in case I get cold."

After they'd looked at their menus, ordered their meals, and glanced around at the others dining nearby, Claire put her elbows on the edge of the table. She leaned over the table and whispered something.

"I didn't hear you," Jacob said.

"Come closer," she said softly.

He leaned over his place setting.

"I wish we had champagne."

Her eyes were rounder than normal, rings of white showing around the blue, her pupils like dark, deep holes drawing him inside. Was she trying to trick him into talking about the work he did for her brother-in-law? She couldn't possibly know about it. What would she think of him if she found out? It had been a constant worry since he'd started picking up the alcohol deliveries. Maybe she wasn't tricking him, maybe she knew and was trying to let him know she didn't care. She'd said it so boldly, unconcerned with whether her desire shocked him. He wasn't sure how to respond.

The waiter arrived with two salads. Jacob leaned back, and she looked down, hiding whatever was in her eyes.

They ate and talked about how the ship felt nothing like a ship. They might as well be eating in any restaurant on dry ground. They talked about the orchestra that would be playing in the Rainbow Ballroom after dinner.

When his baked salmon was half eaten, he started thinking about how he was going to ask her to marry him. He'd thought through the words he would say, but he hadn't considered how close together the tables would be. He hadn't thought about all the voices surrounding them, about making himself heard. He hadn't considered interruptions from the waiter, or wondered if others nearby would stop talking and listen to what he was saying. Claire might be distracted. There were so many ways it could go wrong, maybe asking her while they ate dessert wasn't a good idea. But when? It would be equally challenging in the ballroom. He could ask her to walk outside, but she'd been cold when the sun was just starting to go down, she'd shiver uncontrollably now that it was dark.

He glanced up and saw Henry and Lorene enter the restaurant. Behind them were William and Margaret Sharp. Now he would definitely have to change his plan. He'd known they were coming to the grand opening. He'd even known they'd be arriving while he and Claire were at dinner — he'd seen the car, washed and polished for the short drive to the pier, but he hadn't thought about how their presence would affect his proposal. They were seated on the other side of the room, which was a relief, but he still couldn't ask Claire to be his wife with them sitting right there, possibly watching. He felt on display.

A marriage proposal should be private, filled with romance. The ship restaurant was romantic in a mysterious, unique way, but it wasn't what he'd imagined. If he hadn't been waiting for this day for so many weeks, he would consider choosing a different setting on a different night.

The waiter brought their desserts — apple pie for Jacob, chocolate cake for Claire. He returned with a silver coffee pot and filled their cups.

Claire cut a piece of cake and put it in her mouth. She didn't seem to chew, letting it dissolve inside. Her lips were dark, and a smear of frosting remained on her lower lip. She took another bite. After a few minutes, she pushed her chair away from the table. "I'm going to the Ladies' lounge."

He nodded. This would give him a chance to work out the rest of the evening in his mind without trying to carry on a conversation at the same time. He sipped his coffee and cut a piece of pie and put it in his mouth.

"Hello, Jacob."

He turned. Mrs. King was directly behind him. He stood up, set the fork on his plate, chewed, and swallowed. He put out his hand. "Hello."

She didn't take his hand. "Sit down, you're attracting attention." She moved around to the side of the table.

He seated himself. He felt like a child looking up at his schoolteacher.

Lorene frowned. "I'll be brief."

He nodded.

"I want you to know I saw you brawling a week or two ago. Rolling around in the mud with a brutish looking man." She shivered.

"He's…"

"I don't need to know his name. Or anything about him, I'd rather not."

"But he…It's not…"

She put her fingertips on the edge of the table, leaning closer and lowering her voice. "I haven't mentioned it to Henry. And I won't. But he wouldn't be pleased. It doesn't look good. He trusts you to be a business partner, not a hooligan."

"I…"

"Please don't interrupt me. I only have a minute, and I see Claire headed our way. It would be appreciated if you'd take a step back in your pursuit of her. She's very young, almost a child. If you take your time, I won't say anything to Henry — about your fistfight." She glanced in Claire's direction. "And don't mention this to Claire." Lorene didn't wait for his answer. She turned and walked across the room, nodding at Claire as they passed.

Claire yanked out her chair and flopped down. A few strands of hair had come loose and hung over her cheeks. She pushed them out of the way. "What did she want?"

"Nothing." And that was the truth. He was confident Lorene's influence with Henry was more significant in her mind than it was in reality. After all, nothing had come of the San Francisco proposal she'd made. Thinking back on it, he was certain Henry had just been polite, nodding at her suggestion, hardly listening to it, his mind racing ahead to the responsibilities and pay raise he'd offered later that evening. Jacob would not allow her vague threat to prevent him from asking Claire to marry him. He'd been planning this for too long. Besides, Henry wasn't concerned about how he managed his private life, as long as he was discreet. When he'd asked about taking Claire out, Henry had shrugged it off as casually as if Jacob had asked for a scrap of paper to write a message on. He was confident of Claire's acceptance, despite the diamond necklace. Together, they would face Lorene.

"Should I ask the waiter for more coffee?" he said.

She shook her head and cut a piece of cake. She lifted the fork to her mouth. Her small pink tongue darted out and licked at the frosting. The sight of her tongue made his bones feel like pudding. "Do you want to walk around the deck before we go into the ballroom? You could borrow my jacket if you're cold."

"That sounds nice. But I won't be cold, with you beside me." She smiled. "So *why* was Lorene talking to you?"

"She just came over to say hello."

"Really? She waited until I was gone and walked all the way across the room to say hello?"

"Yes."

"She looked very serious."

"Oh, she saw me fighting with my brother a week or so ago. She thought it gave a bad impression, thought it might reflect badly on Henry if his employee was seen *brawling*. She didn't let me explain it was my brother. That's what brothers do." He laughed.

"She likes to give advice." Claire stabbed her fork into

the cake and broke off a large piece. "I can't wait for the dancing to start. I haven't gone dancing since I moved here."

"I'm looking forward to it. But a short walk will be nice, to digest our dinner." He patted the space below his ribs.

Claire smiled, but he had the feeling she saw the gesture toward his stomach as…brutish. How could a girl so much younger than he make him feel immature? He supposed it was her grace, her way of keeping so many of her thoughts to herself.

He paid the bill, and they left the restaurant. He forced himself to keep his face turned away from the table where Henry and Lorene were seated.

Outside, they walked toward the bow of the ship. His heart thudded against his ribs, the force increasing with each step forward. This was the right place. It was perfect, full of magic. Behind them, lights strung along the ship's buildings and mast glittered in the moonlight. The moon itself was as thin and delicate as one of Claire's eyelashes. They were alone. It was cool and the only sound was water splashing against concrete. He stopped at the railing and put his arm around her waist. He leaned toward her and moved her hair away from her ear. He spoke softly. "I love you."

She sighed and leaned into him. He wished she would say the same, but it wasn't her way. She needed him to take the lead. He reached into his pocket and pinched the ring between his thumb and forefinger. With his other hand, he turned her slightly until they were both facing out toward the horizon. "Will you marry me, Claire? I know I can make you happy and provide you a comfortable life. Being with you makes me feel like the most important man on earth. When I look in your eyes, I feel as if the whole world belongs to me. Will you be my wife?"

He took her hand and slid the ring onto her finger.

She straightened her arm and spread her fingers. She studied the ring. She curled her hand into a loose fist. "Let's not rush," she said.

He swallowed. What did that mean? *Yes?* Or *no?*

She turned toward him. "I can wear your ring, but maybe on my right hand? I'm only just seventeen."

"Why? Don't you love me?"

"I'm too young to really know, don't you think?"

"I think you know what you want."

"I haven't finished high school."

"Does that matter?"

"It's something I should do, and then I'll feel old enough to be married."

"I love you. You're all I think about."

"I feel the same, but I think we should go slowly."

"I don't see why."

"It's just better."

"Is there another man? Is that where you got the

necklace?" He hated himself for mentioning it. He sounded desperate, and crass, thinking about jewelry instead of her heart, unconcerned about what her hesitation might be. He sounded jealous and unsure of himself.

She was quiet for a long time. More than ever, he wanted to know who had given her such an expensive gift, but it seemed she wasn't going to reveal that information. He wasn't going to ask about the diamond again — his or the other one. She hadn't said *no*. That was a good thing. But waiting? For a year, or more? And he couldn't understand why she would wear the ring on her right hand. Their engagement would be a secret. The ring would seem to be a companion to the necklace. He couldn't ask for it back.

She slipped her right hand into his. He felt the cold, hard stone on her finger. She'd already moved it to the wrong hand while he'd been trying to make sense of her answer.

They danced for hours. Jacob was perspiring, and his legs ached, but his mind was numb. Claire seemed happier than ever — laughing and chattering, stopping to talk to her classmates. She was friendly and charming to Lorene, asking how she was enjoying the evening, putting her hand on Lorene's arm and leaning close, as if she were posing for a portrait — sisters at a party.

Claire's vague response to his proposal had shaken him

to his core. He felt he was acting a part as he pointed out interesting features on the ship and asked about her final exams, anything to keep her talking, to keep his mind from veering off to unanswerable questions, and to keep from falling at her feet and begging her to tell him why she wouldn't marry him.

Throughout the evening, Jacob had noticed at least seven or eight men, all of whom he recognized, and a few women as well, slipping outside. The men, not too subtly, patted their coat pockets to feel for flasks. Others that he'd never seen before, joined them. They returned, laughing more loudly, smiling more broadly, their dance steps a little looser. He hadn't noticed Henry slipping out even once. Henry's extreme caution was impressive. It was one thing for an average person to be caught taking a sip of liquor, but not a man who had a cellar full of the illegal stuff and an employee working nearly full time to supply his customers.

It was close to eleven-thirty when couples began drifting toward the door. The orchestra was scheduled to play until midnight, but the beat was more sedate now, softer notes like tired bodies, the music offering the subliminal suggestion that it was time for a quiet after-party, or sleep. Jacob and Claire were seated on a small sofa. She held a teacup, and was taking tiny sips, listening attentively to a girl from her school who was describing a cake she'd decorated — her first. The girl went on in such detail, Jacob imagined he felt the cloying presence of her green and blue and yellow frosting on his tongue, clogging his esophagus. He closed his eyes for a moment and saw ribbons and swirls of nauseating pastel borders. He opened them quickly.

From several yards away, Henry glanced at Jacob. He nodded once and tipped his head toward the exit. He whispered to Lorene, turned, and strolled toward the door leading to the starboard side of the ship.

Jacob touched Claire's elbow. "I'm going outside to get some fresh air."

She winked. "You're not sulking, I hope."

A surge of anger rushed through his chest. He stood up. "I don't sulk. It's stuffy in here, and I can't breathe."

She smiled.

He walked quickly toward the door, not caring whether he attracted attention. The key to remaining above suspicion was a confident demeanor. He wasn't going to skulk out of the ballroom. He wasn't going to allow Claire to think he was devastated. If she didn't come around, maybe he'd go out with other girls. See how she'd like that. No rush indeed. There were plenty of pretty girls around, and he was becoming known as Henry King's right-hand man. A man with a solid income and a great future. He stepped outside. The wind grabbed at his jacket. Spray from the waves flew against his face. He turned so the wind was at his back. Henry stood at the bow of the ship, looking out to sea as if he were the captain of the sunken vessel. Another man stood beside him. Henry looked at Jacob. He said something to the other man, who then crossed to the port side and walked toward the ballroom. Henry gestured for Jacob to join him.

The wind was stronger at the bow, unchecked by the structures that housed the restaurant and ballroom. Jacob pulled his coat more tightly around him. It didn't do much to protect him from the cold, but the tension in his back made him feel as if he were warming himself.

"Great night," said Henry.

Jacob nodded. He clenched his jaw to keep his teeth from chattering. Henry seemed unaffected by the wind and the steady spray of moisture.

"This is what we've been waiting for."

Jacob nodded. "It's perfect. Darker than I expected out here."

"Exactly. But in some ways, it's riskier. The deliveries will be larger, with more cash involved. That can attract interest from competitors."

"I can handle it." Jacob felt reckless. What did it matter? Maybe Claire had turned him down because she didn't want a comfortable life. It had been a mistake to use that word. She wanted a lavish life. She didn't want anything less than what she had right now in the magnificent King house, with people to cook and clean, a woman to help raise her children. He had no idea what her life in San Francisco had really been like. She talked about parties, about friends, but she'd never mentioned whether there was a household staff. Perhaps she'd experienced even more wealth than he'd realized. No wonder she had a diamond necklace. Maybe she thought his ring wasn't good enough to show off on her left hand. "I want to make the most of all the opportunities you offer," he said.

Henry handed him a roll of bills. "I need you to stay out here after everyone leaves. There's a boat coming in at one o'clock."

Jacob's first thought was of the wind and the steadily falling temperature. Then, he thought of Claire and the unresolved question between them. "I can come back after I take Claire home."

Henry shook his head. "Won't work, more risk of being seen. You have to find a place where you won't be observed and wait until the boat arrives."

"But what about…"

"Lorene and I will take Claire home."

Jacob didn't like that. Claire would think he'd abandoned her. She'd feel like a child, riding in the backseat, Lorene like a queen in the front. "I don't think she'll like that. And I feel like I'm not looking after my girl properly."

Henry put his hand on Jacob's shoulder. "It doesn't matter what she likes. I'll explain it to her."

"What will you say?"

"That you're not feeling well. Migraine headache."

"She…I…we…I can't…" Claire would think he was sick with devotion, unable to face her rejection. This wouldn't work at all.

"Spit it out," Henry said.

Telling Henry about the proposal left hanging indefinitely, would make him appear weak. "It's nothing. I'll talk to her tomorrow."

"Perfect."

"I need to say good-night."

"It's better if you don't go back inside. Gives your story more credibility. When the motorboat arrives, you'll need to help load the crates onto the ship here. I've arranged a compartment down below where it can be stored. We'll move it ashore as needed." He handed a roll of cash and a set of keys to Jacob. "The large one gives access to the arcade and the stairs below deck, and the small one opens the space where you can stow it. If you see anything else going on down there, I don't want to know about it. Got it? You're to be *hear no evil, see no evil, and speak no evil.*" He laughed.

Jacob nodded. "It seems like more work, more chance of exposure, making a lot of trips."

"Overall, there's less chance of being seen. Out on the beach, anyone could be passing by or walking along the cliff."

"I suppose."

"Make yourself scarce," Henry said.

"I will."

Henry thumped Jacob's shoulder and walked back toward the ballroom.

About twenty minutes later, Henry and Claire emerged. Claire was laughing, folding her wrap around her neck and shoulders. She didn't look angry or upset. Either Henry had done a very good job explaining Jacob's headache or Claire was happy to be rid of what she decreed was a sulky boyfriend. Thinking about it made him feel sulky. He needed to shake it off. Let her think what she wished. He'd prove he was a catch and the more he thought about it, the better it made him feel to consider playing the field a bit. Let *her* beg for *him*. He moved to the side of the ship, watching their backs as they moved toward the pier.

A moment later, Lorene emerged from the doorway. She paused and looked out toward the water. Instead of hurrying after her husband and sister, she stood there for several minutes. She looked directly at Jacob. She cocked her head slightly.

Jacob turned and took a few steps toward the bow. She'd recognized him. He was sure of it. He needed to tell Henry to explain to her that fresh air helped his headache, or something. He had to believe Henry would handle it with ease. He was more adept at these things — managing women, covering his tracks — than Jacob would ever be.

He sat on the deck, hugged his knees to his chest, and

pressed his body into the point of the bow.

The guy operating the motorboat that pulled quietly up to the side of the S.S. Palo Alto at twenty past one refused to help Jacob unload the liquor. Jacob was left to carry forty small crates up the rope ladder he'd attached to the side of the ship. By the time he was finished, his face was wet with salt water, and sweat glued his shirt to his back. He took the inventory list provided by the boat operator, wiping moisture out of his eyebrows before it crept down and blurred his vision. He pulled the roll of bills out of his pocket and handed them to the guy. After unwrapping and leafing through the stack twice to check his count, the guy touched his hand to his hat, and started the engine with a low purr. He backed away from the ship and motored quietly to the southwest. When Jacob could no longer see the boat, he heard the engine speed increase, but after a moment, the waves swallowed the sound as easily as the darkness had covered up the boat and its lone occupant.

Carrying a box containing two liquor bottles under each arm, Jacob walked along the length of the deck, down the metal stairs to the room below, and stacked the crates in the compartment. When he was finished moving the entire delivery, he locked the compartment door and the door that led below deck, testing the handles on both to be sure they were secure. He slipped the keys in his pocket and started toward the stern of the ship. He studied the shoreline and the pier. The hairs on his arms hardened like slivers of steel, making his skin ache. The thud of his heart and shallow breathing sounded as if he'd run up the hill. Above, the cliffs were dark, but someone might be standing back from the edge with a light he couldn't see, able to watch every movement.

When he reached the pier, he walked quickly, hands in his pockets, trying to think of a story to tell if someone happened to approach him.

He reached the street without an incident. His car was the only one for as far down as he could see. He hurried to it, got in, and drove up the hill, turning left toward the King home. Henry had instructed him to go directly to his office in the back of the house. The yard was dark. Away from the water, the air was warmer. As he rounded the side of the house, the air was filled with the odor of cigar smoke. Henry was sitting on the veranda.

Jacob climbed the steps. Henry gestured to the chair next to him. Without speaking, Henry took out his flask and handed it to Jacob. He took two quick sips and handed it back.

"Have another, if you need it," Henry said. "It takes nerves of steel to do what you did. I'm impressed with your tolerance for risk. You'll be well-rewarded."

The sound of twigs breaking punctuated his words. Jacob froze. "Is…?

"A raccoon," Henry said. "Relax. No one followed you,

did they?" He laughed. He put the cigar in his mouth and sucked on it, making contented noises, like an animal himself.

"I'm a little jumpy. Mrs. King looked right at me as she was leaving the ballroom. I know she saw me, and recognized me."

"Don't worry about it. If she says anything, I'll take care of it."

Jacob held out his hand for the flask and Henry gave it to him. He took two more sips.

Henry took the flask and swallowed some whiskey. "This will be a regular thing."

"Okay."

"Probably two nights a week, at first. Then possibly five nights a week."

"Won't that attract more attention?"

A branch snapped. Jacob stood up and walked to the edge of the veranda. He strained to make his eyes see in the darkness. The house had a magnificent oak tree at the back left corner. Birch trees were clustered in a grove that ran from there to the opposite side of the property. Even with the light on the veranda, the trees were almost indistinguishable, darker shadows in the night. "You're sure that's a raccoon?"

"Sit down," Henry said. "Have another snort."

Jacob remained standing. He took a step closer, and Henry handed the flask to him.

"We get all kinds of critters up here. Coyotes, raccoons, deer, sometimes. Your nerves are on edge because of what you just did. You've become a wary bootlegger." Henry spoke softly.

"I thought you didn't like being called a bootlegger," Jacob said. "We're businessmen."

"Just giving you a hard time." Henry puffed on his cigar.

Jacob moved closer to the edge of the veranda. "Thank you again for the opportunity."

Henry raised his flask at Jacob and took a swallow.

Jacob went down the steps and around the side of the house. When he was out of Henry's line of sight, he paused and looked back toward the trees. He hoped Henry was right. He wouldn't put it past his brother to follow him to the grand opening and wait through the evening, curious about what kept his little brother so busy.

Sixteen

Lorene didn't wake until mid-morning. She bathed and put on a yellow dress with red peonies. She smoothed the skirt over her hips and buckled a narrow red belt around the fitted waist. When she opened the drapes, the fog was blowing rapidly out to sea. It would be a beautiful day to take Mary to the beach. They could bring a small picnic and stretch out on the warm sand. They would go wading and collect shells and small stones. She looked in the mirror and brushed her hair until there wasn't a single tangle. She wove it into a braid. She leaned closer to the mirror. When she wasn't smiling, delicate lines spread out from the corners of her lips. The skin beneath her eyes had a slight papery feel. It was getting more fragile every year. Soon, it would burst into a spray of tiny wrinkles. She opened the jar of cold cream and patted some around her lips and eyes and between her eyebrows. Using her right ring finger, she gently spread it until the white cream faded into her skin. She closed the jar and stepped back.

Claire would join their picnic. It was important to get her out of the house, fill her mind with nature instead of letting her lie around all day dreaming of Jacob, writing passionate letters to men whom Lorene had never met, gazing at the diamond teardrop. Maybe in a casual conversation, Claire would let the giver's name slip out. If there was a giver.

Neither Mary nor Claire were anywhere on the first floor. It didn't surprise her that Claire was still sleeping, or daydreaming in bed, but Mary was normally up at sunrise, often outside on the swing hanging from the oak tree, or hunting for frogs. She had an ungodly love for frogs. She crept through the shrubs after sunset, tracking the sounds of their croaking, trying to see them in the darkness, stroking their bodies that looked so soft and slimy but Mary insisted were not. She spent early mornings at the back of the property where a slight hollow behind the trees collected rainwater, and the surrounding rocks attracted the frogs into their dark hiding places. Lorene shivered every time she saw Mary holding one of the gooey looking creatures. Their eyes quivered, and their limbs pushed against Mary's hands, thrusting through the spaces between her fingers, desperate to leap to safety. Lorene was terrified one would leap out of Mary's cupped hands and smack into her face. She shuddered.

She made a pot of coffee and took a cup to Henry's

study. When he answered her knock, she walked slowly toward his desk, waiting for him to look up. She put the cup near a small obelisk that acknowledged his contribution to the Church in 1928. She stepped back. "Are you working all day today?"

He lifted the cup — "Thank you." He took a sip of coffee. "Until this afternoon, I think."

She nodded. She wouldn't invite him to the beach, he would decline, and her disappointment would increase. She leaned over and kissed his cheek.

"Thank you for the coffee," he said.

"You already said that."

He nodded, took a fresh sheet of stationary out of the box near the top of his blotter, and began writing.

She returned to the kitchen and made herself a piece of toast. She spread strawberry jam on it. She poured a cup of coffee and carried her plate and cup to the screened porch. She settled on the wicker love seat and put her feet on the low table. It wasn't very ladylike, but it was comfortable, and no one was around.

When the toast and coffee were gone, she went back inside and cleaned up the kitchen. She climbed the stairs to the third floor. A moment after she knocked the second time, Claire opened the door. She looked fresh and alert, as if she'd been awake for hours.

"Mary and I are going to the beach for a picnic. Would you like to join us?"

Claire shook her head.

"It's a gorgeous day."

"I'm seeing Jacob for tea."

"Oh." Lorene smiled weakly. "He's feeling better?"

"Yes."

"Well…enjoy your afternoon."

"Thank you." Claire closed the door.

Although it shut with a gentle click, Lorene felt as if the door had been slammed in her face. It made knocking on Mary's door seem like an effort, all the pleasure drained out of her plans. Between Henry's distracted mood, never truly paying attention to her, and Claire's combative attitude, she felt the house was gripped by something she couldn't see or understand, as if the boards and plaster and tile, the wallpaper and paint had turned against her, breathing toxic fumes into her heart. Her soul was turning to something dark and sour, always cowering in fear of criticism or a mocking grin. Beyond her assurance that an Inner Light provided her guidance and companionship, she tried to steer her thoughts away from anything supernatural, even though she had several friends who sought comfort from psychics. She didn't believe in ghosts or demons, and didn't think there were evil spirits that drifted across the earth, attaching themselves to people or houses. But she could see it would be easy to think that a malevolent entity had entered her house when Claire came to stay with them.

Mary was sitting on her window seat reading a book.

Her diary and a pen lay near her feet. She was dressed in her white nightgown with blue rosebuds printed on the fabric.

Lorene kissed her forehead. It was cool and smooth. "Did you sleep well?"

Mary nodded, keeping her eyes focused on the pages of her book.

"Did Annie tuck you in and give you a glass of water?"

"Not really."

"What does that mean?"

"I can put myself to bed, you know."

"Yes. I guess you can."

Mary put her book face down on the cushion.

"It's a perfect day. The fog is gone. We should take a picnic to the beach," Lorene said. "We can walk out on the pier and visit the ship."

Mary shrugged.

"I know you're disappointed you weren't able to go last night, but it's just as wonderful during the day. You'll see."

Mary slid off the window seat. "Okay."

Her expression was so glum, Lorene had a momentary thought of suggesting they go frog hunting. She shivered again. The beach and the concrete ship, even in the daylight, would return the smile to Mary's lips.

With two chicken sandwiches, two apples, and two bottles of pop tucked into a cloth bag, Lorene and Mary walked along Seacliff Drive toward the road leading down to the beach. Mary carried a blanket. They wore sun hats and carried sweaters in case the fog returned. They started down the hill, walking in silence, gazing ahead at the gently rolling surf — deep blue edged in white.

When they reached the sand, they spread out the blanket and set the bag of food on one corner.

"Should we walk to the pier, or do you want to go wading for a bit first?" Lorene said.

"Let's go on the ship."

She was pleased that Mary had shaken off her gloom over missing the party. From what Lorene had observed of the drinking going on outside of the ballroom, flasks passed around, giddy laughter, she was glad children weren't permitted. She'd heard there was even more drinking below deck, men and women fondling others who weren't their spouses. Some women had come to the grand opening alone, looking for men who might exchange sex in a dark corner for a pint of whiskey that had doubtful quality. The boat seemed custom-designed to stimulate children's imaginations, and she felt Mary's disappointment sharply. If people followed the laws, moral and legal, maybe they wouldn't have to bar the most enthusiastic segment of the population from enjoying the ship.

They stood on the port side, looking toward the Monterey Peninsula. Mary asked what they'd eaten for dinner and how the orchestra sounded. Then, she was quiet for a few minutes. "It doesn't feel like I'm on a ship," she said. "I guess because it's not floating."

"And it felt even less like a ship when we were inside and couldn't see the water."

"What's a bootlegger?" Mary said.

"Where did you hear that word?"

"What is it?"

"Someone who sells illegal liquor."

"Why are they called bootleggers?"

"I don't know. Where did you hear about that?"

"Jacob said it."

Jacob was proving himself to be an unfit companion for Claire. First the fistfight she'd witnessed, now this. Was that why he hadn't taken Claire home last night? She'd seen him lurking near the bow of the ship, and she'd known something wasn't right. Were bootleggers using it now for their illicit deliveries? It was heartbreaking, so typical of criminal minds, to take something lovely like the concrete ship and turn it into a vehicle for crime and decadence. They would turn the lovely ship into another cavern for gambling and drinking, filled with ladies of the evening, just like the Deer Park "Teahouse" which no longer served tea and fine desserts, but kept its name in an attempt to hide what went on there.

She sighed. She wished more than ever that Claire had agreed to come to the beach with them. There must be a way to open Claire's eyes to Jacob's true character, to help her notice appropriate boys her own age. There was no reason she should be seeing one boy exclusively. She was too young. No matter what it said about Lorene's marriage at the same age, seventeen was much too young for an exclusive relationship that would lead inevitably to marriage. Why couldn't Claire learn from Lorene's mistake? She didn't like thinking of her marriage as a mistake, and overall, it wasn't, but there was no doubt she'd been too young. She saw that so clearly now. She'd been too young to know how to live with a man. She'd been too young when she became a mother, uncertain about how to raise a child. If she gave birth now, she'd have a much better understanding of what was required. She wouldn't have made as many mistakes.

"Did Jacob say he was involved with bootlegging?"

Mary shrugged. "Maybe ask Claire if he is."

"When were you talking to him?" she said.

"I wasn't. I just heard him say it."

"When?"

"Last night."

"We were at the grand opening last night," she said.

"After that."

So. He'd arranged to meet Claire after his illicit business was done. He'd come back to the house, and she'd snuck out to meet him. There were so many things going on while Lorene was asleep. She felt as if she lived in a different world from everyone else in her household.

"We didn't get home until after midnight. What were you doing awake at that hour? And Jacob didn't ride with us. So it must have been even later."

"I was angry that you went without me. I climbed the oak tree and stayed up there for a long time."

"In the middle of the night? Where was Annie?" Of course, Lorene knew where Annie had been. She'd fallen asleep. Her days were long. It really was an imposition, asking her to stay late to look after Mary. It needed to stop. Annie was too agreeable. Even though Annie appreciated the extra money, it was too much to ask of her. "You could have fallen and hurt yourself. You might miss a branch or… a wild animal could have attacked you. It's so dangerous. There are bad men out at night."

"I was angry."

"That's not an excuse. You shouldn't do something foolish just because you're angry. You need to talk about your feelings."

"I have. No one cares. And no one was home."

"I care."

A gull flew overhead, dipping low. Lorene ducked, even though she knew it was an illusion that the bird seemed to be only a foot or so above her head. The gull moved higher and hovered over them, its wings floating on the breeze. It watched them with hopeful eyes, or so she imagined.

"Then why can't I go on the boat at night?"

"It's not my rule. I've explained this before."

Mary leaned over the side, peering down into the water. It lapped gently against the sides now that the tide was pulling out. Lorene bent over to see what she was looking at. Fish flashed by, close to the surface, silvery and moving like they were made of liquid.

"I'm sorry," Mary said.

Lorene took her daughter's hand. "I'm sorry you can't come out here at night, but it really is not what you think. It's no different from any restaurant, from any ballroom."

Mary nodded.

Lorene squeezed Mary's hand. They continued walking around the boat, peering in the windows so Mary could see how uninteresting the interior was. After a while, they returned to the beach and ate their sandwiches. They took off their sandals and walked to the edge of the water. The tide was completely out now, and they spent the next hour picking up pebbles and seashells, wading in the shallow, quietly moving water.

The door to Henry's study was closed. Lorene knocked, more firmly than usual.

"Come in."

Henry stood behind his desk. "I was just finishing. Should I meet you in the parlor for tea? Or on the veranda?"

"I need to talk to you."

"I'll be there in about five minutes."

"Now. Privately."

"Why isn't the parlor private?"

"I don't want Mary to overhear. She's heard enough. Or Claire, for that matter."

He sat down. "What's going on?"

She sat in one of the red leather armchairs facing his desk. It had been ages since she sat here. She usually didn't come into his study except to bring him a cup of coffee or ask him if he was ready to come to dinner. The last time she'd sat in one of these chairs was…she tried to think. Maybe when her mother died? To talk to him about Claire coming to stay with them. She'd felt like he was an adult and she was a child, asking permission to invite a friend to stay over. It shouldn't be that way. This was just as much her home as it was his. Why had she thought she had to ask his permission to have her sister live with them? Although right now, she was wishing she'd never done that. She was too kind, too worried about her baby sister. She should have insisted one of her aunts take the girl. Managing Claire was beyond Lorene's capabilities. Another instance where she was too young. Would she spend her entire life always feeling a step behind, always at a disadvantage, as if she'd never fully entered the adult world, learning how to live after it was too late?

"I have a very serious concern about Jacob," she said.

"Yes?"

"I think he's involved in bootlegging — illegal transportation of liquor."

He laughed. "I know what bootlegging is."

"You need to fire him."

"Why on earth do you think he would be involved with something like that?"

"Mary heard him talking to Claire about it."

"I find that hard to believe."

"Mary wouldn't lie."

"She must have misunderstood."

Lorene clutched the arms of the chair. They were huge, thick and stuffed so tightly there was no give. Her fingers ached with trying to stretch around the ends. She put her hands in her lap. "She didn't know what the word meant — bootlegging — so I don't think she misheard."

"Will you stop saying that."

"Saying what?"

"Bootlegging."

"Why? That's what it's called."

"It's a foolish word."

She shrugged. "That's beside the point. He shouldn't be anywhere near our home, now that we know. Is he the one supplying your liquor?"

"No."

"If he brings a criminal element to our home, if he… you need to fire him, tell him to stay away from Claire. Tell him we never want him anywhere near our house."

"Please don't think you can tell me how to run my business."

"Don't you care what he's doing?"

He leaned back in his chair and gazed at the ceiling. "You've given me no proof he's *doing* anything."

"Mary said…"

"Mary is a ten-year-old child, Lorene."

"I know how old she is!"

"Calm down."

"Don't tell me to calm down. I have good reason to be upset. Do you know bootleggers carry guns and work with gangsters? Do you know federal agents often have to shoot them, they're so reckless and violent?"

"I didn't realize you were such an expert in criminal activity."

"It's common knowledge."

"Is that right."

"Don't patronize me."

He smiled. "I'm not. But you can't tell me who to hire and fire. I shouldn't have humored you when you suggested Jacob working in San Francisco. The home and Mary are your areas of concern. Business matters are mine."

"A lot of men seek their wives' council."

"Do they?"

He should respect her input and value her as his equal, but talking about that would have to wait for another time. Protecting Mary and Claire was more important right now.

It wasn't a stretch to say it was a matter of life or death, and it was infuriating listening to Henry behave as if the threat wasn't real. He seemed to think Mary wasn't very bright or she was lying. Lorene wasn't sure which was worse. It was possible he had no idea how intelligent his daughter was — how much time did he spend conversing with her? "This isn't just about business. It's about protecting our family. I want you to dismiss him."

"I'm not going to do that. You have no proof. You have an overheard piece of conversation, maybe, by a little girl. That's no cause for firing my most valued employee."

"Then you need to confront him about it."

"Stop telling me what I need to do."

"I'm extremely concerned. I'm afraid for Mary."

"So I see."

"Maybe hire a private detective and have him followed, get proof of what he's up to, if you really think you need proof before you take any action."

He laughed.

"This is serious."

He pushed out his chair and stood up. "If it makes you feel better, I'll ask him what he was talking about."

"Doesn't it worry you that he's talking to Claire about illegal activity?"

"I said I'd discuss it with him."

"Immediately?"

"When I see him. On Monday."

"He's out with Claire, now. Maybe you should go look for them."

"Hunt him down and drag Claire home by her hair?"

"Stop mocking me."

"It's hard not to. You should listen to yourself."

"I saw him on the ship, by the way, when we were leaving. He was trying to hide near the bow. When he said he was ill and couldn't take Claire home, he was lying."

"I talked to him before we left. He was in a lot of pain." Henry pressed his hand to the side of his head as if he was nursing pain of his own.

"Maybe when you saw him, but ten minutes later, he looked fine."

"Did you talk to him?"

She gripped the chair arms again. "I didn't speak to him. He was frightening, lurking in the darkness like that."

"Why don't we go have our tea now." He walked around the desk and held out his hand to her.

"You're dismissing my concerns."

"Lorene! I said I'd talk to him. That's more than I should be doing. It's insulting to his integrity. But I'll try to bring it up without accusing him."

She stood up. "If anything happens to Mary or Claire because of this, I'll never forgive you."

He put his arm around her waist. "Everything will be fine, I promise."

She didn't believe him. He couldn't promise that.

Henry never mentioned the overheard conversation about bootlegging again. After a week or two had gone by, Lorene asked him about his conversation with Jacob. Henry informed her it was all a misunderstanding, everything was settled. She didn't need to think about it anymore, and she should talk to Mary about her eavesdropping habit. It was low class. Didn't she agree?

Spring & Summer 1931

Seventeen

After ten months spent looking at the diamond ring on Claire's right hand, Jacob was fed up. She obviously didn't feel the same way about him as he did about her. Over those ten months, his passion had withered, reshaping itself into a needle of pain directly below his heart. Next month, she would graduate from high school. Despite wearing the diamond ring in the no man's land of her right hand, she hadn't mentioned marriage or his proposal once during the entire ten months. Ten months! At least he hadn't had to look at the diamond teardrop dangling from her neck since that night on the concrete ship. For all he knew, she was keeping several men in a state of uncertainty similar to his own.

Managing the liquor deliveries had changed him. He'd developed nerves that remained taut and steady in nearly all situations. His confidence gave him a bold stride, and he no longer hesitated over decisions — except for whether he should break it off with Claire. He supposed that was a decision worth deliberating over. He was sure Henry would agree.

Even the problem of David had been resolved through Jacob's careful control of the situation. Late last summer, he'd approached Henry and asked whether David might be hired to stock shelves in the market. George wasn't a young man, and stocking shelves required lifting boxes that weighed between fifteen and thirty pounds, in some cases. George was still responsible for checking inventory and shipment arrivals, so there was no risk of undetected theft. Besides, when he'd stolen the pop, David had been just a kid in many respects, still finding his way after the death of his father and the loss of their family home. Lots of kids had a few foolish moments. Jacob had been tempted to point out that bootleggers weren't in a position of moral superiority, but decided that fact was either already obvious to Henry, or it would be considered irrelevant because Henry was focused on protecting his self-interest, not debating ethics. It was better to stick with a simple argument, and he'd been right. Henry agreed to give David a job, under the close supervision of George. The job offer spoke to Henry's respect for Jacob, his trust in Jacob's judgement.

Hiding his nighttime work from David hadn't been as difficult as he'd imagined. In fact, it had become even easier — David worked long hours doing physical work that left him exhausted at night, too tired to be checking up on his brother.

There wasn't a flicker of guilt when Jacob went about his evening activities because he'd come to realize he provided a necessary service. The sale and distribution of alcohol kept money flowing through the economy at a time when money seemed to be drying up like seed pods, blown away by the gentlest breeze. His increasing confidence led him to the decision that he wasn't going to marry a woman who was only mildly interested in him. He'd worked hard for her, saved his money, treated her like a duchess. Much of the time she managed to avoid looking him in the eye. His feelings seemed to be an unimportant part of her life. There was no sense that she admired him, that she wanted to be with him only. He felt like he was a diversion, one of many. She acted as if he were disposable, easily replaced.

He pulled into the curved driveway in front of the King home. Claire stood on the front porch. She began winding a black silk scarf around her neck as he pulled around. Normally he had to ring the bell and wait for Annie to wander through the house looking for Claire. He often sat in the foyer for five or ten minutes before Claire appeared, waiting for him to stand up, turning her cheek for him to kiss.

Now, even before he came to a full stop, she was walking down the steps. She opened the door and got into the car. They were going to dinner in the restaurant on the concrete ship. The ship's dancing and dining offerings had been in a state of uncertainty, not unlike his relationship with Claire. Business overall had been slow as the economy floundered and the ship was closed through the winter. A week earlier, a grand re-opening had been held. It wasn't nearly as grand as the original, and the anticipation was minimal. Claire had suggested attending, but he felt it would simply be a repeat of the disastrous original opening. Dining there this evening seemed appropriate. He would end their relationship where he'd once hoped their future might begin.

He wasn't aware of even the suggestion of grief or heartbreak. He was mostly tired. It surprised him how love was able to transform itself into something heavy and ugly, as if the beautiful thing he remembered never existed at all. It made him think of the yellowish cast that came into his mother's green eyes, the way her once round, firm shoulders turned to bones with skin stretched across them, and her cheeks seemed to sink inside of her skull as she lay there trying to breathe through her last days on earth.

A few weeks earlier, his attention had been drawn to a woman he'd met at an Easter picnic. Claire had been sick with the flu all of Easter week. While he waited in line to receive a slice of ham on his plate, Sarah had looked across the serving table and smiled at him. Later, she'd asked him to be her egg-hunting partner. Together, they'd filled a large basket with dyed eggs. They'd laughed at the thought of consuming so many eggs before they spoiled.

Sarah had dark hair, cut to her shoulders — glossy and moving like water all the time. Her bright blue eyes were shocking beneath the bangs that covered her forehead. She laughed constantly. He hoped she wouldn't turn sulky and secretive like Claire. He hoped it wasn't a trait shared by all women.

As he drove down the hill toward the pier, Claire sat quietly beside him. He couldn't think of a single thing to say to prompt conversation. He worried they might rattle around in a nearly empty restaurant, making the silence between them even more pronounced. It would be gloomy if there were only four or five occupied tables, the rest spread out like a sea of deserted snow-covered islands in the large room.

They walked the length of the pier, still not talking. Gulls circled overhead, a huge crowd of them today, as if they'd spotted something dead to feed on. They were low, menacing with their sharp orange beaks ready to tear and devour rotting flesh. He wanted to wave them away, but it wouldn't do any good. They were relentless. He quickened his pace. Claire lagged behind, and he grabbed her elbow and propelled her forward.

"What's your hurry?" she said.

He realized he wanted to eat, go for a stroll along the beach, and drive her home as quickly as possible. He'd tell her at the end, sitting in the car, cutting short the period of awkwardness. He wouldn't even have to look at her.

The waiter seated them beside a window near the front of the restaurant. As he'd feared, they were surrounded by empty tables. It was early still, but he'd expected more than two other couples. The room echoed with the lack of human presence. White plates on white tablecloths made his eyes ache.

Claire propped her menu at an angle that prevented him from seeing her face. She studied it as if she was preparing for one of her final exams. He'd made a decision for his entree and dessert, and still, she perused the list of offerings. There weren't that many selections. Was she even reading it, or was her mind elsewhere and she'd forgotten she was supposed to be choosing a meal?

"Do you know what you want?" he said.

"Not yet." The menu remained steady, so he was unable to see a flicker of her eyes or the hint of a smile that might soften the words, spoken without inflection.

He set his menu on the edge of the table and took a sip of water. A shot of Henry's scotch would be nice. It worried him how attached he'd grown to the stuff. Now, instead of drinking it to be polite when he met with Henry, he found himself tapping his fingers on his leg, waiting for Henry to extend the flask in Jacob's direction. It wasn't good to be thinking about it while he was waiting for dinner. He hoped he wasn't becoming addicted to it. He rarely took more than a few sips, was never drunk or even close to it. The heat of the liquid in his veins and the easing of his thoughts, always searching in the darkness for someone watching him, soothed him. It would unknot the tension that had formed between him and Claire. He wondered if she felt it. She never mentioned it.

"Do you want me to make a suggestion?" he said.

She lowered the menu and peered over the top. "Why would I want that?"

"You're taking an awfully long time."

"There are too many good choices."

"Choose one this time, and you can have one of the others the next time."

"Business isn't doing well on the ship, you said so yourself. There might not be a next time."

He shrugged.

She placed her menu on the table. "I'll have the filet mignon."

Of course she would. The most expensive item. He could afford it, but he resented the smile that accompanied her decision. There was a suggestion of victory in it. Her ring flashed as she picked up the water glass. He wasn't planning to ask her to return it. The tiny diamond was a reminder of failure. He would never want to give it to another girl. He'd buy a new one — for Sarah, maybe. He hoped. She seemed a lot more enthused about him than Claire ever had. Now, he could afford a much nicer ring.

He ordered Claire's steak, medium rare, and stuffed

sole for himself. Because Claire had taken so long to make up her mind, the garden salads were delivered as soon as the waiter took away their menus. Eating gave him something to do. He cut the lettuce into small bites with the side of his fork. Claire talked about a graduation party she was invited to. She made no mention of whether she'd be asking him to escort her. Maybe breaking their engagement, if it were an engagement at all, would be easier than he'd thought. It seemed as if she cared for him less and less. She was just too lazy to take any action herself. Or maybe she liked having a diamond on her finger, even if it meant nothing.

Claire declined to have dessert. It was disappointing to miss the banana cream pie he'd been thinking about, but at the same time, he was relieved they could reach the inevitable conclusion more quickly.

As they strolled around the ship's deck, a pod of dolphins frolicked a few hundred feet past the bow. They stood for a while, watching them swim in large circles, herding fish into clusters so they could eat. Their sleek gray bodies shimmered in the gold light of the descending sun. The small younger animals leapt in the air, making perfect arcs as if they'd been trained for that purpose. Claire laughed and wound her scarf several times around her neck. She leaned over the edge of the ship, refusing to continue walking, unable to take her eyes off them. For a few moments, watching her laugh and cheer each time one jumped, he thought he could love her again. But then he saw her naked left finger. He shoved his hands in his pockets. It didn't matter whether he could find a way to love her, she didn't love him.

"You seem more gloomy than usual this evening," she said. She looped her arm through his as they walked back toward the pier.

"I'm not gloomy. Ever."

She laughed. "Yes you are. You sulk more than a girl."

It wasn't true. She was trying to make him angry. Maybe she really did want him to break their non-engagement.

"See, you won't even talk. You're sulking right now." She grabbed his hand and yanked hard.

There was a popping sound in his elbow. "Ow!"

"That didn't hurt."

She was right it hadn't, but he didn't like it. He walked faster.

"Slow down. You're in such a rush with everything — walking out to the ship, ordering dinner, hurrying back. You didn't even enjoy the dolphins."

"Yes I did."

"Could have fooled me." She pinched his cheek.

"Don't do that."

She giggled.

He pulled his arm away from her and walked faster, taking long strides so she had to hurry to catch up.

"What are you so grouchy about? You're spoiling our evening. You make me wish I'd stayed home tonight."

He stopped. "Me too."

"What?"

"I wish you'd stayed home. In fact, I think we should stop going out with each other."

She folded her arms. Her hair whipped across her face as she turned into the breeze. She didn't brush it away. "What are you talking about?"

"I'm not in love with you anymore. I'm ending our engagement. Not that we're actually engaged since you refuse to wear the ring on the proper hand or tell anyone about it."

"You're breaking up with me?" She stepped forward, raised her hand, and smacked his face. "How dare you?"

His cheek burned. He imagined he looked like a child with a bright red mark across it. He grabbed her wrist. "How *dare* I?"

"You can't break up with me."

"Well, I am."

"You aren't going to humiliate me like that. I'll tell everyone I broke up with *you*." She yanked the ring off her finger.

For a moment, he thought she would hurl it over the side of the pier. But she dropped it in the side pocket of his jacket. "Take your itty bitty diamond."

He started walking.

She ran after him and grabbed the back of his jacket, forcing him to stop. She moved in front of him and tilted her head up. She glared at him, her chin jutting out. "You'd better tell everyone what I say. You better tell them I broke up with you."

"Say whatever you want. It's not important." He was angry he'd blurted it out. His nerves hadn't grown as steely as he'd thought. At least not with her. Now he'd have to listen to her berate him all the way back to the car and on the short drive to her home.

"It's very important. All kinds of men are interested in me."

"I'm sure they are." He had a splitting headache. It would be so nice to just pick up her small, slender body and drop her over the side of the ship. Let the sharks have her.

"I can have anyone I want."

"That's fine."

"You don't believe me?"

"Yes, I believe you."

"So I can have you if I want."

She stabbed her finger into his breastbone. It hurt but he wasn't going to let her know how painful it was.

"Maybe I just don't want you." Her voice was getting louder, shrill.

He glanced around. He didn't need to draw attention to himself. He had to avoid having a face that was easily recalled. "That's fine. Then we're agreed."

"You better not go telling people you dumped me!"

"Let's get in the car. You made your point clear." He tried to keep moving, but she grabbed his coat again, slowing his forward momentum.

"You haven't promised," she shouted.

"I'm not going to promise anything so ridiculous. Why would you think I'd talk about you at all?" He opened the car door, and she got inside, yanking it closed before he released his grip, wrenching his shoulder.

She carried on during the short drive up the hill and along the street to her sister's house, telling him she was too high class for him, complaining about how small the ring was and if he'd really wanted her, he would have sacrificed for something more impressive. She informed him he wasn't very good looking and not intelligent at all. He took it all in silence. Her fury was like a two-year-old's tantrum. He wasn't going to argue with someone who was clearly losing her senses, looking for every cruel thing she could find to throw at him. All she was doing was cementing his decision.

He stopped near the end of the driveway. Henry's car was parked near the porch.

"Why are you stopping here?"

"You're home."

"Take me to the steps."

"No."

She punched his arm. "You can't treat me like this.

Take me to the steps!"

He turned off the engine and folded his arms across his ribs.

She lunged at him, pounding her fists into his shoulder and arm. She grabbed his ear and twisted it. He cried out. She twisted harder.

He forced his voice to remain low and steady. "Get out of the car."

"You haven't promised."

"I'm not going to. It's stupid."

She moved until her back was against the door. Saliva flew out of her mouth as she spoke. "I will destroy your life. No one dumps me and acts like he's too good for me. No one!" She flung open the door and nearly fell out of the car. She left the door open and ran up the driveway. She stomped up the steps, opened the front door, and slammed it behind her. He wondered what she would say to Lorene or Mary or Annie. Or Henry, if he heard the racket from his study.

Two days later, Jacob met David at the diner for breakfast. Over pancakes, he told David he'd broken up with Claire.

"Maybe I should ask her out," David said.

"That's not a good idea."

"Why? You don't think she would have me?"

"I have no idea, but if she did go out with you, and things went sideways, she turns into a terror."

"What happened?"

Jacob gave him a cleaned up version of Claire's tantrum.

David stared at him, his fork poised midway between his plate and his mouth. A piece of pancake began losing its grip on the fork. A moment later, the pancake tore and fell into a puddle of syrup. "Do you think she'll sabotage your job? Or mine?"

Jacob shook his head. "Henry has a lot of respect for me." He was confident, more than he sounded because he didn't want to explain why he was so certain. There was no way Henry would risk the damage Jacob could do if they had a falling out. Even aside from that, Henry relied on him for errands that were too sensitive for others. Jacob still handled the bank deposits for the legitimate businesses. No, he was confident Claire could spin into a frenzy, and Henry would simply turn away.

"I don't know. That's a pretty definite threat," David said.

"Don't worry about it."

"Maybe you should be more worried. Maybe you should be thinking about how to get the upper hand, make the first move."

"What kind of *move*? What are you talking about?"

"Solidify our positions. Maybe tell Henry she needs to be locked up."

"It was a temper tantrum, she's not insane."

"It sounds pretty crazy to me," David said. He cut a wedge out of the pancakes and stabbed his fork into the bite-sized stack.

"She was emotional, that's all."

"Are you sure?"

Jacob nodded. He was queasy from too much syrup and butter. He pushed his plate away.

"Lost your appetite?"

"It's a lot of food."

David shoved a forkful of pancakes into his mouth. "We need a plan." The fog was burning off, and the sun suddenly shone through the window, surrounding David's face and upper body with blinding light. "I'm serious. We need to protect our interests."

"*Our* interests?"

"Yes."

David seemed unaware of the sarcastic tone. He continued shoveling sopping pancakes into his mouth. After a moment, he chewed furiously, swallowed, and put down his fork. "She threatened you. She has the inside track. She can talk to Mrs. King. She has Henry's attention at dinner every night of the week. She can even utilize Mary."

"How would she *utilize* Mary? You're the one who sounds crazy." Jacob laughed.

"I don't know. Women have ways. They can be very crafty. You should know that."

"Not all women are the same."

"In that way, yes they are. Just like all men are saps for a pretty girl."

"That's completely different."

"Trust me on this."

As far as Jacob knew, David hadn't had more than one or two girls, with long gaps in between where he didn't even ask a girl out. How could he possibly believe he was an expert on all women? As if you only had to read a book and you knew how they operated. He watched David eat for several minutes. The sunlight moved slowly until it fell on the table between them. Jacob closed his eyes against the brilliant light for a moment. He opened them and waited for David to speak.

When the plate was empty, the excess syrup mopped up with a piece of toast, David pushed it to the side. He put his elbows on the table and leaned forward. "What's the plan?"

"We don't need a plan."

"You're being naive."

Jacob laughed.

"Don't laugh at me."

"Everything will work out. Henry doesn't care what Claire does."

"How do you know that? She *threatened* you!"

"It was a tantrum."

"You were pretty shook up when you were telling me. I don't think you really believe it was just hysterics."

Jacob signaled for the check. David moved his hand to

his hip pocket, as if to reach for his wallet. "I have this," Jacob said.

"Thanks."

He pulled out a few bills, ready when the waitress came with the receipt.

As they stepped on to the sidewalk and turned to keep the sun out of their eyes, David grabbed Jacob's elbow. "Be careful. You've helped me out, I want to return the favor. I'll try to come up with a plan."

Jacob shrugged. They didn't need to plan anything, his position was secure. But if it made David feel things between them were somewhat equal, he didn't need to squash him into an inferior position. Despite David's flaws, Jacob loved his brother.

Out of professional courtesy, Jacob decided to tell Henry about the breakup, just in case his brother had had a glimmer of wisdom and foresight. It couldn't hurt to have the news come from Jacob rather than venom pouring out of Claire's once kissable lips. Henry was meeting him at the entrance to the pier that evening. He had extra cash for Jacob because he'd been informed the boat was carrying a larger load than normal.

In the darkness, Henry appeared menacing. Jacob could easily see him wielding a machine gun like any gangster ready to defend his assets. Hopefully, Jacob would remain one of those assets, although right now, Henry would primarily be concerned with liquid assets. He laughed softly.

"What's so funny?" Henry slid his hand inside his coat and removed an envelope from the pocket. He handed it to Jacob.

"I don't know," Jacob said. "Just one of those senseless thoughts that comes from nowhere."

"Don't be laughing at nothing when you're unloading crates. It makes you sound unhinged."

This was not a good segue to his news regarding Claire. He coughed. "Don't worry. I would never do that."

Henry grunted. He turned away from the water.

"By the way, just a quick bit of news," Jacob said.

Henry turned back. He looked anxious, as if any unexpected news couldn't be good.

Jacob coughed again. "I just wanted to let you know Claire and I are no longer seeing each other."

"Why would I be concerned with your social life?" Henry said.

"Just wanted you to know. So there are no secrets between us."

Henry nodded. "I appreciate the sentiment." He touched his hat brim. "Be careful."

"I always am."

Henry turned and walked along the footpath.

From where he stood, Jacob couldn't see the car. Jacob stepped onto the pier. Claire wouldn't pose a problem. As

Henry had indicated from the start, he had no interest in her comings and goings.

Eighteen

The dining room was much too warm, even though the windows were open, straining to capture the delicate breeze and draw it into the room. At six-thirty in the evening, the temperature was still eighty-two degrees, and no one wanted to be eating a formal dinner, but Lorene insisted. Sunday was one night she could ensure Henry was at home to eat with them. A little warm air never killed anyone. She looked at the salmon fillet covered with a creamy dill sauce. The dill had a cooling effect, but the roasted potatoes and steamed Brussels sprouts were winter food, meant to warm the inside of your body. She wished Annie had made a potato salad with tomato wedges on the side, but it was too late now. She sliced a Brussels sprout in half then split each piece again and ate one.

No one spoke. Their resistance to the fancy dinner was more pungent than the sprouts. "We should have ice cream for dessert," she said. "Let's eat it on the back veranda.

Doesn't that sound nice?"

"Chocolate?" Mary said.

"I think we have chocolate."

"Can we finish dinner before we think about sweets?" Claire said.

The only sounds were utensils on china and the occasional soft thud of a water glass on the covered table.

"How come there's nothing interesting to talk about?" Mary said. "I don't like the Brussels sprouts. They smell like the dirty clothes basket."

Lorene frowned.

Henry pushed his plate to the side. "I agree with your thoughts on the Brussels sprouts, Mary. And it's too hot for conversation."

"I have something to talk about," Claire said. "Although it's not a conversation exactly." She took a sip of water. A fly buzzed over the serving dish of salmon to her left where a few small pink pieces of fish remained. The fly landed and began nibbling. "Ew." Claire waved it away. She folded her hands in her lap. "I wanted to tell you that I broke up with Jacob."

Lorene pressed her lips together, trying to keep a smile from taking over her face. It felt as if a breath of fog-laced breeze had poured through the window, easing all her discomfort.

Henry was staring at Claire. His brow had a deep crease at the center. His lips were parted. He seemed about to say something. Slowly they closed. He continued studying Claire, tilting his head to the right as if to get a better look at her, hoping it would provide insight.

"So," Claire said. She pushed back her chair. "That's over."

"Jacob mentioned something about that," Henry said.

Claire gripped the back of her chair. "Don't believe his nonsense."

"I've never known him to speak nonsense," Henry said.

"Did you return his ring?" Lorene said.

Claire turned. "How did you know about the ring?"

Lorene smiled. Her sister must think she was an imbecile.

"And just to answer your question, of course I returned it. Why wouldn't I?"

"Are you feeling okay about it?" Lorene said.

"Yes. I'm just fine, thank you. I was tired of him. I have other men in my life that are much more sophisticated."

Lorene glanced at Henry. There was still a sense that he wanted to say more. He seemed puzzled by Claire's announcement, but unwilling to speak up. It wasn't like him. She had the impression he knew more about the breakup with Jacob. Had Jacob's illegal activities forced Claire to break off their engagement? It had been strange from the start — Claire wearing the ring on her right hand, never mentioning the engagement. At first, Lorene hadn't even been sure the ring came from Jacob. Then one day last fall, she'd overheard Claire in the screened porch, talking to a friend from school about it. She couldn't make sense of any of it, but Henry definitely had something on his mind.

He stood up. "Let's go outside. Lorene, ask Annie to bring us ice cream. And maybe some iced tea, or lemonade." He left the room.

Lorene went into the kitchen and spoke to Annie about the ice cream, then she returned to the dining room where she stacked the china and carried the plates to the kitchen. She scraped the leftovers into the garbage. She asked Annie to take out the trash after the ice cream was served, and instructed her to leave the dishwashing until morning. It was too hot.

They sat on the screened porch holding chilled bowls filled with chocolate ice cream, drinking lemonade, and listening to Mary talk about her plans for the summer. Every day she would swim in the ocean. She and her friends were writing a play. They would perform on the veranda in a few months. She would climb the oak tree and read books up there when it was too hot in the house. Lorene suggested she was too old for tree climbing. Mary glowered, and no one spoke for several minutes.

After a few more spoonfuls of ice cream, Mary sat up straight. She put her bowl on the low table and leaned forward. "I finished that book I got from the library."

"Which one is that?" Henry said. "You read so many." He grinned at her, his lips dark and slick with ice cream.

"About Nellie Bly."

"Who's Nellie Bly?" Henry said.

"I told you."

"I forgot. You know so much, I can't keep up," he said.

Lorene tipped her head down and hid her smile as Mary contorted her face into a grimace, deflecting his patronizing comment.

"She was a reporter. She got herself committed to an insane asylum to write about the horrid things they did to inmates."

Henry nodded. "Not the most edifying reading material."

"It's interesting."

"Why?" Henry sounded genuinely curious.

Mary's eyes glittered as she looked at their faces, assessing their interest, ready to take the center of the stage.

"It's interesting because Mary knows what it's like to live with mental cases," Claire said.

"Claire!" Lorene stood up. "That's rude and… completely untrue!"

Claire laughed.

Mary began talking softly about the poor treatment of the mentally ill in the last century, but no one was really listening. Lorene kept her eyes on Mary, hoping she felt they wanted to hear her thoughts, but her own mind wandered to Claire.

Soon after that, they drifted off to their bedrooms to

read and try to get some rest. The night was cooling slightly, but the breeze was still too mild to make its way through the screens.

Once they were in their bedroom with the door closed, Lorene turned to Henry. "You seemed troubled by Claire's announcement."

"I heard a different story from Jacob, that's all."

"Oh?"

"He said he broke it off."

"Is that all?"

"It struck me odd. But you're right, it's nothing."

"Do you think she's seeing someone we don't know about?"

He shrugged and started to undress.

"Do you?"

"She's not our child. Her decisions are her own."

She knew he was right, but she worried. If her father or mother were still alive, they would have some say over Claire's life. Now, Claire did whatever she pleased, and it wasn't good. It would lead to heartbreak for Claire, and possibly come back on Lorene and Henry. She didn't understand why he couldn't see that.

She changed into one of her summer nightgowns and got into bed, pushing the blankets against the footboard.

When Henry was beside her, they lay on their backs in the darkness. Crickets chirped with such a racket it seemed as if they were clinging to the sides of the house, trying to get inside, like the start of a Biblical plague. Henry took her hand, but his grasp was limp and she wished he wouldn't bother. She couldn't remember the last time he'd held her or made love to her. He was so rarely in bed when she was awake. Everything was about business, and if she complained, he told her to be thankful they had a comfortable life without worries. A lot of people were destitute. He reminded her that money didn't just flow in on the tide.

She knew she couldn't manage Claire's life, couldn't stand in for her mother, but she'd tried and failed to shake off the aching sense of responsibility. Someone had to watch out for the girl. Claire hadn't finished growing up when their mother died, and now she drifted through life without anything to keep her from crashing on the rocks. When Lorene tried to talk about seeking the Inner Light, or anything related to the beliefs they'd grown up with, Claire gave her a smug look and said nothing.

It wasn't fair that she had to feel burdened by something so far outside of her control. It was exhausting and all-consuming. It was leeching the enjoyment out of her life. When she tried to look inside and listen to the Quiet Voice, she heard nothing.

She lay awake for a long time. She wondered about the other man, or men, Claire claimed to have in her life. No one else came to the house to pick her up. Lorene had never heard another man mentioned by name, and yet, there was the diamond necklace.

Henry was snoring long before she fell asleep.

When she woke, Henry's side of the bed was vacant. The sheets were cool, and the smell of him was gone. She turned over and tried to find her way back to sleep. She felt she'd only slept for a few hours, the night torn apart by partial dreams that upset her but didn't leave behind enough images for her to know the reason why. Even with her restlessness, she hadn't been aware of him leaving.

Sleep refused to come. Her mind raced. Providing a home and a family for Claire had surely given Lorene some rights to act as a parent. Now she realized she'd squandered the months before Claire turned eighteen. It had become an obsession — thinking she could still find a way to gain influence. The first step would be to find out whether Claire was stealing. If that were the case, maybe Claire could be committed to a hospital for observation, for psychiatric care. It would be an alternative to offer, rather than time in jail. The rumored horrors of a women's prison might make Claire compliant. But how would she find out where the necklace had come from? Words slid off Claire's tongue without meaning. It was impossible to tell when she was lying and when she was truthful. She pulled the covers over her face, blotting out the light so she could return to a dream state and her subconscious might work out in flimsy images the solution to her problem. Her mind still refused to quiet down.

This wasn't about Claire having any affection for Lorene or even respecting her — it was about protecting Claire from permanent damage. Or was it simply about removing her from their lives, from Lorene's life in particular, being free of the worry and the constant challenge to her authority? Claire behaved as if Lorene was nothing more than an interfering housekeeper! She was the mistress of this house! Claire was staying here because of Lorene's devotion to the family. Claire owed her an explanation about that necklace. It might be that time resting in a sanitarium for the mentally ill would be good for Claire, would allow her to express her grief — something she'd never done. It would get her away from boys until she had a chance to mature, and help her understand what was causing her desire to steal. Claire was on a course that could destroy her life, and she needed to be saved from her worst impulses.

Either a man with depraved intentions had given her the diamond, or she'd stolen it. An appropriate boy her age would not be able to afford a gem like that. The amount of time Claire had spent with Jacob over the past year, and the lack of evidence of any other man, pointed to the latter. In fact, maybe these other *men* she referred to were nothing more than figments of Claire's imagination, similar to the imaginary friends of childhood. Yet another reason that time in a sanitarium specializing in the intricacies of the human mind would be beneficial.

Sleep was not coming back. She flung the covers off her face and sat up. She stretched and got out of bed.

It was nine-thirty by the time she was washed and dressed. Instead of going downstairs for a cup of tea and some toast, she went up to the third floor. Heat from the previous day had accumulated near the top of the house. The door to the storage room was closed as was Claire's door. Warm air had settled like a film of dust into every crevice of the hallway between the two rooms and the top of the stairs. Lorene smiled, confident she'd made the right decision. Although she hadn't heard the gentle whispering Voice, she was certain the Inner Light had led her to this mindset and the action she was about to take. Confessing her suspicions instead of harboring them inside would spur Claire to be honest in return. She knocked firmly on Claire's door. She waited for several seconds. She needed to remain calm, control the conversation and especially her emotions. She waited another moment, then raised her hand.

The door opened.

Claire looked at her with sleepy, hooded eyes. If Lorene didn't know better, she'd think the girl was drunk, or drugged with some sort of sleeping aid.

"May I come in for a few minutes?" Lorene said.

"Why?"

"Because I asked."

"I'm kind of busy."

"With what?"

"None of your business."

"I need to talk to you."

"We can talk right here."

"It would be better sitting down, friendlier."

Claire raised her eyebrows but said nothing.

"You know Claire, you're a guest in my home. You owe me the courtesy of a few minutes of your time."

Claire turned and walked toward the center of the room.

Confidence fluttered inside Lorene's chest. She'd won the first battle. She entered the room and closed the door. It was unlikely Mary would come upstairs, but she couldn't take any chances. She went to the armchair that faced the window seat, turned it slightly, and sat down. "Have a seat."

"I'm fine." Claire stood near the unmade bed. She folded her arms across her chest. Her hair was brushed to a fine silken sheen, but she still wore her nightgown. It had a slight odor from having been slept in a few nights too many. Or maybe it was just the heat that made it rank. The room was uncomfortably warm.

"You should sleep with the window open. It would stay cooler in here. It's better for you."

"I don't like to be cold. And I don't want insects to get in."

Lorene glanced at the window. The screens were

secure. Claire must have a phobia of some kind.

"So what did you want to talk about?" Claire sat near the foot of her bed.

Lorene studied the cluttered surface of the dresser. There were so many expensive perfumes and lotions. It was possible Claire was also stealing money. Or perhaps Jacob had been giving her large sums of cash. Bootleggers dealt in cash, and they had plenty flowing through their fingers — so much they hardly remembered what they had. They might as well be printing counterfeit bills. Maybe he was doing that, too.

It was such a relief to be rid of him, at least from seeing him at the dinner table, watching him hold her on the dance floor, knowing he had his hands and his mouth all over Claire's body. It was still worrisome that he had so much responsibility in Henry's business affairs. He might be stealing from Henry, skimming a bit here and there off bank deposits or receipts from the stores. She shook off the thought. Henry was too smart, too careful to let something like that happen. He checked his books and accounts daily. He would notice even the slightest discrepancy. She couldn't let her imagination run away. Or, maybe Claire was lying about that! Both of them were lying. Maybe she and Jacob hadn't broken it off at all. Maybe she was helping him with the bootlegging. She might be standing watch for him, or carrying cash. Most people wouldn't suspect a woman of being involved. The fact that she'd announced so dramatically that she had ended it, especially when Henry was told a different story, was suspect. Just because she wasn't wearing the ring didn't mean anything. Maybe they'd pawned it because they needed money immediately.

"What *is* it?" Claire said.

"I saw the necklace you wore to the grand opening."

"What are you talking about?"

"Last year, on the cement boat."

"Last year?"

Lorene nodded. "I waited too long to mention it. I wasn't sure how to bring it up."

"I have no idea what you're trying to say." Claire pulled up her nightgown and scratched her kneecap.

This wasn't a time to be polite and gracious. She needed to make sure there was no misunderstanding. "Where did you get the diamond necklace, the teardrop?"

"Why do you care?"

"I'm concerned."

"About what?" Claire flopped onto her back. Her lower legs still hung over the side of the bed. The angle of her body made it impossible to see her face.

"Will you sit up please?"

Claire yawned with a loud groan. "I'm tired. Get to the point."

"I'm concerned you stole the necklace."

Claire bolted up. "Are you calling me a thief?"

"Yes, I suppose I am."

"I'm tired of your insults."

Lorene didn't know what she'd said that Claire found insulting, but she wasn't going to be diverted. "Then where did you get it?"

"A man."

"Jacob?"

Claire laughed.

"Was it Jacob? If it was, you should return it with the ring."

Claire spoke in a falsetto. "It wasn't *Ja-cob*."

"Then who was it?"

"Why do you think you have the right to pry into my personal life?"

"Because you're my sister. I care about you and I don't want to see you get hurt."

"I can take care of myself."

"Claire, please. I'm trying to help. A respectable man doesn't give a young girl expensive jewelry."

Claire laughed.

"Stop laughing at me."

"But why? You're too funny." Claire flopped back down on the bed. She pulled her nightgown up to her hips and scratched her inner thighs, leaving long ugly welts in her pale skin. She turned her head and saw Lorene looking at her legs. She scratched harder.

"Stop it."

Claire wriggled her hips. "But it feels so good."

A headache blossomed near Lorene's right eye. She pressed her finger against her temple, trying to suppress the throbbing.

"Am I a headache?" Claire said.

"You want to be treated like an adult, but you act like a child. Actually, you sometimes act as if you're deranged."

"You're jealous because I have a beautiful, very expensive diamond. I know, because I had it appraised. I think it's worth more than your diamond ring."

"That's beside the point."

"Is it?"

"What man gave it to you?"

Claire sat up. She pulled the nightgown over her legs until it settled demurely around her ankles. "I'm eighteen. I don't have to explain my love life to you."

"Were you seeing two men at the same time?"

"This is getting really tiresome. What, exactly, do you want to know? Whether I've done the deed? Whether I might be at risk for having an illegitimate child? Whether I'm still a bad influence on Mary? Whether I might steal from you?"

All of those things. It was every single one of those things. Lorene looked at her sister's sleepy, seductive eyes and wondered where she'd learned so much. Maybe she hadn't learned it anywhere, maybe her hubris and ability to control a conversation were inborn.

Claire grinned. "All the things I mentioned worry you, don't they." She didn't pose it as a question.

Lorene felt the girl could read her mind. She felt taunted and laughed at and demeaned, and she wasn't sure why it was so upsetting, because no matter what Claire said, or how she tried to pretend sophistication, she was immature, still a little girl in so many ways. Lorene was a happily married woman with a respected husband, a beautiful, intelligent daughter, and a lovely home. She had friends and an active social life. She had so many good things, sometimes she wondered what she'd done to deserve so much.

"As long as you didn't steal it," Lorene said, "you have a right to your secrets, I suppose. Although I worry about what kind of man would give such a gift to a girl your age, to a woman who isn't his wife." She stood up. She'd lost the battle, despite the earlier impression she was winning. "If you bring any kind of trouble into this house, tarnish Mary's innocence, damage the reputation Henry and I have built for this family in the business and social community, you'll need to find another place to live. I think you should give some serious thought to your future and how much longer you really need to stay under our care. Since you don't seem to want our care, unless it's financial."

She turned and walked out of the room, leaving the door open. She hurried down the stairs and went into her bedroom. She took three aspirin, closed the drapes, and climbed into bed fully clothed. Her skull seemed to be splitting open, as if someone had taken a meat cleaver to it. Buried under the covers, hearing Claire moving around above her head, gave her the feeling a monster lived in the attic of her house, biding its time until it devoured them all.

Her headache didn't abate until four o'clock that afternoon.

She crawled out of bed. Her eyes hurt when she blinked and it seemed as if her mouth and throat were filled with sand. She went to the window and pulled the drapes. She opened the window wider to let fresh air into the room. A burgundy car with a cream-colored roof sat in the driveway. The passenger door hung open. She heard women's voices. A moment later, Claire pranced down the front steps, one of her silk scarves trailing behind her. This one was pale yellow and hung past the hem of her skirt. She shrieked with laughter and climbed into the car. She slammed the door, and the car drove too fast around the curve and out of the driveway. Lorene ran to the bathroom, used the toilet, and combed her hair. She opened her bedroom door. The hallway was empty. She hurried to the stairs and went up to Claire's room.

The room was as stuffy as it had been that morning. All the drapes were closed. She turned on the light. She stood in the center of the room, trying to think where she'd missed searching the time before. She went to the bed and felt between the mattresses. The box was still there. She went to the window seat and lifted up the cushion. Sheets of paper, covered with blue ink and tied with a white ribbon lay in the center of the wood frame. She couldn't believe it had been so easy. She sat down on the floor, her back against the window seat, and began reading.

The letters were in a man's handwriting. After reading a few lines, she didn't need the handwriting to tell her they were from a man. All were signed — *Yours completely* — no name. There was no information to give her any clue to his identity beyond the mention of places they'd visited in San Francisco. For all she knew, the letters were from Jacob. Maybe he'd lived in San Francisco before coming here. She wished she could remember — had Henry hired him first, or had he started seeing Claire and then Henry offered him the job? The past year was foggy in her mind, details clouded by the tension of Claire's unsettling effect on the household.

The letter writer repeatedly mentioned his despondency that Claire had to leave the city following her mother's death. The rest of the words made Lorene's neck and chest so warm she could hardly breathe. He described every inch of Claire's body with overwrought but strangely moving passages about her soft, creamy skin, the shape of her breasts and hips, the endless sweetness of her mouth.

After three letters, she couldn't read any more. She felt voyeuristic, and although she tried to shove the thought to the furthest corner of her heart — very, very jealous.

Nineteen

Mary sat on her window seat watching Claire in the garden below. Claire was walking dreamily among the rose bushes, peeling a single petal off each of the blossoms. She ignored the ones going to seed, tearing off fresh petals as if she were ripping flesh off someone's body. She would cup the blossom in one hand, bending it slightly with her thumb, tearing with a quick twist of her fingers. Mary felt as if she heard the roses screaming.

The mutilated roses made her think of the people tortured inside the insane asylums. Supposedly that didn't happen nowadays. Miss Bly had helped bring reforms, but that was in New York. Mary worried it might still be going on in California or other states. Who was really checking? Normal people never visited those places. Some of the women Miss Bly wrote about weren't even insane. People were afraid of madness. Once, when she was walking with her parents, a man had run past, shouting at someone only he could see. Pillows of foam spilled out of his mouth and his eyes seemed to be twice the normal size, as if they were about to burst out of his skull. Lorene's hand had trembled in Mary's, and her father began walking too fast, urging them to keep up. She wished they would buy her the book by Nellie Bly, but they'd never agree to it. She wanted to read it over and over. She could check it out from the library again, but it wasn't the same as owning it yourself.

If she went down into the garden, would Claire stop what she was doing, or would she try to convince Mary to join her? It seemed as if Claire wanted to get Mary in trouble, or at least wanted to persuade her to do things she didn't want to, to talk about things she'd rather not discuss. Still, she loved Claire. She wished they were sisters and that things could go back to the way they were when Claire first came to stay with them. Having a sister was the most wonderful thing in the world. She would never have a sister or brother. Her mother had told her several years ago it wasn't possible. It wasn't fair that a sister, even if she wasn't a true sister, had been dangled in front of Mary's eyes, and then ripped away.

She turned her back to the window and pulled her diary out from under the pillow. She wrote about Claire tearing up the roses. She wrote about the whale she'd seen in the bay the day before. It was so large, she knew it was entirely possible it could swallow her whole. She thought about the story of Jonah living in the belly of a whale and wondered what that would feel like. It might be cozy, although it probably smelled awful — like when you threw up. She was certain it would smell awful, maybe as terrible as the dead seals that sometimes washed up on the beach. Sobs pushed against her chest when she saw them — their flesh torn away in spots, turning strange colors, developing a pulpy appearance. They were so cute when they swam by, it seemed as if they stopped and treaded water, looking directly at her, wanting to say *hi*. And then they turned up dead.

There was a knock on the door. The knob turned, and her mother came into the room.

"Are you writing in your diary?"

Mary nodded. She closed the book, leaving her pen in the spot where she'd been writing.

Her mother walked to the window seat. She leaned over Mary and looked out. "What is Claire doing?"

"Torturing the roses."

"How do you mean?"

"She's tearing off the petals."

"Oh! I should…" A pained expression threaded its way across her mother's lips. She appeared to swallow it and turned to face Mary. She sat at the opposite side of the window seat.

"It's summer. It's a beautiful day. You should go outside. What are Elizabeth and Theresa doing today?"

"Elizabeth went to visit her cousins."

Lorene nodded. "And Theresa?"

"She's sick."

"Oh. That's too bad."

Mary shrugged. It was nice to have some time to read and draw pictures. Sometimes Theresa talked too much. She was probably being punished with her laryngitis. She smiled to herself.

"I was thinking," Lorene said.

Mary waited. Her mother sounded uncertain which wasn't like her. Usually, she simply said what was on her mind, but now, she was fiddling with her rings, twisting her bracelet around her wrist.

"Remember when you said you heard Jacob talking about bootlegging?"

"That was a long time ago."

"It was. Do you remember if he said anything else?"

"Like what?"

"I don't know. Anything you forgot to tell me."

"I don't remember any more."

Lorene nodded. She pinched the seat cushion piping between her thumb and index finger. It looked as if she wanted to tear it off, like Claire was doing with the rose petals. Was this what happened to girls when they became women? Did they all become insane? Lunatics that were impossible to understand? One of her mother's friends had been sent away for rest, but when her father mentioned it, he moved his hand in a circle by the side of his head. Was that why it was so easy for Nellie Bly to pretend she was a lunatic?

"Has Claire ever said anything about bootlegging?" Lorene said.

Mary shook her head.

"Do you remember anything she said?"

"When?"

"When Jacob was talking to her about bootlegging."

"He wasn't talking to Claire. He was talking to Daddy."

Lorene stared. It looked as if she hadn't heard what Mary said, or as if she didn't recognize the name, that she was trying to figure out who Daddy was.

"Jacob was talking to your Father about bootlegging?"

Mary nodded. "Was I not supposed to say?"

Her mother put her hand on Mary's ankle and squeezed it gently. "No. Of course you were supposed to say. I was just confused for a moment. I assumed…" Lorene stopped talking and stood up.

Mary felt that her mother was lying, but she wasn't sure what part was a lie, or why she needed to lie about any of it.

Fall 1931

Twenty

The quantity of alcohol being delivered to the bow of the concrete ship was staggering. Jacob now made five nighttime trips out to the ship every week. Despite the cast iron sheath he thought had grown around his nerves, the frequency of his visits gave him the jitters. People loved the ship, even though it was failing as an entertainment venue and the Seacliff Amusement Corporation was rumored to be going out of business. Couples and families walked on the pier in the evenings, admiring the ship. By the time he went out to carry cartons off the motorboats for storage below, it was past midnight, but it was impossible to know when someone might be enjoying a late dinner out and decide to end the evening with a walk to the cliffs and a look at the bay and its lone ship.

On top of that, David was once again eaten up by curiosity over the details of what Jacob did for Henry King. The comfort of steady employment had grown familiar, and now David griped about the tedium and grueling physical effort required by his job. He wanted something that paid more and didn't break his back. Something like the work Jacob did. At least once a week, David pestered him. *How hard can it be to put cash into a bank account? Why can't I run errands? I have a drivers' license. Why do you get the easy work and I'm treated like a dumb mule?*

Jacob hadn't mentioned any of it to Henry, but it worried him. He was constantly looking over his shoulder, afraid that one night, David would not go off to drink beer with his friends, would not collapse into his bed at ten or eleven o'clock and be as good as dead until morning. David's curiosity would blossom, and he'd get it into his head to follow Jacob.

He wanted to be thinking about Sarah and how nicely their relationship was progressing, not about his brother. He was tired of the repetitious conversation and tired of feeling responsible. Henry would never trust anyone else in the same way he trusted Jacob. Why couldn't David grasp that simple truth?

There was a faint drizzle. The weather was colder than normal for September, and a chill gripped his arms and legs and crept inside his bones as he drove down the hill toward the pier. He followed Beach Drive for several hundred yards so he was parked far from the ship. It was too risky to leave his car any closer now that business on the boat was dead. An empty car anywhere near the ship shouted that it was out of place. The Sheriff might be called.

He walked back along the deserted street, turning onto the footpath that ran along the base of the cliff. He wished the misty rain would stop. It spread across his face and seeped into everything. It tricked him into thinking there wasn't much to it, and suddenly his coat and hat were sopping wet. He wiped his hands across his face and shook off the water. He went another twenty yards or so and stepped onto the wooden ramp that led up to the pier. He hurried out toward the ship. This was the worst part. The pier was completely exposed. Even if he ducked and tried to make himself less visible near the railing, it was easy to see when a man was out there.

From beyond his line of sight, he heard the soft hum of the motor on its lowest speed. Jacob broke into a slow jog. Lately, the driver of the boat was as edgy as Jacob. The longer they succeeded in their deliveries without detection, the more their luck was tested. Even though it was safer than coming right up to the beach, risking getting mired in sand, visible for a quarter mile in either direction, the concrete ship attracted its own kind of attention.

When he reached the bow, the motorboat was emerging from the darkness. He waited for the boat to pull alongside. He tied the rope ladder in place and lowered it over the side of the ship. The driver cut the engine, and the motorboat drifted closer. The driver grabbed the ladder and pulled himself into position.

Carrying wooden boxes of bottles up and down a rope ladder should have been a three-man job. Jacob had to climb partway down, the other guy handed him a small crate containing two bottles, and with it tucked under one arm, pulling at his shoulder, Jacob made his way back up, wedging his feet between the side of the ship and the ladder rung as he lifted the box onto the deck of the ship. Every single time he wondered whether there wasn't a better way to move the boxes. He was covered by darkness, but still felt exposed. It was exhausting work that had left rock-hard calluses all over his palms and fingers. If David thought he was the only one doing backbreaking labor, he would be disappointed to see what was required to earn a more lucrative salary. Even if David could be trusted, he could also be counted on to complain endlessly about the difficulty.

By the time Jacob had transported thirty small crates up to the deck, he couldn't distinguish the sweat from the drizzle falling on his skin. He felt as if he'd been plunged into the ocean. He longed for a drink of water, or a moment to sit down, but there was no time. Speed was important. Minimizing exposure was key.

The motorboat backed up slowly, turned, and headed into the darkness.

Jacob picked up the first crate and walked the length of the deck. He went into the arcade and down the stairs. He unlocked the cabinet and tugged on the handle. The door remained shut. He set the crate on the floor and pulled harder. It refused to open.

The ship was freezing up, shutting him out, just as Claire had done. It wanted nothing to do with him. He shook off the thought. Every time he set foot on this boat, he thought of the naive, hopeful, wildly in love man he'd been the first night they ate dinner on board and he asked her to be his wife. He might be drawn to Sarah, but Claire's suddenly cooling affection and her lashing out had cut much deeper than he'd realized. There was a tiny pain, deep in his stomach that made itself known from time to time, as if there were a thorn that his skin had grown over, seemingly healing the wound, but it remained, always ready to work its way to the surface.

He yanked harder on the door and it flew open, sending him stumbling back. His foot twisted and he came close to falling. He was not going to indulge in fanciful thoughts, imagining the ship had a soul or some nonsense like that.

Of course, a lot of men who worked on ships believed that was the case. Why else call ocean-going vessels *She*, believing the soul of a woman inhabited the spaces below the deck, filled the sails on schooners? It was nuts. Those were superstitious thoughts that came from too much time out at sea, not seeing firm ground for weeks at a time, utterly helpless and dependent on the floating structure beneath their feet. Ultimately, only that frail piece of human construction kept a man from the voracious jaws of the sea and the powerful, silent creatures that lay in wait below the surface.

It felt as if someone had whispered the thought in his ear. He turned toward the darkness behind him and shivered.

It was nothing. Just damp skin and his body finally cooling from the exertion of climbing the rope ladder. He needed to get busy and stop daydreaming, allowing ridiculous fears to take over his mind. Perhaps his sanity was being challenged. He'd spent too many nights alone on this ship, scurrying up and down in the darkness, trusting it to keep his secret.

As he climbed the stairs for the next boxes, his footsteps echoed. He didn't recall hearing an echo in the past. His nerves were getting the best of him. Ironclad indeed. All he'd done was suppress his anxiety over the danger he faced out here alone. Just as he'd suppressed his feelings for Claire. He still loved her. He hated her, yet he loved her. It wasn't just her physical beauty that captivated him. She had a wild spirit that took hold of every part of his being. Sarah was contented and smiling, easy to be with, equally beautiful. But she wasn't Claire. She didn't consume his soul. He shook his head and ran along the deck to pick up the next box. He stacked four on top of each other and struggled back to the doorway. If he concentrated and used all his strength, he could get this done in half the time.

Down below, the door to the locker had swung closed. He looked around the empty room behind him, trembling at the thought of someone watching, closing the door to force him to turn and notice he'd been discovered. The room was dark except for the weak beam of his flashlight that didn't reveal anything beyond the immediate area around his feet where it lay. He put down the boxes and picked up the light. He shone it across the room. It was empty.

There was a sudden drop in temperature. Something touched his cheek. He cried out. The flashlight crashed to the floor and went out. He clawed at his cheek. Someone standing right beside him, hidden in the blackness. He turned, he thrust his arms out to his sides and turned several times in a full circle. Nothing, but now he was dizzy from turning too fast. He knelt and patted the floor, hunting for the light. This was taking too long. Henry would be expecting him, waiting as he did every night there was a delivery, ready to review the inventory list.

His fingers closed over the light, and he pressed the switch to turn it on. It was dimmer than earlier, but it was simply the sweat leaking into his eyes that made it seem that way. He had an overwhelming urge to cry — something he hadn't done since he was a small child. Even when Claire ignored his proposal, or rather postponed it, whatever it was she'd done, he hadn't cried. Perhaps because he'd still been hopeful, at first. The hope drained so slowly, it never brought him to tears. The fading hope had turned to anger, but that was a shield for his true feelings. Now, he wanted to sob — for Claire, for the early deaths of his parents, for the home ripped out from beneath him and his brother when they'd needed it most, for the weight of helping his brother find his footing, most of all for Claire…and for the fact that he'd ended up a criminal. Maybe that's why she'd turned on him. She knew what he was doing for her brother-in-law.

What he did for a living could be justified all kinds of ways, none of which would matter if he was caught. They'd take away his money and car. How could he think of marrying anyone, buying a home, knowing it would all evaporate with one wrong step? And what future did he have? If he told Henry he was finished, what kind of employment reference could he expect? The very best would be no recommendation at all, and there was a real possibility Henry would be so angry at the loss — which he would perceive as betrayal — that he'd maliciously prevent Jacob from finding employment at all. Jacob would be back to working as a laborer, earning pennies. If he could even get something. Farms and businesses were failing all over the place.

He swallowed. He needed to get a grip. Finish the task at hand. Standing in the bowels of a deserted ship with a closet full of illegal liquor, and more piled on the deck above, was not the right time or place for reviewing his choices and reflecting on where his life was headed.

He yanked open the door, nearly wrenching his arm out of the socket. He stacked the boxes inside, went to the stairs, turned off his flashlight, and tucked it in his waistband. He ran up the stairs two at a time. He worked quickly and furiously, as if Henry were standing right there, cracking a bullwhip to make him run faster.

When everything was stowed in the cabinet, he slammed the door, and locked it. He sat on the bottom step to catch his breath.

After a few minutes, he stood, shut off the light, and turned to climb the stairs. The light was never to be seen on the deck. He was used to making his way up the stairs in complete darkness. He put his foot on the first step and felt the cool breath on his cheek. He shivered and went up two more steps. He was exhausted. His mind was playing tricks on him. He took the next steps two at a time and then, couldn't seem to move forward. It felt as if he'd run into a heavy drape. He fell back. His foot landed three steps below. The ankle, already tender from his fall earlier, gave way with a searing pain. He bit his tongue to keep from shouting, tasting blood.

He righted himself and risked turning on the light. Nothing was there but the narrow metal stairs leading up to the catwalk that surrounded the hollow room. He turned off the light and climbed slowly, taking care with his nearly useless ankle. Henry would be waiting for him, wondering what was taking so long, worrying they'd been caught.

At the same point on the stairs, he once again encountered something solid, preventing him from climbing higher. The breath raced across his cheek and down his neck.

"Who's there?" His voice was shrill. He batted his hands in front of him, feeling nothing, but he still couldn't move forward. "What's going on? Is someone up there?"

He heard nothing but the echo of water sloshing inside the hull where it had been allowed to enter to keep the ship solidly on the ocean floor.

"Hello?" If someone was up there, or standing in the room outside the perimeter where his flashlight beam traveled, they would think he was weak. Terrified. It was not the voice of a man in control of his destiny. He coughed and tried to push forward, but the solid thing blocked his way.

A voice that echoed with the same hollow sound as the water spoke. *I'm dying.*

"Who is it? Who's speaking?" He was shouting now, not caring if something made of flesh and blood discovered him on the ship. This was far worse than a fight with his fists, handcuffs, a jail cell.

Just when he thought he might fall down the stairs, weeping, the cool breath touched his cheek, and the space around him felt open and full of air. He climbed the stairs. Nothing was there.

When he emerged from the arcade, he pulled the door

closed and locked it. He limped as fast as his ankle would allow, along the deck and onto the pier. He pushed harder, enduring the screaming pain until he reached the footpath. Gasping for air, he hurried along the path and up to the street. He opened the car door, fell into the front seat, slammed the door, and locked it. As if a door and a lock could keep out whatever he'd encountered back there.

Four days later, he was still shaken by the experience. The crates seemed twice as heavy now when he carried them up the rope ladder. His hands shook as he stacked them in the locker below deck. In the past, he'd moved quickly, sure of himself. Now he had to pause as he lifted each one, check to ensure his wobbly hands didn't lose their grip, sending the box crashing onto the floor, spilling glass and liquor, spreading the penetrating odor that would give them away.

When he arrived home, David was sitting on the porch of Jacob's boarding house, smoking a cigarette. It was nearly three in the morning.

"I'm tired. What do you want?"

"Sit down and have a smoke with me."

"We can't talk here, we'll wake my housemates," Jacob said.

"They sleep like the dead. I know because I knocked on the door for ten minutes and no one answered."

Jacob slumped into the chair beside his brother, took the offered cigarette, and let David light it for him. He was too tired to strike a match. He wasn't sure he had the energy to draw on the cigarette.

"How much do you know about the businesses Henry is involved with?" David said.

"Are you nuts? I'm beat. I don't want to answer your questions."

"I ran into Mrs. King."

"Is that right."

"She came into the market looking for aspirin."

"Okay."

"What exactly are you doing for him at three in the morning?" David said.

"I just deliver stuff. I've told you that."

"It sure takes a long time. What kind of stuff?"

"I don't read his personal things. Envelopes — letters, I suppose. Account books."

"Why does it take all night?"

"Sometimes I have to wait for him. Stop with all the questions. I'm tired of it."

"Mrs. King has a lot of questions too."

Jacob didn't answer. Crickets chirped. Somewhere a few houses away, two cats snarled at each other, then began growling. After a moment, they screeched and were silent.

"She wanted to know what I did for her husband," David said.

"Wasn't that obvious, if she saw you in the store?"

"She wanted to know if I did other stuff. Like you, I suppose."

"So?"

"She asked who I was, found out I was related to you. She said she saw us fighting once on the cliff. Remember?"

Jacob nodded. He didn't care whether or not David could see his response in the inadequate light coming from the three-quarter moon.

"She seemed awfully suspicious of her husband."

"How do you know that?"

"She gave me twenty bucks to follow him. Made me swear on my mother's grave I wouldn't tell anyone or betray her confidence."

"You're telling me she walked up to a total stranger and asked you to spy on her husband?"

"I guess I have a trustworthy face."

Jacob didn't have to see David's face to know he was feeling smug, that now he was the one who was trusted over his brother.

"I find that hard to believe."

"That I have a trustworthy face?"

"That she would ask such a thing. She doesn't even know you, no matter how trustworthy your face might be."

"She seemed kind of frantic."

"What does she expect you to do?"

"Find out what he's up to."

"That's a rather open-ended request."

"Yup." David struck a match. The light flared in front of his mouth, making it look like his lips were on fire. "Do you know anything?"

"Anything about what?"

"Does he spend his nights at the "tea house" with ladies of the evening? Maybe he has a mistress, and he keeps you busy delivering illicit love letters. Is that why she's so upset?"

Jacob felt the tight cords in his back and shoulders slide away from each other. There was nothing to worry about. David could follow Henry until the cows came home. Henry was a very cautious man. It would be nearly impossible to follow him without him noticing. He could lead David anywhere. Lorene was just feeling insecure and upset that her husband was out of the house in the evenings. Everything was fine. She'd get over it, once David told her there was nothing to worry about.

Jacob wanted to laugh, he felt so good. He was safe. Despite the hard night and the lingering anxiety over his encounter with some kind of presence inside the ship, he felt light and confident for the first time in a while. He was lucky to be associated with a man who was so clever, who covered his tracks so meticulously.

"I was thinking, if he's up to no good, maybe there's an opportunity," David said.

"What do you mean?"

"A business opportunity."

"What are you talking about?"

"Blackmail, brother. If he's up to no good, maybe he'll pay to make sure his secrets stay secret. Don't you think?"

"No. He's not doing anything that would make him a blackmail target," Jacob said. His confident tone shocked him. Maybe battling his fears below the ship's deck had given him a new kind of strength. He smiled and asked David for another cigarette. His exhaustion had been replaced by a surge of adrenaline that felt very pleasant.

Twenty-one

Lorene buried her bare feet beneath the warm, dry sand. She wore a large hat to keep the sun off her face, and a dress with narrow straps that allowed the sun to bathe her arms. It was a spectacular Autumn day. The temperature was mild and the breeze gentle enough to keep her from getting too hot. At the edge of the surf, Mary filled her bucket with water, making multiple trips to the moat she was building around a large sand castle. It was embellished with rocks, gull feathers, and intricately shaped slivers of driftwood. The castle looked as if it might turn into something real — miniature people would begin moving about its feathered gardens, rowing small boats in the lake and along the canal that ran down to the ocean.

Life seemed tranquil, although Lorene worried it only appeared that way because she allowed all of its disturbing parts to slide past her without objection.

Last summer, when she'd demanded that Henry tell her

why he'd discussed bootlegging with Jacob, he hadn't spoken to her for two weeks. He accused her of not trusting him, of being an ungrateful wife. He'd accused her of paranoia, of allowing her mind to manufacture stories around subjects she knew nothing about. He accused her of insulting him. He'd said it was simply a casual conversation and what the hell was Mary doing sitting in a tree in the middle of the night? He suggested that instead of throwing darts at him when he was working himself to the bone trying to provide a nice life for her, maybe Lorene should consider the lapses in her mothering that allowed her child to leave the house undetected.

When the silent battle was over, she was limp with defeat. During the evenings when he was out, she sat in the parlor. Two candles provided the only light as she tried to look within, to determine where she'd made a mistake, to find insight from the Quiet Voice. All she heard was an echoing silence. She and Henry lived in the same house, ate dinner at the same table, slept in the same bed, but they inhabited two different worlds. She didn't know how to invite him into hers, and he'd locked the gate to his.

She removed the top of the thermos and poured water into the cup. She took a few sips. The sun and the steady, quiet waves made her sleepy. She opened her bag and took out the October issue of *Good Housekeeping* magazine. It was a silly title, since she did nothing to keep their house, abdicating all of it to Annie. What would become of her once Mary had a husband and home of her own? She cared for her roses, did a bit of crocheting, read books and magazines. She visited with her friends, gossiping and talking about clothes and children. Henry wanted nothing from her except a captive audience to his views on politics and business. He wanted her beside him at social events. He stayed far away from her in bed, except for an occasional kiss goodnight on the rare evenings when they slid beneath the blankets at the same time.

The magazine pages fluttered in the breeze. She'd forgotten what article she'd wanted to read. They all seemed unimportant, or something she'd read before.

Mary rushed up to the edge of the blanket and fell on her knees in the sand. "I'm thirsty."

Lorene poured a cup of water and handed it to her.

"And hungry."

Lorene opened the bag and Mary took two crackers out of a waxed paper sleeve. Lorene folded the wrapper back into place.

"What are you building?" Lorene said.

"An insane asylum!" The expression in Mary's eyes was unreadable. Her smile seemed slightly manic, although maybe Lorene was reading into it, upset that her daughter was so fixated on something so ugly. And yet, Mary's fixation turned Lorene's thoughts to Claire. She continued to entertain the fantasy of having Claire locked away somewhere, even though it would do nothing to solve the problems between Lorene and Henry, so what did it matter?

"You think about those things too much," Lorene said.

"It's interesting."

"It's sad and sordid."

"Brains can get sick just like bodies. It's harder to fix them."

"I suppose." Lorene nibbled on a cracker. "But it would be torture, to be locked up for the rest of your life, like a bird in a cage." She looked up at the sky, watching the birds soar and glide.

"People disappear in their make-believe worlds, and sometimes they never come out." Mary sounded quite confident of her opinion. "Is that why you locked the door? So I can't play make-believe in the storage room anymore?"

"I didn't lock the door." Lorene gazed out at the ship. Its buildings glistened white. It looked as if it wanted to break away from the pier, reclaim its engines, and charge out of the bay, crossing the ocean, exploring the world. She wondered if she'd ever see any part of the world outside the Central Coast of California and San Francisco. They'd visited Lake Tahoe once, but that was all.

"Someone locked it," Mary said.

"The storage room?"

Mary nodded. She shoved her hand into the bag and took out the box of sugar cookies. "May I?" She settled on the blanket.

Lorene nodded. "Who would lock it?"

"You, Daddy, Claire, or Annie."

"It wasn't me."

"I like playing in there."

"I know you do."

"I like to dress up in the old clothes, and pretend I'm having the vapors on the couch."

"I'd like to see that." Lorene smiled.

They each ate two cookies, and Mary drifted back to her replica of an insane asylum. Lorene flipped through the magazine. Too bad there weren't any articles on how to reclaim a husband's attention. He'd worshipped her when they were dating, and during the first years of their marriage. Even after Mary was born, he was devoted to *both his girls*. More so to Lorene, of course, always gazing at her, going on about how beautiful she was, how lucky he was to have her, how Mary reflected all of her beauty. Now, he sometimes looked up from his newspaper with a puzzled expression, as if he'd forgotten who she was.

A few weeks ago, she'd gone into his grocery store to purchase aspirin for her near constant headaches. She felt the headaches were telling her she was thinking too much, spending so much time gnawing on her heartache that her brain was wearing itself out. She'd known immediately that the man stocking the shelves was the same one she'd seen fighting with Jacob the year before. And now he worked for her husband? She'd blinked, trying to change what she saw right in front of her.

When she'd approached him and started chatting, he'd been quite talkative. Even though she suspected that he'd have his hand in any illegal activity that might be going on, she felt a certain amount of anonymity with him, perhaps because she'd never seen him at the house, didn't have the added complication of watching him court her little sister. She'd asked him to keep an eye on Henry. She'd handed him four, five dollar bills, and watched as his eyes widened and his lips separated into a look of hunger. She'd been vague about what she thought Henry might be up to. She just wanted a little information about where he went at night. She didn't really know whether he was involved with illegal liquor, or something else entirely. Gambling, maybe — she'd heard there were gambling parties below deck on the concrete ship.

There were too many questions Henry refused to answer, too many meetings at night, too many hushed conversations right on her own veranda. He wasn't going to treat her like a stupid, decorative but unnecessary, piece of furniture any longer. So far, David Archer hadn't discovered anything, but it didn't change her certainty that Henry was hiding things from her. If he didn't respect her enough to share his life with her, she would no longer show him the loyalty she'd given him for all these years.

When Mary was finished with her sand structure, she made Lorene remove the camera from its thick leather case and take a photograph of Mary kneeling beside her work of art. They packed up their things and walked up the hill. Mary chattered about crazy people all the way home.

After Lorene rinsed the sand off her feet and hands, removed her hat and combed her hair, and changed her clothes, she went down to the pantry. There were three large rings filled with keys. She wasn't sure which fit the locks upstairs, so she took all three rings and went up to the third floor. Claire was out with her girlfriends, which was where she was most days. Lorene wondered when, or if, the man who'd given her the diamond necklace would propose. Or maybe she'd return to Jacob, or find someone else entirely. She just wished it would happen soon and Claire would be out of the house. Maybe being rid of Claire *would* improve things between her and Henry. At the very least, they'd no longer have a smirking audience when Henry dined at home.

The storage room door wasn't locked after all. She put the key rings over her wrist and opened the door. Nothing looked any different than she remembered. The room smelled slightly less dusty, but that was all. It was filled with racks of garments, unused furniture, and a few wooden chairs with broken backs or legs. Why were they even keeping those chairs? At the time they were stored, she'd probably planned to have them repaired. Now, they were simply mismatched pieces that no longer had a place in the house.

She stepped out of the room and closed the door. It did stick slightly. Maybe Mary thought it was locked, although Mary was very precise and it was hard to imagine her giving up and making an assumption without putting in effort to force it open.

She returned the keys to the pantry.

Several days later when Mary was at school, and Claire was out God knows where, Lorene went up to the third floor again. She couldn't stop thinking about the room being locked. Maybe Henry was hiding liquor in there. Although, then it would be locked all the time.

She tried turning the doorknob. She rattled it, certain it was stuck as it had been the last time. She shoved her shoulder against it. No, it was definitely locked. She went back down to the first floor, got the key rings and retraced her steps. When she reached the third floor, she was breathing hard. Nearly every day she went for a long walk, climbing the hill from the beach to the top of the cliffs. Two flights of stairs shouldn't exhaust her. Either her heart was working overtime because she expected to find something upsetting, or perhaps she'd hurried up and down faster than usual, eager to satisfy her curiosity.

She tried the first key. The door opened before the key was fully inside the keyhole. It hadn't been locked after all. Was she losing her mind? She was sure the door had been locked before she'd gone to the pantry for the keys. Positive, in fact.

She went into the room and put the rings of keys on a dresser to the right of the doorway. She closed the door behind her. The room smelled fresh. Everything else was the same — the furniture pushed up against one wall, the fainting couch that Mary loved, a small round table beside it, the last century clothes that fed Mary's imagination. She turned slowly, trying to decide where to look for something out of place. She ran her hand over the clothing hanging beside her. She went to the next rack and slid the hangers along the bar — nothing. When she'd finished looking through all the garments, she searched the dresser where she'd left the keys. The drawers were empty. The same was true of every other piece of furniture that had drawers or shelves. She sat on the couch and looked at the window. Dark blue drapes hung on either side, left open so there was plenty of light. She went to the window and looked out. The sill was free of dust, suggesting the window had been opened recently. That's why it smelled so fresh.

After a few minutes, mindlessly staring out the window, she crossed the room, picked up the rings of keys, and went out. She left the door standing open.

For the next few days, the room was all she thought about. Several times each day she went up to the third floor. The storage room door was open, as she'd left it. She asked Mary repeatedly if she'd been playing in there.

Mary said she was too busy with schoolwork, she hadn't had time. Besides, her friends weren't interested in make-believe anymore. "I'm growing up," she said.

"Not that quickly," Lorene said. How could Mary have moved from make-believe to thinking she was too grown up in the space of a few days? Lorene laughed.

"It's not funny. I am, and I decided I don't want the dolls in my room anymore."

"It's a long time before you're too old for dolls," Lorene said.

Mary shook her head. "I'm already too old."

"Well, they're not bothering you on the shelf. So it's not important right now."

Mary scowled and said nothing. When Mary left the parlor, Lorene went upstairs. The storage room door was still open. She was tired of repeated trips up and down the stairs, but it was becoming something she felt she had to do on a regular basis, curious to see when she'd find it locked again. She couldn't make a cup of tea without going upstairs while it cooled enough to drink. She couldn't wash her face or brush her teeth at night without going up there. Claire's door was always closed, so as far as she knew, Claire wasn't aware of her obsession.

Now, she found herself going up to check the storage room every time the clock struck the half hour. It was always unlocked, and she stopped bringing the keys, but couldn't stop herself from checking. Over the course of the next two days, she found it locked only one time. No one answered when she rapped and called out, asking who was inside. She'd thought about returning for the keys, but another idea began to form.

She couldn't make herself stop. She sat in the chair, listening to the clock chime, gripping the arms. She picked up her crocheting but couldn't finish more than a few stitches before her legs trembled with the desire for movement. The piano sat in the corner of the parlor, untouched for nearly a year. She'd lost her desire to play. Her body needed more intense activity, but even a hike failed to calm her nerves for more than a few minutes. She stood and stretched her arms overhead. She might as well check the room. The compulsion formed a tight knot in her stomach.

On Friday evening, Henry wasn't home for dinner. She ate shepherd's pie with Mary and Claire and then both girls disappeared to their rooms. A few minutes after Claire went upstairs, Lorene followed. The storage room door was locked. She tapped her fingertips on the door. "Who's in there?"

She was greeted with silence.

After breakfast the next day, she dressed in slacks and an old sweater. She went to the side of the storage room where all the furniture was shoved up close together. She squeezed behind a bookcase that was about four feet tall. She settled down on the floor, crossing her legs at the ankles, and waited.

Several hours passed. She dozed. She woke. Her

muscles cried out for activity. Finally she stood up. She would try again the next day, and the day after that. She would hide in the room until she found out who was locking the door from time to time. Maybe it was Mary after all. Maybe Mary's unhealthy interest in people suffering from insanity had damaged her own brain. Maybe she was still playing make-believe in there, despite protesting she was too old, and she was embarrassed to tell her mother. Maybe her games were something she wanted to keep secret.

On Tuesday, Lorene went into the room after dinner and settled behind the bookcase, bending her legs to the side and tucking her feet close to her hip. Twenty minutes later, the door opened.

A woman giggled — Claire. She should have known.

The door closed softly. The lock turned.

A man's voice emitted a sound somewhere between a groan and a satisfied hum of pleasure. He spoke in a low voice. "You taste so sweet."

Lorene bit her lip hard, trying to swallow blood mixed with the bile that surged up from her stomach, filling her mouth. The groaning, sighing, whispering man was Henry.

She pressed her hands over her mouth, digging her fingertips into her jaw. She pinched her knees together and made herself as small and tight as possible. If she could have, she would have held her breath. Showing herself to them would be even more humiliating than what burned inside, making her heart and lungs, liver and stomach, raw and tender. Every soft, silent breath cut through her like a razor blade.

For what seemed like hours, but was probably twenty or thirty minutes, she was subjected to sounds that would surely worm their way into her ears and haunt her dreams until the day she died. Listening to them filled her with disgust at herself for witnessing something she shouldn't, but she would not subject herself to Claire's triumphant smile by stepping out of her hiding space. She would not allow Henry to offer pity or apologies or whatever filthy lie he might manufacture. The only power she had left was knowledge. It was a slender advantage.

Finally, they were finished. The sounds of them struggling into clothing, whispering silly, shameful words of devotion made her head ache. Then, the door opened and closed and she was alone.

She wrapped her hands around her arms, hugging her legs to her chest. She pressed her face against her knees and let thick, warm tears run over her hands and wrists. What a fool! Bootlegging indeed. Henry had sworn to love her until she died. He'd promised at the altar, in the huge Catholic Church where he'd forced her to silence the Inner Voice and memorize words and repeat articles of faith she didn't believe. Perhaps lying to the Catholic God had delivered a lying man into her arms. She'd betrayed her own God, and now Henry and his Latin-speaking God, had betrayed her. All the things she'd sensed were the truth — he didn't need her thoughts or opinions in his life. He was disinterested in her body. He no longer loved anything about her.

And Claire!

Part of her wanted to rush into the girl's room right this minute, open the window, and shove Claire to her death. But was a three-story fall enough to end Claire's life? She had no idea. She'd done everything for her sister, welcomed her into her home, provided loving guidance, sacrificed her daughter's cherished bedroom, fed her and clothed her and allowed her freedom that Claire had used to steal and lie and mock.

Maybe Claire hadn't stolen the diamond. Instead, she'd taken Lorene's husband. Maybe the diamond teardrop was a gift from Henry.

The letters. They'd been lovers for years! Since Claire was a girl. When their mother was alive and Claire lived in San Francisco and Henry went up there weekly for business.

Lorene lay down on her side. The headache was gone. Her whole body felt empty and very, very tired. So tired, she thought she could close her eyes and give herself over to sleep that would last for eternity.

Twenty-two

Every time Jacob drove down the hill and along Beach Drive at night, he argued with himself over whether he should tell Henry to watch his back. As he walked in the darkness back to the pier and out over the water, his footsteps thudding on the wood planks, he mumbled out loud. The same phrases cycled through his head with maddening sameness, as if his brain were locked onto a small, tight track. Henry was a clever, careful man. He was perfectly aware of the dangers they faced. He knew who his enemies were — the women's temperance union, the clergy, the men who wanted a cut of what he had, and the men who wanted to put him out of business. He had more enemies than Jacob had friends, and surely Jacob's brother, a laborer who hadn't finished high school, didn't pose a worrisome threat.

Jacob imagined his brother following Henry when he left a restaurant or his office. David's footsteps would be loud, his presence obvious as they passed streetlights, or even in the darkness as David assumed he had plenty of cover, but Henry would hear his breathing, sense the heat of a man moving too close.

But what if he didn't? What if Henry was only alert to cars passing with excessive speed or creeping at an unusually slow pace? What if he was over-confident, proud of his cleverness, believing his intellect was so superior there was nothing to worry about?

Jacob was furious with David for taking Lorene's money in payment for spying on her husband. A wife should trust her husband. Had she forgotten how she enjoyed that enormous house and the lovely garden, a staff of employees taking care of all the dirty work while she spent her days strolling to the beach and drinking tea with her friends? It horrified him to think of being married to a woman who paid a stranger to spy on the man she was supposed to love and support, the father of her child. When you asked a woman to be your wife, how did you know whether she would remain loyal? Would Sarah be loyal if she suspected his involvement in illegal activities? Would Claire? Was there any chance left with Claire? He wanted to stop thinking about her, stop longing for a miraculous change in her heart, but whenever he thought of his future, he had trouble imagining it without her.

Occasionally, he hoped he might escape to another kind of life. When his mind wasn't circling around the fear of

David discovering the liquor distribution operation, it strained to see a way to change his own circumstances, but it was like trying to see the horizon from the bow of the ship at night. He knew it was there, he felt he'd be able to see it if he stared hard enough and long enough, and yet, there was nothing. Just water and darkness stretching out forever.

His footsteps echoed in the empty space between the pier and the surface of the water. He slowed his pace. It was a delicate balance — moving quickly, yet keeping his boots from thumping so loudly that someone on the footpath might hear and look toward the pier. He stepped onto the boat. The surf crashed against the sides. Spray rained down on his face. It was a high tide with larger than average swells even though no storm was in sight. He walked to the bow and leaned against the side, waiting.

It seemed as if he stood there for hours. After a while, he risked turning on the flashlight to check his watch. Ten minutes past one. Only fifteen minutes had passed. He shivered and hunched his shoulders, which did nothing to warm him. He turned off the light and shoved it back in his pocket. The waiting didn't use to be so painful, but that was when he thought it was exciting to be out at night, the thrill of hiding in the dark, thinking of his ever-swelling savings account. Now, all he could think of was David creeping around after Henry, Claire's hatred, and his mild feelings of boredom toward Sarah. He wanted it all to stop.

The surf grew quiet for a few minutes between breakers, and he heard the low sound of the motorboat. Finally.

He attached the ladder to the side of the ship and watched the boat emerge from the darkness, rolling furiously on the swells. It bobbed like a small log, pitching up so that it almost seemed vertical. He hoped it would be able to draw close enough to unload.

The driver dropped wood cylinders over the side to protect his boat as it was shoved against the concrete. Still, the small boat bobbed and rocked and banged against the S.S. Palo Alto. Jacob felt queasy watching the driver's body move with the rhythm of the motorboat. Jacob dreaded climbing down the ladder, balancing the boxes of liquor, trying to prevent the rough water from wrenching them out of his hands. Henry allowed for one damaged box a week. Any additional damage was attributed to Jacob's carelessness. He had to cover the loss. So far, his pay had never been docked.

He climbed over the side of the ship and started down. It seemed to take forever, securing a box under one arm, carrying it up the ladder, putting it on the deck, and climbing back down, close to the crashing surf. His pants were soaked with salt water. They turned stiff and heavy until he felt as if he had pieces of plywood strapped to his legs. The boat operator was methodical and careful as he lifted each box and handed it to Jacob. They managed to unload the entire shipment without dropping a box into the surging water.

As the motorboat pulled away, climbing a swell and disappearing on the other side, Jacob pulled up the sopping wet ladder and went to work carrying the boxes below deck.

By the time he was finished, he felt like lying down in the arcade and napping. A strange mixture of sleepiness and nerves raced through his body. The nerves would triumph, and he wouldn't be able to sleep anyway. He sat on the bottom step of the staircase and lit a cigarette. It would quiet his thoughts and steady his shaking hands and legs. The cavernous space below deck seemed to have no temperature and no odor. The smoke from his cigarette hung motionless in the air, smelling of nothing. It more closely resembled a cloud of his own breath. Inhaling and blowing thin streams of smoke calmed him. His muscles ached less, and his seawater-soaked pants were less of a burden.

He closed his eyes and listened to the water beating against the sides of the ship. It sounded far away. Where was the motorboat now? Would the operator make it safely back to whatever harbor he'd come from? Jacob didn't know where the shipments originated. He didn't know the name of the man who drove the small boat, and he had no idea whether the guy worked for Henry or was connected to one of his business partners. For a man involved up to his neck in an illegal operation, he was very ignorant.

The ship seemed to fold itself around him, comforting and at the same time agreeing that he was ignorant. He was trapped into a life that had a very good chance of ending in an early, violent death. Landing in a jail cell until old age was the upside. He put out his cigarette. He stood up, stretched, and rubbed his hands together to warm them. He turned to climb the stairs. Something clutched at his neck, pressing into his throat so he couldn't breathe. He grabbed at his neck but all he felt was his own skin. The hands he thought were squeezing his throat were phantoms. He struggled to breathe, coughing and gagging. He flailed his arms out to the sides, trying to locate the man who was pressing the oxygen out of him. His vision blurred and he thought he might pass out. He fell forward and grabbed the handrail on the staircase. He tried to climb but his feet wouldn't move. His boots felt as if they were filled with wet cement. Dragging his feet along the floor, he managed to inch forward, but couldn't lift either one to the bottom step.

He cried out. "Let me go!"

The pressure increased. He clawed at his neck and collarbone, trying to wrench the man or the thing away from him, but nothing was there. "What's happening?" His voice was faint and shrill without oxygen. Any moment, his lungs would be empty, and his body would collapse in a damp pile of limbs and slack muscle. "Please! I don't want to die. Please don't do this."

The pressure eased away from his neck. He put his own hands there, trying to protect himself from the next attack.

I'm dying.

"Who are you? What do you want?"

I'm dying.

"I can't help you if you don't show yourself."

I'm dying.

"Stop! Stop saying that!" He was shouting now, pushing his hands against the sides of his head, but still, the voice was there as if it had taken root inside his brain. Maybe it was a memory, and not a voice at all.

The words, repeating as they did, in a voice that sounded like rusted steel bars rubbing against each other, made him think of his mother. She was in her bed, the shape of her body barely visible under the blankets, her voice rough as she told him over and over she was dying. No matter what he said to her, no matter what he asked her — if he could bring soup or water, another blanket — she'd moaned, "I'm dying."

For days he'd heard nothing else. His father refused to enter the house, unable to listen to her wailing, unable to face the inevitable. Instead, his father sat on the porch, sleeping in the rocking chair at night, asking Jacob to bring him a piece of bread and coffee at mealtime. David stayed even farther away, sleeping and eating at friends' homes. Caring for her fell to Jacob. He changed her bedding, cooked pots of soup and fed it to her a half spoonful at a time. After a while, she couldn't manage the heavy vegetable or beef soups, and Jacob began helping her sip broth from a cup.

On the last day of her life, he went into her room. The steadily repeated lament was inaudible unless he put his face close to her lips. Her head, the only remaining weight of her, was sunken into the pillow like a stone. She grabbed his shoulder. Her voice rasped like a fork on corroded metal. "Listen to me. You have to look after your brother. He's not as clever as you. It would be so easy for him to get in with the wrong kind of people. I need you to take care of him. Please. Please!" As if so many words had drawn the last threads of life out of her body, her lips collapsed around her teeth. She fell asleep, and in another hour, she was gone.

Until now, Jacob had forgotten what she'd begged him to do. The words had been buried under the strain of their father fading out of their lives, followed by his rather sudden death. There was the loss of their house, and then, the thrill of Claire and his exciting new job. His mother hadn't waited to hear whether Jacob promised to do as she'd asked, and maybe that's why he'd forgotten. He hadn't promised. He hadn't said a word. But did a failure to speak the promise let him off the hook?

He tried to pull himself up. His body felt as if it had tripled in weight.

I'm dying. I don't want to die alone.

"Who's speaking?" He turned. "Is someone here? Show yourself to me."

There was silence.

Finally, he lifted his foot onto the first step. It required monumental effort. He clung to the railing and tried lifting his other foot, but it was too heavy. He stood for several minutes, holding onto the railing with both hands, frightened he would never leave the partially submerged caverns of the ship again. He would die here. But someone came regularly to remove the liquor Jacob stored in the locker. Surely Henry, or another faceless employee of Henry's, would find him. In the morning, a bit of light would filter down here, wouldn't it? He'd be able to see the person speaking to him. He'd be able to understand why control of his body had slipped out of his grasp.

The silence grew heavier, a thick blanket settling around his head and shoulders. He could hardly hold himself upright. He put his full weight on the handrail and closed his eyes. He thought about lighting another cigarette, but wasn't sure he had the strength to raise his arm.

A piece of fabric, or maybe a finger glanced across his cheek. He opened his eyes but saw nothing. The thing touched him again. He let go of the railing and dragged his fingers across his face, trying to feel where it had gone. The ability to move his hand to his face gave him confidence he could now climb the stairs, but when he tried to lift his foot, it was still impossible. He turned and sat down heavily. He pressed his elbows against his leg and rested his chin in his cupped hands. He stared into the darkness, terrified, but resigned to the fact he wouldn't be able to move until whatever force was assaulting him decided he should be released.

Several minutes passed. He closed his eyes again. By now, surely Henry had come down to the pier looking for him. He would be pacing, wondering where the hell Jacob was. Henry liked keeping distance between the delivery of his product and the exchange of cash. It was hard to predict what he would do if Jacob never showed up. How long would he wait? And what would the consequences be? No pay for the entire night? Fired from the delivery job? Fired altogether? He opened his eyes.

About twenty feet away stood a grayish figure. The thing was easily twenty feet tall. The head brushed the ceiling of the long room. There was no face to speak of, but he felt it was studying him, looking directly into his eyes. It wanted something. It moved slightly. Jacob's hands trembled and he felt his lips wobble uncontrollably. Would it approach him? Touch him? It already had. The choking sensation, the tickle of something on his cheek.

Perhaps it had even grabbed his legs, making his feet heavy, as if they were weighted to the floor, in the same way the cavities of the ship had been filled with water, sinking it onto the bottom of the ocean where it was impossible for it to move ever again. A ship that could no longer ride across the waves, choosing its direction, ruling over the ocean and carrying men and their cargo to other countries. He felt the shame of the boat, solidly on the ground, barnacles collecting on its skin, eating away at the concrete. Waves crashed against its sides. It was only a matter of time before a fierce storm turned the ship into a punching bag. He could hear the surf now, relentless, thrashing furiously, oblivious to the object in its way.

"What do you want?"

I'm dying.

He couldn't see that the thing was speaking, but he heard the words, felt them inside his mind, clear and direct.

"I can't do anything about that," Jacob said. "Please let me go. Don't take my life."

The thing faded. It was still visible but more like a wisp of smoke now.

After a moment, he was able to move his feet.

What was this thing? What did it want with him? He'd never heard anyone mention it, but then, he didn't know anyone who spent time down here alone.

He climbed the stairs, lifting each foot slowly, marveling that now it felt as if his feet were so light he wasn't aware of their solid substance, as if his boots had melted away.

At the top, he looked over his shoulder. The thing hovered in the far corner, faint and watery. There was still no recognizable form to it. Even so, he knew it was filled with grief. He felt its ache consuming the space, weighing down on his own heart. He went out the door and was glad for the cold night air and the mist rising off the breaking waves, brushing his face, glad to comprehend what it was that now touched his skin.

He started toward the center of the ship. When he passed the structure that housed the dining room and dance hall, he saw Henry at the end of the pier near the entrance to the ship. He paced back and forth. He stopped, looking at his watch. The spread of his legs and set of his shoulders gave off an aura of rage.

Jacob paused, trying to formulate an explanation.

As he looked toward the beach and the dark cliffs beyond, there was a flash of light at the top of the cliff. He moved sideways, close to the ship's mast. Another tiny light, the flame from a match? His back and legs froze. David was up there, smoking and keeping an eye on Henry.

Henry began pacing again. He stepped onto the ship, looked out toward the invisible horizon, and again shone a small light at his wrist to read his watch.

Jacob waited. If David saw them speaking…

Henry turned and walked quickly along the pier and onto the footpath. He turned toward his car, parked a few hundred yards from the pier. Jacob waited while Henry walked to the car, got in, and drove back past the pier, turned, and headed up the hill. Jacob continued staring into the darkness. There was a final flash of light on the cliff and then nothing. He waited for another thirty minutes to be sure.

The next morning, Jacob was awake before dawn. Sluggish and trembling from two hours of terror-filled dreams, he got up, heated water on the single electric burner on his dresser, and dropped several teaspoons of instant coffee into a cup. When the water was boiling, he poured it over the granules. He took the coffee down the hall to the bathroom, unoccupied at such an early hour. He showered quickly, then sipped the burning coffee while he shaved and dressed. He wanted to be waiting outside Henry's office when the sun came up. He wasn't sure if Henry would be worried or angry, but he guessed that even if Henry had been worried a few hours earlier, the worry by now had turned to anger. If it hadn't already, the transformation to anger over being left in the dark would happen rapidly once he saw Jacob was alive, once he was informed the shipment had arrived and been safely stored.

Instead of parking in the driveway of the King home, Jacob pulled off the side of the road by the iron fence a few hundred yards from the entrance. Leaving his car in front of the house would pique Lorene's interest if she happened to be awake this early, happened to look outside.

He hadn't decided whether he would mention the light at the top of the cliffs. First, he needed to provide an excuse regarding why he hadn't appeared on time. Trying to explain the unsettling experience with that…that thing, was impossible. Instead, he would exaggerate the rough surf, water splashing over the bow, and suggest it had taken much longer than usual to unload and make his way along a slick deck as he carried boxes below.

Henry's study was dark.

If Jacob were seen sitting on the veranda, it would raise the same questions as his car in the driveway. He walked along the path leading to the thick grove of birch trees at the far side of the yard. He moved into the center, hidden from view by the branches that hadn't dropped their leaves. His body swayed as he tried to keep from falling asleep. It was an odd mixture of discomfort from the cold, coupled with hunger and an aching desire to curl up on the wet grass and sleep. He leaned against one of the trees. It kept him steady, but made his eyelids even more determined to close. He stood up straight and walked to the side of the grove, turned and walked back.

About fifteen minutes later, a light shone faintly through the drapes in Henry's study window. Jacob hurried across the lawn and up the steps. He wiped his feet on the mat outside the office door and knocked. There was no answer. He stepped back to get a better look at the window. He was sure a light had come on. He waited for a few minutes and knocked again, more firmly this time.

Henry opened the door. "Well." He stuffed a piece of

paper in his pocket as he stepped back for Jacob to enter.

At least Henry wasn't going to fire him on the spot. Of course, he was waiting for his inventory list. There was no telling what might come after it was turned over.

Jacob took a seat facing the desk. Henry remained standing. "What happened to you?"

"The surf was rough last night."

"I didn't notice. Was the shipment held up? Damaged?"

Jacob stood up and pulled the inventory sheet out of his pocket. He handed it to Henry. "It took a lot longer than usual getting it up the ladder. I was soaked to the skin, and the deck was covered with water, so I was extra careful carrying everything below."

"I see." Henry studied the sheet and put it on the desk.

"I'm sorry if you were concerned."

"Sorry would have been more useful five hours ago. I came out looking for you. Why didn't you consider I might be out there and try to make contact?"

"I guess I didn't think about it. I was concentrating on getting everything put away."

"I pay you a lot of money to think on your feet."

"You do, and I'm very sorry." His voice sounded weak, like a child who was about to be punished, afraid to discover how painful it would be.

"It was nerve-wracking. Not knowing if you'd been caught. Drowned. The shipment lost or damaged."

Hearing his drowning put in the same list with an arrest

and a financial loss was disturbing. Henry's caution was understandable, not coming out onto the boat while the liquor was changing hands, but didn't he have even a little concern for the life of his most trusted employee? And what would have happened if Henry had seen that apparition? *Would* he have seen it, or was it all some sort of waking nightmare formed inside Jacob's imagination? "Sorry. I should have…"

"Stop repeating yourself. I don't need an apology, I need to know what's going on. Always. Information is currency."

Jacob nodded.

"I'm not sure how to handle this," Henry said.

Jacob waited to hear that he'd not only be losing out on last night's payment, but perhaps have future salary cuts. It wasn't fair. He was the one doing the hard work and taking most of the risk. All the risk. The motorboat could speed away into the darkness. Henry could deny any knowledge. Whoever picked up the bottles and carried them on their final trip to shore was a mystery to Jacob, and Henry had equal deniability for that piece. None of them knew the others' names, or even their faces. The man driving the boat wore a hat pulled low, a collar tugged over his jaw. He kept the side of his body turned toward Jacob. In the dark, Jacob couldn't even guess the color of the hat or the shape of the man's nose.

"You put me at risk. I was standing out there for too

long, in plain sight. If someone saw me, they'd wonder."

Jacob's palms and neck turned clammy, and he worried they released the odor of sweaty skin. Whether or not it was David, someone had been smoking on the cliff. From that vantage, there was an unobstructed view of the entire shore. Even in the darkness, the surface of the water, the foamy edges of the breakers, the light of the moon all came together, bathing the beach and the footpath in a soft glow. Even someone who hadn't set out to watch Henry's movements would have noticed him, and wondered.

Jacob clasped his hands. "I'm very, very sorry. I guess I was cold and wet, and I just wasn't thinking."

Henry gripped the back of his chair.

Jacob stood up. He wouldn't mention David. He didn't know for sure who'd been standing on the cliff, and if it had been David, the blame might fall on Jacob…even if he revealed Lorene's role. After he spoke to David, he'd decide what to do. "There's nothing more I can say. It won't happen again."

"It better not," Henry said. "I need to know everything that's going on. I can't run a business blindfolded. *Everything*. Is that clear?"

Jacob nodded.

Henry reached into the desk drawer and pulled out an envelope. It looked to be the same thickness as always. Jacob's heart thudded. He swallowed. Henry held out the envelope, and Jacob leaned across the desk and took it.

"Thank you."

"*Everything*."

"Yes. Everything, I'll make sure of it."

Henry nodded. He reached into his pocket and pulled out the letter he'd been holding when Jacob arrived. "And there's this." He tossed it on the desk.

Jacob picked it up. The letter had no salutation and consisted of three lines.

I know what you're doing.

Leave fifty dollars in a brown envelope under the flowerpot outside the bakery.

If the envelope is there by ten o'clock Monday night, I'll keep your secret.

Jacob stiffened his hand to keep it from shaking. He put the letter on the desk.

"Any idea what this is about?" Henry said.

Jacob shook his head.

"It's juvenile."

Jacob nodded, maybe too eagerly. He stopped moving his head and shoved his hands in his pockets.

"I want you to keep an eye on the bakery Monday. Find out who this character is."

"I don't…"

"You don't, what?"

"I don't know if, what if he…I think…it's possible he might…"

"Are you trying to say something?" Henry smiled, but

his eyes were hard and steely.

"I doubt he'd come himself."

"How do you know that?"

"I don't know it for certain, but if it were me…I would expect you to be watching. I'd send someone else. I might even hire a kid to pick it up."

"Then you can follow this mythical kid you think will be hired."

"Okay. But I…"

"Is there a problem? You seemed baffled."

"I'm just…I'm in shock, seeing this. I'm a little scared, actually. Do you think someone knows?"

"Someone always knows something. It's probably nothing. A prank. It's quite vague, don't you think? Fishing for a chance to extort. My wealth is common knowledge, and someone wants to try to take advantage."

"That makes sense," Jacob said.

"So go watch the place. Don't be seen."

"What about the delivery?"

"This is more important right now. Someone else can handle the delivery."

Jacob hadn't known there were others taking deliveries. He was less secure in his position than he'd realized. And if this joke of a letter was from David…it was definitely David…Jacob had no idea what to do. "Where did you get the letter?"

"It was lying on the floor when I came in."

Jacob nodded. Maybe another letter…David could leave another letter, taking back the threat. He almost laughed. It was a ridiculous idea, but he had to do something to make David stop. Lorene hadn't helped the situation because now David felt justified, his suspicions fueled by hers. His head ached. He badly needed some sleep. After a good rest, an idea would come to him. "I didn't really sleep last night. I'm going to lie down for a few hours, and I'll do the banking after that, if it's okay with you?"

Henry nodded. "I don't need you functioning below par."

"Thanks." Jacob turned and went to the door. He wanted to look over his shoulder, gauge the expression on Henry's face, try to interpret his mood, but he didn't dare. It would make him look nervous. Henry would lose more confidence in him if he read the terror on Jacob's face.

David was standing near the trashcans behind the market when Jacob arrived. He was lighting a cigarette. He pulled out another, touched it to the burning tip of his own, and handed it to Jacob.

Jacob took a puff and glanced to either side. The alley behind the shops was empty except for the two of them. He yawned. The three-hour nap hadn't done much to refresh him, but at least his brain felt as if he could generate rational thoughts instead of the soupy mess that swam around inside when he'd faced Henry a few hours earlier. He took another puff on the cigarette, held the smoke inside for a moment, and released it slowly in a narrow stream. "What the hell were you thinking?"

"Huh?"

"Leaving that note for Henry — are you out of your mind? He's not going to just give you fifty dollars. And what a stupid amount. You might as well announce that you're going to ask for more on a regular basis."

David laughed. He lifted his foot to the side and tapped his cigarette against the sole of his boot. "He told you about that? He absolutely does trust you!"

"Of course he told me. I'm one of his most valuable employees."

David stretched his lips into an expression that Jacob assumed was supposed to mimic his own.

"I know how he thinks. He's not going to pay you," Jacob said.

"Yes he will."

"You're messing with the wrong guy."

"Oooh. Scary." David laughed.

"I'm serious. He's not going to hand over a single dollar, knowing you'll be back for more, proving to you there are secrets he wants kept. He's not going to let someone have that kind of power over him."

"He has no choice."

"He has a lot of choices."

"Like what?" David said.

"You have no idea."

"Empty threat. I think you're scared that your position is jeopardized. If I bleed Henry dry, what will be left?"

Jacob turned away from his brother and looked toward the end of the alley. At his left was a solid wall of buildings, the back entrances to the market, the bakery, a shoe repair shop, a tailor, and a flower shop. He took a puff on his cigarette and tried to think. If he told David he'd been ordered to spy on him, it would create a bigger, more complicated problem. David might try to pull him into it, insisting Jacob mislead Henry. Words failed to take shape in his mind. He couldn't look at his brother, the leering expression, so triumphant. How had this happened?

The tormented memory of that thing on the ship and the reminder of his mother's request nagged at him. His mother had been concerned about the wrong son. Jacob was the one mixed up with a bad crowd. The pieces of his life were spilling all over the ground, rolling downhill like marbles pouring out of a cloth bag, bouncing and skittering in every direction. He couldn't even follow them with his eyes, much less chase after them and capture them in time. He dropped his half-smoked cigarette on the ground. He stepped on it, twisting his foot as if he could grind all his problems into a pulpy smear of tobacco and paper and ash. He turned. David blew a cloud of smoke in Jacob's face.

"Look, you really do not know who you're dealing with," Jacob said.

"Sounds like you have a lot more information than you're letting on. What's he up to? Liquor? Gambling? *Does* he have a gal on the side? Is that why Lorene is so desperate that she's willing to pay a stranger to sneak around after him? Maybe he's involved with supplying women to the "tea house", is that it?"

"It doesn't matter. What you need to think about is that he's a powerful guy. People in this community look up to him. People fear him."

"I'm not afraid of anyone," David said.

"You should be."

"Why? If you're so worried about it, he must be worried. Sounds to me like I'm on to something. I don't know what it is, but it's enough that I saw him standing out near the ship in the middle of the night. I don't have to know the details. I hear enough stories about what goes on below deck. A swimming pool!" He laughed. "More like liquor, gambling, prostitutes. Any one of those things will make him pay for my silence."

"You can't accuse him of any of those things. You have no proof."

"I don't need proof, baby brother. It's called guilt by association. If he's not guilty, he won't pay, and nothing is lost on my side. It's a perfect setup."

"You're making a mistake."

David grinned. “You should see your face. You look as worried as an old lady.”

“I’m not worried.” Jacob shoved his hands in his pockets. If Henry knew this conversation was going on, if he had any hint of the subtle betrayal, Jacob would lose his job. He owed his loyalty to his boss, and he shouldn’t be suggesting that Henry would respond to the blackmail threat with violence. He was implying that Henry was indeed connected to something dangerous. Jacob had never seen him with a weapon or heard him speak of guns, but it was common knowledge that bootleggers were armed. Sometimes Jacob wondered why he hadn’t been told to carry a gun. Not that he wanted to, absolutely not, but they were involved in a business that was run by underground characters. Jacob had become one of them — flouting federal law. It sounded horrible when he thought of it in those terms.

“You look worried sick. In fact, you look like you’re gonna puke any minute.”

“I didn’t get much sleep.”

“Why not?”

“I’m not here to discuss my health. I’m telling you Henry will not leave cash in an envelope under a flowerpot, of all things. And if he finds out you sent that ridiculous note, you can kiss your job goodbye. Who knows what else.”

“What’s he gonna do, shoot me?” David laughed.

"Does Mrs. King know you're blackmailing her husband?"

"This has nothing to do with her."

"She paid you for information, and you haven't given it to her."

David glared at him. "Well, I don't have information. I saw him standing by the pier at two in the morning or something like that."

"Then how can you blackmail him?"

"I told you. He was up to something, hovering around the ship at that time of night. If his conscience is clear and he doesn't pay, no harm done. But I think he will."

"He won't. I guarantee you he won't get trapped into making payments, even if he's worried about what you might know. Especially when there's no guarantee you won't spread rumors about him. In fact, he thought your letter was a joke."

"Then why are we talking about it?"

They stared at each other for several minutes. The sun rose over the tops of the buildings. Under its warmth, the alley came to life with the smells of rotting fruit discarded in boxes behind the market, and stale bread from the bakery. The odor reminded Jacob of how badly he wanted to lie down between clean sheets and sleep, without any thoughts twisting themselves into troubling dreams. "I think you should send another letter. Tell him you changed your mind."

David gave a laugh that sounded like a braying donkey. "Changed my mind?"

"You're playing a dangerous game — juggling Henry and his wife."

"It's not dangerous. I can handle both of them."

Jacob took a step closer. He grabbed David's shirt front. "Send another letter. I can't tell you what I know, but Henry is a dangerous guy, and he won't allow you to get one up on him. I promise — it will go badly for you."

"Are you threatening me?"

"No. I'm trying to help you. Tell Mrs. King you discovered nothing, which is the truth. And send another note. I mean it."

"Or what? You are threatening me."

"It's possible Henry knows people that wouldn't hesitate to kill someone who's causing trouble for him."

"What do you know? What are you doing for him anyway?"

"Never mind. Just do what I said. And if you tell anyone, then I'll make sure you lose your job. You'll end up in a poor house, and if you go on about any of this, people will just think you're nothing but a bum and a lunatic."

"Let go of me."

Jacob released his grip on the shirt. He turned and walked toward the end of the alley where it opened into an area with benches facing a small vacant lot.

"My kid brother isn't going to threaten me!" David shouted. "You proved he's involved in something. His wife was right, and I'm right."

Jacob started running. He had no idea how he was going to fix this or what he would tell Henry.

Twenty-three

A low, opaque fog covered everything, which was somehow appropriate for what Lorene was about to do. She'd asked Henry to drop her off at the town center for a bit of early Christmas shopping. The decorations in the shops were understated this year, an acknowledgment that not everyone anticipated a lavish, merry holiday. Most windows were lined with simple garlands, a few had woven a string of colorful lights around the greenery. The endless ropes of tinsel and banners draped across the storefronts that had been typical a few years ago were missing. Wreaths were few and far between. Lorene walked past the row of shops and continued up two blocks. She turned right onto a street lined with small cottages. A two-story farmhouse stood on the last lot of the dead-end street. It was surrounded by a field that was filled with wildflowers in Spring and early Summer. Now, nothing grew but long brown grasses and thick weeds. A few leafless trees stood at irregular intervals. She walked up the front steps, across the worn planks of the porch, and knocked on the door.

A woman answered. Her brown hair was streaked with gray, cut in a twenties-style bob. She wiped her hands on her green smock. She tucked her hair behind her left ear and smiled. “Hi.”

“I’m looking to rent a room,” Lorene said.

“We have four vacancies.”

“Yes. I read the ad in the paper.”

The woman stepped back from the doorway and Lorene went inside. The woman walked into a tiny sitting room that faced the street. Lorene followed. The woman turned and clasped her hands in front of her ribs. “I’m Betsy. I’m not the owner. I fix breakfast and lunch and do light cleaning, but I can take your information and a deposit for Mrs. Harmon.” She went to a small desk in the corner, removed a notebook from the top drawer, and picked up a pen.

They sat beside each other on a beige and blue floral sofa with a low table in front of it. “I need your name, age, and current address, as well as the names of two references,” Betsy said. “And a deposit of five dollars.”

“I’d like to pay for three weeks up front.”

Betsy nodded and made a note in her book. “Two of the rooms are upstairs, and two on the first floor. The first floor rooms are suites, so they’re ten dollars a week. Upstairs rooms are eight dollars for the one facing the field, six for the one on the street side."

"Second-floor street side is fine."

"And your name and age?"

"It's for my sister — Claire Farmington, age eighteen."

Betsy wrote the information in her book.

Lorene provided her current address. She named herself and Margaret Sharp as references. The minute she got home, she'd need to telephone Margaret.

"There's no smoking, and it goes without saying, no booze," Betsy said. "Everyone needs to be in promptly by nine p.m., except on Saturdays. No male visitors in the rooms, only in the sitting room, dining room, parlor, and of course, the front and back porches." She smiled as if pleased that she'd been so thorough.

Lorene wondered where the kitchen fell in the list of forbidden rooms, but she smiled and nodded, pleased that she was not only rid of Claire, but that Claire's wings would be clipped. She counted out the bills and handed them to Betsy. She put the makeshift receipt, written on a scrap of paper, in her purse and said that Claire would be moving in on Saturday. "Do you know of anyone for hire who has a truck to move a few pieces of furniture?"

"Oh, the rooms are furnished," Betsy said. "I thought that was mentioned in the ad."

"I must have missed it. Even better. I still need a truck though, for boxes."

"There are plenty available. I'll get you a name and

phone number." Betsy stood up. She returned the notebook and pen to the desk. "Do you want a cup of tea before you go?"

"No thank you."

While Betsy went for the truck information, Lorene stood by the window looking out at the street. Claire would consider it dead. Fog blew past, drifting onto the porch. It was so thick now, the house across the street looked like it was disappearing right in front of her eyes.

"Here you go." Betsy's voice behind her was crisp and cheerful.

Lorene turned. She took the slip of paper. "Thank you."

"We'll look forward to meeting Claire. I hope she's sociable."

"Very."

Betsy nodded. "That's important. Everyone here gets along."

As Lorene walked back toward the shops, she thought about Claire's sullen looks and her silence during meals. She thought about the diamond teardrop, definitely a stolen piece of jewelry, despite Claire's boasting about the men she knew. Lorene hoped nothing happened that would tarnish her own, or especially Margaret's reputations. But serving as a reference was only a formality. Hopefully, by the time Claire's true nature was revealed, Mrs. Harmon, and Betsy, and the occupants of the boarding house would have forgotten all about Lorene King and Margaret Sharp.

The next day, Claire went out with her girlfriends. The minute the car disappeared from sight, Lorene got the key to the storage room. She hurried up to the third floor. She went into the storage room and picked up a cardboard box with several smaller boxes nested inside. It would have been easier to ask for Annie's help, but the satisfaction of doing this herself was too great. She carried the boxes into Claire's room and dropped them in the center of the floor. She returned to the storage room and emptied a shipping trunk that was stored behind the couch, dumping the contents on the floor. No one would be in here for a while, it didn't matter if she left a mess. She dragged the trunk across the floor. It scraped on the wood floor, but Henry wouldn't hear it, far away in his study at the back of the house. Mary was also out of earshot, reading a book on the screened porch, despite the damp weather. Lorene maneuvered the trunk through the doorway and into Claire's room.

She locked the storage room door, removed the key from the ring, and dropped it into her pocket. She placed the ring on the top step so she wouldn't forget to take it back to the pantry.

It took only an hour to stuff all of Claire's dresses into the trunk, her shoes into boxes, and her other clothing and books and correspondence into three additional boxes. They made a sad, small stack in the center of the room.

Lorene stood beside the bed, unsure whether to pack the diamond, or leave that to Claire. She glanced out the window. A seagull soared past. A moment later, it returned and hovered there, as if it were trying to see inside the room.

Packing the diamond herself would represent a small victory. Claire would have a moment of panic when she realized it was gone. She slid her hand beneath the mattress. She felt around the spot where she remembered putting it the last time, but it wasn't there. Of course, Claire might have shifted its placement. She stood up and shoved the mattress off the boxspring. She pulled off the blankets and sheets. The small box with the diamond wasn't there.

She put the sheets and blankets in a pile near the door. Everything needed washing. Bleach, too. She glanced at the window seat. It would be good to take down all the curtains, replace them with something new, erasing every trace of Claire from the room. Would Henry agree to new carpeting? She hadn't decided whether she wanted Mary to sleep in this room again. Mary would demand it, of course, but ghosts lurked in the corners, wicked thoughts circulating beneath the ceiling, things that might infect Mary with whatever was wrong with Claire.

After considering the disassembled bed for several minutes, trying to muster up energy to replace the mattress, she turned away and moved toward the window seat. She'd forgotten the packet of letters. She lifted one of the cushions off the frame.

"What are you doing?" Claire's voice was shrill.

Lorene startled and dropped the cushion.

"What are you doing in my room? And what's all this?" Claire's hair had been chopped off to her earlobes. The effect was startling. She looked like a woman of twenty-five. Her eyes were more heavily made up than usual, and they simmered like black holes in her face. "Get all these boxes out of here and fix my bed!"

Lorene glanced at the window seat frame. She picked up the packet of letters and put them on the floor. She replaced the cushion and sat down, suddenly tired from the frenzy of packing. "It's time for you to move into a place on your own."

"I'll move when I'm ready."

"No. You're an adult now, as you keep pointing out. You've stayed here too long." Lorene stood up and ran her palms down the front of her slacks. She felt the key pressing against her leg through the thin cotton of the pocket lining. Even though it had been there for some time now, it still was cold against her leg.

"I have nowhere to go. Are you trying to hurt me by pointing that out?"

Lorene laughed. Did Claire really imagine that Lorene could hurt *her*? Claire didn't know the meaning of the word. She'd torn Lorene's heart into bloody ribbons of flesh. Claire hadn't done it alone, of course, but the ache was too enormous to consider yet how Henry should be dealt with. His turn would come. She hadn't decided if she wanted to be rid of him, or if she wanted to see him suffer. She was mostly inclined toward the latter, but no good came of rushing into things. It wasn't possible to make him feel the pain she had experienced during that afternoon in the storage room when she'd listened to her husband and her sister making love with such tenderness and desire. Every time the memory arose, her knees turned to liquid, and she thought she might collapse. Without the steady, persistent guidance of the Inner Light, she had no idea what to do about anything. Every movement had a heavy, numb quality, somewhat like a marionette with the dead weight of its limbs lifted by invisible strings, but she had no idea who was operating the strings. Possibly Henry and Claire.

Claire walked to the center of the room. She unfolded the flaps on one of the boxes and began pulling out shoes, dropping them on the floor. When she'd removed four pairs, she scooped them up and turned to go into the closet.

Lorene blocked her way.

"Move," Claire said.

"Put them back. You can't stay here anymore. I've rented a room for you."

"A room? I'm not living in some boarding house for spinsters."

"Yes, you are. That's what young women without families do. It's perfectly respectable."

"I have a family."

Lorene grabbed two pairs of sandals out of Claire's arms and let them fall to the floor. "I've hired a truck to pick up your things. They'll be here in about an hour."

"No. This is my home." Claire kicked the sandals out of her way and headed toward the closet.

Lorene grabbed her arm. Claire wrenched away and stumbled sideways. She cried out and collapsed at Lorene's feet. "You hurt my wrist."

"Don't be dramatic. I'm not putting up with a temper tantrum. Put the shoes back in the box and check the room to see if there's anything I forgot to pack."

Claire pushed herself to her feet. She stood in front of Lorene, thrusting her face close so Lorene could smell the powder on her skin and the styling cream in her hair. "I'm not leaving. Unpack my things."

Lorene crossed her arms.

"You can't do this."

"I can. You're all grown up, you're finished with school."

"You have no right. I'll tell Henry."

Lorene stepped back. "Will you?" She hoped her mild expression made Claire uncomfortable, if only for a moment. But there wasn't even a suggestion of guilt on Claire's face. The girl had no conscience. That was the problem. Somehow, despite her Quaker education, the Inner Light had not taken root in Claire's heart.

Claire turned and hurried toward the door. Lorene rushed after her. She grabbed Claire's arm and yanked her back. Claire fell against her, and they collapsed on the floor. Memories of their childhood flashed through Lorene's mind — tumbling on the floor with her baby sister, tickling her. Lorene had thought it was a game when she listened to Claire's magical, flute-like laughter. Then, Claire's giggle faded. She turned her face and bit Lorene's lip. Lorene cried out as Claire's sharp, tiny teeth punctured the skin and blood seeped into her mouth. It hadn't been a game. Or maybe it was a more dangerous game than Lorene realized. Claire had won. And Claire would always win. No matter what happened now between Lorene and Henry, Claire had already won. Lorene could send her away, but she could never erase the sounds of their lovemaking, the unfettered desire pouring out of Henry.

Tears spilled down her cheeks. She let out a choked sob.

"Are you crying?" Claire laughed. "What are you crying about? I'm the one being mistreated. And I know Henry will not approve of this. I'm not leaving this house until he says so." She tried to pry Lorene's fingers off her arm.

Lorene tightened her grip. She pushed Claire onto her back. She sat on the girl's legs and pinned her arms beside her. "This is between you and me. I'm the one who decided you should live here. I had to make a case to Henry. I'm the one who has decided it's time for you to go. Henry doesn't make all the decisions around here."

Claire laughed. She stuck her tongue out at Lorene, wiggling it wildly.

"That's mature of you," Lorene said.

"Then get off me."

"I'll get off you, and we'll go together to tell Henry you're leaving, and then I'll ask him to drive us to the boarding house."

Claire smirked. "Why would I do that? If you want me out, you tell him. And we'll see what he says."

Lorene stood up. She brushed her palms across the front of her pants, as if they'd been soiled by contact with Claire. "I'll do that." She left the room and went downstairs.

Without waiting for Henry to respond to her knock, she turned the knob and entered his office. "Sorry to disturb you, but I need to discuss something right now."

He put down his pen and looked at her.

"I've decided it's long past time for Claire to move out. She's eighteen, she has her own friends, her own life, and I don't want Mary exposed any more to…"

"I agree." Henry leaned back in his chair.

She was about to blurt out, *you do?* She managed to reshape her open mouth and the sounds in her throat into a forced cough. The next words that rose to her mind were *thank you*. Those too, she suppressed. She was in charge now. She asked him to drive her and Claire to the boarding house immediately. He agreed to that as well. It would be an uncomfortable ride for Lorene, maybe for those two as well — Claire sulking like a child in the backseat. But Lorene would survive. She'd managed to hold herself together so far. In many ways, it was getting easier.

Maybe Henry felt the power of her rage and interpreted it as confidence. He gave her a funny look, but she refused to ask him what it meant. She refused to ask, as she so often, too often, had asked — *what are you thinking?* She didn't give a damn what was inside his head. She wanted that girl out of her house, out of her life, and then she'd decide about him.

Claire thought Henry made all the decisions. Not any more.

Twenty-four

Although Mary liked reading on the screened porch, liked hearing the birds in the nearby trees, liked smelling the fresh air, it was too cold. The quilt over her curled up legs had helped for a while, but now the cold had soaked into the fabric, making her feel as if she had a blanket of wet sand over her legs. She closed her book and stood up. She finished the hot chocolate in her mug and carried it into the kitchen. She wandered into the parlor. Her mother was sitting in the green armchair. Lorene had turned the chair so it was facing the window.

"What are you doing?" Mary said.

Her mother continued staring out the window.

"Mother?"

Lorene turned. She smiled. Her face was pale, not peachy pale, but white, almost the color of the sheer curtains that partially covered the window.

Mary fingered her necklace. The stone and its silver

setting felt heavy and cold on her collarbone.

"What is that?" Lorene stood up and crossed the room. She moved Mary's fingers away from the diamond. "Where did you get that?"

"Claire gave it to me."

"Take it off."

"Why?"

"It doesn't belong to you." She held out her hand, palm up.

"Yes it does. Claire gave it to me."

"She stole it."

"She did?"

"Yes."

"She said that was just a story she made up."

"Of course she did."

"I'll ask her again," Mary said.

"Give me the necklace. And you can't ask her. She's gone."

"What do you mean?"

"It was time for her to move out by herself, so our family can get back to normal."

"But she's part of our family!"

Lorene walked behind her. She lifted Mary's hair to the side, exposing her neck.

"Where is she?"

"Your father and I took her to a nice rooming house where other young women live. She'll be happier there.

She'll be close to the shops and her friends. A truck is coming for her things."

"Is that why you were staring out the window?"

She felt her mother's fingers undoing the clasp. The pendant dropped slightly as it was unhooked. Her mother reached around Mary's shoulder, caught it in her hand, and took the necklace off. She closed her fist around it.

"She said it meant she was special."

"Well, she's not."

The rough tone of her mother's voice was frightening. What was wrong with her? She acted as if she hated Claire. "Can I have it back later, if you find out she didn't steal it?"

"No."

Mary sighed. Something was wrong, but she had no idea what it might be. She tucked her book under her arm. "Can I go to the beach?"

"*May* I," Lorene said.

"May I go to the beach?"

Her mother nodded. "Be sure to come home before sunset. I don't like you walking up the hill in the dark."

"I will." She kissed her mother's cheek.

Lorene turned to the window again. It seemed as if she were looking for something more than the truck. It made no sense that Claire was suddenly moving out of their house. Mary didn't understand why her mother thought Claire had stolen the necklace. She didn't understand anything, but when her mother didn't want to explain something, it was useless to keep asking. She went upstairs and changed into warm pants and a pullover sweater. She got her coat and scarf and a felt hat and went out.

Walking to the beach alone made her feel grown up. The beach was perfectly safe, and she didn't understand why she hadn't been allowed to go alone when she was younger. She imagined building sand castles without her mother constantly watching, studying everything Mary did. Now, she didn't enjoy building sand castles as much. She preferred to read, or just walk along the edge of the water and feel the wind on her face, tickling her nose, brushing across her lips. She liked walking on the pier and looking at the ship. It was sad, now that the restaurant was closed most of the time. No bands had played there since early in the summer. She'd never had a chance to dance on it or eat in the fancy restaurant. They said most people couldn't afford things like that now. When she looked at the ship, sitting in the water, waiting, it seemed as if the ship was sad. It was foolish to think a ship had feelings, but she couldn't stop the thought from popping into her head.

The beach was nearly deserted. Not many people liked to go out there when it wasn't sunny and warm. Maybe that was why the concrete ship was doomed before she even reached her permanent port. Three men stood on the west side of the pier, fishing poles extended like delicate antennae, staring at the gray-green water. Gulls stood nearby, hoping to steal a catch, although they never did.

She took off her shoes and socks and left them on the footpath. It was cold, but she liked feeling the sand on her feet. She walked up close to the water and stood for a while, lulled by the rhythm of the waves. She turned and began walking, thinking of nothing much, glad of the chance for her mind to be empty and quiet. Her mother sometimes spoke vaguely of quieting her mind, seeking the Inner Light, but her voice was low, almost a whisper, and she quickly changed the subject. Her parents had agreed that Mary would be Catholic. She was curious about the Inner Light, but it was impossible to get her mother to say much about it. Mary had read a library book about Quakers, but it left her with a lot of questions, and she wondered why her father got to decide what they would believe as a family, as if he thought they shared a single brain.

When the sun slipped close to the point at the far side of the bay, she turned and walked back toward the ship. Only one fisherman remained. Another man stood on the deck of the boat. He faced the horizon, shoulders hunched, his hands in his pockets.

She went up to the footpath, brushed off her feet, and put on her socks and shoes. She went onto the pier and walked halfway down. The fisherman pulled his line out of the water. The hook was empty. He put the cover on his bucket of fish, secured his line, and began walking. As he passed Mary, he nodded. She leaned on the railing and watched the sun melt out of the sky. Her mother would be upset when Mary arrived home after dark, but she wouldn't do much about it. She'd simply complain, repeating her worries.

Mary studied the man on the ship. He looked like Jacob. She moved along the pier. Yes. He glanced over his shoulder and lifted his hand in a greeting. She walked onto the boat and over to where he stood.

"Your mother let you come out here alone?"

"As long as I get home before it's dark."

"That's in a few minutes."

She smiled.

"She doesn't punish you if you're late?"

"It's a stupid rule. She just says don't do it again. Nothing will happen to me."

"Bad things happen on the ship," Jacob said.

"What bad things?"

He leaned his elbows on the edge of the ship. "Never mind. I shouldn't have said that. Sometimes I think too much, and words spill out before I can stop them."

"What bad things?"

"Adult things. Never mind. Tell me what you saw on your walk."

She moved closer to his side and turned, facing the water. If she didn't look him in the eye, he'd talk more. The sky glowed orange and lavender with streaks of pale gray clouds.

"I'm tired of people telling me what I can and can't do,

or what I shouldn't think about, because I'm not an adult."

He laughed.

"So what bad things? I know all kinds of bad things. I know about insane asylums and people stealing jewelry and drinking champagne and throwing up."

He laughed again. "You're too smart for your age."

"I'm almost twelve."

"Still a little girl."

"Not so little." She glanced at his shoulder, only a few inches above hers.

"Fair enough."

"Then tell me."

"People have private parties and drink liquor out here. They gamble. Do you know what gambling is?"

"I'm not stupid."

"I didn't think you were, but not knowing something doesn't mean you're stupid. I was just checking."

"Okay. What other bad things?"

"Isn't that enough?"

"Gambling and drinking aren't anything out of the ordinary. You sounded scared, like it was worse than those things."

"Did I?"

"Yes."

He rubbed his face with his hands. "I don't know… maybe the ship is haunted. If you believe in that sort of thing. Do you believe in ghosts?"

"I never thought about it. I mean, I've heard ghost stories, and it's easy to believe they're real when you read a story, but I never thought about whether I might see one."

Jacob didn't speak.

"Did you see a ghost?" she said.

"I'm not sure."

"What happened?"

"You can't tell anyone."

"Why would I tell anyone?"

"Sometimes people share secrets, and the other person reveals the secret when they shouldn't."

"Is the ghost a secret?"

"I don't know. I've never heard anyone mention it. They'd think I wasn't very bright if I went around talking about ghosts."

She laughed. "I don't think that's it. They'd think you were insane."

"You're right."

"I won't tell anyone."

"I was down in the area below the arcade, at night. Alone."

"Why?"

"That part isn't important."

She wasn't sure about that, but if she wanted him to tell the story, it was better not to interrupt with questions.

The remaining light of the sun hugged the cliffs at the northwest corner of the bay. Soon, it would be quite dark.

But she had Jacob to walk her home, and her mother couldn't be upset about that. She might be worrying right now, but she also might not even be thinking about Mary. Her mother seemed concerned about a lot of other things besides walking on the ship after dark.

"Tell me what happened," she said.

He told her about not being able to lift his feet to climb even a single step up to the deck, about something brushing his cheek. He described the thing he'd seen, its hugeness and its undefined shape, its lament about dying. He said the voice sounded like a woman.

When he stopped talking, she waited a moment before she spoke, to be sure she wasn't pushing her way past any important details. "Why would it moan about dying? If it's a ghost, it's already dead."

"So you believe me?"

"Why would you lie?"

"People lie all the time."

"Yes, I believe you."

"Maybe those were the last words she said, before she died?" Jacob suggested.

"It sounds scary."

"It was."

"Did anything else happen?"

He was quiet. She felt there was something else, but she was pretty sure he wasn't going to tell her. Maybe he'd cried and was ashamed of it.

"That's about all," he said.

"Should we go down and see if the ghost is there now?"

"It's locked."

"Then how did you get in?"

He didn't answer. The sky grew dark. It was cold, but there was hardly any wind, so it wasn't the kind of night that made you shiver so badly you'd do anything to get back indoors as soon as possible. She liked talking to him. After that first bit, he'd treated her like an adult. She'd been wrong to hate him. It wasn't his fault that Claire was sometimes cruel. She was already that way, it just wasn't noticeable before she started going out with Jacob. And now Claire had stopped loving him altogether. That must be very painful — knowing someone loved you and then changed her mind.

"I have a key," he said.

"Can we go down? And see?"

"What if something happens?"

"What could happen?"

"I told you I couldn't climb up the stairs. I couldn't move at all."

"But then, after a while, you could."

"You're very bold," he said.

"Mostly curious. I want to see a ghost."

"Okay, sure. Why not." He stepped away from the side. "Go ahead, I'll follow you."

They walked for several yards until they reached the

door leading to the arcade. Jacob took a key out of his pocket and inserted it into the lock. He shoved the door open, and they stepped inside. Their footsteps echoed as they descended.

"Why were you down here?" Mary whispered.

"I can't talk about that. So please don't ask."

When they reached the lower level, she stopped on the last step. "Now what?" she said.

He laughed softly. "I don't know. It was your idea."

They stood quietly for several minutes.

"Should we sit down?" Mary said.

"Okay."

They sat beside each other on the bottom step.

In a low voice, as if she knew she shouldn't disturb whatever was hovering in the shadows, Mary told him about her history class. She talked about Claire moving out. She thought that might make Jacob say something about Claire, but it didn't. She chattered on about the ship, how disappointed she was that she'd never been to a party on it.

"Shh," Jacob said.

"What is it?"

He put his hand on her shoulder and whispered again, "Shh." His voice was so soft, it sounded as if he was simply blowing air between his teeth. "Did you hear that?"

She held her breath. There was a sound like wind moving through something hollow. It had a slight echo, and at the end, it seemed to sigh. "It's just the wind."

"I don't think so. Stop talking for a minute."

He said it kindly, so she didn't feel as if he was telling her to shut up. She listened to the faint moaning, the distant sound of water splashing against the ship. It was dark, but her eyes had adjusted, allowing her to see Jacob's form beside her.

After a while, her feet began to itch as her skin warmed from the icy cold water she'd splashed in while she was walking along the shore. That, and the granules of sand that hadn't come off when she'd brushed at them before putting on her socks. She curled her toes, tightening her muscles in an attempt to stop the itching. She squirmed. Jacob patted her arm in a soothing way, and she uncurled her toes and took a deep breath. It would be so exciting to see a ghost.

It seemed like hours. Her mother must be frantic. Then, a shadowy form began to take shape in the far corner of the room. Every thought of the world that existed outside the belly of the ship slipped out of her mind.

Mary's fingers felt like ice. She shivered. Jacob's arm quaked, echoing the trembling of her own. She clenched her hands together. Her breath came in rapid bursts. It was terrifying and thrilling at the same time. She'd seen dead animals. She'd never seen a dead person, but she knew all about the sorrow people felt when someone they loved slipped out of their body and left behind cold flesh and vacant eyes. Was it really possible that some part of them still existed? The Priest and the Nuns said only in heaven, only if you were good, only if you were Catholic. Otherwise, your spirit was caught in burning flames. And there was no communication between the two worlds. Seeking the face or the voice of someone who had died was a sin. She'd forgotten about that when she urged Jacob to go into the ship to see whether the ghost might be there.

She felt as if she knew the spirit was always here, not always visible, but constantly listening, watching. Only occasionally speaking.

I'm dying.

Mary clutched Jacob's elbow. The voice wove around inside her head, something *Other*, but not…as if it was putting its feelings right into her brain like the doctor injected medicine through a needle into her arm.

All alone. I'm dying.

"She sounds so sad," Mary whispered. Tears filled her eyes. She blinked so they wouldn't blind her from the grayish figure filling the corner of the room.

"Shh," Jacob said.

They sat for a while. Every few minutes, the figure moaned, repeating the same words. It shifted slightly, but remained far away from them. Mary was glad about that. She might be terrified if it tried to come close.

Then, it started to dissolve. It slowly faded out of sight while the gentle moaning continued.

"Who is she?" Mary said.

"I don't know." Jacob stood up. "She's frightening, but

sad. It's confusing."

"Yes."

"I'll walk you back to the house, your mother must be worried about you. Thank you for staying here with me. I don't feel so crazy now."

"I never thought you were crazy."

They climbed the stairs and stepped out onto the deck. Jacob closed and locked the door. The air was sharp and cold. Although the sky was clear, the stars shone with a blurry light. The tide was low, and the water sounded like the gentle lapping of a lake rather than the fierce ocean.

The ship felt dark and empty behind them. "Maybe it's the ghost of the ship," Mary said.

"What do you mean?"

"She's dying — the ship. In some ways, she was already dead when they brought her here. They took out her engine and made her into nothing but a building stuck in the water. She doesn't get to float ever again."

"Maybe so," Jacob said.

She had the impression he didn't agree. Maybe he knew who the ghost was, maybe it had said something else to him when she wasn't there. She wished she could come back by herself, but there was no way to persuade him to give her the key. She'd have to be content with what she'd seen. After all, it was exciting to know she'd seen a ghost. If she got to talk to Claire again, this time she would have the best story.

Claire would see that Mary was special. She didn't need a diamond necklace to prove it.

Twenty-five

Jacob didn't know why he hadn't thought of it sooner. The solution to his brother's ridiculous attempt at blackmail was so simple it was laughable. Standing on the concrete ship, brooding over the situation and the trapped nature of his life, it had come to him. Perhaps the ghost had given him the suggestion. He laughed. Despite Mary's childlike reassurance, it seemed that he was slightly off his rocker after all.

He would simply write the letter himself. He'd send a retraction using the words he'd suggested to David. When David showed up to look for the envelope, and there was nothing, what could he do? He could send another note, which Henry would certainly view as a joke, or a simple annoyance, something from a madman who wanted to frighten him. If Jacob made the retraction sound mildly deranged, all the better.

At first, David would be angry that Henry was ignoring

him, but once he had a day or two to think it over, he'd see that he'd been outwitted. He'd understand that Henry would never be afraid of a silly, anonymous note. Writing a second note would also take care of the need to fabricate a story for Henry about someone loitering by the Bakery, waiting for an envelope of cash. He composed the letter with a few words, scribbled quickly. *I thought I saw you somewhere you shouldn't have been, but I was wrong. I'm not gonna ask for money, so you're off the hook.*

It seemed believable. It was short, like the first note, and proved the person writing it was fishing and didn't have concrete information. Henry would accept it, glad to push the annoyance out of his mind. He folded the paper twice. An envelope wasn't necessary. A loose note would add to the impression that it was a childish prank.

After he'd finished unloading that night's shipment, he drove home and walked the mile and a half up the hill and along Seacliff to the King house. He made his way along the edge of their driveway, cautious, even though the house was completely dark. He glanced up at the third floor, feeling as if he'd seen Claire's face at the window. But of course he hadn't, she was gone.

It irked him that whenever he found a few minutes during which his mind could wander, as he waited in the dark for the motorboat, or stood in line at the bank, or waited outside an office for a meeting to conclude, his thoughts rushed to Claire, not Sarah. Why couldn't he have an obsessive desire for a girl who obviously adored him, who looked at him with such love and longing? He knew Sarah felt uncertain, wondering why he'd said nothing about marriage. She'd make a beautiful, charming wife, and yet his body, his soul, ached for Claire.

He moved onto the grass, walking close to the trees that divided the King property from the farmland next door. The lack of light didn't mean no one was awake, walking around sleepless, making a cup of tea, or pouring a shot of scotch, looking out one of the many windows. When he reached the backyard, he took off his shoes. He walked through wet weeds and onto the stone pathway. He crept up the stairs to the veranda and moved along the side of the house to the exterior study door. He squatted, shoved the folded letter through the surprisingly wide gap below the door and sat down for a moment, his back against the wall. A feeling of relief came over him, although it was probably premature. He stood and forced himself to walk just as soundlessly down the stairs and back to where he'd left his shoes and socks.

When he reached the street, he ran down Seacliff Drive and all the way back to the center of town. He rounded the corner, headed toward his rooming house. As he drew closer, he saw David on the front porch. He was sprawled in a reclining wooden chair as if he lived there. Jacob's stomach clenched. He worked half the night at hard, physical labor that was more intense than David could begin to imagine. Then, he worked all day, running errands, kowtowing to Henry's associates. He stopped at the foot of the steps.

"The money didn't show up," David said. He shoved himself out of the chair and walked down the steps.

Jacob wanted to ask what money, but he knew. And David would know that he knew. "I told you he didn't take it seriously."

"I find that very difficult to believe."

"Believe what you want. You know, I was thinking…"

"Don't change the subject." David slung his arm around Jacob's shoulders. "Let's go for a walk."

"It's the middle of the night."

"That never stops you from whatever else you're up to."

Jacob's eyes felt as if sand had been kicked into them. He pressed his fingers against his closed eyelids, afraid to rub them and irritate them further.

"What did you say to him to make him not leave the money I asked for?"

"I didn't say anything. I'm not getting involved."

"You're already involved. In fact, I think you know a lot more than you're saying. You're his Man Friday. That guy tells you everything."

"That's not true."

"Almost everything."

"Still not true," Jacob said.

"Let's get some beer. I know where…"

"I know you do," Jacob said. "I don't want beer. I'm tired, and I need to sleep."

David grabbed Jacob's arm and turned him so they were facing each other. A streetlight behind David shone in Jacob's face. He squinted. For some reason, the light made him yawn.

"Yeah, yeah, you're tired. But listen to me. This is our chance to get ahead. Why are you so set on protecting him? Even his wife knows something's up. So I know you do too. We could get ourselves set for life."

"That's not how I want to do it. Besides, I told you — it won't work. You need to trust me on this. He will not pay someone week in and week out, even if he's worried you might have information he doesn't want you to have. He'd find a way to bring you down."

"Fine. I'll figure it out myself." David let go of Jacob's arm and started walking.

"Wait. I have an idea." Jacob ran after him. "I was thinking…I should rent a house. We can live together. And maybe we could figure out a way to go into business. Start a delivery or messenger service, or something. The Archer Brothers."

David laughed. "You're kidding."

"I'm not. I have a lot saved. I can afford a cottage. We could work out of there."

"Who's paying money for a delivery service? Businesses are closing, not looking for ways to burn money doing something they can get one of their clerks to do."

"I don't know, I just got the idea. I haven't thought it all through. I just think we need to get out from under Henry King." His voice trembled. Would Henry let him out? Or would he decide Jacob knew too much? "Maybe we should move away from here. Start over. There are more opportunities in San Francisco. Or even Los Angeles."

"I dunno," David said. "Why all of a sudden?"

"I don't want to work for one guy all my life. I don't want to just be his errand boy. And we've always stuck by each other."

"What about your girlfriend?" David said.

"Tell me what you think about my idea, *I'll* worry about her."

"Maybe. I've always lived here. I like the beach."

"There are better beaches in Los Angeles. And it's warmer."

"And Hollywood," David laughed. "Is that what you're thinking? All those rich movie stars need a messenger service?"

"See, you're thinking already."

David turned his head slightly. He spit on the ground. "Don't talk down to me, if we're going to be partners."

"That came out wrong. It's not how I meant it. I'm tired. Let me get some sleep, and we'll have breakfast together and talk."

"Okay. Sure." David slapped Jacob's back. "I'll see ya. Eight-thirty?"

"My treat," Jacob said.

"Everything is."

"Not for long. We need a fresh start."

They turned toward their respective boarding houses. Jacob felt like running. He didn't know where the idea had come from, and he wasn't convinced it would work, but they had to try. It had to be better than this. Unfamiliar scenery would wipe Claire out of his heart once and for all. This entire town was haunted — by his dead parents, by the thing lurking in the ship, and by the specter of Henry King over every part of his life. Most of all, by Claire. Hopefully, Henry didn't have tentacles that reached to Los Angeles. But even if he did, he'd have no way of knowing that's where Jacob had gone.

He jogged up the steps and went into the house and took the stairs up to his room two at a time. He felt as if he'd shed a water-soaked wool coat.

Over pancakes and an entire pot of coffee the next morning, they talked about Los Angeles. Jacob had found a map of California on the bookcase in the parlor of his rooming house. He pushed their plates close to the table edge and spread the map out between them. They looked at the multiple thick black lines indicating the major streets of

Los Angeles and the surrounding area. Aptos was an insignificant dot in comparison. They drank coffee and tried to figure out how they would find customers. David's face developed a reddish cast when Jacob told him there was enough money in his savings account to rent a small apartment and keep themselves fed for at least six months while they figured things out.

After breakfast, Jacob headed back toward home. His feet felt strong, and his steps were firm on the pavement, his shoulders no longer locked tight as they had been for the past six months, maybe longer. Their plan would work. It had to work. They'd figure it out. They were young and strong, and David could be charming and persuasive when he wanted. So what if the business outlook was dismal. It wouldn't stay that way forever. Prohibition wouldn't last forever, and his heart wouldn't always ache for Claire. He walked by the pharmacy, looking in the window at a display of perfumed lotions. As he rounded the corner, he stayed close to the building, then stopped suddenly as he nearly crashed into the woman turning right. Claire.

"Hello, Jacob."

She said it as easily as if she'd planned to meet up with him, as if they'd had lunch together just a few days earlier, as if nothing was wrong between them. He stared at her. She'd cut her hair, and it swung around her face like a curtain blowing in the breeze. She pushed it away from her eyes. "Like it?" She tipped her head and smiled.

"It looks nice," he said.

"Thank you. How have you been? Let's walk together."

"I need to get to work," he said.

She pouted. "Oh, come on. Henry won't mind if you're a few minutes late."

It must be some sort of a sign, running into her like this. Her suggestion proved that Henry had enormous reach. His fingers touched every facet of Jacob's life. The man owned him completely.

Claire took his arm. "We haven't talked in ages. What's new with you?" She started walking in the direction he'd come. He walked beside her, wanting to slip his arm away from her hand. At the same time, he longed to pull her closer, press their bodies together, smell her skin, bury his fingers in her short, seductive hair.

"Don't go all silent on me." She squeezed his arm. Her grip was so tight he felt as if he'd been caught in the tentacles of a squid.

"Tell me what you've been doing, who you've been seeing," she said.

"Mostly working."

"Not all the time." She laughed and looked up at him. She winked.

"Actually, yes."

"I'll have to speak to Henry about that."

"It's not necessary."

"I heard you have a new girl," she said.

"Where did you hear that?"

"It's a small town, Jacob. Everyone knows everything."

"I don't think so."

"Don't be so sure about that."

Now he was glad of her death-like grip. His arm would tremble if she didn't have such a hold on it. She spoke as if she had a closer connection to Henry than Jacob had realized, suggesting she could influence his decisions. She implied it was small-town gossip that alerted her to his relationship with Sarah, but was that just a decoy to cloak the knowledge she had through Henry? Surely Henry hadn't let Claire in on their side business, had he? Yet, Henry had suggested there were others besides Jacob receiving liquor deliveries. Was it possible boats were coming in every night of the week? Maybe they came several times a night and liquor was stored in other hidden lockers below the deck of the ship. Claire certainly wouldn't be unloading booze and storing it, but she might be doing something else for him.

"Why are you so quiet?" she said.

"I don't have anything to say to you."

"Oh, that's not very nice. Haven't you forgiven me for breaking up with you?"

"That's not how it was." Why did he bother? It didn't matter. She'd spread whatever stories she wanted, she believed whatever truth she invented inside her inscrutable mind. It was frustrating to be so drawn to her and at the same time, see her for what she was — no good for him. He was enticed by what he wanted her to be, not by the woman she truly was. He yanked his arm out of her grip, which had the effect of shoving her away from his side.

"That's rude," she said.

Was she subtly threatening him, telling him not to be so sure that everyone didn't know what he was up to? But if he asked about it, he'd give himself away. And if she already knew and were indeed delivering a sugar-coated threat, he would make himself appear weak. Still, he needed to know what she was talking about. "Why do you think everyone knows everything about other people?"

She laughed.

"Why are you laughing?"

She laughed harder. She turned to face him. She tilted her chin up so her hair slid back from her temples. She was so beautiful. He longed to kiss her. He took a step back. His heel hit the edge of the sidewalk, and he wobbled.

Claire giggled.

"Stop laughing."

"You're just too funny."

"Why did you say that?"

"Because it's true, dummy."

He needed to stop talking right now. He extended his hand and took hers. He shook it once and let go. "I need to be on my way. Have a pleasant morning."

"Aren't you going to say it was nice seeing me?" She

smiled, pursing her lips slightly.

"If I'm anything, I'm an honest man." He turned.

"I don't think that's the case at all. Not at *all*."

He walked away. It sounded again like a sweetly-delivered threat, but it was impossible to know what she intended. It was impossible to know whether she planned to do something to hurt him. Still, she couldn't damage him without hurting Henry, so the odds were in his favor. She only wanted to upset him. It seemed to be her greatest pleasure.

When Jacob arrived at the King home, William Sharp's car was in the driveway. This was his punishment for wasting time listening to Claire. Maybe that had been her plan — ensure he was late to work, insert a small needle of mistrust in Henry's mind. He sat on the veranda. The sky was clear, a painfully bright blue, filled with bitterly cold air. He should have worn gloves. Maybe by the start of the new year, he'd be living in Los Angeles and never have to wear gloves again. He'd sit on his own porch looking at palm trees. Of course, there were palm trees here, but not as many, and they looked out of place among the Monterey Pines and Cypress and Redwoods.

It was ten o'clock when the office door opened, and William stepped onto the veranda. He nodded at Jacob and hurried down the steps. What had they been talking about? Jacob wasn't sure what the two of them did together.

Looking at the physical appearance of the two men — William with his pale skin and patrician nose, Henry with his broad shoulders and muscular neck — it was easy to imagine Henry was a thug, getting his hands dirty while William kept his distance. Maybe for all his bravado, Henry was as trapped and nervous as Jacob.

Jacob stood up and went to the office door.

Henry didn't look up, but seemed to know Jacob was there. "Where were you?"

"I ran into Claire. Sorry I'm late."

Henry picked up the note Jacob had shoved under the door. "Wait 'til you read this. It's funny."

"What's that?" Jacob closed the door. He stood in front of it, eager to leave the minute he could, anxious to free his thoughts so he could plan his new life.

"That idiot who tried to extort money from me changed his mind."

"What?"

"It sounds like a kid. Playing games, just as I thought. It says I wasn't *observed after all* and I'm *off the hook.* Can you believe it?" He laughed. "Off the hook. As if I was on any hook to begin with."

Jacob laughed. The sound rattled around the room.

Henry glared at him. "We should take it as a warning."

"How's that?"

"I think someone did see something, they just aren't sure what it meant. I think he…or she…you never know…

lost his nerve, or decided more proof was needed. But something prompted this. Something gave the impression there was meat for blackmail. I've decided I don't want you driving your car down to the beach anymore. The car attracts curiosity, sitting there so late at night. It's easier to keep yourself hidden if you walk."

Jacob felt tired, thinking of climbing the hill after all the trips up and down the unstable ladder into the rocking boat, followed by traipsing up and down the stairs with armloads of bottles. Assuming that thing living down below allowed him to climb the stairs at all. Maybe the next time, he'd be trapped below forever, killed by something inhuman.

Henry pointed to the corner of the desk. "There are the cash deposits for both banks. And you need to deliver that envelope to William."

"He was just here. Why didn't you…"

"Don't question what I ask you to do, Jacob. Deliver the envelope to William. It needs to be there by noon."

Jacob nodded. Maybe he could find a way to extricate himself from Henry by Christmas. He had a constant headache. His back was twisted into knots. He lived under a steady spray of seawater soaking into his skin. Even if he earned half the pay, a quarter of the pay, somewhere else, there was enough saved to get on his feet. He was done with Henry and done with Claire. The only way to get her out of his head was to move far away.

He took the cash and the envelope.

"Oh, and that." Henry pointed to a small box in the corner. To Sam McIntyre."

"Yes, sir."

"Hurry up. The day's slipping away."

Jacob picked up the box and left without saying goodbye. He needed to start planning the words for his final good-bye. He needed to consider whether it might be best to simply send a letter, disappear at night and never speak to Henry again. He would gladly forfeit his final paycheck.

Twenty-six

Lorene sat in the parlor. The door was closed and a single birch log burned in the fireplace. On the table beside her was a white china cup painted with yellow pansies. Her tea steamed, not yet ready to touch her tongue. Beside the cup was the diamond teardrop. The chain pooled next to the stone like spilled tea. At first, she'd been inclined to think Claire had stolen it, because it was difficult to imagine Claire knowing a man who could afford something like this. The diamond was easily a carat and a half. Then, she'd clung to her assumption of theft because she didn't want to think about her young sister being involved with an older, financially secure man. And maybe, simply because she felt her sister was cunning, and stealing completed that picture.

Now, she was certain she'd had it wrong. The diamond was a gift from Henry. But then, why had Claire passed it on to Mary? Was she expecting a larger diamond, one for her ring finger?

Lorene put her hand to her throat. It felt as if the airway was closing up, wrapped with the silver chain, suddenly yanked tight. She coughed and leaned forward, as if pressing her chest against her legs would force air out of her lungs, bursting through the tight space. She felt worse. She stood up and walked to the window, straining to take in small gulps of air. After a few minutes of filling her lungs until she thought they'd burst, she returned to her chair. She scooped up the necklace, dropped it into her pocket, and sat down. The steam had evaporated from the surface of the tea, but she wasn't sure her throat would allow even a slender thread of liquid to make its way through.

She was over-reacting. Of course, Henry wouldn't divorce her to marry Claire. He loved her, despite what he'd done. There must be another explanation for the necklace, but she had to get herself under control before she confronted him. Claire had been gone for more than a week now, and it had been nearly two weeks since she'd overheard them in the storage room. Henry strutted through the house as if life was a glorious party. She couldn't allow that to continue.

The tea was cool and too sweet. She drank it anyway, faster than she should have. Her stomach ached as a result. She went up to their bedroom, used the toilet, washed her hands and face, and applied rose-colored lipstick. She brushed her hair. There was no need to pinch her cheeks to bring a glow of blood to the surface. Two red spots burned on either cheekbone.

When she entered his office, Henry wasn't at his desk. It startled her, not seeing him in his usual spot, thinking for half a second the room was empty. He was sitting in one of the armchairs facing the desk, reading a newspaper.

"I'd like to talk to you," she said.

He patted the arm of the chair beside him. He folded the newspaper as if he planned to put it aside, but continued reading while she seated herself. This was better. They were equals without the imposing desk between them. She waited for him to put down the newspaper.

After several minutes, he turned the folded paper over. Without looking at her, he said, "I have to go downtown in about half an hour, so if you want to talk, don't be pussyfooting around."

"Will you put down the paper, please."

"You haven't said anything. I'm making the most of my time." He glanced at her and gave her a charming, slightly mocking smile.

She stood up. She reached into her pocket and dropped the necklace onto his leg. It slid to the floor and lay there glittering like a fallen star.

"What's that?" He glanced down. He leaned forward and slapped the folded newspaper on the desk. He hadn't reached far enough, and it fell to the floor. He bent down and picked up the chain. The diamond spun. "Oh. Where did you find it?"

"I didn't find it anywhere. Claire had it. She'd been hiding it under her mattress. She wore it once — to the grand opening last year. Didn't you notice?"

"I…"

"Yes. You bought it for her."

He closed his fingers over the diamond and looked at her. His eyes were unreadable. "Of course not."

"You're having an affair with her."

He put his other hand on her arm. "Lorene. How could you even think…"

"I heard you."

"You heard…what? Is one of my competitors slandering me?"

She stood up. She put her hands on her hips and glared at him. She wasn't sure whether he was playing at being stupid or if he truly didn't understand. It didn't even cross his mind that he could make love to another woman — not just any other woman, his sister-in-law — in his own house, directly above the bedroom he shared with his wife, and they might be overheard. "You really don't understand?"

He shook his head. He'd adopted the expression of a confused little boy. She hated it when he did that, making her the harsh mother to his playful child. She wanted to smack him, but that would make her feel he'd won before she even knew what he might say. "I heard you and Claire having sex in the storage room, you idiot!"

The blood drained out of his face, and the faux-innocent expression slipped off as if his head had been doused in water. Quickly, he recovered his composure and smiled. "You must have been dreaming."

"I wasn't dreaming. I was in the room."

"What?"

"I hid in the back of the room. I heard you and Claire come in. Your voices were quite distinct."

"That's disgusting. How pathetic."

"What is?"

"Hiding and participating in something like that. It's sordid."

"I'm sordid?!" she was screaming. Where was the Inner Light? Where was her sense of calm, her determination to maintain her pride?

"Yes, don't you think so?"

"I think you're a nasty beast. It makes me sick what you did, and that you bought her such expensive jewelry. Your gift made her feel superior, as if you belong to her!"

He stood up. He dropped the necklace on the desk and reached for her hand. She twisted out of his reach. "Now that I've gotten over the shock of what you did, let me explain," he said. "It was only once. I'm not in love with her, if that's what you think." He stepped closer and took her wrist, curving his fingers gently around it, as if he knew she'd yank her hand out of his grasp. "I bought that diamond for you, Lorene. Claire took it out of my desk drawer. I didn't know where it had gone. When you said, she was stealing…"

"Don't," she said. Despite herself, she glanced at the necklace. It was so beautiful, but it looked tawdry lying there, something that no woman would want now. Part of her longed to believe he'd bought it for her. The other part of her was ashamed for wanting it, for wanting to think he'd planned to surprise her with such a lavish, romantic gift. "Don't lie to me. Don't treat me like I'm stupid and so easy to manipulate."

"I wouldn't lie to you."

He touched her cheek, drawing his finger across the bone. She imagined the red spot was growing brighter, letting him know he was having an effect on her. She turned her head.

"Listen," he said. "I'm telling the truth. She…she tempted me. You remember how you were when you were younger. So alluring, your wiles impossible to resist. For any man." He laughed nervously. "And…you remember how you drew me in. How I couldn't help myself. But the difference was, I fell in love with you. And I still love you." He let go of her wrist, and put his arms loosely around her waist, pulling her to him.

She wanted to shove him away, but his arms were so warm and strong. She'd missed them for weeks, months. A year? She needed him. She hated him, and she needed him. The last time he'd held a woman it was her sister. He'd run his fingers across Claire's skin, pressed his face into her hair, removed her clothes and looked at her young, firm, flawless body… She pulled away from him. "Don't touch me."

"You liked it."

"I liked it when you were mine, now…"

Tears filled his eyes. They looked ready to spill over, but they remained pooled around his lower eyelids. "I'm telling you the truth. Please believe me. I'm weak. You need to forgive me. I was so relieved when you told me she wouldn't be living with us anymore."

"You wrote letters to her!"

"I didn't."

She wavered. There was no proof the letters were from him, or that Claire hadn't stolen the necklace after all. But she'd heard them. She didn't need proof of that, and hearing them, knowing what they'd done, knowing he wanted someone besides her…"I read some of the letters."

His eyes were dry now. "I made a terrible mistake. The worst mistake of my life. But you have to believe me. It was only once. It was…"

"I needed you! I loved you!" she shouted. "I gave my whole self to you. And you…" She gasped, trying to breathe, "you…" She started crying. She turned so he wouldn't see her contorted face. Then, she whirled back and hammered her fists against his chest. She felt like a woman in a film, playing a part, going through the motions of betrayal and rage and wanting to hurt him but she could never hurt him the way he'd hurt her. She could punch his face, bloody his nose, knock out a tooth. But she couldn't shred his heart. It didn't matter where the necklace came from or if the letters were his. He'd taken off his clothes, and held Claire, and stroked her skin and gushed on and on and *on* about her exquisite body. Had he forgotten the things he'd said? Because she'd heard every word, and she remembered each one. They burned in her head like hot spears.

He picked up the necklace and took a step toward her. He opened the clasp and held out the two ends. "I want you to have it. I bought it for you, and she should never have…"

She backed away. "I don't want it."

"Please."

"Get it away from me."

He placed it on the desk. "I want to fix this. How can I fix it?"

"You're too late. The way to fix it was by loving me, only me."

"I do."

"No, you love *her*."

"Please, Lorene. Let me hold you." He moved toward her, his eyes filling up again with tears.

She shoved him. He stumbled back and rammed his thigh against the corner of the desk. He winced.

"You keep forgetting. I *heard* you!" she screamed. "I heard all the wanting, craving, needing things you said to her. Every single word!" She was sobbing. "I heard every sound and all your disgusting groans and her…" She could hardly breathe she was crying so hard. This wasn't how she'd wanted it to go, but the pain was unbearable. Words flew out of her mouth before she even knew what she was thinking. And he just stood there, looking sad, or frustrated, or whatever it was. Not hurting at all. She was ashamed of the hurt. She felt exposed, as if she were standing naked in front of a ballroom full of people, all staring at her, looking at every imperfect part of her body, frowning with pity and disgust.

"Are you divorcing me?" he said.

He looked more afraid than hurt. Even with that. There was no way to hurt him, he was a block of soulless concrete. He was probably thinking about money, or the house. Or, he was thinking about how to get her out of the house so he could move Claire in as his wife. She wiped her face, spreading tears and mucous to the sides of her cheeks. She must look hideous — red and swollen, her skin slippery and completely undesirable. When she spoke, her voice was clogged and muddy. "I haven't decided. But it will be *my* decision."

"Tell me how I can make it up to you. Please."

"You can't *make it up*, Henry. You betrayed me."

"She…she touched me. She got me into a state where I

couldn't stop. It was like a drug was injected into me. I couldn't think. It doesn't mean I don't love you."

"I *heard* you, Henry! Don't tell me how it was, what she did, when I heard every word."

She grabbed the necklace and walked out of the room. She left the door open behind her. She ran up the stairs and slammed her bedroom door, regretting it the minute it was closed. No sounds escaped from his study, Mary wouldn't have heard the shouting, but she might have heard this. She locked the door and threw herself across the bed. She tossed the necklace on the floor. It glowed brightly against the dark wood.

She pulled one of the pillows toward her and hugged it, curling her body around it. No matter how she burrowed into the quilt, her hands and legs were icy cold. She should get under the covers, but she wasn't finished. She needed to see Claire. She couldn't make it go away, couldn't make Henry love her, but she could certainly punish her sister. Claire would never again come close enough to Henry to touch him. Every single person they knew would learn that Claire was damaged goods. The boarding house wanted respectable women. Not tramps. Claire would be forced out. She'd have to go back to San Francisco, try to find a friend there who might take her in. No man would want her now. At least no decent man.

Twenty-seven

Meeting Claire onboard the concrete ship seemed fitting. Lorene had worried Claire wouldn't agree to the location, that she'd complain it was too far to walk, or too cold, or too dark. She'd ask why they were meeting at sunset. The wind would tear through their clothing like a shark's teeth.

But Lorene knew a way to overcome all of Claire's objections. *I have something for you. From Henry*, she'd said.

Claire had sounded nervous after that. *Can't you bring it to me here?*

Lorene was not going to sit in the parlor with other boarders and have a conversation with Claire. She needed absolute privacy, no chance of anyone overhearing a single word. The ship was perfect for that. The gulls were the only audience. Even someone taking a late afternoon stroll on the footpath wouldn't be able to hear what Lorene had to say. The waves drowned out everything.

She was mildly surprised that Claire hadn't demanded to know what Lorene had from Henry. She hadn't even asked. It made Lorene wonder whether her sister was expecting something from him. A letter? Another piece of jewelry? Money? It didn't matter. She wrapped her long wool cape tightly around her body. It was like wearing a blanket, much warmer than a coat. She wore a cashmere scarf and beret and gloves — a matching set of dark green.

The decorative lights on the ship had been turned off for months. The buildings were shuttered. The gulls behaved as if they owned the place now, sitting along the sides and on top of the buildings. They dropped their soft, white excrement for people to slip on. She stepped carefully as she made her way down the side toward the bow. Claire was nowhere in sight.

It was what she'd planned for — she'd arrived twenty minutes before the scheduled time to make sure that was the case. She would keep control of the conversation from start to finish. No breaking down in thick, choking tears as she had with Henry. Of course, that was completely different. He was her husband. She loved him with every cell in her body, even while she despised her weak, clinging heart. Claire was another story. Lorene had come to hate her younger sister. It was impossible to believe they came from the same family.

After standing at the bow for several minutes, gazing at the deserted footpath and watching the waves wash onto the beach, she saw Claire walking toward the pier. Lorene tucked her hands inside her cape and watched Claire's approach. She wore delicate shoes and a short dress. Her coat was very stylish but covered only her hips, leaving her legs exposed to the wind. One of her completely useless silk scarves was draped around her neck. Her head was bare, and her hair fluttered elegantly in the wind. Once she was out beside the deep water, she'd freeze. It was laughable, but it also meant Lorene had to get quickly to the point of their conversation. She would return the necklace and disabuse Claire of any notion that she had a future with Henry. Lorene was the one who possessed the marriage license and the wedding ring. She was the one who had given birth to Henry's daughter. Never again would Claire be allowed to mock her or treat her as if she were stupid. Lorene would wipe that superior expression off her sister's face like she'd wiped milk off her lips when she was a baby.

Claire's ballet slipper shoes brushed the pier. She reached the entrance to the ship and looked directly at Lorene to be sure her sister was watching. She laughed. As she stepped onto the boat, she flung her arms out and twirled around. There was something seriously wrong with her. Lorene wasn't sure why she hadn't noticed it a long time ago. Maybe even when Claire was a child who laughed, then suddenly bit her sister's lip hard enough to draw blood, licking her own lips and giggling as if she'd enjoyed the taste of human flesh.

When Claire reached Lorene's side, she lifted her face to the sky and shook her head to brush the hair off her face. The minute she lowered her chin, her hair blew across her eyes. "So what's all this about? So much drama. So much mystery."

"I thought you liked it out here," Lorene said. "A man I know said he sees Jacob out here all the time in the middle of the night. Is this where you meet him? Giving yourself to any man who will have you?"

"I never slept with Jacob. Besides, we're done. I told you that ages ago. Jacob's out here at night doing Henry's dirty work — collecting his liquor deliveries."

Lorene swallowed.

"Oh, I guess you didn't know."

"I…"

"Poor thing — in the dark about so many pieces of your life."

She wasn't going to listen to Claire's raving. She'd think about that later. "I have something for you."

"So you said."

"Can you turn around? I'll put it on."

"What?"

Lorene held up the chain. The diamond twisted and danced in the wind.

"Oh, I don't want it. I gave it to Mary, didn't she tell you?"

"Yes. But it's yours. He bought it for you."

Claire stared at her. She smiled uncertainly. "I don't…"

"Turn around, and I'll put this on."

Slowly, a skittish look in her eyes, Claire turned halfway. Lorene pulled the silk scarf out of the way and hooked the chain around Claire's neck. She re-wound the scarf around Claire's throat. She took the girl's shoulders and moved them gently until Claire turned to face her. "You had sex with my husband."

Claire pushed her lips into a pout. "You're confused."

"Don't play innocent. I heard you. I was in the storage room when you and Henry came in."

"Ooh, that's nasty."

"You can have the diamond, but Henry belongs to me. You'll never see him again."

"You can't do anything to stop it." Claire smiled, pretending a look of pity.

"I'm telling your housemates and Mrs. Harmon about you. I'm telling all my friends and…"

"Won't *you* be the laughing stock."

Claire was right. The humiliation would be tremendous, but it was worth it. The hurt was so much worse than the shame, and no matter how many people knew, the hurt couldn't cut any deeper. She'd been split in two, her insides bleeding out of her every time she took a breath. "You'll need to move back to San Francisco."

"It's nineteen-thirty-one. People don't care about that."

"Maybe some people don't care, but most do."

"You don't own him. You can't keep him away from me."

"He made one mistake. I've forgiven him."

"Is that what he told you? A single mistake? You are so much stupider than I thought." Claire shrieked with laughter.

Lorene's eyes filled with tears. It was the wind, the air was biting cold.

"Don't cry. It's just that it's my turn now."

"He doesn't want you. He wants his family and his daughter and the life we've created. He wants me."

"You are so wrong." Claire tugged the sides of her coat, as if that would warm her. She shivered, then stiffened her shoulders, trying to keep control of her body. "He promised to love you as long as you were beautiful. Don't you remember? But you're not beautiful. You're getting a little wrinkle here and a little crease there. Everything is sagging. *Everything*." She giggled. "Maybe you don't see it in your mirror, but he sees it. I see it." Claire laughed.

Lorene slapped Claire's face. The force was so hard, Claire was knocked sideways. She grabbed the edge of the ship. The skin of Claire's face had felt cold and hard. It hurt Lorene's fingers possibly more than it burned Claire's cheek.

"You can't hurt me. You can slap me all night, and it won't make you young again. It won't make me old. You can throw me over the side of the ship to the sea gods. Then I'll never get old like you. I'll be a luscious corpse." She smiled, her lips as white as her skin.

They were empty words. Claire was too arrogant to want to die. She thought she'd escape the normal process of aging. She believed she would always be desirable. It was impossible for the young to imagine their flesh decaying. "Shark food is more like it."

"I might as well die young and beautiful. He'll always want someone new. Didn't you ever wonder about his first wife, just slipping over the cliff, as if that happens every day? She *threw* herself off the cliff. All his women need to die, before they're eaten up by age." She giggled.

Lorene gave her a thin smile. None of that mattered. "You should have listened to me. You should have learned what our parents taught us about the beauty that's inside. Men want a woman who makes a beautiful life for them, not just a pretty face. But that's beside the point. I work in the garden every day. I care for my roses single-handedly." Lorene moved to the side

"What does that have to do with anything? Have you gone mad? You want to talk about gardening?"

Lorene stroked the two ends of the scarf hanging down Claire's back. "No. I haven't gone mad. Sometimes the stems of roses are tough. If the shears haven't been oiled, or the blades are dull, it takes a lot of strength to make them work. I have extraordinarily strong hands." She gripped the ends of the scarf and pulled.

Claire let out a single cry, then the sound turned to a rough, inhuman screech. She thrashed her hands at her throat. She twisted her body this way and that. She tried to kick, but kicking backwards was ineffective, and where her heels did manage to make contact, Lorene's legs were protected by her long, thick cape. Lorene continued tightening the scarf. The girl was gasping, flapping her arms as if somehow that would cause oxygen to flow into her lungs. After a moment, she collapsed on the deck. Her skin had turned a purplish color, a color that was beautiful when it splashed across the sky after the sun disappeared, but monstrous on Claire's face.

Lorene leaned against the railing, waiting for her heartbeat to slow. Her shoulders and back ached. This was the worst thing a person could do, far worse than what Henry had done to her. But it was for Claire's own good. And for Mary's. And really, also for Henry. He needed his family and their well-established life. Claire would destroy all of that, and in the end, Henry would regret it. Because despite Claire's confidence, she wouldn't always be young. And then Henry would need to find someone else. Even Claire knew that, his first wife knew that. It would never end. But Lorene had something more powerful than youthful beauty. She had a strong will. She was the mother of his child. She was bound to him forever. The Inner Light had deserted her so long ago. She didn't have to listen to know it would have guided her in another direction than this, but once the Light was gone, she was on her own, and this was the most practical solution.

Lifting Claire's body up and over the side of the ship would require tremendous effort, but she had plenty of time. It was nearly dark now. In the winter, the beach and the footpath were deserted. She undid the brooch on the front of her cape. She took the pin and dragged a scratch across Claire's cheek. She made another, carving deep so plenty of blood began to seep out, a scent for the sharks. She scooped Claire into her arms like she was lifting a child. She moved a few steps to her right where the side of the ship had a cutout for rope. She bent her head over her sister's unconscious body. A faint whisper of breath touched her lips. She kissed the soft, slack lips, and heaved her over the side. The splash was almost indistinguishable from the sound of waves hitting concrete. She leaned against the side and breathed deeply, trying to ease the terror that overtook her now that she'd done it.

Although the deck was wet from waves splashing across it, she sat down. Her cape would keep her dry for a few minutes. She needed to be quiet. Even though the Inner Light had abandoned her forever, she needed to take a moment for her raging thoughts to subside. She closed her eyes and leaned her head against the side of the ship. As the waves beat at the concrete, she heard unfamiliar sounds. She pulled her cape tightly around her, willing the echoing thuds to be something else — not Claire's unconscious body tossed against concrete. Was she dead yet?

She shivered. Something brushed against her cheek. She touched her face but nothing was there. The sounds weren't thuds after all, more like a strong wind echoing through the empty spaces below the deck, designed for storing oil, never used.

I don't want to die alone.

She opened her eyes. Was that a thought entering her mind from out of nowhere, or had she heard a voice? She stood up. She squinted, as if it would help her peer through the darkness. Had someone been watching? Did they know what she'd done? She whimpered softly.

I'm dying. Both of us have been abandoned, but we don't have to die alone.

She began trembling uncontrollably.

I don't want to die all alone. Come with me.

Lorene cried out. "Who's there? Why are you doing this?"

The sound seemed more like the wind now. Was she losing her mind? She wasn't sure if her thoughts had turned against her or someone was speaking. She started to walk toward the rear of the boat. It was time to go home, she needed warm tea and a fire. Mary would take her thoughts off of this. She took a few more steps and felt she couldn't continue. She looked behind her.

A figure with long silvery hair, distinct even in the

darkness, stood near the bow. The wind whipped her hair out to the side, but her face wasn't visible.

"Who are you? What do you want?" Lorene shouted.

The figured remained motionless. It didn't speak. Had she been crying about death, or was that all inside Lorene's mind and this woman was watching her fall to pieces? She started walking slowly toward the bow. A moment later, the woman disappeared. Lorene shivered, she turned and ran to the stern, taking small steps, careful not to slip on the wet concrete. When her feet touched the wooden pier, she ran as fast as her cape would allow. She was crying. Maybe it would be better to die. She'd committed the worst crime of all. She could never take it back. The Inner Light was gone, and her husband didn't love her, even if she'd managed to remove Claire from their lives.

It was nearly eight o'clock when she arrived home. The house blazed with light. It looked as if the lamps burned in every single room on the first and second floors. The only dark windows were those on the third floor. Before she'd left, she'd turned on the bedside lamp in her own room. She'd wrapped a little string of red beads on the doorknob that let Mary and George and Annie know she had a migraine headache and was trying to rest. It wasn't impossible that one of them had knocked to see how she was doing, but it had never happened before, so she felt fairly certain her absence hadn't been noticed. The trick now was getting into the house and up to her room without being seen. She hadn't expected a house pulsing with light, and presumably, activity.

It might be best to walk around to the back edge of the yard, linger among the trees, freezing, but hidden, until Mary went to sleep and Annie left for the night. But then she risked Henry coming into their room and finding she wasn't there after all. She hadn't thought this part through as well as she should have. She was so used to Henry not being home, and there was his car, gleaming in the driveway — polished green and black paint as seductive as a woman in green silk and black lace lingerie.

Murdering Claire hadn't been a definite plan in her mind, but the thought had been there when she arranged the meeting, a whisper below the surface, ready to be drawn out. The things Claire had said…tears filled her eyes as she remembered the cruel words. Silencing the girl forever was the only way Lorene could go on living. And maybe she had planned every detail after all, or why leave her light on and the indication of a migraine on her doorknob?

Claire's tongue had been cruel and disrespectful from the first day she came to live with them. Where was her appreciation toward her older sister for taking her in? She could have ended up in an orphanage! Well, it didn't matter now, but Lorene still seethed over the lack of appreciation. And the things Claire had done with Henry! It was appalling. He wasn't free of blame, not at all. He was more to blame, but if Claire had behaved herself, none of it would have happened. Lorene had won. Claire wouldn't feed disgusting stories to Lorene's daughter or touch her husband's body or laugh in her face ever again.

The dining room light winked out. A moment later, the parlor went dark. Annie was closing things up for the night. There was no sign of Henry. She hoped he was in his study. Maybe he was thinking about how to win back his wife. She laughed softly. It was said that if something sounded too good to be true, it usually was, and she supposed that was the case — imagining Henry filled with regret and an accompanying desire to woo her like he had when she was young. And beautiful. Her throat spasmed. She put her hand to her neck and thought of Claire's gasping fight for life. At the same time, Claire had urged Lorene to kill her, chanting about how she wanted to be thrown into the sea, to die young. She never wanted to be old and tossed aside like Lorene.

The front-facing windows on the first floor were all dark now. At the side of the house where Henry's study window looked out on the side yard, a faint light spilled out on the path. She squeezed her eyes shut. It was time to move forward in her life, repair what damage she could, reclaim her place in Henry's life, if not his heart.

There'd been all that talk about the illegal liquor. Claire mentioned it so casually, as if everyone knew. So, it was true. He was involved in something criminal, and he'd lied about that as well. She coughed again. She put her hand to her throat. The necklace. She'd heaved Claire into the ocean still wearing the necklace. Would Henry ask where the necklace had gone? Or Mary? When Claire's body was found, if it was found, would the necklace give away Lorene's involvement? If she were found, would they wonder how Claire had gotten it back? She took her hand away. It was easily lied about. She'd think about what to say when, and if, that happened.

She crossed the yard, tiptoeing past the empty veranda and the screened porch. She opened the door to the mudroom and crept inside. She removed her shoes. From there, she walked through the breakfast room to the parlor and into the front hallway. She took a breath and ran lightly in her stocking feet up the stairs, past Mary's bedroom, and opened the door to her own room. Inside, she closed it carefully. She pulled off her cape and hat and gloves and tossed her clothing and shoes onto the floor of the closet. She stripped off her dress and stockings, pulled on a nightgown, and crept into bed without combing her hair or brushing her teeth. The most important thing right now was to breathe carefully, slowing her pulse so that she was asleep when Henry came in. She was exhausted. Sleep shouldn't be difficult.

Winter 1932

Twenty-Eight

Lorene sat in the living room. Two cups of tea were on the coffee table — one for her and one for Henry. The doors were closed, and Henry sat beside her at the edge of the sofa, ready to stand up at any moment. Seated across from them in one of the armchairs was the Sheriff. Not a deputy from the Sheriff's office, but the Sheriff himself.

"Explain to me again why a stranger was packing up Claire's things?" Henry said. "That should have been done by her family."

"It doesn't matter sir."

"It certainly does. It's not right."

"The point is, we found the note." The Sheriff pointed to an ivory envelope on the coffee table. He brushed his palm across his closely cropped hair, then patted his head as if he was searching for the hat that was sitting in the chair beside him. The Sheriff was a tall man, intimidating even without the dark green uniform. He was taller than

Henry, at least six-feet-four inches.

Lorene worried Mary was outside the door with her ear pressed against it. She'd been told to stay in her room, but Mary rarely did what she was told anymore. She was too curious, and too defiant. It seemed as if Claire had had a bad influence on her after all, or maybe it was just part of growing up. Lorene supposed her own mother had considered Lorene defiant when she announced she was marrying Henry, stomping on Sylvia's heart, as she'd been accused of. Maybe everything that had happened to Lorene the past few months was punishment for what she'd done when she was so young and full of herself.

The Sheriff turned his dark brown eyes on her. "When did you last speak with Miss Farmington, Mrs. King?"

"I don't remember," she said.

"Have you spoken to her since Christmas?"

"No."

"And you had no idea she was missing until I came here today?"

"That's right."

"Did you spend the Christmas holiday with her?"

"We had a falling out."

"May I ask what that was about?"

"No," Henry said. "You may not. It's private family business."

"It may not be private business for long," the Sheriff said.

"It was difficult, having a wild girl like Claire in our home," Lorene said. "We have a young daughter. It was best for all that Claire moved out, but she developed hard feelings over it."

"Lorene," Henry said.

"Maybe I should talk to Mrs. King alone," the Sheriff said.

"That's not possible," Henry said.

"If we make an arrest…"

"Who's talking about an arrest? A girl drowned, she wrote a crazy letter as if she knew she was going to die. That sounds like suicide to me."

"It's not your call," the Sheriff said. "Please let me ask your wife, I mean, Mrs. King, a few questions. If you keep interrupting, I'll take her to the Sheriff's station."

"Just show more respect," Henry said. "She's a lady."

"I'm well aware."

Lorene picked up her cup and took a few tiny sips of tea. Maybe, if she kept the cup near her mouth, her face wouldn't give her away. She'd have time to think before she answered. Evidently, Henry didn't like her telling the Sheriff anything about Claire. But there was no way the Sheriff, or Henry for that matter, could find out what she'd done. Despite Claire's note, it wasn't as if she could come back from beyond the grave and give them the missing details. She took another sip of tea.

"So, Mrs. King, you haven't seen Claire at all since she

moved out of your home?"

"That's right."

"Why would she write a note like this?"

"I really don't know. To punish me, I suppose."

"Why would she want to punish you?"

"She was a very troubled girl," Lorene said. "Over…"

Henry held up his hand. "No need to get into Claire's personality. It's not important."

The Sheriff glared at him. "I said…"

"I'm not interfering. But keep in mind who we are. I want my wife treated…"

"I don't think I was being disrespectful. I'm trying to understand why a young woman would write a note like this."

"She was troubled. My wife already told you."

Lorene smiled behind her teacup. Hearing Henry call her his wife warmed the cold heavy feeling inside her chest.

"I'd like to understand Mrs. King's views on why her sister had a desire to punish her — in her own words."

"She was vindictive," Lorene said. "She defied me. I tried to reign her in, to step into my mother's shoes after she died, but Claire didn't like it. So there were hard feelings. I did the best I could."

Henry patted her knee. He left his hand there. She thought about drinking from his teacup. Hers was almost empty, and it was soothing, the act of mindlessly sipping the warm liquid, not thinking too hard about what was happening, and what might come of all this.

"The note sounds as if she knew she was going to die." The Sheriff rubbed his head again.

"I'm sure she did. If she had decided to take her life," Lorene said.

"A sin," Henry murmured.

The Sheriff nodded. "And you think that she implied you might want to kill her because she was vindictive, as you said?"

"Yes. I think so."

"That sounds extreme."

"She liked drama," Lorene said.

"It's an unusual case," the Sheriff said. "I've never heard of anything like it. And the note…it seems to suggest…"

"Suggest what?" Lorene said.

"Would you like to read it again?"

She nodded and set her cup on the saucer.

The Sheriff picked up the envelope, removed the note, and handed it to Lorene. She unfolded it and read slowly, more carefully this time, since she'd been terrified at the first reading. She'd hardly comprehended what the words were saying.

Only the good die young, so I guess that means I'm good. I always wanted to be good, tried to be good. But I also tried to experience everything. That's more important than being too good. Like Lorene. Too full of religion and all that.

I think my dear sister might be planning to kill me. She hates me so much, although I understand why. Maybe it's better to die before I get wrinkled and flabby and saggy like her. I'll always be beautiful, always be a goddess. But if I end up dead, my blood is on her hands.

Lorene folded it carefully and placed it on the table. She should be thankful for small things, starting with the fact that Claire had enough discretion to avoid mentioning Henry. Surely the Sheriff would be asking much different questions if he knew about that. She looked at the Sheriff and gave him a small, sad smile. She picked up her teacup. It was empty. Of course, Annie wasn't there to notice, she was shut out of the room along with Mary.

"She said her blood is on your hands."

"So dramatic," Lorene said. "A lot of young girls are. I know I was at her age."

"She says some insulting things about you." The Sheriff's face turned red.

"Vindictive, as I said."

Henry patted her leg again. She felt powerful and weak at the same time. It was remarkable how Henry was standing by her side, treating her like a queen. But she was furious at Claire, believing she could have the final word. How typical. She was not going to win. Absolutely not.

"She thought you were planning to kill her. Why would

she think that?"

"*Might* be..." Lorene coughed. "She wrote *might be*. She's crazy."

"There's more to it than that. Nothing else about the note indicates she was out of her mind. It's very lucid, thoughtful."

"Have you studied psychiatry?" Henry said.

The Sheriff deliberately kept his face turned toward Lorene. It looked as if his new strategy was to simply pretend Henry wasn't in the room. "It needs an explanation," he said. "As to her thinking."

"Well I can't explain someone else's thinking," Lorene said. "Especially not Claire's."

"How would you interpret it?"

"That she's insane. I already told you."

"There were scratches on the face. Her skin was very damaged, of course, disfigured. I won't go into details. But there were scratches, like marks that might be made by a needle or a straight pin."

Lorene shrugged. "I imagine she looked awful."

"We don't think she simply fell into the water and drowned. There are other..."

"I forgot where you found her," Lorene said.

"The body washed up near Capitola."

"And how do you know it's Claire?"

"There was a silver identification bracelet around the wrist. It was engraved with her name."

"I see."

"And you're sure you had no indication she was missing?"

"Mrs. Harmon said something about it, in passing. But I thought Claire had gone back to San Francisco. She missed it terribly. Maybe for the holidays. So I didn't think much of it."

The Sheriff scowled. She wasn't sure how to interpret his unhappy expression. Maybe he thought she wasn't a very caring sister. But it wasn't her fault! She'd tried to be a good sister and Claire wouldn't have anything to do with it. Why didn't he ask about that, take notes about what Claire was like, instead of acting as if everything was Lorene's fault? He'd tried to ask more about Claire, but Henry stopped him. Maybe this would go better if Henry wasn't listening and re-interpreting everything she said, forcing it to conform to his view of the world. She could imagine what he'd have to say after the Sheriff was gone.

"What do you think the note means?" the Sheriff said.

"I already told you." Lorene smiled, hoping to show she was being cooperative but wouldn't be twisted into contradicting herself.

"Vindictive is a broad term. She wrote that her blood is on your hands."

Lorene laughed. "She didn't *bleed*. She drowned."

The Sheriff raised his eyebrows.

"I know it's just a metaphor, but it's funny, don't you think?"

"Nothing about a young woman's suspicious death is amusing to me."

"Are you sure she even wrote it?"

"Yes, I'm sure."

"Did a handwriting…"

"Miss Farmington wrote the note. Please tell me why she thought you *might* kill her."

Lorene put down he teacup. It clinked and rattled, failing to settle properly into the depression in the saucer designed to fit the bottom of the cup. As she pulled her hand away, it trembled slightly. She grabbed it with her other hand. From the corner of her eye, she saw the Sheriff watching. She held her breath for a moment, and when she spoke, her voice wavered. "I don't know why she would think that. I did everything I could for her. It's terrible to find out she might be dead and to think she would ever imagine I'd want to hurt her. It's the complete opposite. I wanted to help her live an admirable life, and she pushed me away." A few tears dribbled out of her eyes. What she'd said was the truth, and it made her sad. She lifted her head and looked directly at the Sheriff. He seemed unmoved.

They sat in silence for several minutes.

The Sheriff cleared his throat. "People are very observant, Mr. and Mrs. King."

"What's that supposed to mean?" Henry pulled his hand

away from Lorene's leg and stood up.

"You seem to have very little information about Miss Farmington, who lived in your home for nearly two years. There's a reason she felt Mrs. King wanted to harm her, and others may have noticed more about their relationship than you realize. If you have nothing else to tell me, I'll wait until I can interview others. After that, I'll have more specific questions for your wife." He stood up and put on his hat. "I wanted you to have the opportunity to give your point of view first."

"It sounds like you suspect my wife of harming her sister and I resent it. The girl was unbalanced. We can't help what she wrote in a foolish suicide note. Whether it was pure fantasy or some sick game, I don't know. But we haven't seen her since she moved out of our home."

The Sheriff touched his hat. "I'll come by when I have more questions." He walked to the living room door, opened it and stepped into the foyer. He closed the door slowly. A moment later they heard the front door open and close.

Henry went to the window. Lorene couldn't see the Sheriff's car, but assumed that when Henry turned away, the car had pulled out of the driveway.

"I don't like this at all," Henry said.

"Neither do I." She suppressed a smile. Although the suggestion that she was being blamed for Claire's death was frightening, she was thrilled that Henry was so interested. He behaved as if nothing had ever happened between him and Claire. He was protecting his family, standing up to the Sheriff on Lorene's behalf. In the end, Henry hadn't challenged a word she'd said, as if he believed her simply because she was his wife. He *loved* her. The things that happened between him and Claire had been washed away by the ocean as it carried her body away from the concrete ship, depositing it in a soggy, lifeless heap, two miles up the coast.

She stood up.

Henry came to her side and took her hands. He looked into her eyes. "Why would Claire think you wanted to kill her? Didn't she know you at all? You're the gentlest woman who ever walked the earth."

She leaned her head on his chest. He felt so warm and good. She would never ask about his involvement with liquor distribution, and she'd never mention his passion for Claire again. Everything Claire said was a lie.

A few days later the Sheriff had returned, but his questions weren't much different from the first time. Now, Lorene was glad of the whispers about bootlegging and the tough reputation Henry had built around town. It seemed that no one wanted to say anything critical of Mrs. King. No one had seen Claire leave her boarding house that evening, no one had seen her near the water. No one had any idea there was a falling out between Lorene King and her sister. No one knew anything at all.

When the Sheriff returned for a third visit, he was carrying a small metal box.

Henry heaved a large sigh as he ushered the Sheriff into the living room. Once again, Lorene was on the sofa. There was no tea this time. "Are you asking me the same questions all over again?" Lorene said.

"That's what I wanted to know," Henry said.

The Sheriff stood in front of the coffee table. Henry remained by the door leading to the foyer, his hand on the knob.

"We didn't show you this before because we were hoping to find the shop where it was purchased." The Sheriff placed the box on the table. "It was found on Miss Farmington's body."

He waited.

Lorene folded her hands in her lap. She leaned on her forearms. Her knuckles poked the insides of her thighs. She relaxed her arms. She was not going to ask what was inside the box. The clock chimed the half hour. Outside, the clouds seemed to be rearranging themselves, because sunlight that hadn't been there a moment earlier burst through the window into the semi-circle alcove at the front side of the room.

The Sheriff opened the box and removed the diamond teardrop. It didn't look as if it had spent time at the bottom of the ocean. The diamond glittered, and the chain was polished to a lovely gleam. “Have you seen this before?”

She wanted to look at Henry, to read a suggestion on his face of what he might be thinking, but if she glanced in his direction, the Sheriff would know the necklace had a story. Even so, she couldn’t deny having seen it. There were too many people who knew — Mary, Jacob. Very likely Annie had noticed it at some point, perhaps when Mary was wearing it. He wouldn’t dare question Mary without her mother beside her, but it seemed he dared to do a lot of things she felt he shouldn’t, so what did she know? “I’ve seen Claire wearing it.” Her voice was soft, too hesitant, and she worried it sounded like a lie, or only a slender thread of the truth, an uninteresting and unimportant thread.

“No one at her rooming house had seen it.”

Lorene looked up. The Sheriff met her gaze. “I don’t know anything about that,” she said. Her eyes felt as if they were twitching in their sockets, begging to look in Henry’s direction, but the Sheriff continued studying her closely. She couldn’t take a breath without him noticing how quickly she inhaled and whether or not she held it for a moment too long.

“Where did she get it?” the Sheriff asked.

“She was somewhat vague about that.”

“We spoke to her former boyfriend, Jacob Archer. It wasn’t a gift from him. He said she’d worn it once or twice. He thought she might have had it before he met her.”

“Why would he think that?”

"It was his impression. He said she was very casual about it, for such an expensive piece of jewelry."

"I don't think his *impression* matters." She took a deep breath. It was best to stop talking.

"Well, it was his impression. So we checked jewelry stores in San Francisco."

She waited.

"We weren't able to learn anything about it."

"That's too bad." She hoped she sounded sincere. The Sheriff wouldn't stop staring at her. She felt as if he knew…he *knew* she'd put the unwanted diamond around her sister's neck, then yanked on the scarf until her sister passed out, that she'd managed to heave the unconscious body over the side of the ship. She thought he even knew about Henry and Claire. But how could he? It was a secret shared by only three people. One of them was dead.

"We did learn it's worth quite a lot. The stone is one and a half carats. A very fine cut."

"It is beautiful."

The Sheriff put the lid on the box. "We'll keep investigating."

"I'm glad to know you care so deeply about getting justice for my sister," Lorene said.

The Sheriff grunted.

When he was gone, Henry left the room. He returned with his flask and two glasses. He poured some in each glass.

"I don't drink that stuff, you know that," Lorene said.

"It will calm your nerves." He took a sip from his glass.

"My nerves are perfectly fine."

"You sounded anxious."

"Anyone would be anxious when a Sheriff treats them like a criminal. It's very upsetting."

"Does he know something about you that he's not saying?" Henry said.

"It's upsetting to be treated this way."

"How did Claire get the necklace? You had it when we spoke in my study a few weeks ago, so you must have seen her since she left."

Lorene touched the edge of the glass with her fingertip. Would the whiskey calm her? It might make her head ache and prompt her lips to spill out things they shouldn't. She pushed it away.

"Have a sip," Henry said. "It's good for you."

"I don't think so."

He swallowed half his drink and poured a bit more out of the flask. "There's something you're not saying. I certainly hope you didn't lie to him about the last time you saw her."

"Why not? You lie. All the time. Our entire lives are an enormous lie." It seemed that her lips were going to take on a life of their own with or without the whiskey. She picked up the glass. It smelled like something that shouldn't be put inside the human body.

"Let's put that behind us," he said.

"I have."

"Do you know how she drowned?"

Lorene said nothing.

"I can't help you if you're not truthful with me."

"I don't need your help."

"I think you do. You're hiding something. It's all over your face. You're too honest for this type of thing." He put down his glass and took her hand in both of his. "Don't worry, we can take care of this."

"I'm not worried."

As if she hadn't spoken, he went on. "I can have you committed to a sanitarium for the mentally ill. Law enforcement won't be able to touch you there, I'm fairly certain."

She put the glass to her mouth, poured the fiery contents across her lips and tongue. It enflamed every piece of flesh in its path. She slammed the glass on the table and stood up. "Why would you even think of that? There's nothing wrong with me."

"I'm concerned you murdered your sister."

"How dare you accuse me of something so heinous! You…"

"Settle down."

"No! You think that poorly of me? You think that's the sort of person I am? I didn't steal someone else's husband. I didn't lie to the woman trying to comfort and shelter me after my mother died, the only woman on the entire earth that would take me in. I don't flout the law selling illegal liquor!"

"Stop shouting. Mary will hear you."

"Don't accuse me of committing murder or threaten to lock me up and I won't shout."

The room had grown unbearably hot. The sun poured in through all the windows in the alcove and the large window to the right. It had spread across the floor and draped itself over the sofa. The back of her neck and her forehead were sweaty. Her scalp was on fire, her thoughts glaring like bright lights, shining out of her head, allowing Henry to read every single one. She waved her hand in front of her face, knowing it would do nothing to reduce the temperature of her body. She moved to the armchair, escaping the sunlight.

"You have to tell me the truth. There's a reason Claire wrote that note."

"I have no idea what that girl was thinking. She was the one who needed to be put in an asylum."

"So you took matters into your own hands?"

She glared at him. She wanted another sip of his whiskey, but she didn't dare admit it. And if she did have one, it would make her ill. She closed her eyes. Why had the Inner Light deserted her so easily? Maybe because she'd stopped sitting quietly and waiting for it. She'd closed her heart. It was too late for that now. "She wrote that note because she planned to kill herself and she decided to punish me from beyond the grave. Tormenting me in this life wasn't enough for her. She was an evil girl."

"I don't think Claire had the courage to kill herself."

"How can you possibly know that?"

"I knew her quite well."

"Isn't that nice. Rub my face in it." She began crying. She didn't want to, but the sobs and a gush of tears rushed out of her as if there'd been a geyser building up pressure inside of her and now it had to be released.

"Keep shouting and getting hysterical, and I can drive you to an institution right now. They'd take you with no questions asked."

"I hate you," she whispered.

"And I hate you." He said it calmly, in a normal tone, as if he were concluding a business meeting, glad to speak the final words of agreement. "You need to tell me what you did, and you need to do it soon, or I'm having you put away. I'm deadly serious."

She spit at him. The tiny spurt of saliva didn't even make it to the coffee table.

He stared at her with a horrified grimace on his face.

Twenty-nine

Claire was dead. Every time Mary thought of it, tears rose up out of nowhere and spilled down her cheeks. She'd never said good-bye! Even though Claire was mean and confusing, she was the only aunt that Mary had ever known. And she was fun, in the beginning. How could something as exciting as having your aunt come to live with you, share your bedroom, be a friend that was partway between a classmate your age and a grown-up, slowly turn into something that made her throat ache, and now made her feel like her heart had been torn out of her chest?

She'd drowned, her parents said. No one knew where or how. Her body was found at Capitola Beach. It was hard to stop thinking about that — Claire's water-soaked body washing up on the sand. It was hard to think Claire would never speak or laugh or tell secrets again. Her father said Claire was probably in hell because she hadn't been baptized in the church. That had to be a lie. No kind-hearted God like the one hanging on the cross, looking sad, but loving, would make Claire burn in fire the rest of eternity. It couldn't be true.

Since they'd found Claire, ferocious storms had battered the shore, and all of Monterey and the surrounding counties. Mary had lost count of how many days it had been. They said part of the road leading down to the beach had washed out. Pedestrians could use it, but it was closed to automobiles. Worst of all, the beautiful, majestic, magical concrete ship had cracked in the center and was temporarily closed. It looked like temporary was going to turn into permanent. Tears swam across her eyes every time she thought about it. The ship might fall apart before she was eighteen and allowed to participate in its *adult* activities. People were saying that the company operating it was going out of business, and there wouldn't be any more dinners or music and dancing.

She felt like the whole world was falling apart.

The sound of her mother's sobs had been faint all evening, through one closed door, down and across the hall, and through another closed door. Mary couldn't sleep. She turned on her side and listened to rain spatter against the glass surrounding the window seat. She liked hearing the rain, but every few minutes her parents' voices rose, drowning out the soft patter. She couldn't make out their words. Something was terribly wrong. They'd been locked in the living room with the Sheriff two weeks ago, and then again, a few days after that.

As her mother cried and her father talked, Mary heard Claire's name once or twice. She heard her father's voice, punctuating her mother's sobs with the words *for the best... the safest way.*

For a while, Mary sat in the armchair in her bedroom. The door to her room had been locked from the outside! It was tiresome being treated like a child. She was not a child. Small breasts were swelling beneath her dresses, but her father didn't know that. Even her mother didn't seem to be aware. The dolls sitting on the shelf across from her mocked her womanhood. They stared at her with their porcelain faces. With the paint on their lips and cheeks, they resembled clowns, the glass eyes hollow and watery making them appear infinitely stupid. And they were. She was too old for dolls. Her mother said she had played with her dolls until she was thirteen. Mary laughed. That was not going to happen. When she was thirteen, she would be sitting on the beach, watching boys strut past, trying to capture her attention. Already, boys glanced her way every single time she went out. Another thing her mother and father didn't seem to notice.

The dolls stared at her, laughing at her predicament. Locked in the bedroom like a lunatic was locked up. It wasn't really that way, but it was fun to pretend for a few minutes. Crazy people were interesting. Scary, but interesting. She liked the horror of the lunatics who did things no respectable person would do. They were so sad, so lost inside their own heads. How did the doctors decide someone was mad? Was there a test? It hadn't been very difficult for Miss Bly to pretend she was insane. She'd talked nonsense, expressed irrational fears, and that was it. Maybe they locked people up more easily back then. Nellie Bly found it far more difficult proving they'd made a mistake locking her up — she'd needed outside help to get released. People seemed eager to lock up anyone who didn't follow the rules. Sure, some of them rambled on with senseless stories, or abused their own bodies, or tried to kill themselves. They needed to be locked up, but not all of them. Nellie Bly died two years after Mary was born, which was disappointing. Mary would have liked to meet her and ask her a few questions.

Did her mother think Mary was a lunatic and tell her father to lock her up? Mary had read that sometimes women who invited excessive interest from men were considered candidates for an asylum. Maybe her mother had noticed Mary looking at boys, or boys looking at Mary.

Mary's dresses were exactly the same as the clothing she'd worn when she was five — dresses like sacks that were only fitted to her figure when a huge sash was tied around her middle in a big fat bow. They said Mary was too young to understand. She was not allowed to know why

Claire had moved out. She wasn't allowed to hear what the Sheriff was talking about. She didn't want to be a child anymore. She *wasn't* a child.

And the dolls.

There were eleven of them. Each one wore a unique outfit. Every year, she felt less pleasure in their inevitable appearance when she lifted the lid off the gift box. She didn't remember how she'd felt about the dolls she'd received when she was two and three years old, but she did remember opening the box on her fourth birthday. The doll was dressed in a red, white, and blue dress and held a little American flag in her stiff hand. Mary couldn't wait to take it with her to the Independence Day parade. The doll had long, dark brown hair and real eyelashes. When she was four, she didn't notice the horrific stare in those blue glass eyes. She didn't notice the lips were sealed closed with pink paint.

Now, the dolls glared at her, telling her she wasn't being very nice. They heard her thoughts, she was sure of it. The nuns said God watched everything Mary did, and noticed every single thought, but she knew better. The dolls were the ones who knew her thoughts. She couldn't see God, but she saw the dolls, and they saw her. Their eyes were open all through the night. It was difficult to sleep, knowing they sat on that shelf, staring down at her, pursing their lips at Mary's unladylike dreams. In her dreams, Mary saw the boy who sat in the back row in her class — a boy with black hair. He was several inches taller than Mary, with a tenor voice that made her insides feel like pudding. The boy looked steadily at the back of her head until she could feel his eyes burning through her hair, lifting it up and exposing her neck. His name was Charles. In her dreams, Charles took her hand and held it in his. He kissed Mary's lips. He touched her hair and whispered that it felt like expensive silk.

Every morning when she woke from the dream, the dolls' eyes stared, their gazes penetrating her skull. When Mary had her back to them, they talked about her. Sometimes they spoke so softly, it was impossible to understand what they were saying. Their voices took on a hissing quality — *whisper, whisper, whisper*. It sounded like a shelf full of serpents.

The doll with blonde curly hair who wore a pink nightgown and pink slippers was the meanest. She got the others going. She murmured that if she were allowed to sleep beside Mary in her bed, like she used to, she would put a stop to those dreams. The doll complained that she'd been stuck up on the shelf because Mary knew she was being a bad girl. It didn't prevent the doll from knowing what was going on. Oh, she knew. And Mary knew that she knew.

Mary stood up. She walked to the dresser and looked at herself in the mirror. The sash looked silly. She reached behind her and yanked the end. The bow unfurled, and the sash fell to the floor. She leaned forward and studied her face in the mirror. Did anyone notice her baby fat was sliding off her cheeks like melting ice cream? Blue eyes stared back at her, full of life, eyes filled with the interesting things she'd read and all the interesting things she planned to do. They weren't vacant caverns like the dolls' eyes. She closed her eyes and tried to think.

If she opened the window and climbed out, she risked hurting herself. There was a tree nearby, and she might be able to reach a branch, but it wasn't a very large one and what if it broke? She'd fall a long way, and one of her bones might break. Her father would be angry that she'd disobeyed him, that she'd done something sneaky. Her mother would cry that Mary might have died. Without even turning to look, she felt the dolls nodding in agreement that those were exactly the things her mother and father would say. But she didn't want to be here. Her father had been so eager to leave, after all the crying during the night. Mary hadn't heard a sound from her mother all day. Their house was a lunatic asylum. She wanted to escape and check on the boat. She needed to be sure the crack wasn't so big they couldn't mend it. If the boat split and fell apart before she was old enough to go dancing and dining there, she would die. It was the first day it hadn't rained in over a week. She needed to go outside and do *something*. She could not stay in this room with those dolls another minute.

She walked to the window, turned the lock, and pushed

it open. She put the hook into the eye to keep it from sliding back down on her. She dragged the chair to the window closest to the tree and used it to pin the curtains to the wall so she wouldn't get tangled in them as she climbed out. No one could see this part of the house — it faced the side yard, so that was good. She put on a sweater. She took off her shoes and socks. She tucked her socks in the toes and dropped her shoes out the window. The brief silence followed by the soft thud as each one hit the ground made her feel as if her stomach had been hollowed out.

She only owned two pairs of pants, and they were in the wash, so she folded her dress up, grabbed the sash she'd abandoned earlier, and wrapped it tightly around her waist to keep it out of the way. She stretched her leg up and out through the open window, turned, and hoisted the rest of her body up onto the sill. She put both legs out and sat there for a moment. The tree was farther away than she'd realized. She was going to have to lean to grab the branch. She closed her eyes and pictured herself putting her feet on the branch just below, which was thicker and stronger than the one she had to grab onto.

There was no sense sitting around imagining it forever. Either the branch would hold her, either she'd be able to grab it without falling, or she wouldn't. If she did fall, it wasn't so good that no one could see this part of the house. She might lie in the muddy garden for hours.

She held the window frame with one hand, leaned out,

and touched the branch. It swayed gently. She grabbed at it and pulled it down so she could get her other hand around it and let her body fall away from the windowsill. The branch lunged down, and the thicker one below scraped at her shins. She squeezed the branch, letting it move her up and down until it had adjusted to the extra weight. She kicked her legs, found the branch below, and curled her feet around it like the robins that perched higher in the tree and sang to her in the mornings. She stood there for a moment, still holding the branch above, steadying her breathing. Once her heartbeat returned to normal, it was easy to climb to the ground as she'd done many times before in other trees.

As best she could, she wiped the mud from between her toes onto the grass and put on her socks and shoes. She untied the sash and draped it over the fence. She slipped out the gate and headed to the road leading down to the beach.

The boat looked whiter than ever under the gray clouds. A few fishermen were on the pier, but the boat was deserted. She approached the pier and went up the ramp. She walked across the rain-soaked boards, hearing nothing but the thud of her feet and the roar of the waves. None of the fishermen turned to look at her. They stared over the railing, looking into the water as if they could find the fish by sight and move their lines to the right place. As she drew closer to the boat, she saw there was a bar across the entrance area. It was secured with a chain and padlock, but it was only a single bar. How silly of them. She could slip under that without even putting her knees on the deck.

She glanced over her shoulder. The fishermen were still busy. She smiled at her good fortune. She ducked under the pole and hurried around the side, past the building that housed the arcade. She approached the larger structure. Above was the restaurant that had glowed with lights in the evenings. She stopped and looked through a window at the dance hall, waiting for summer. Waves slammed against the sides of the boat. Even though the storm had passed on, the ocean was still unusually rough. She turned and continued walking.

Ahead, four men were leaning over the side, looking into the water. How they could see anything but waves, she had no idea. They were talking loudly, but the surf covered over their words. It almost sounded as if they were shouting at each other. They must be discussing the repair. Maybe the crack was larger than they'd realized. Maybe the water crashing against the concrete was making it worse. She hoped not.

She walked right up to where they stood, and still, they seemed unaware of her presence. She wasn't sure why she was walking toward them, she should hide. The minute they turned they would hurry her off the boat, punish her for coming on without permission. She leaned over the side to see the crack. She hadn't noticed it from the beach, but surely it was visible here.

There was a short lull as the waves fell silent between swells.

"We need to call a diver," one man said.

"We can't wait," another said.

"Do something. We can't just stand here talking about it."

It had cracked days ago. Why were they so anxious, as if something had to be done right that minute? She leaned over as far as she dared. She could hardly see the side of the boat. How were they able to see so clearly from where they stood? They were much taller, of course, but it was still an awkward angle.

Waves smacked the side of the ship. Saltwater splashed up at her. She felt the spray on her cheeks and tasted it. If the sun were out, if it were summer, she would dive over the side and go for a swim, although if the waves were as fierce as this, they might dash her against the concrete.

One of the men cursed.

"Do something!" another one shouted.

A third man turned toward a storage cabinet. He dragged a large net and a pole with a hook on one end out of the cabinet. He handed the net to the others, and they tossed it over the side of the ship. They pulled a rope that ran through the edges of the net. Two of them began dragging the net out of the water, rope scraping at the side of the ship, while the other two wrestled with the pole, helping to secure the weight of whatever they'd captured.

When most of the net was on the deck, the men with the pole dropped it and positioned themselves next to the railing. All four of them heaved something up out of the water and over the side. It smacked onto the deck.

Mary screamed. They turned. Their mouths moved, their arms waved, but she couldn't hear them. A roaring sound filled her head and her lungs, drowning out their voices and the ocean.

Wrapped inside the enormous net was a woman's body. Her hair was plastered over her face and twisted around her neck. Her arms were bound to her sides by a cream and turquoise shawl that Mary's father had given her mother for her last birthday. The body was all wrong, like it was coming loose at the joints. The part of her face that was visible was purple and red — enormous bruises that ran into each other like splashes of wine.

Mary screamed and screamed. One of the men ran toward her. He grabbed her and turned her around so her back was to the others, and she could no longer see that awful thing in the fishing net. He hurried her toward the stern of the ship where it joined the pier. Behind her, despite the roar of the waves, she heard ugly thumps as they unwrapped the net from around her mother's body.

After that, she didn't remember much. The man hurried her off the ship, and he must have asked her name. She remembered sitting on the pier, staring at the ship, thinking how stupid it was to have a boat made of concrete — something that sinks. She remembered crying and feeling sick to her stomach, throwing up on the pier, leaving an ugly puddle of creamy liquid with chunks of something orange. And then her father was there, carrying her down the ramp. He carried her all the way up the washed out road to where he'd had to leave his car.

Thirty

A doctor came to the house and gave Mary a small pill to swallow. As soon as the doctor and her father left her bedroom, assuming she would burrow beneath the covers and move quickly to unconsciousness, she slipped out of bed. She waited near the door, listening for their footsteps thumping down to the first floor. She heard them talking in the foyer, but their voices were nothing but hums and mumbles. She carefully opened the door and ran up to the third floor. She found a cardboard box and carried it down to her room. Standing on the chair for her writing desk, she looked into the dolls' eyes. They glared back at her, fearing their fate. The first to go was the blonde doll in the pink nightgown. She thought she was so smart. If they knew so much, why hadn't they warned her? If they knew what people were thinking, they should have known what her mother was planning. They were stupid. Their heads were full of air, and their lips were sealed shut. It was childish imagination, thinking they might be alive in some way that wasn't immediately obvious.

The doll stared up at her from the box, the eyes blank and cold, like her mother's. Mary cried out. She turned the doll on her face, and grabbed three more. She dropped them on top of the first. When the shelf was cleared, she folded the flaps and shoved the box toward the door. She opened the door and pushed the box into the hallway. Annie or her father would take care of it. She went back into her room. She yawned as she looked around.

Her mother would never enter this room again. She would never sit on the window seat, never ask to see Mary's homework. She'd never laugh or push Mary's hair off her face. Tears filled her eyes irritating her sore, swollen eyelids. She stumbled into her bed and pulled the covers up until she was completely buried. The light was a dim glow through the blankets and quilt. She was so tired. They shouldn't have made her take that pill. If she slept and didn't dream of her mother, wouldn't her mother be sad, knowing she'd already been forgotten, if only for a few hours?

She'd heard the men on the ship whispering. And then talking in low voices to her father. Her father and the doctor. Jacob had come by, and there was more talking in quiet voices, meant to keep her from hearing. More than ever, they were treating her like a child. But she heard part of what they said, at least the important part. Her mother had killed herself. She'd never learned how to swim. She'd gone out to the ship before dawn and pinned her shawl around her shoulders. She'd thrown herself over the side. They wouldn't say why. Her father murmured to everyone who came to the house — *She didn't leave a note. Not even for Mary*. His voice sounded more angry than sad.

It was impossible to stop yawning. She was so tired, but each time she closed her eyes, she started to cry. The inside of her head felt as if it were filled with water, gentle waves pushing her thoughts this way and that.

When she woke, it was raining. Water. Something was wrong. Something about water. Something bad had happened. She turned over…

Her mother's body wrapped in the net.

She started to cry. She closed her eyes and saw her mother again, soaking wet, her face a horrid color, her body slack, reminding Mary of a dead fish she'd seen on the beach once. She turned over and shoved her face into the pillow. It felt as if she was the only person in the house. She turned on her side and tried to listen for voices, or the sounds of Annie moving about. Nothing but silence. Was it this way every morning when she woke? She'd never paid attention. Maybe the house had always been silent, but she didn't notice because she felt her mother's presence, even in the quiet.

Normally, Mary would be out of bed already, dressing

for school, but before the doctor gave her the pill, her father had said she wouldn't be going to school for a few days. She needed to grieve, he'd said. She wasn't sure exactly what that meant, and wasn't sure how she was expected to do it. If only her mother had told her more about that Inner Light. It sounded like something she'd want to notice right now. It might be comforting, to know someone was living inside her, that she hadn't been left all alone. The rosary in her desk drawer was pointless. How would touching beads and repeating the same words over and over make her feel better? It wasn't any different than memorizing her multiplication tables.

Finally, she couldn't bear listening to the chatter in her head. Maybe she wasn't alone after all, her skull was crowded with unfamiliar thoughts, torn pieces of conversation that she couldn't make sense of because they kept whispering. Getting rid of the dolls hadn't helped as much as she'd thought. She got up, washed her face and combed her hair, and put on pants and a sweater. Maybe she wouldn't wear a dress ever again, now that her mother wasn't here to tell her a dress was preferable. She started to cry.

Downstairs, there were people after all. Her father was in the living room drinking coffee and talking to a man she didn't know. The sound of Annie beating eggs in a glass bowl came from the kitchen. Jacob was sitting in the foyer. He stood up.

"Mary."

"Hi."

"Can I give you a hug?"

She nodded and felt the tears start running out of her eyes again. Was this how it would be for the rest of her life? Every time she had a new thought or someone spoke to her, she'd start crying?

Jacob patted her back. He didn't say stupid things like the people who had come by the house yesterday afternoon, telling her everything would be okay, telling her that Lorene was with the angels now. One lady had said Mary's mother would be with the angels after she finished her time in purgatory. Only God knew how long that would be, but the woman imagined it might be fifty years, even a hundred, possibly. Lorene had committed murder. Taking your own life was murder, and her mother needed to repent. Mary thought about kicking the woman's thin leg. Instead, she'd turned her back on the woman with her green dress and her bony feet that were stuffed into pumps that looked too small for her.

Jacob released her shoulders. He wiped his eyes. "I'm sorry," he said.

The only time she'd seen a man cry was when the captain of the S.S. Palo Alto said good-bye to his ship. "It's not your fault."

"I'm sorry for you, for…my mother died when I was fourteen."

"I'm sorry."

He patted her shoulder. "I shouldn't be talking about my mother. Yours is the one that matters right now."

A shiver ran across her shoulders. Did that mean someday her mother wouldn't matter? Other mothers would die, hundreds of mothers, thousands. Her own mother was lost in a huge crowd of mothers who left their children to fend for themselves. The whole inside of her body felt hollow.

They went into the living room. Her father waved his hand at them to leave the room, so they went to the kitchen and sat at the small table, watching Annie make breakfast. Her eyes were red, and her face looked like a sponge that had mopped up blood.

Annie sat beside Jacob, and the three of them ate scrambled eggs and toast and ham. Mary thought she wasn't hungry, but each time she put a forkful of food into her mouth, the fork found its way to the next spot on the plate. She finished all of it before the others.

Annie offered a cup of coffee to Jacob. He accepted.

"May I have coffee?" Mary said.

Annie smiled and laughed softly. "Absolutely."

The rest of the morning was like walking around the beach in thick fog, everything blurry and far away, the sounds muffled as people came and went, talking mostly to her father.

By three o'clock, Mary wished she'd gone to school. It

was impossible to concentrate on reading a book. The rain had floated down all day, a fine mist that seemed like it would stop at any moment, but didn't. There were dead leaves in the foyer, wet and goopy as they slipped off the soles of shoes, coming and going. Her father had explained that one of the men was the undertaker. Another man was the coroner. She recognized the priest. He'd stayed for a very long time, and her father's voice grew loud, close to shouting — "There's no proof! You can't make that judgment."

The last man was there to talk about insurance.

Finally, they stopped coming.

Her father knocked on her bedroom door. "Mary?"

"Yes?" Mary waited for him to come in as her mother always had. He knocked again. She went to the door and opened it.

"We should eat some dinner. Annie made turkey sandwiches. Come downstairs."

"I'm not hungry."

"Annie said you had the same opinion at breakfast, but you gobbled down your food." He smiled.

"I'm sorry."

He put his hand on her head. "Don't be sorry. Life is for the living."

Tears swam across her eyes.

"You need to eat."

She nodded, feeling his arm shift with the movement of her head.

They sat in the dining room. Her father took his usual chair with the wooden arms and Mary sat to his left, where Claire used to sit. Beside her father's plate was a glass with golden-brown liquid. He'd never had whiskey at the dinner table before. He took a sip. He paused, staring into the glass. He took another sip. He continued holding it in front of him. "Your mother's funeral will be on Friday."

She nodded.

"The church won't allow her to be buried there, so she'll be at a lovely place in Monterey."

"Why?"

"Because the priest is an ignorant, obstinate fool."

"But why?"

He took another sip of his drink. "Because she had the shawl pinned around her to prevent her arms from moving, they're considering her death a suicide. That's…"

"That lady, Mrs. Wharton, she said my mother will be in purgatory. For killing her own self."

He nodded.

"I don't understand. Why would she kill herself?"

"I don't know, Mary. I really don't."

"Is it because…"

His spoke over her, his voice louder. "We don't know. That's the end of the story. You can't know everything in this life. People have their own thoughts and we never really know what's inside their heads. Which is why Father Martin is an idiot. He has no idea what your mother was thinking. She might have fallen. She might have…"

"But no one thinks that, do they?"

He shook his head and took a long swallow of his drink. He reached inside his coat pocket and pulled out a silver flask. He unscrewed the cap and poured some into the glass.

"Didn't she love me?"

"Of course she did. Don't ever think that. Not ever. You were her whole life."

"Then why would she leave? Why would she leave us alone?"

He shrugged. "It's inside her head. It has nothing to do with you."

"But how do you know? If you can't know what's inside another person's head?"

"I just know. You're all she talked about. You should have seen her when you were born. She couldn't take her eyes off you. She hardly wanted to sleep."

"But maybe she didn't love me as much now that I'm grown up."

Her father shook his head. He took another swallow of whiskey.

"Is drinking all that whiskey going to make you throw up?"

"Why would you think that?"

"Claire told me."

"Your mother loved you every day, no matter what age you were. And she'll always be with you. She's an angel now."

She nodded. There was no way he could know that. But it was nice to think about.

"Do you know how you get the flu sometimes? Or a bad cough?"

She nodded.

"Your mother was sick. But it was in her head. Now, she's at peace."

"Was she insane?"

"Not insane, just…not feeling well."

She wanted to ask how he knew that, but it was becoming clear that even though he was certain no one could know what another was thinking when they were alive, he was also quite certain about what her mother was thinking in death.

"You should say the rosary for her. And it wouldn't hurt to pray for yourself, that you won't follow the same path as your mother."

"Why would I do that?"

He was quiet for a long time, taking small sips of whiskey, his head turned as if he was looking out the window, even though the drapes were closed. "It's just better to be safe than sorry. Cover all your bases."

She nodded. She pulled the turkey out from between the

slices of bread. It was limp and clammy. She picked up the bread with lettuce and butter and ate the lettuce sandwich. Her father didn't say anything about not eating the turkey. His sandwich sat on his plate. He refilled his glass and took another sip.

Thirty-one

Why couldn't her father ever understand how tiresome it was that he, and everyone else, treated her like a small child? Maybe not Annie. Annie let her drink coffee, as long as she had lots of sugar in it. But Annie didn't have answers to Mary's questions. Her father refused to tell her everything that had happened, saying over and over that some things were only for grownups to know. He didn't understand that only grownups should have to think about suicide and since Mary had to think about it, that made her a grownup. He shushed her and told her to put it out of her head. When she tried to explain that she already knew a lot, and having large dark, unexplained spots made it impossible to concentrate on anything else, he repeated himself — he didn't know why her mother killed her own self. Mary didn't believe him. Every time he said that, his left eye squinted closed, and he looked at something on the other side of the room.

The only good thing was that she still didn't have to go to school. Although she wanted to sit in her classroom and listen to the teacher, she did not want to hear her friends and classmates talking quietly, stopping mid-sentence when she got too close. She didn't want to see them peeking at her when they thought she wouldn't notice. At the funeral, that's exactly what had happened. She felt as if she was floating around inside a glass ball, like a figure inside a Christmas ornament, watching mouths move and heads nod, but hearing nothing. Treated as if she were invisible.

Eventually, she'd have to go back to school, but for now, she liked it. She walked to the beach every day and spent most of her time on the pier, even when it was raining. She wore her slicker and rain hat and rubber boots, nestling herself inside a flannel and rubber cocoon.

Three days after her mother's funeral, she was sitting on a bench on the pier, facing the Monterey Peninsula. It seemed so close, it felt as if she could swim there. But her father had driven Mary and her mother to Monterey quite a few times, and it had taken forever. Maybe that's what Claire thought when she went into the ocean. She thought she'd have an invigorating swim. Possibly, Claire had jumped off the concrete ship. Her mother couldn't swim, but maybe the Inner Light had whispered it wasn't that difficult, and so her mother jumped, forgetting the shawl pinned around her like a straightjacket.

As Mary thought about how it would feel to be under so

much water, unable to breathe or move your arms, your clothes dragging you down to the bottom, a pair of dolphins showed their fins, undulating through the water like needles weaving through fabric. A moment later, three more dolphin fins poked out of the water and disappeared again. Another seven or eight followed the first group. It was always hard to count them because they sometimes looped around, and they went up and down, constantly moving. She watched until their dorsal fins became specks that she couldn't distinguish from the birds sitting on the water.

She heard footsteps on the pier and turned. Jacob was walking toward her. He waved.

When he reached the bench, he sat beside her. "Mind if I sit here?"

"You already are."

"But do you mind?"

"No."

"What are you thinking about?"

"Watching the dolphins."

He squinted at the water.

"You can't see them anymore. They're going to Monterey."

"Oh. That's funny you…"

She turned to see if he was going to finish speaking. He stared out at the water. There was a strange expression on his face, sadness, maybe. Was he thinking about his mother? "What were you going to say?"

He shook his head.

"I wish people wouldn't act like I'm a child," she said.

"How are people treating you like a child?"

"Keeping secrets. I know there are things they won't tell me, because they think I'm too young. But it's not fair. I deserve to know what happened to my mother."

"Well, they believe she drowned herself. It wasn't an accident."

"I know that."

"Then what?"

"Why did she throw herself into the water?"

"She must have been very sad."

"I heard her crying. And my father was talking about a mental health sanitarium. Is that why?"

"Are you sure you want to know adult things?"

She nodded.

"You might wish you didn't know."

"I don't think that will happen," she said.

"The Sheriff thinks your mother killed your Aunt Claire."

"Why? Why would she do that?"

"I don't know why, but maybe your father wanted your mother in a hospital so they couldn't arrest her. Jail is a terrible place."

"How do you know?"

"You hear stories about it."

"When you're an adult?" she said.

He laughed. "Yes."

"But why would he lock her up?"

"Either way she'd be locked up. That way, it would be cleaner, better conditions. She wouldn't be in as much danger, a better place to stay. If you have money."

"Oh."

"I don't think she would kill someone!"

"Maybe your Aunt Claire did something unforgivable, and your mother did it before she had time to think."

"Unforgivable?"

"I don't know. I really don't. But Claire said vicious things to people, very hurtful things. And she did a lot of things your mother probably didn't approve of."

"That's no reason to kill someone. I don't believe that."

He shrugged. "That's just what I've heard. I think the best thing is to think of everything you know about your mother, and remember the best. If she did murder Claire, she was probably so upset she couldn't think straight."

"And so she needed to be in an insane asylum."

"I wouldn't call it that."

"I miss her. I miss Claire. Everyone just disappears."

His face twisted into an odd shape. She thought he might start crying. He stood up and looked past her at the ship. He put his hand in his pocket. He pulled it out and held up a key. "I want you to have this. It's the key to the arcade. But you can't go in there after midnight. You shouldn't be out on the ship, or the pier at all after midnight, it's not safe. Okay?"

"Okay."

"Maybe you'll see the ghost again, if you're not too scared. Although I have a feeling you're not afraid of very many things."

"Maybe not."

He handed the key to her.

"Why are you giving it to me?"

He glanced over his shoulder, as if he thought someone had crept up behind him. "Can you keep a secret?"

She nodded.

"It's really important. You can't tell your father, especially. But no one, really. At least not until tomorrow. Can I trust you?"

"Yes."

"I'm going away. After you said that about people disappearing, I didn't want to be one of them. But my brother and I are moving away."

"Why?"

"We need a fresh start, a new life. We've been planning it, but then Claire died, and I…" His eyes teared up. "I loved her. A new place, new people will help me not think about her so much. I hope."

"But why can't anyone know? Why can't my father know? Won't he be mad that you quit working for him without telling him why?"

"He'll know why."

She looked at him, waiting. "Aren't you going to tell me? Or is this an adult thing and I'm just a little kid?"

He sighed. He sat down on the very end of the bench. "I really can't. It's not my place. I can't work for your father anymore, but I can't talk about his business."

"Is it bootlegging?"

His eyes widened. They were dark brown, warm and affectionate. She didn't understand why Claire stopped liking Jacob. He'd turned out to be one of the nicest people Mary knew. His eyes were so kind. And he'd shown her a ghost!

"How do you know about bootlegging?" he said.

"I heard you talking to my father about it. The night of the grand opening. And my mother told me what it is."

He nodded. "You can't talk about it."

"I never have. Except to my mother."

"That's good." He stood up again. "You'll be okay Mary. I know your life is really hard right now, but you're smart. And strong."

"I guess so."

He smiled. "You know it's true, I can see it in your eyes."

She wondered if her eyes said as much as his did.

They hugged each other and said goodbye three times.

When he was gone, she felt in her coat pocket for the key. She squeezed her hand around it, letting the teeth dig into her skin so she wouldn't cry.

After Annie cleaned up the kitchen and went home, Mary tiptoed downstairs. The house was dark. Her father was in his study. She went into the kitchen and packed three oatmeal cookies and an apple in a paper bag. She crept back up the stairs. She went up to the third floor and opened the door to Claire's room. Her room. Tomorrow she would tell her father she wanted it back. If he said no, she'd move in here anyway. How would he know? She could stay in both rooms, pretend to go to sleep on the second floor, and come up here later. She turned on all the lights. She turned the clock on the nightstand to face her. Eight-thirty. She thought she would go out to the ship at ten. It was late enough that no one would be around, especially in the winter. She sat in the window seat and ate one of the cookies.

When it was close to ten, she took the bag of food, returned to her room, and put on her coat and hat, scarf and gloves. It was easy to get out of the house when her father was in his study. The house could catch on fire, and he wouldn't notice until the flames ate his study door.

There wasn't much wind and walking down the hill to the beach was quiet and pleasant. There wasn't a car in sight anywhere along the shore or on the pier. The hazy three-quarter moon allowed her to see the pier and the ship, but if someone was out there, she wasn't sure if they'd be visible. She hoped she was alone. She was more alone than she wanted to be. She'd liked going below with Jacob, but now it didn't seem as exciting. What if the ghost trapped her down there? What if it hurt her? What if it was the ghost that dragged her mother over the side of the ship? Maybe the ghost dragged Claire into the water. The Sheriff wouldn't know about that. If it could keep Jacob from climbing the stairs, the force of it might be able to do whatever it pleased. But if the ghost was a piece of someone dead who was hanging onto the living world, it might know where her mother was. It might be able to tell her if purgatory was horrible. It might even be able to tell her what her mother was thinking right now, even if it couldn't tell her what she'd been thinking before she drowned.

It was difficult getting the key into the lock in the darkness. She had to take off her gloves, feel around for the keyhole with one hand, and then insert the key. She didn't have a flashlight, so all she'd brought was a small candle and a box of matches. If there was a draft down there, she might not have any light which would be so scary she wasn't sure she could bear it, but she had to see that ghost. And if they closed down the ship as they were threatening to do, this might be her last chance.

She stepped inside. She struck the match, but nothing happened. She dragged it across the strip again, pressing her fingertip harder this time. It flared, and she touched it to the candlewick. It gave off a soft glow, and the empty room looked much less frightening. She dropped the match on the stair. Right now, Jacob was probably on his way to wherever he was going. Her father wouldn't know he was gone until tomorrow, wouldn't start wondering about his key until tomorrow. She had no doubt the key in her pocket belonged to him.

When she reached the bottom, she sat on the last step and held the candle with both hands. Her stomach grumbled. She took her left hand off the candle and pressed it to her stomach. It was too late now. She'd left the food on the pier, and it was a good thing. Keeping track of the key and matches and candle was much more important than eating. Her stomach grumbled louder. She bent forward slightly to squish it into silence. A drop of wax spilled out from the puddle at the top of the candle. It ran down the side, but stopped before it reached her finger. The flame trembled. She clutched her wrist to steady her other hand. The flame bent over and began dancing wildly. A breath of air tickled her cheek. She gasped and pressed her lips together.

"I know you're here," she said. "I'm not afraid of you. I'm looking for my mother." Her voice sounded soft and not like her own. She sounded like a very little girl.

I'm dying.

"Who are you?"

I'm dying.

"I'm sorry. What's your name?"

I don't want to leave.

"Please tell me who you are."

The breeze against her cheek grew stronger. The candle flame danced as if it were terrified.

I don't want to be alone. I don't want to leave the beach.

"Please. Tell me who you are."

There was silence. She didn't see the figure like she had with Jacob, but she felt as if someone were sitting beside her, wrapping herself around Mary's shoulders, pressing into her back, cradling her head.

"Do you know my mother?" Mary whispered. Her voice sounded more grownup now.

Lorene.

"Yes."

Claire.

"My Aunt."

I don't want to be alone.

"Did you take them?"

A faint image appeared a few feet in front of her.

Mary opened her eyes wide and held her breath. "Mommy." She felt something warm inside of her. The figure faded as quickly as it had appeared.

They came to me.

Mary felt her eyes starting to close. The breath on her cheek was warmer, but almost imperceptible now. "Don't leave. I have so many questions."

She touched her cheek. Was it still there? The candle

wavered, and the point of the flame sank, growing slightly curved, then straightened again.

It was gone. She couldn't say how, but she understood that, for now, hers was the only breath in the bottom of the ship. She wished she could stay inside the ship forever, feel the arms around her and the breath on her cheek.

Spring 2033

Thirty-two

Mary's spirit drifted through the openings below the deck of the concrete ship. She never stopped marveling that so many souls, an entire ocean, a universe, were contained within a place that looked crumbling and dark and full of decay to those viewing the exterior. From here, her mind could float among the stars. Here, she drank tea with her mother on a sunny afternoon and talked to her about the Inner Light.

Another winter had passed. The ship was broken in so many places now, it was like a series of enormous stepping stones leading out into the ocean. The dolphins and seals still swam nearby, and the gulls and pelicans and cormorants rested for an afternoon on the broken pieces of concrete. A long time ago, when she was alive and walking on the earth, she'd thought it was entirely possible the concrete ship was swarming with ghosts, and she'd been right. All those people who had danced in the ballroom, splashed in the swimming pool they'd imagined and dreamed of, longing to be submerged in fresh water beneath the sea. People who had eaten meals and enjoyed games, talking and laughing. People who slipped into the room beneath the deck to sip illegal liquor and kiss those they shouldn't have under the cover of darkness and the roar of the ocean. All their longing and craving and wanting and needing lingered inside the concrete shell.

The depths of the ship pulsed with love. Her mother. Claire. The people Mary had loved who had lived parts of their lives on the ship before *She* took them to be with her. Jacob and his brother, Caroline and Danny. There were so many… Even her father, leaving behind his inadequate love for her mother along with his physical form. But most of all it was filled with James. Mary heard his voice in her ear, inside of her as the space between them was no longer tangible. It was the voice she'd felt she'd known all her life, the voice that sounded so familiar the moment she'd met him for the first time. The voice that lingered in her mind after he died, as clear and crisp as if he were seated beside her.

She remembered walking on the pier the week after James died. Her eyesight was failing, but she could still find her way easily, could still see the water splashing against the ship. She carried a small handful of his ashes. Scattering human remains into the water off the side of the concrete ship was forbidden, but that's exactly what she'd planned to do. She held the ashes tightly. She didn't want them drifting between her fingers. Neither did she want her mind to drift, causing her hand to spontaneously unclench, scattering ashes before she was ready. They were meant to go on the water, not across the weathered boards of the pier.

As she drew near to the point where the pier joined the ship, she saw a fisherman who'd caught a large salmon. The glistening, thrashing fish was two feet long, maybe more. The man who caught it was having a terrible time wrestling it over the railing. He was balancing on aluminum crutches to walk, with bands designed to support his forearms. The lower part of one leg was missing just below his knee, and his other leg was weak and wobbly. Trying to maintain his balance, to keep the crutches in place, and hang onto the fishing rod seemed almost impossible. If she weren't holding a fistful of her husband's ashes, she would offer to help.

She'd considered quickly tossing the ashes away. What did it matter? James was gone. It was symbolic for her, it comforted her that part of him would be in the ocean, but it was only for her. He didn't care anymore. Would he even know? Still, it was impossible to let go of that promise. She'd assured him she would do this for him. And she wanted to do it. There were others who could help the man land his fish. She stepped onto the ship. She walked as far as she could up the port side.

When she reached the farthest point, she leaned over

the side. She brought her fist up to her face and kissed her knuckles. She closed her eyes and thought about James. She spoke in a whisper. *Are you here?*

Her skin was warm despite the fog. An equally warm feeling ran through her bones and convulsed across her belly. She opened her eyes and slowly uncurled her fingers. She held her hand out and let the loose ash fall over the side. It caught on the breeze and hung for a moment. A breaker swelled beside her and caught the remains. She smiled and brushed the rest off her fingers. She stood for a few minutes, thinking of nothing.

She almost hadn't bothered, thinking for those few moments that it didn't matter. She'd been so wrong in thinking that way. It mattered more than anything. It was the most important promise she'd ever kept. Because now his spirit lived within the ship.

The *Spirit* of the ship herself kept them all.

Here, it was more beautiful than she'd ever imagined. And she watched the beach, loving the place she'd lived all her life. Watching. Listening. Speaking, to those who paid attention, echoing back to them the thoughts buried inside their hearts.

Throughout Mary's life, the ghosts had tried to assure her there was consciousness beyond the grave. They weren't there with malice, they weren't haunting the beach to resolve unfinished business.

All we want is to stay forever near the beach we love.

Acknowledgements

The "cement ship" has been with me since I first set foot on her as a child. When I saw her after a gap of twenty-five years, the decay caused by decades of pounding surf haunted me, and the story of the people and the ghosts who lived in her presence began to emerge.

The structure of the trilogy — going backwards through time — is the brainchild of my husband and business partner, Don Grant.

Many thanks to John Hibble of the Aptos History Museum for his entertaining historical facts about the ship and the town of Aptos. Thanks also to David W. Heron, author of *FOREVER FACING SOUTH — the Story of the S.S. Palo Alto, "The old cement ship" of Seacliff Beach*, for historical details of the concrete ship.

A Note From Cathryn

Thank you so much for choosing to read *Haunting the Beach*. Your support is greatly appreciated, and I hope you enjoyed the book as much as I enjoyed writing it. If you enjoyed the book, I would be extremely grateful if you could take a few moments to leave a quick review. It's always great to hear what readers think and it can also help others discover my books. Any recommendations to friends and family are also very welcome! I love hearing from readers so please feel free to let me know what you thought via my Facebook page or Twitter. You can even contact me directly through my website. To make sure you don't miss out on my upcoming releases and more, you can sign up to my mailing list at my website: CathrynGrant.com

Thank you again for all your support – it is greatly appreciated.

Cathryn.

www.ingramcontent.com/pod-product-compliance
Lightning Source LLC
Chambersburg PA
CBHW021120260626
47169CB00005B/1368

* 9 7 8 1 9 4 3 1 4 2 2 2 4 *